PRAI

"I cannot recommend this book high enough, it is an energetic, carefully written adventure into a world that could be, a place that wouldn't be out of step in our nightmares, and full of characters that you are willing them on to succeed with every page. An absolute triumph of a book, utterly entertaining...."
—Author Martin Skate

"Overall, the author played my emotions like a virtuoso. Every chapter plucked emotional chords that were played with dexterity. This is not improvised jazz, but a carefully crafted composition of emotion and adventure."
—Eric Morrison, *Amazon customer*

"What I loved the most about the book was that it didn't shy away from being gritty and real and hardcore. These characters are tough! There were some parts that were even hard to read, but it was those parts that made me feel so deeply about the book and characters."
—Author Amy Bartelloni

"The Treemakers is one of my favorite stories I have read. Mrs. Rozelle's bleak and terrifying dystopian world is utterly amazing! I found the book original and I was very emotionally invested in the characters. While each one is trying to make a life in a world that is destroyed and devoid of caring adults they become a family of friends, brought together by their desire to live freely and to love openly."
—Caelan Cox, *age 17*

"The Treemakers is an original concept that's very well written. An emotional and wonderfully imaginative story that will enthrall you from the very beginning. Believable and descriptively beautiful, I did not want to put this book down. It's definitely action-packed with enough twists to keep you guessing until the very end."

—Angela Berkley, Amazon customer

"This is by far one of my most favorite stories that I have ever read. This author is amazing at keeping you at the edge of your seat throughout the entire book. I am so excited to find out where she takes this story."

—Michelle Kluttz, Amazon customer

"A wonderful book, filled with action, mystery, depth of character and a believable setting, written by a gifted storyteller. Christina L. Rozelle has brought to life a world that could be, if our penchant for using the earth without giving back doesn't cease. She has created images both brutal and terrifying, while holding tight to the promise of one young woman. A girl, really, Joy has been through the hardships inherent in "The Jungle" by Upton Sinclair. She has memories infused with hope. She has the "youngers" to care for that look up to her. She has "olders" who rely on her to know what to do. She has challenges enough to daunt the strong of heart, but she perseveres. When you read this book, you feel these things penetrating your heart. Read this book, and you'll be thanking yourself."

—Lawrence Parent, Amazon customer

"The images are STRIKING! You are given every detail of this world and as the scenery changes, you will love the flow! It's heartbreaking and yet breathtaking ! Joy's world is ugly yet you will see so much beauty!"

—Author Leslie Cox

"The Treemakers is very unique. And the plot twists are amazing. The author took on some very painful and disturbing topics with poise and bravery. I loved the book and look forward to the sequel!"

—Author Casey L. Bond

"This YA Sci-fiction novel is well-written, very descriptive and a novel with originality, in which is very rare, which gains this author major points! As I read this novel, I had no problem keeping up and imagining exactly what the author wrote. With each book, I look for whether or not I was emotionally invested...and with this novel, I was. Not only did I love this book, I did not want it to end. But when it did, I found myself searching to see when the next book will be out. So you can count on me to read that one, as well. I will be eagerly waiting. Kudos to Christina Rozelle for a wonderfully emotional, adventurous YA Sci-fiction book!"

—A Bibliophile's Review

CHRISTINA L. ROZELLE

FOR MY CHILDREN, Savanna, Sierra, Skyla, and Miles. You are masters of love, patience, encouragement, understanding, joy, kindness, and forgiveness. You've been my beacons in the night, so bright, a bleak world of blindness has disappeared into this new dawn. A million thank-yous and kisses would never be enough to express my deepest gratitude, honor, and humility, that I've been blessed with another chance to be your mother.

ONE

Last week, Pedro looked out the window one second too long and lost his left hand in the chopper. Everyone knows the blade comes down in four seconds, even if you've never worked this station before. Because although it's not the Tree Factory's most dangerous machine, it's right next to the only window. That's what makes it so hazardous. That, and the huge appendage-slicing blade that slams down at sixty miles an hour to dissect two-inch titanzium plates.

Pedro won't be coming back. He's useless to the Superiors now. He can't build trees, so he's gone to who-knows-where. Probably the cannibals somewhere east, because no one will trade anything worthwhile for a cripple, and missing a hand apparently doesn't change the flavor of one. Or so says Diaz Superior. Pedro's younger brother, Miguel, went red when he heard that, and the Superiors locked him in the dungeon for two days. While his sobs and screams echoed through the pipes below the Orphan Dorms, we dreamed of vengeance. Pedro's the only blood family Miguel had left. I swore I'd help him get his revenge one day. When the time comes.

I breathe in deep, and rub my gloved hands together as the chopper revs up.

Another glorious day at the Tree Factory! I imagine Mona Superior saying in that fake, singsong voice of hers.

"Yeah, right," I mumble.

The chopper's light blinks green, and a sheet of titanzium drops down the chute from Abrilynne upstairs. My eyes slip to the window. Sunlight reflects purple twinkles on the sill, a layer of dust with tiny fingerprints dotting it. Our trees circle the factory and the Superiors' private bunker a hundred yards away. Beyond that stand ghost-Bunkers B and C, baked by the raging sun. Farther, the eastern aboveground tunnel's sealed-off entrance. No one's used that thing in years.

I focus back to the blade, slide the metal to the gridlines, grip the safety handles, and count.

One.

Two.

Three.

Four.

The blade squeals down and slices the sheet into perfect, even halves. I send them along the conveyor belt to Samurai, who douses them with a chemical that helps to retain heat, before blasting them with the sun torch. Then, with giant mechanical tongs, he shapes them into rainwater-catching and-storing cylinders.

I'm glad I don't have that job. After watching Molina burn to a crisp, I have a hard time even glancing in that direction.

As I'm cutting, Samurai drops the new cylindrical base into water to harden. Then, Johnny removes it to solder its seam. His part has to be perfect; any holes, and the base won't hold water, and the tree won't operate correctly. From there, Miguel inspects the quality and attaches the spiky roots and top brackets to hold the oxygenizing branches in place.

In the scrap rooms, Toby and the younger children sort scraps and fabricate branches that draw in poison air and send it to the photosynthesis solenoid to be released as oxygen. Then, they attach two-foot-long spiked roots that lock the trees into the ground. We treemakers have a whole mess of jobs, but the most important one belongs to my best friend, Jax. He carries the life of Bygonne on his shoulders.

Jax spends all day upstairs in the Brain Room, constructing new photosynthesis solenoids—the heart, brain, and lungs of the trees. Without them, our trees would be useless. His poor apprentice, who's been learning this job for a year, knows a lot, but the Superiors like Jax's speed. His apprentice is anything but fast, though if something ever happened to Jax, at least his knowledge of solenoids would still be around.

Another sheet drops down, and again I look outside. *What was it like out there?* When sunlight was still precious, nourishing...? Now, it fries everything through that lovely hole in the sky. The Superiors have a safety suit in their office for when Humphrey has to fix a tree malfunction, and for when they need to be replaced every six months because of the harsh climate's wear and tear. They have to give him liquor, of course, or he wouldn't go. Who'd want to?

I position the sheet into place and grip the handles. The blade slices it, and I send the halves down to Samurai. Here, where you work depends on your age, and how strong and quick you are. And since I'm the strongest and oldest girl at sixteen last May, the Superiors assigned me the chopper once Pedro left. I even had the "privilege" of cleaning up his blood. Disgusting, but I bit my tongue and did it, because this was my daddy's last station seven years ago before he died.

Before this, I worked upstairs for two and a half years with Abrilynne, and before *that*, I spent nine years of my young life sorting in Scrap Room A, sneaking off to visit my daddy at the chopper every chance I'd get, down to the last day of his life. There were only two Superiors then; it was easier to get away with things. I remember the smell of my daddy's sweat as he handed me a stale, stolen cookie—back when they still had them—hidden in his sleeves for the occasion. He'd pull one "from behind my ear" and feed it to me. I'd giggle, and he'd send me back to the Scrap Room.

I hated it there. Cramped, dark, reeking of waste, oil, and burnt wire sheath.... I'd stare through blurred tears at stained walls, trying to hang onto the memory of my mother's face. Horrible times. Hiding behind mounds of scraps as "those who did not perform adequately" were whipped to unrecognizable shreds by the Superiors and their ragged-faced militia men. And with hundreds slaughtered in the uprisings, it was naïve to be hopeful any longer. Even so young, I knew that wretched truth.

Now that everyone else in Greenleigh is dead, we're safer. Someone has to build trees for Bygonne. But that doesn't mean we're the lucky ones. Whether slashed or slaughtered, devoured by the noxious air of freedom, or rotting gradually from the lungs outward... there's a plethora of awful ways to die.

I learned that firsthand with my parents; my mother, then a few years later, my daddy.

Not a day goes by that I don't see him standing here next to me. His hands reflect in the gray metal of every cut I make, thanks to his gloves that protect my own. The day he died, I snatched them from the ground here and measured one to my own hands. *I'll never fill these*, I thought.

But here I am, wearing them, feeling the heat of fresh-cut titanzium through worn brown leather, breathing in the open-air dust that swirls around my head, like he did. I'm closer to him now, standing where he stood, gripping the same safety handles he gripped as the chopper's blade comes down. Gazing out the same window between cuts at two of the six windowless bunkers encircling us.... When he was alive, they were, too. Greenleigh was a living, breathing city.

Bygonne didn't exist a hundred years ago, until our idiot

ancestors burned a hole in the sky a thousand miles wide. Those who made it out before The Wall went up ... they were the lucky ones. The rest were banished, forced underground. Most died. Those who survived had to adapt in a dead world. I wish they had all died. That way, none of us would be here, until our last breath, building trees for Bygonne.

At least they came up with bunker air-filtration systems which allow us halfway-decent air. And heat-resistant titanzium for trees and bunkers, so we don't have to be underground. Knowing you're beneath the earth, especially for long periods of time, is confining and utterly maddening. A glance outside brings much relief. It would bring even more if we could see The Wall from here.

Supposedly, The Wall's thicker than fifty men and a thousand feet high, with a force field to the Stratosphere to make sure we stay on this side and not "infect" the Outsider's portion of the Earth with our bad air and stupid genes. We're forbidden from even knowing what's outside of Bygonne, much less going there. Thank goodness for the Other Side's secret charities who feed us and channel us fresh water. Not that the food's anything to be excited about, but ... it's better than being hungry, though not by much. And without their fresh water, the most abundant thing we have here, we'd perish in no time at all.

A zillion titanzium slices and a million daydreams later, it's almost lunchtime. My hands are killing me; I haven't built up calluses in the right spots yet.

A sweaty and distraught freckled face appears in my peripheral. "Where's Toby?" he demands. This is one six-year-old you don't want to piss off. Another sheet squeals down, and I guide it to the gridlines.

"I don't know," I reply. "Wasn't he with you in Scrap Room

B this morning?"

"Yeah, but he left thirty minutes ago, and hasn't come back yet." He's red hot with anger; he may spontaneously combust.

The chopper cuts, and I send the plates down the line. "He probably went to the washroom." I rub my aching hands together. "Give him a few more minutes."

He glares and stomps off toward Scrap Room B.

These children are irritatingly dramatic. The pressure of the work doesn't help, I'm sure. But we all know how important our jobs are, even with the dark and twisty crevices the Superiors hide their evil in. That's life in Bygonne. You take the dark with the light and build on.

If we didn't make trees, we wouldn't have enough oxygen to breathe—period. In the same way we, the treemakers, act as one body to fabricate trees so Bygonne breathes another day, our trees give life where there'd otherwise be none. Bunker air-filtration systems clean out some of the poisonous ozone gases, but without our trees, they wouldn't have enough oxygen to filter in, and we'd all die. A hundred trees circle the Tree Factory alone. Even if it's not perfect air, it's most likely the cleanest in Bygonne. One positive to being a treemaker.

Another sheet squeals down, and I gaze out the window. Bygonne's a burner today; not a cloud in the sky. I start to guide the sheet into position, when something moves outside. My heart skips a beat, then hits the floor. I jerk back as the chopper blade comes down, slicing uneven halves, and slam my hand on the emergency alarm button, racing to the window.

"Toby!"

Screams are coming from somewhere, and I realize they're from my own mouth. Beneath the murderous morning sun, Toby's flimsy breather melts from his face into the dirt. His clothes catch aflame, his dark skin bubbles and pops, the blood boiling beneath it. He drops to his knees.

I drop to my own beneath the window. My brothers and sisters leave their stations and crowd around me.

"Joy, what happened?" Jax crouches beside me.

"Toby…" I point above my head. "Toby… went… outside."

"What?" He stands to peer out with the others, pushing to get a peek. "How did he get out there?"

Miguel stares at his shoes.

"Miguel… what?"

"He asked me this morning how to disable the alarm for the flush chamber—"

"And you told him!" I scream.

"I thought he was just curious!" He takes off, slamming his fist into a wall and sending a broom flying as he disappears down the hallway.

Jax wraps me up in his arms as I cry. "He didn't know," he whispers. "How could he?"

"I know." I wipe my eyes. "You should go talk to him. I'll be okay."

He helps me to my feet and, giving my arm a squeeze, takes off after Miguel.

The speakers crackle overhead. "Attention all treemakers," says Mona Superior. "Please report to the common area immediately."

I stand on shaky legs and look outside again.

For weeks, Toby's been saying he wanted to be free. I didn't think anything of it. We all want that. He said he wanted the sun to free him like it did his ma. I didn't understand what he meant. I do now, seeing him there, arms outstretched like a scorched angel.

I think he may even be smiling.

TWO

"COME ON," I say to everyone still crowding around the window. "We have to go."

Chloe trembles in the corner, sucking her thumb. At only five, she shouldn't witness things like this. I crouch down beside her. "Chloe? We have to go to the common area now. Would you like a ride?"

She nods, wide-eyed, and plucks her thumb from her mouth. I swing her up onto my back and everyone stares. Our rules state: No talking, laughing, playing, or physical contact of any kind during working hours—which are from six a.m. to six p.m. Two uneven cuts already cost me lunch. Now, I'll lose dinner too, for "fraternizing." But I don't care.

Abrilynne puts Baby Lou on her hip—the one exception the Superiors make, because she can't walk well enough on her own yet.

When we get to the common area, Mona Superior, with frizzy reddish-brown hair and high black boots topped with bulging knee fat, arrives on the catwalk, rolling her oxygen tank behind her.

"Jax Grayson," she calls down. "Miguel Ramirez. To your seats—now."

They emerge from a corner of the common area and take their places at the table; Jax next to me, and a red-faced Miguel down at the other end.

"Joy Montgomery," she says, smoothing the front of her blouse over her protruding stomach.

"Yes, madam?" I set Chloe down in her assigned seat, while the stench of nutrient-fortified slop and the misleading delicious aroma of foul-tasting bread find their way into my stuffy nose.

"You operate the chopper, correct?" Mona Superior places her oxygen mask to her face, takes a deep breath.

"Yes, madam."

Something clanks to the floor on the other side of the factory, sound reverberating through the silence. Rats.

"What happened to Toby?" She takes another deep breath into her mask.

"He went outside, madam."

She holds the mask out from her face, vapors of life rising to the heavens like a virgin child's death.

"How exactly did he go outside without sounding the chamber alarm?" she asks.

Miguel stiffens.

"I don't know," I say casually. "I suppose he figured out how to shut off the alarm so he could go out without alerting attention."

"Hmm." Her eyes flit around faces and backs of heads, pausing a moment on Jax's and Miguel's. "And why exactly would he want to do that?"

"He... he said he didn't want to be a treemaker anymore, madam."

"Ha!" Another deep breath into the mask. "You have the honor and privilege of being treemakers for Bygonne. A fine, noble privilege. See what happens when you aren't thankful for the blessings you have?"

I clench my fists behind my back in silent reply.

"I trust there'll be no more uneven cuts today, Miss Montgomery?"

"No, madam, of course not." I dig fingernails into my palms, fuming.

"I pray this event will not interfere with adequate performance?" She sneers. "Because I'm thinking a few of you may benefit from time alone in the dungeon with the rats...."

My stomach quakes at the thought of my previous stay in the dungeon; days alone in utter darkness—famished, dehydrated, sick from bad air, losing track of time and my grip on reality, fighting off jumpers ... it's enough to change a person for life, to make you do anything to keep from going back there.

I stare Mona Superior down and don't let on that I'm worried.

Humphrey's hacking, wet cough—the telltale sign that it's end-of-days for him—interrupts through the kitchen door.

Mona Superior looks away and fidgets with her shirt hem. "I will extend the lunch period by ten minutes to allow all of you to process this ... event." She sucks her teeth and, tilting her head up, fans herself with a lacy thing. "Work will resume in precisely forty minutes." She tugs the chain above her head, ringing the giant bell that signals Humphrey to serve our slop. I guess I'm eating today. Debatable whether that's a punishment or a "privilege," as she likes to call everything.

It's a "privilege" to spend your life making trees, a "privilege" to eat snotty slop every day, a "privilege" to watch your brothers and sisters die or get maimed one by one as the days go by. Losing their minds. Making trees to breathe another day ... in a life they hate living.

"I will give you ten minutes of verbal privilege, while I go to the office to update our records," Mona Superior adds. "And when I return, I expect you'll be silent, if you wish to eat dinner." She scowls past an enormous hairy mole on her nose, before turning back toward the office, tugging the satin rope attached to her oxygen tank. It rolls behind her, clacking against the metal grates.

"Forty minutes to grieve our brother's horrible death right outside our window?" Jax says. "And verbal privileges? She must be going soft on us."

Humphrey dishes out slop down our two long rows. I'm still not sure which stinks more: Humphrey, or the slop. Weeks ago, I pulled a long, curly, black hair from my mouth. Since then, I spend more time trying not to think about which of his body parts it came from, than what the slop ingredients are. No one knows for sure, and listening to rumors is usually worse than not knowing. He ladles some into my bowl, and I hold my nose. I've seen stuff come out of Baby Lou's nose with more appeal than this. But I dig my spoon into the slimy, curdled filth anyway, and shovel it down until there's nothing left. Better to eat it fast; you don't taste as much that way.

After lunch, I beg Aby for Baby Lou; I need the distraction. She helps me wheel the rickety old playpen in between the chopper and the window. I've got no desire to look outside anymore today. Probably ever again. No one will clear away Toby's remains. Our only window is forever stained with heartbreak.

Jax's green eyes twinkle in the fluorescent lighting as he climbs the catwalk steps two at a time, headed back to the Brain Room.

I focus again on Baby Lou. Jax gave her an old worn pipe and she's been playing with it for an hour now. She keeps peeking through it at me, and it's adorable. I crack the faintest smile, and for a second, I long to be her, oblivious to the sinister world that awaits when she's old enough to take orders, and strong enough to move metal.

"Hey there, little miss." I tickle her soft brown chin, and she giggles, showing off short rows of teeny teeth. "I've gotta get the chopper running now."

She doesn't understand me, but I like talking to her anyway, and she likes hearing my voice. She coos and babbles, and bops me on the head with her pipe as she raises it to peek through. I peek back, and she laughs.

An hour into my running the chopper, she starts to cry, and the pungent odor tells me she needs changing. I press the blue button, signaling a momentary stop on the assembly line. All machines cease and quiet. The Superiors don't like it, but they know we have to take care of Baby Lou to give them another worker in the coming years. One of the few reasons we have to stop working.

I spread a dingy blanket from her playpen out onto a nearby workstation tabletop, pushing aside scattered tools used to fix the chopper when it breaks down. I lay her on the blanket, clean her with water from my bucket and a spare towel, then tie her back up with fresh cloth.

When I try to put her into her playpen again, she cries and clings to me.

"Ugh, Miss Baby Lou. It's hard for me to work with you on my back all day. Can I please put you in the crib?"

More crying.

I heave a sigh, snatch her blanket from the tabletop, and affix her to my back. She's happy there. Of course she is. Within minutes of my resuming work, she's fast asleep, snoring softly against my neck. This makes me grateful for my years of hard labor here. Otherwise, finishing my two-hour baby-watching shift while operating the chopper this way would be impossible.

She sleeps soundly for an hour, through all of the screeching, squealing, pounding and grinding. It's when she sleeps best. I'd prefer it, too, I think. It's easier not to think about things. At night, when it's so quiet you can hear the mad wind howl across the rooftop, it's easy to lie in bed and remember everything you've ever thought in your whole wretched life.

Occasionally, out of habit, my gaze slips to the window, but I yank it back when it reaches the dark spot on the ground. I shudder and fight back tears, recalling the night I met Toby two years ago, when he was shipped here in a cargo box from Taborton. He was traumatized. For a week, he didn't talk to anyone and hid in the corner of the boys' dorm and cried. They tried to force him to work by taking meals away, but that only made it worse.

So one night, I sat by the hole in the wall between our dorms, next to his bed on the other side, and started telling him about a little boy named Billy who had a pet dragon. He said no one had ever told him a story before. Those were the first words he said to me. At that moment, I could see in his eyes, he knew he was home. We were family. He had brothers and sisters who cared for him, who took care of each other. Together, we'd take the dark with the light and build on.

I'd never told a story before. I read them often, but never made one up from my own imagination. So, from then on, I was the storyteller. I still tell them every night to the little ones; it's the only way they get to sleep now. A few of them call me Momma Joy, and that makes me feel good. They deserve to have someone love on them, and tell them stories and whatnot.

Tonight's story will be rough.

Anger rises to the surface, and I slam the next titanzium slab to the gridline with too much force, making the chopper rattle. The new sound stirs Baby Lou. I rock her back to sleep and force my tears to go away. The chopper's no place for your emotions to get to you, unless you want to lose a body part. And I happen to be very attached to mine.

Some time later, the line stops again, and Aby slides down the pole near me. "Guess I'll be taking her now." Her face is rosy from the upstairs heat.

"How hot is it up there today?"

"Toasty, as usual. But she'll be fine." She ties her hair up. Even with the building's thick titanzium roof, it still climbs to ninety degrees upstairs. I don't want to hand over Baby Lou; she's comfortable on my back. But unfortunately, my muscles are starting to give out. At least it hasn't rained recently, so the humidity isn't bad.

Aby's face grows serious as I fumble with the blanket knot at my waist. "Are you okay, Joy?"

"I will be."

"Why are the machines stopped!" Mona Superior's shrill voice carries down from the catwalk.

"Sorry," I call back. "We're just trading off Baby Lou."

"Well, hurry it up if you want to eat tonight!" She spins around, headed back toward the office.

"Yes, madam."

"Hey, cutie," Aby whispers, removing Baby Lou from the sling. She sneaks a snort into Baby's chin, making her giggle. Aby's only fourteen, but she's like a momma, too. Or a big sister to some. She's impossible not to love, with her long red curls and dimples and puffy, heart-shaped lips—one of those faces you could stare at all day.

"Winding down now," she says. "Only four hours to go."

I drag the playpen to the freight elevator and load it on with them, then give Baby Lou a kiss on her soft cheek. She tugs at my short brown strings of hair before she and Aby disappear in the dim lighting behind the rattling door. For a few seconds, I stand there, as if they'll change their minds and come back. I'm not ready to return to the chopper yet.

Now, there's nothing between me and the reality of what happened today.

But I stumble back, reluctant to push the "ready" button. An invisible force draws my eyes over to the window, where an "X" of ash and bones—Toby's remains—lie on the ground. I cover my mouth to muffle my sobbing, because there's no stopping it.

"Goodbye, Toby," I whisper. "We'll miss you so, so much."

§

At dinner, we're left with Humphrey to watch over us. He growls for us to hush until Mona Superior is in her office, then he settles his stout self into a chair to snooze. A small relief, though still no one talks much. Everyone keeps glancing over at Toby's empty chair. One thing losing my parents—and now, Toby—has taught me: you don't realize how big somebody was in your life, until you measure the space of their absence. And his is so much bigger than this thin, shabby chair.

Once he opened up, Toby was that brother you'd confide in, and he'd drop everything and listen like nothing else mattered. He cared about people. When the twins first came, he gave them his slop, because they'd eaten theirs and wanted more. Who knows how long they'd been without food? They were begging for snotty slop, so they must've been starving. Toby had no second thoughts about it. He was thoughtful, generous, unfailing... but haunted.

"You okay?" Jax asks. "You're quiet."

I stab my cold slop with my spoon. "Don't feel much like talking."

Jax leans closer. His breath tickles my ear. "Tonight."

"Did you talk to him?"

He eyes our snoring, good-for-nothing night guard. "I signaled. As long as he gets his, you know?"

Humphrey, the man who can be coerced with a jigger full of washtub liquor.

I sigh. Usually, I'm the instigator. But tonight, I'd rather fall asleep in my lumpy bed and never wake up.

"Come on," Jax says. "We need supplies."

He's right. But his eyes also say he means to distract me from the pain of losing our brother today.

"Okay." I sigh again. "Let's do it."

THREE

AFTER DINNER, we file toward the Orphan Dorms, ushered by Emmanuel Superior wearing a purple satin gown and bright red lipstick, which has smeared across half of one front tooth. What a freak show. Platform shoes, paint-chipped beads, rancid perfume. A baby-smooth face and waxed sideburns. I wonder if he has any clue how completely idiotic he looks. He's gotten much worse over the past few years, prancing around the Tree Factory like he's queen of all the land and we're his royal subjects. His emerald-green oxygen tank sits on six tiny wheels and follows him around like a slave. Long tubes from its spout insert directly into his mouth and nose, so he breathes fresh at all times.

Emmanuel Superior—the main reason I lie in bed at night and fight to keep from crying.

He once slapped me for helping a little boy who tripped over a piece of wire and landed on the floor. Sliced my face right open with his sharp purple fingernail. I still have a scar.

"He'll never become a man with little girls babying him!" He spat rot in my face with each word.

How would you know anything about becoming a man? I thought, blood rolling down my cheek. I expected to die within a week from infection, but I didn't have to defend myself. My daddy did. And I wish he hadn't.

Emmanuel Superior never looks me in the eye for more than a second or two. He knows I'll trace his matching scar with my eyes. From the corner of his thin upper lip to the crest of his cheekbone, my stare will scream at it in the silence. He covers it with so much caked-on makeup it's hardly visible, but it doesn't matter. I have it memorized, along with the rage on my daddy's face the moment he gave it to him… the moment he chose to die for me.

With a corkscrew from his satin robe pocket, Emmanuel stabbed him—Zephyr the Magnificent, Greenleigh's only living magic—three times in the chest. And he laughed.

I shrieked as my daddy's dying body was ripped from me, taken by Arianna Superior, like all of the injured and dying men and women before him, like my mother. Still, in my panic, I knew I had to act fast. It wouldn't be long before they cleared out our quarters and sent me to the Orphan Dorms. So I raced there and stuffed a few things away—his old boots; a pack of playing cards missing an Ace of Spades; a worn-out, faded book of magic tricks full of scratched notes in his handwriting—into the empty bag he usually kept his magician stuff in. Someone had stolen its contents from our room before I got there.

Now, Emmanuel Superior counts us—sixteen girls and twenty-three boys—then takes Jax by the ear. "One of you is missing," he snarls. A fake eyelash hangs loose from his eyelid. "Who is it, and where is he?"

Mona Superior, of course, didn't bother to tell him about Toby.

"It's Toby, sir," Jax replies, unfazed by the intimidation. "He's dead."

"Dead?" Emmanuel Superior releases Jax and smoothes down his satin robe. "How?" He adjusts the bra strap peeking out from under his lapel.

Jax stands motionless. "He went outside today," he answers, and for a second, I sense fear in Emmanuel Superior's beady black eyes. Hard to tell, though, with all of that turquoise eye makeup. But it's gone with a deep inhale into his nose tubes. He brushes a brown wave of hair from his face like it's the most precious thing he's ever done in his life. "Hm. Just as well, he was worthless anyway. Off to sleep, all of you. We have a large shipment of materials early in the morning. You'll need to be in tip-top shape at six a.m."

With fire in me, I lead my girls into our room, and he shuts the door with a bang. Seconds later, the boys' door slams closed next to us. The girls huddle in their usual groups to chatter, and I go to the hole in the wall and unscrew the tack. Jax is already waiting there, leaning against the wall, straight black hair tucked behind his ears.

"What an ass," he says. "Don't let what he says get to you. You know that's what he's doing."

"I know, I'm trying not to."

"Good. So, after storytime, we leave. Square?" I guess he sees my sadness. He comes nearer and puts two fingers on the lip of the hole. I link mine with his. "It's okay," he whispers. "I know it'll be hard, but you have to. For them. They're upset enough already." He nods toward the younger boys behind him.

"I know," I whisper back, breathe deep, and prepare to act strong, even if I don't feel it. "Anyone who wants to hear tonight's story," I announce, "must first hose down, brush, and use the toilet. Once everyone's ready, I'll begin."

We have to be stern with the rules, otherwise things would be all finfannery and crockus—nothing would be in order.

All at once, thirty-something sets of feet thunder across the two rooms as children scramble for the wash areas. Aby's on spray duty tonight; she'll hose down all the littlest ones while they wash. Once they're finished, the olders will go, two at a time, holding the hose for one other. Hygiene is very important; if you develop something that was preventable, like a cavity or an infection... it's not your day.

Last year, Molina let a wound get infected and couldn't work for a week. When she was well, the Superiors punished her by taking away two meals a day "until further notice." By the end of the first week, she was famished and wobbly, and couldn't concentrate. She pushed the wrong button on the sun torch and it backfired, burning her up in seconds. Had I been working the chopper back then, I might've saved her. The Superiors, of course, claimed it was merely one of those "factory accidents"—a terrible stroke of luck. But we all know the truth.

One by one, the girls finish up and, freshly washed, take their seats at my feet. I scoot my storytelling stool to the corner by the hole where I sit every night so the boys can hear me, too. As I scan slicked hair and clean faces, I notice a lot of them match mine. Sad. Confused. Angry. My palms begin to sweat. Jax is right there, closest to me on the other side of the hole, where he usually is. But right behind him is an empty space on the bed in the corner where Toby sat every night, eagerly awaiting my story.

He'll never hear another one again.

There's a lump in my throat. My strength threatens to cave as my vision wades through tears. Crying for someone you love is a natural, healthy thing, but I have to be strong for the little ones. If I start crying, then they may think, *Who'll take care of us, now that Momma Joy has lost her strength?* No. Poor things have been through enough. I sit up straight and breathe in deep. Everyone's seated, and Aby holds Baby Lou in her lap. At least she's too young to understand the horror that occurred today.

"What story you gonna tell tonight, Momma Joy?" Chloe

asks. The hair-braiding chain begins at my feet and curves in a semi-circle around me; little girls learning the ways of girl things, like hair, and giggles, and secrets. On my other side, another group has curled up in blankets, chins rested in their hands, staring up at me.

"Okay." My voice is crackly and weak. I clear my throat, and start again. "Okay, first, I want to have a moment of silent reverence for our brother, Toby, who died outside today. He was loved and cherished by us all, and he'll be greatly missed." I lower my head to hide my tears, and wipe at them while I say a silent prayer that God, or Who or Whatever is out there, took our brother to someplace beautiful.

"May Toby go to Paradise today," I say, "where he'll dance, play, and be loved forever."

"And so it is," we say in unison.

I lift my head, wiping wetness from my face again. "In honor of Toby, I'll be retelling the first story I ever told, the one I made up the night he became our brother: the story of Billy's Dragon."

A hush falls over the room, and I close my eyes to lose myself in it. Jax says I've got a gift; not everyone envisions things in full color, with intensity and complexity. I didn't even know I could, until that first night.

"Once," I begin, "there was a little boy named Billy. He was sad, because a giant storm came and swept his town away, with his whole family, too. Everyone drowned, except for Billy. Soon, the water filled up his house, so he climbed inside a washtub, scared. He floated out the second floor window and away in the washtub with only a pocketful of magic stones his daddy had given him for his birthday. If only he could've floated by the kitchen on his way out, then maybe he could've gotten some food.

"Hours went by as the roofs and treetops disappeared beneath the water, and still he floated farther and farther away. Billy cursed his daddy for lying to him about the stones' power. He'd tried for months to get them to do something, give him wings to fly maybe? Or even X-ray vision to see through things.... But nothing he'd wished for had ever come true.

"When he'd asked his daddy why the stones didn't work, his daddy said, 'They'll work when you need 'em most. You have to believe.' Billy thought it was stupid, that his momma and daddy were treating him like a baby. He'd thought every day about throwing the stones in the garden, not that anyone would notice. They were just stones. Plain ol' ugly brown rocks. Nothing special about them.

"Still, he kept them in his pocket every day, until the storm came. They were all he had left. That, and his washtub. On the third day, he was so parched from the sun, and surrounded by saltwater, leagues deep—"

"Momma Joy?" Chloe tugs my pant leg. "Is that the ocean?" she asks.

I wink down at her and nod.

"And Billy knew his time had come to die," I resume. "Angry, he took the stones from his pocket and hurled them into the sea—"

"I thought it was the ocean," Chloe says again.

"Chloe, shh," says Aby. "It's the same thing." She waves at me to go on.

"He threw the magic stones into the sea," I continue, "and a second later, a great green-and-blue dragon shot up from the water with a splash and flew over him. At first, Billy was scared; he'd never seen a dragon before, and it was enormous, it could very easily eat him up if it wanted to. But it didn't. 'Hop on my back,' the dragon said, 'and I'll take you to Paradise....'"

Twenty minutes later, as I finish the story, half of the girls and boys are asleep on the thin floor pallets. I told it a little longer than usual tonight because I was lost in it. In my mind, Toby was Billy, living happily ever after on his dragon's back, flying through the heavenly blue skies, dipping down into the crisp blue ocean and back up again. I desperately want to believe my brother is there now.

Sometimes I wonder, though, if it's foolish to think that there's some kind of paradise after death. Mother never believed it, but Daddy did. And I'm torn. I don't know what to believe. I know what I want to believe, yet I hear my mother's voice as she argued with my daddy from her deathbed behind closed doors: "There is nothing left. No happy ending," she said.

No happy ending on this Earth, I believe. Except in my stories. But what comes next, after the dead Earth, and the tragedy of death before life has even been lived? What then?

Aby and some of the older girls help me get the little ones tucked away safe in their beds, and I meet Jax at the hole. Sliding the metal cover up and affixing it to the latch, I peek in to scope out the boys' side. Jax sits on the edge of the twins' bunk, talking softly to them. Their sad eyes hit me like fists to the stomach. Toby was a big brother to them more than most.

If I could shut off my brain and never think again, I might.

"Hey." Jax's voice startles me from my daze.

"Hey."

"Ready?"

"Yeah."

I flip the cover back over the hole, and find Aby braiding her hair in the greenish-yellow glow from a liqui-light lantern on our shared bedside table. "Hey," she says. "You leavin'?"

I nod.

"Humphrey's gonna let you go, after what happened

last time?"

I shrug. "I guess he's over it."

"Where're you going?" She ties off the braid's end, then gives the lantern a shake. The light intensifies to illuminate her face in a sickly green color that clashes with her red hair, making it dark-brown. "You gonna need one?" She taps the safety glass.

"I don't know. I think Jax still has a few light sticks. They're easier to manage down there."

Aby stretches and tilts her head until her neck pops in three spots. She repeats it on the other side. "Yeah, true."

A sniffling in the corner of the room grabs my attention. Someone's crying. Maybe one of the little ones. I start to go to her.

"No," Aby says. "You go. I'll take care of it."

"You sure?"

She nods. "Please be careful."

"I will." I peek at Baby Lou sleeping soundly in her crib.

"We'll be fine," Aby assures me. "Tell Jax I said hi."

"Okay. And maybe next time you and Miguel can go with us."

"Really? That would be great! It's been like a month—"

"I know, it's time." I hug her, breathing in the nasty scent of Tree Factory soap on her skin. Someone taps on the door.

"Be safe." Aby blows me a kiss. "And have fun."

FOUR

I TIPTOE TO THE IRON DOOR, yank down on the partially corroded handle, and it opens to Jax leaning against the wall, arms crossed and tattered backpack slung over one shoulder. Humphrey lies in his too-small cot, his round, hairy gut protruding from under his too-small dingy shirt.

"Better not get caught." He flops a fat arm across his forehead, stares up at the ceiling. "Or it'll be all our asses. Fried in the sun, like your friend."

"Brother," I correct. "He was our brother."

"Whatever. Don't get caught." With a sick slurping sound, he sucks grime from his teeth, then scratches a disgusting armpit. "And I better get something good this time. I don't know what that hogwash was last time, but it nearly killed me."

"Yeah, yeah. Quit your whining," says Jax. "You said it was good when you were dozed."

"Just hurry up, and don't get caught." He dangles a ring of keys from one finger, and glances up at us for the first time. "And watch out for monsters," he says, winking and pursing his pudgy lips.

"Right. The monsters," I say. "Thanks for the reminder." I snatch away the keys and affix them to the belt loop of my jeans. But their weight makes the fragile strings rip apart, and they clunk to the floor.

"Stupid ancient clothes," I mumble.

"I got 'em." Jax scoops them up and drops them into his huge back pocket.

I laugh. "God, you could fit another body in there."

"I know, aren't they ridiculous?" He eyes me and grins. "Good to see you smile."

As soon as he says it, though, my smile fades. "Let's go."

We leave Humphrey behind to fight his cot for a more comfortable position and head to our exit. How the Superiors would entrust such a worthless oaf to be our night watch, I'll never understand. Either they trust him more than they should, or they're complete idiots. Or maybe they know we have nowhere to "escape" to anyway.

Past Greenleigh, which is now a ghost city with the exception of us orphans-turned-treemakers, it's miles to the next town. Trolley tunnels are somewhere, though we still haven't found them. Once we get into the bunkers, our amateur lock-picking skills govern how far we get. The keys will get us through the main thoroughfare connecting the corridors from Bunkers A through E, but we've only broken into A and B so far, and only made it down six levels. The bunkers go much deeper than that. How much deeper, we don't know. Not even our parents knew that, although everyone had speculations.

The only sure way out of Greenleigh is the aboveground tunnels, where temperature-controlled Haulers come twice a week to pick up our trees for distribution throughout Bygonne. But the last kid who tried to escape through one of those, ended up a very effective threatening device for the Superiors—when a bag of bones and ashes is dumped in front of you, you do what you're told. And you definitely don't plan to follow in his footsteps.

The cuffs of Jax's baggy jeans drag the floor as we shuffle softly through the building, stirring dust cyclones beneath our feet. His shaggy black hair shines blue beneath the few flickering bulbs left on to illuminate the place. I smooth down my own hair and tuck it behind my ears. Jax swings his bag around to his front and peeks back at me.

"Ah," he whispers, "you're beautiful as always, Momma Joy." He digs into the bag, takes out two breathers, and hands me one.

My cheeks warm. "Thanks, Papa Jax." I affix the breather to the top of my head in preparation for when we go deeper underground.

"Ugh, don't call me that," he says, strapping his own to the top of his head and slipping his arms through the backpack's straps. "I hate it."

When we finally get to the main factory section, the floor changes from dirt to rough concrete. To our right, a small square of purplish-black glistens in the moonlight behind it, casting a soft glow across the chopper's surface. We slow at the staircase leading up to the catwalk. "Stay here." Jax releases my hand and ascends, the stairs squeaking softly with each step.

Each time we sneak out at night, we have to first make sure the Superiors aren't in their office. Most of the time they aren't, but we once found Diaz Superior up there, slurring to himself like a drunken lunatic. Luckily, at halfway up the stairs, if you don't see a light on, then no one's there. I've always wondered what would happen if one of them came while we were gone and found the door unlocked.... Or worse, if they locked it while we were still down there. But even though the thought scares the pigment from my skin, it isn't enough to keep me from going. Nor are the meager hours of sleep.

Seconds later, the steps squeak again, and the dusty air shifts as Jax slides in beside me. "All clear." He takes my hand again. I've grown to love Jax's hand in mine—the roughness of his skin, the calluses I've memorized, the warmth I don't want to let go of.

When we get to the back corner doors near the washing station, the pungent odor of industrial soap makes me plug my nose. I'd rather smell the dungeon's mold-stink. Nothing says "Welcome to the Tree Factory! Your Hell-on-Earth until the day you die" more than the chemical scent of that soap. Rumors once circulated through the adults that it was made from the fat of the dead. Horrible, nasty stuff.

Maybe we'll find some good soap again. We once found some inside a little jar in one of Bunker A's deteriorated wash-rooms, one I remember using a few times as a young girl. We made that soap last for a month, rationing only a drop for bathing in the evenings. The girls' broad smiles as they smelled each others' hair afterwards was worth the risk to hunt for more. But that was months ago, and we haven't found any since.

For a year, we've been sneaking around underground, and not once have we been caught. At first, we were terrified we would be. We'd let a month or two go by before we went out again. But as time passed, we got braver and braver, and now we go once or twice a week. Humphrey covers for us as long as we find good stuff to bribe him with, though not once in the past year has he had to.

It'd be easy to let our guard down, so we're careful not to get too over-confident. One thing you learn after working your whole life in the Tree Factory: over-confidence will get you killed. My daddy's voice echoes in my mind: *Stay on guard. Be aware of your surroundings. Notice the nuances. Cover your tracks. Always be prepared. Question everything. This is how you stay alive, Joy. And this is how you keep the ones you love alive.*

Jax moves the heavy shelf away from the wall—first one side, then the other—leaving a space wide enough to squeeze through to the hidden door. After everyone was dead and the Superiors closed off the bunkers, they moved this shelf in front of the door, thinking we'd forget. But everyone we loved once lived beyond that door, once walked those corridors, hands clasped, laughing, singing....

How could we ever forget?

And not get back there as soon as possible?

Jax jiggles the key in the lock, and it clicks. As always, I hold my breath, remembering the first time we went down. Most terrifying, yet exciting, night of my life; the night I realized I have my daddy's spirit and the Superiors would never fully control me. Now, my stomach flip-flops like it did back then. A few years have gone by since they locked the doors, and us inside the Tree Factory, forevermore. If they caught us, it would surely be our deaths. Still, what kind of life are we living anyway?

We step into the dank darkness, and I close the door quietly behind us. Blindly, I reach for my spear leaning against the wall. The roughness of its iron and the weight in my palm brings me comfort. Someday, I may bring it inside the factory and turn the place upside down. The Superiors' blood would paint the walls, and I would usher my brothers and sisters underground, to—

—utter darkness, bad air, and living off rats.

The fantasy's always grand, until it ends there, particularly with the rats. Their scratchy scurrying through the wall crevices makes me shiver. Of all the animals left last, why rats? I hate rats. My stomach knots up remembering the warmth dripping down my chin because hunger won out that time.... A chill devours me. "Light?" I say to Jax, trembling.

He takes something from his pocket, gives it a shake, then his hand is glowing bright whitish-blue. "We'll have to go to Bunker A's warehouse first," he says. "This is the last light stick we have."

"Okay. Where else are we going? I mean, did you have a specific destination in mind, or are we just exploring?"

"Both, kind of. Remember that freight elevator in B?" He heads down, and I follow close behind.

"The one that doesn't work because there's no electricity?"

"Yeah. Maybe there's a hidden staircase nearby that goes to the same place. I know there has to be more than six sub-level floors. And they had to have more stairs for emergencies, you know, in case of power failure...? We might find the trolley tunnels, or... or even the reservoir where our water from the Other Side comes from, then we'll have a way out—"

"And, what? Swim to freedom?"

"If we have to. Come on, we've gotta find a way to get farther down."

Farther down.

I want to, as much as I don't want to. Not even our parents knew what lay on the lower levels—if there were any. They all had stories supporting their speculations, of course, like science labs for creating new animal species that lived on less oxygen and were useful to us remaining humans.... And this was their reasoning behind the jumpers. Jumpers were one of the scientists' "mistakes," like the other, larger "mistakes" that escaped and killed off half of the population.

Old Jonesy, the drunken storyteller who swore he knew all of Bygonne's secrets, slurred on and on about the lower floors being overrun by beasts the scientists created, and how everyone was gobbled up. Then, he'd laugh and drink more, embellishing the story every time he told it. At first, the creature was as black-as-night and bigger than five grown men, then it was a two-headed, fire-breathing beast with ten eyes and wings as black-as-night... or something stupid like that. He had a thing for "black-as-night." People would listen long enough for a moment's entertainment, before pushing him off to the side, where Old Jonesy would slump alone in a corner somewhere. Exactly how we found him, years later. Last man standing in the Greenleigh bunkers wasn't standing at all; he was slumped and alone, and still is.

"Farther down," I finally repeat with a sigh.

Jax holds the light above my face. "You aren't scared, are you?" He wraps an arm gingerly around my waist to bring me closer.

"Of course not." I stare, unwavering, into his green eyes.

"Joy Montgomery…" He kisses me without warning, his lips lingering on mine before he backs away. "Your bluffs don't work on me."

My body numbs, warms. "You… kissed me."

"Did you like it?"

"I'm not sure yet."

"We can do it again if you—"

"No, it's okay.…"

"Ouch." He lays a hand dramatically over his heart, then tugs his breather into place over his mouth and nose.

I pull mine on, too, tighten the strap, and activate the air lock. "Let's just… get to the warehouse."

§

After a long walk in awkward silence, winding through dark and littered corridors, we reach the busted warehouse door of Bunker A. Perched on a sewage pipe, a red-eyed rat twitches its whiskers at us, and I freeze. Jax holds out his hand for the spear, and I give it to him slowly as we stand in silence, holding our breath. I pray for the rat to scurry off and, after another few seconds of it sizing us up, to my relief, it does.

"It's been a while since we came across a jumper, huh?" Jax whispers.

"Don't say that."

"Why?"

"Every time you do, seconds later, a frothy-mouthed, blood-thirsty killer dives at us from the ceiling." My eyes travel up to the iron support beams where jumpers like to hide. I let out a long breath as we climb over a fallen door to push aside the tilted one leading into the warehouse. Ransacked crates—torn through by the Superiors, maybe; or by the last of the living—lie spread open, covered in years of dust.

"Is it me," I say, "or are there fewer of those things every time we come down here?"

"Rats? Oh, I dunno. But, seriously… you didn't like the kiss?"

"I didn't say that, but…" I stop in my tracks, searching for a good explanation. "You're my best friend," I say. "Like a brother, even…."

"Oh, come on. You can't honestly tell me you've never thought about kissing me."

"I didn't say that, either." We lock stares for a few seconds, and a slight grin slips through.

Jax puts his arms around me. "I knew you did."

"Jax, no"—I push away—"it's not right. Like, bad timing, maybe? Toby—"

He puts a finger to my breather, over where my lips are. "You're breaking rule number two."

Right. Rule number two: Leave all of the bad stuff upstairs. This is our time together to be free, and that means free from all of the darkness in our minds.

"Sorry," I whisper.

Shuffling from somewhere in a dark corner snaps both of

our heads in that direction. Jax waves the light stick, illuminating the shelves and crates scattered here and there. Too many places for them to hide. I glance up, and right as I do, I lock eyes with a gigantic rat—fat and white, barely able to fit on the support beam. It hisses, displaying four blood-stained, razor-sharp teeth. Jax grips the spear in the ready position—slightly under and behind the beast. If it knows he's there, it doesn't let on. It seems to have dinner plans for me.

I ease back and step on something both squishy and crackly. I glance down, and scream at the bloody, half-eaten carcass of a smaller rat lying there, freshly enjoyed. When I turn back, the jumper lunges. I scream again, and Jax impales the creature straight through its middle. It screeches and thuds to the floor with a clank from the spear. Another twitch, and its eyes close, its body goes limp.

"Dinner?" Jax jokes.

"Not funny."

"I know, I know. Sorry." He yanks the spear free from the jumper's belly, using his foot to hold its body to the ground. My stomach threatens to turn inside out, as well.

I shiver. "Let's get out of here."

Visions of being gnawed to the bone while still alive has been the source of many-a-nightmare.

"Here." He hands me the spear. "I need to grab some supplies. Cover me."

We make our way to the side room door Jax busted the lock on when we first started coming down here. To our amazement and delight, it's filled with supplies: clothes, blankets, tools, light sticks, books, and some things we have no name for. But unfortunately, no food or medicine. Those, we still have to rely on the Superiors for. Unless, of course, we find it while scouring the living quarters five floors below, where our families once lived. But we've already torn that apart.

Jax starts stuffing his backpack: a handful of light sticks, a couple blankets for the new boys to share, and some clothes I'll have to hem to make them fit anyone. Most of the clothing we find are adult sizes. Jax whistles and holds up a slinky black thing that couldn't possibly be an article of clothing.

"What exactly is that?"

"Oh, come on. You're the girl. It's obviously a dress." He tosses it to me. "And it would look great on you."

"Oh, no." I hold it at arm's length. "Not on your life."

"Just take it. Here, I'll put it in the bag. Maybe you'll change your mind about it."

"No"—I toss it back to him—"I won't."

He shrugs, but tucks it into his bag anyway, then digs through a crate full of books. "You ready to try this one yet?" He holds up a book written by somebody named Stephen King. The cover alone would steal the children's sleep for weeks.

I shake my head. "I don't think so. Probably way too advanced for me, anyway."

He tosses it back in the box and holds up a larger book with bent corners and animal pictures on the cover. One of their favorites.

"That's better."

He takes out two books from his backpack and returns them to the box, replacing them with the animal book, then tightens the drawstring and flings the bag over his shoulder. "Let's go down to B to check out the freight elevator first. Then we'll head back over here to A and check sub-level six for liquor. Hopefully, we'll find some this time. Hey—maybe we'll find more loose floor tiles. Remember when we found the Blue Notes someone hid?" He cracks a light stick, shaking it until the whitish-blue glow brings more life to the room.

"Yeah, I remember."

Last time, we had to make a concoction for Humphrey from the bottles of liquids we found around the living quarters. Who knew what they were, or how long they'd been fermenting. Could have been medicines. Or rat poison. We're guessing the latter now, though at the time, we figured they'd be something good because they had long names I couldn't read. We mixed them together, hoped it wouldn't explode, then gave the brew to Humphrey, praying it would do the trick. And it did ... too well. Humphrey couldn't work for two days.

We head from the smaller room into a bigger one, kicking aside dusty debris as we walk. Rats must rearrange things when they scurry around down here; every time we come, things have moved. Unless the Superiors raid the bunkers. We're positive they wouldn't bother, though. The aboveground bunkers, maybe. But there's nothing down here they'd want—that we know of, anyway. We hurry through the short tunnel connecting Bunker A to Bunker B, arriving at the door we busted the lock on a year ago, then we begin our decent into the stuffy, dusty stairwell.

"Evenin'." Jax greets the blackened corpse of Old Jonesy, slumped against the wall, still clothed in overalls and working boots.

"Hey, Jonesy," I mumble, stepping over him. "You need new boots yet?" I ask Jax.

"No, I think I'll let him hang onto those a while longer."

We wind around the dark corridors of Bunker B, sub-level six, where I took my mother to the clinic to get her "medications," which were no more than shriveled roots and stale herbs that only gave her headaches. Seconds later, we stand in front of the freight elevator, our light sticks reflecting in its semi-glossy surface.

Jax knocks on the door. "Hello?" he yells, and jabs the down-arrow button a jillion times. "Anybody home?"

I glare at him.

"What? You never know...."

"How's it supposed to work without electricity, Jax?"

He shrugs. "Magic?"

"Yeah. Not gonna happen. Not in this place."

We stand for another few seconds, before he heads left. "Come on. We haven't checked a couple of corridors down here."

"Okay, but you know we'll find what we always find—nothing."

"Aren't you usually the optimistic one?"

"I have my moments," I say. "I'm allowed."

"That's significantly bordering on breaking rule number four."

"Sorry. I'll be more careful."

As we start down the corridor, an unfamiliar sound behind us makes my heart jump in my chest—a *ding*, and a squeaky whistle. We whip around, Jax aiming the spear toward the noise, and I'm frozen, heart pounding.

A dim light flickers over a breathtaking and impossible anomaly: the elevator door is open.

FIVE

WE JUMP BACK, and Jax drops the spear, which clatters to the ground, sound ricocheting off the long corridor walls.

"Whoa, what the—?" He hurries to retrieve the weapon, while my heart beats against the inside of my chest. A *whoosh* of citrus-scented air swirls around us.

"Jax, how... how did it open?"

"You got me." He breathes in and out heavily, and we stare at the rectangular yellow light that soon goes dark. The door begins to close. In a flash, Jax jumps in front of it, and the light turns on again. The door pushes back into its crevice. "Come on."

"You're joking, right?"

"You scared?" He winks, and offers me his hand.

I hesitate before placing mine in his. "Terrified."

Jax tugs me onto the elevator and into his arms, wrapping me up tight. "I've got you. Don't be scared."

Then, the door closes.

"Enter destination," an electronic female voice says through a tiny speaker, scaring the piss out of me.

Jax points to the four rows of buttons along the wall, all with numbers beside them. "Nineteen more floors down." His excitement meets mine, but it also meets the fear of not knowing what to expect.

"Where do we go?" I say, voice shaking. "And why does it smell like citrus?"

"All the way down. And I have no clue."

Slowly, he moves his finger to the last button, and I slap it away. "What if we get stuck down there, Jax, then what?"

"What if we find the way out?"

After a silent, heated stand-off, Jax, pausing to take a breath, presses the last button. It lights up.

"Sub-level floor twenty-five," the voice says.

The elevator shimmies and begins to descend—quickly. My ears fill with pressure, and my stomach flutters. "Are we supposed to be going this fast?"

"Guess we'll find out in a few seconds." He holds me tighter, and my ears pop. Sounds change from muffled to screeching.

"Again with the not-funny...."

I watch each button light up, then grow dark as the elevator moves farther and farther beneath the Tree Factory. Seventeen, eighteen, nineteen.... I hold my breath the way I do before we open the factory's main room door to go sub-level. Except this time—like the very first time in the factory—I have no idea what to expect. Could be anything down here.

Immediately, my overactive imagination starts replaying every monster story I ever heard when I was younger, until the number twenty-three lights up... and stays lit. The elevator slows to a stop, and the number twenty-five goes dark.

"What the—?" Jax punches the button.

The door opens like the birth of a demon—chilling and unnerving—and makes us retreat against the back wall. Smells waft in like a titanzium brick—years of rot and filth, left to multiply in the dark, mixed with citrus. Charming combination. Right outside the elevator, a dusty yellow bulb flickers, draped with a delicate cobweb that sways gently. The dim light beckons us out. My voice of reason says otherwise, but intrigue wins out when I notice the sporadic green lights along the ceiling—Bygonne's universal symbol for clean air.

"Um, Jax?"

"I have speculations."

"Are they any good?"

"Nope."

He walks us forward, still gripping me snugly around my middle, but I push against him, planting my feet at the threshold. "Uh-uh."

"Come on," he says, "this is awesome. Most excitement we've had in like, what—ever?"

I give in, and he guides me out. As soon as we clear the threshold, the door closes with another *ding*. An oxygauge on the wall next to us is covered with an inch of dust. Jax blows it clean, and we lean in to inspect it. The dial ticks steadily and hovers at safer levels than the Tree Factory has ever had.

"How is that even possible?" I mumble.

"I don't know," Jax says, "but..." He whips the breather off, takes a deep breath. "It's not lying." Then, he makes a face. "Other than that nasty citrus-and-death smell that's much stronger now, the air's good."

I strap my breather to my own head and inhale deeply the impossibility of such fresh, though stinky, air in the most unlikely of places. Ahead, the corridor stretches out bare, with only a couple of metal doors, but nothing else. Not turned upside down, like the upper bunker floors we've been raiding for the last year. The corridor's so long, farther down, the lines, shapes, and lights blend together into a blurry mystery.

"Apparently, no one's cleared out this floor," Jax says.

To our right is another corridor, completely dark.

"Any idea why this corridor is lit, but that one isn't?" I ask.

"I have—"

"Speculations. Right."

We interlace our fingers, and start down the hallway. The

minute squeak in Jax's left boot pierces the silence with every step. He grips the spear in a spring-loaded fist. Lights surge brighter for a second before snapping off into utter darkness for one terrifying moment, then return to their still brightness.

"Okay," I say, "we should go."

"Wow, for a tough girl who's not afraid of anything, you're sure being a softy."

"I never said I wasn't scared of anything. You're putting words in my mouth."

"Oh yeah?" He stops us in front of a closed door, considering this. "Okay," he says, "jumpers. But other than those, name one thing."

"Well, what's behind that door, for starters. The rot smell has to be coming from *something*."

"Yeah...." He winks and presses the dark, square button beside the door. "Time to find out what."

Nothing happens. A jostle of the handle doesn't do it, either.

We move farther down the hall, past two more locked doors with dark buttons, then stop.

"Well," says Jax. "That sucks."

I tap his arm and point down the corridor—"What's that?"—toward a tiny green light set lower on the wall than the oxygen lights.

"Let's check it out."

We continue on cautiously, and the walls ahead start to change from plain, gray stone to magnificent colors. My heart thumps as we come closer.

"Wow...." we both whisper at the most brilliant paintings either of us have ever laid eyes on. Women, twirling in elegant dresses; hundreds of butterflies of all shapes and sizes; children laughing and frolicking in green, rolling pastures; valleys kissing a floral-laden mountainside. As we stroll down in small steps to soak in every last bit, the scenery shifts. From sunny and jubilant, to a delightful murky gloom, with purples and blues and a black sky dotted with gray stars. What appears to be one of our trees is surrounded by a horrific, nightmarish land with jagged lightning shattering an angry sky....

Black paint glistens in the light of a flickering bulb. I touch the wall with my finger, and a lump forms in my throat. Panic spreads on Jax's face.

"It's still wet," I whisper. "How—?"

"Someone's down here." Jax grips the spear tight. To our left, a door similar to the rest stands next to a button that glows green. Farther on, lights in the corridor end.

"Is it just me," I say, "or does it seem like we were led to this door?"

"It's not just you." And before I object, he presses the green button. The door slides open. An overpowering citrus smell rushes out with a light fog or smoke that obscures the area.

Jax chuckles nervously. "It keeps getting weirder and weirder.... The fog's a nice touch!" he yells into the room.

I glare at him.

"What? I mean, obviously someone led us here, right? Come on out!" he yells in again. The fog soon clears, and inside, tiny blue and green lights sparkle in the darkness, lining the walls and the ceiling. I take a step toward the door, but Jax grabs my arm to stop me.

"What?" I say. "Now you're scared?"

He shrugs, then holds his hand out in an "after you" motion.

I step into the room, and as soon as we both clear the doorway, the door slides closed. Seconds later, a hissing echoes around us as more citrus smoke fills the room. The lights brighten—I shield my eyes—until a thin horizontal line of light fans the length of our bodies, and back up again.

"Scan complete," says the same voice from the elevator.

The light explodes in a flash, and we huddle together on the floor, startled. Then, I'm spinning, shooting like a comet through space. Momentum tugs at my insides, while streamers of light-and-black whirl past. I feel for Jax's hand, but it's not there; I reach for him, but he's gone.

"Jax!" I try to scream into the dizzying void around me, though my voice only comes out in a whisper.

Then, everything stops, and I'm hugging my knees. Gradually, my eyes adjust, and I find I'm sitting on smooth, pale wood with thin grooves. In a panic, I glance around for Jax who's a few feet away in the same strange room, staring back at me, his panic matching mine.

"Where the hell are we?" he asks. "What just happened?"

We stand and turn, surveying the small, simple room made of wood. We stop when we finally face a window in the corner, where light pours in to bathe the floor a creamy golden-brown. We clasp hands and ease toward it. To the right of the window stands a red wooden door with a fancy handle. A long rectangular bench on the other side appears to have hand-carved etchings around its edges. Behind us in the far corner lies a mattress with a woven blanket and two pillows. Other than that, the room is bare. The ceiling peaks to a gradual point in the center, where wooden posts meet and hold it all together, and the roof above reminds me of the kitchen broom at the Tree Factory.

When we reach the windowsill, my body goes numb. I must be dreaming. Trembling, I grip Jax's hand tighter. On the other side is a ground covered in green, crawling up a hillside dotted with a rainbow of fluttering flowers. The sky—which I've only ever seen through purple-tinted windows—is an aching, quaking, brilliant blue, that drenches me with bewildering elation. And if that weren't enough... to our right, off in the far distance, is a forever-rippling cobalt—the ocean—sparkling across the horizon.... And all of this, beneath a blazing sun.

"Are we dreaming?" I whisper. Jax doesn't answer but pulls me to the door and opens it. A gust of air blows the hair from my eyes and brings with it the fragrance of an unknown world. Together, we descend three rocky steps onto green ground interspersed with patches of white sand. I squint right into the sun, amazed that I'm not burning to death right now.

"It doesn't make sense...." Jax, releasing my hand, spins in a slow circle. "It's not real," he says. "None of it. It's impossible."

I scoop up a handful of sand, like the stuff we use at the Tree Factory for smoothing out metal. I let it sift through my fingers and blow away into the wind. "But, Jax—"

"It isn't possible!" he insists. "We were hundreds of feet below the ground! We walk into a room, it fills with smoke, and then—*poof*—we're suddenly in a perfect, picturesque world with clean air and life? No." He shakes his head, chest heaving with unease.

"Relax, we'll figure it out." I brace myself against the side of the hut. Maybe I'm telling myself this more than anything.

For a long, silent moment, we absorb the unimaginable splendor.

"Who cares if it's not real?" I shrug. "Let's enjoy it anyway. I mean, look at it...."

He reads my face for a minute, then soaks in the splendor around us. He nods. "Okay. Let's check it out."

With a wide smile, I take his hand and try to search for possible explanations for this, but I come up empty. We start down the gradual hill, wisps of tall green—grass—brushing our pant legs. A few more yards, and mighty trees come into view, swaying in the breeze.

"Jax!"

"I see them!"

We sprint toward them, past fluttering creatures with brightly-colored wings that dip and dive around us in the blue. Something huge and brown and alive appears ahead of us and steals my breath away. I stop and grab Jax, yanking him back.

"What?" he asks, panting.

I point, having trouble catching my breath. I'm not used to running free. My heart beats like it never has before, as the creature lifts its great head topped with long, winding, pointy things.

"Deer," I say. "I think that's what it's called."

It spots us and scampers off through the trees. "If this isn't real," I add, "then how come it saw us and ran away?"

"You got me."

"No speculations?"

"Uh, nope. You?"

"Well... yeah."

"Okay? What?"

"Maybe it's a portal," I say.

"Huh?"

"Like a... a wormhole or something, to the Other Side."

"You've been reading too many sci-fi books."

"Well, how else would all this be possible?"

We walk in silence to the nearest tree, my words echoing through my mind. And Jax's, too, I'm sure. The feelings of both magical illusion and unbelievable reality wash over me like a mighty flood when we draw closer to the trees. Real trees. Now I'm positive everyone has been wrong about God. Because I've found God right here. Swaying in these branches, reaching high into the blue abyss of perfect impossibility.

Rocking gracefully as though there's never been a day of pain, or there has, but it sways on anyway. As if it's always been, and will always be, swaying here forevermore in perfect, unobstructed bliss.

Tears roll down my cheeks as I squint upwards. Sunlight dances enchantingly through its branches, offering glimmers of blinding light. More perfection. We lie down on the prickle-covered ground gazing up at it, unable to speak beneath its majesty. I run my fingertips along the rough brown base that digs deep into the earth, marveling at its inherent ability to create what we have spent our whole lives manufacturing: sweet, pure, oxygen.

§

Chilly air wakes me in a panic, and I open my eyes to sparkling in the dark above, a low grumble around us. Jax is curled up on the ground beside me. "Jax!"

He stirs, then sits up, peering around frantically, then at me. "We're still here."

"Yeah, and it's night. We must've been asleep for a while."

Lightning strikes the ocean, electric branches shooting off through the sky in all directions. It's both beautiful and frightening.

"Storm's coming," I mutter.

"How do you fall asleep and wake up, in a dream?" he asks.

"Yeah, I was thinking that. So, we're definitely not dreaming."

"I don't know how, but...." Jax's eyes drift upward. "Man, check out those stars."

For a moment, we gaze at the twinkling darkness directly above, completely awestruck; the midnight blue is a tattered blanket long-since stretched over the daylight, letting enough light shine through to illuminate an incredible, sleeping paradise. Lightning strikes again, closer, this time followed by louder thunder. A droplet hits my forearm, and my heart skips a beat as I wait for the burn of toxic sky-waste. Yet all I feel is wetness. It slides down my arm as another lands on my head, then my nose.

"We'd better get back to the hut," Jax says.

We jog back up the hill, surprised to find the hut's windows glowing orange as if a light were on inside, though I don't remember there being any lights. Water pours down from the sky, and we take our final few hurried steps toward the hut, whip open the door, and run inside, struggling to catch our breath. I laugh, pinching at my drenched shirt, and Jax chuckles, too, then he tugs me over to the bed. We collapse in a wet heap, shivering more from excitement than from the cold, and his lips inch slowly toward mine....

Then, I'm spinning back through the swirling dark void, shooting through space at a trillion light-years a second until I'm lying on my back on cold concrete. We scramble to our feet, Jax picks up the spear and aims it at the evil around us. "Who's doing this?" he screams into the dark. "Show yourself!"

Silence.

I pick up our discarded breathers. I don't remember removing mine. And then I realize ... my clothes are dry. My thoughts spiral out of control, and I fight the urge to vomit.

Jax pushes the green button, and the door opens. We hurry from the room, then my stomach lurches, and I heave onto the concrete floor. I brace myself against the wall and feel wetness there. Jax paces nearby, fists clenched and spear at the ready, challenging the shadows to come forth and show themselves.

He lays a hand on my back. "You okay?"

I nod, and glance at my own hand. "Still wet," I say. My

body quivers and my forehead grows clammy. Jax's glistens in the light, too.

"That's impossible, we were gone for hours."

I hold my palm up to his face, spread my blackened fingers apart. Then, I point a shaky finger at the handprint in the painting on the wall. "Obviously it's possible. Do you feel sick?"

"A little. Like we were rocketed into another dimension or something, man—shit!"

"And our clothes are dry. I don't underst—"

"Tell us what's going on!" he screams, voice echoing off the walls and into the stillness.

"The paint," I say. "Was it that wet when we went into the room? I have a feeling, somehow, wherever we went, time moved faster there. Or, I don't know... sped up and slowed down again, or...." My head spins from too much conflicting information. Nothing makes sense. It's not possible, and yet... it is. Because we experienced it. It's all entirely incomprehensible.

Once we get back to the elevator, the door opens before Jax's finger even reaches the button. We make uneasy eye contact, then cautiously step on and replace our breathers. The elevator rattles back up to our original floor without our telling it where to go, and when the door opens, I stumble out, weak in the knees and lightheaded. The door closes, and the light above it goes dark. Like nothing ever happened. Only the scent of citrus lingers in a stir of primal dust.

SIX

"WHERE *IS* THE WALL?" I asked my daddy one night while he brushed my hair. We lived in Bunker A, where all of the Tree Factory workers lived back then.

He cleared his throat. He hadn't yet developed "the cough," but "the tickle" had crept in, and he cleared his throat all too often. "The Wall?" he said. "Somewhere east. And you're going to find it one day, I know you are." He poked at my ribs, and I squealed. "I hear," he whispered, "there's an underground passageway that leads straight there."

"You mean like the trolley tunnels?" I'd never been in one, but I'd heard about them. People traveled from city to city in Bygonne through the trolley tunnels.

"No," he said. "Deep underground. Mysterious...." Then he flipped a coin out from behind my ear and made it disappear. He was always doing magic, anything to make me smile. But he kept on and on about how someday I'd be free, through the mysterious magical wall to the green paradise of the Other Side.

I didn't realize it then, but I know now—he didn't say those things to make me feel better, he said them to make himself feel better about leaving me. A few more years and his time would be up, too. No one makes it past thirty in Bygonne.

Except for the Superiors.

Someone shakes me—

"Joy, wake up."

—and I moan in response, covering my head with my

blanket, body aching with need for sleep.

"Joy, it's rise time… and Baby Lou's sick."

My eyes pop open. Aby's sitting on my bed, holding a whimpering brown bundle. I sit up and take her, cradling her to my chest. Heat rises from her dry skin like a furnace. That listless-eyed stare into nothing clamps a vice around my heart.

"We need medicine." Aby wrings her hands, avoids my eyes. She knows exactly what she's asking.

"I'll ask at breakfast."

Arianna Superior, with her motorized, diamond-studded oxygen tank, comes to escort us to the common area this morning. This is unusual; she hardly ever steps a toe off of the catwalk. Usually Humphrey, or her stumbling, muttonhead son, or one of the other Superiors, comes to get us. Rumor has it she's scared of the diseases we might carry, and of getting infected. But I know it's not that. Her eyes are a dark and empty abyss of hatred and homicidal famine. Not one rotten piece of her decayed heart has shed an ounce of fear or care for humankind in a long, long time. No, she has other reasons for floating above us like the angel of death. Waiting for the perfect time to strike and take us from this life, perhaps.

My heart skips a beat. I've been so focused on Baby Lou and my need for sleep, only now am I remembering last night's discovery. Or… was it a dream? It had to have been. I check my hand. Still, it bears remnants of black paint.

Definitely not a dream.

We all march quietly down the hall toward the disheartening smell of another foul breakfast. In my arms, Baby Lou gulps water from her bottle, shivering violently. I wrap her tighter in her blanket, and kiss her. "You'll be okay, sweet Baby," I whisper. "Momma Joy will take care of you."

When we get to the common area doorway, I step aside to

let everyone pass. Then, I walk cautiously—not too bravely, not too feebly—up to Arianna Superior at the catwalk stairs. "Baby Lou's sick with fever," I say. "She needs medicine, or she'll die."

Arianna Superior glances from Baby Lou to me, with no expression. She cocks her head with a click that chills my spine. "Is that so?" She draws out the last syllable like she's sharpening a knife, seemingly amused by the possibility of Baby Lou's death. Maybe she'll help it along.... Or perhaps my begging arouses her lust for our suffering.

She takes a long, dramatic breath into her golden mask, the diamonds on her tank twinkling in the overhead lights, and I remember my promise to Miguel. Someday, they'll get theirs. But today, the bluff of weakness. Done right, you'll get virtually anything you desire. One of the lessons learned from the sparse years I had with my parents—a prostitute, and a gambling magician.

"Please, Madam Superior," I say. "I'll do whatever you want. I'll do extra work, and... and anything I need to. Please...."

Arianna Superior smiles. Except, it looks more like if you dug up a corpse and spread its rotted lips apart. "Very well," she says. "Bring the beast to the office after breakfast. I have something you may do to earn it."

"Thank you, Madam Superior, I will."

I hurry to take my place next to Jax, as Humphrey makes his rounds with the slop pot. Diaz Superior stumbles down the catwalk to his mother and slumps into a chair. With a grimace of disgust, Arianna Superior leaves him to watch over us, and heads to the office. Seconds after she disappears, Diaz Superior closes his eyes and passes out, drunk. Humphrey eyes me as he ladles slop into my bowl, and gives me a slight nod. Jax shrugs at him. With everything that happened last night, we forgot to even look for his "payment," and we had no choice but to sneak by his sleeping body and into our dorms.

I grab his hairy arm and, leaning in close, whisper into his ear: "We found something that might be of interest to you. Unfortunately, we didn't have the right tool for picking its lock. Next time, we've got you covered." I wink and give him a flirty smile; a lesson from my mother.

He rolls his eyes and continues down the line.

"What'd you tell him?" Jax asks.

"You know, about the lock we needed to pick next time?" I nudge his boot under the table.

Whispers rise up as the children take advantage of Diaz Superior's passed-out drunkenness.

Jax nods. "This morning, I thought it was a dream."

"Me, too. In fact, if I didn't have this here"—I show him the black paint on my palm—"I might have still thought it was. Seems impossible, right?"

Another nod. "We need to find an explanation."

"It's our way out, that's the explanation."

"Then why did it bring us back?"

"Well, someone obviously led us down there. Maybe they knew we couldn't leave the children—"

"Why would someone lead us down there, and then not show themselves?"

"I don't know... maybe they're shy...?"

With a roll of his eyes, he stuffs a bite of bread into his mouth. "There'd have to be a better reason than that."

"What are you two talking about?" Aby leans over, breaking away from her conversation with Miguel.

"I'll tell you later," I say, and shovel slop into Baby Lou's mouth and a few into my own, fighting back a gag.

"Oooh, secrets?" Miguel snatches the lump of bread from Jax's plate and rips off a chunk. "Let's hear 'em."

The room falls deathly silent, and Jax lays a finger to his lips, nodding slightly toward the catwalk, where Arianna Superior approaches her son. He's slid halfway out of his chair, probably drunk off of six month's rations. Arianna Superior jerks a leg back in her long, thick, black skirt and kicks with the force of a factory machine. Diaz awakes in an earsplitting scream, flailing to the floor, gripping an ankle bent sideways. Bone protrudes from the skin and red spurts through the metal grates, splattering on the concrete below. With one hand, she grabs him by the throat and drags him behind her toward the office.

Humphrey stands rigid in the corner, like he's peed himself, while the rest of us are frozen in shocked astonishment. I'm thinking Humphrey won't be sleeping on the job anymore.

"What... was that?" Jax says.

"I don't know," Miguel replies. "But it's about time somebody broke a few bones of his, right?"

Nervous laughter flits around the room for about two seconds before it's cut off. Mona and Emmanuel Superior appear above us, no doubt gossiping. Mona's wild hair has fat pink and green curlers in it today.

"Sunday," Jax and I mutter at the same time.

She always wears those ugly curlers on Sunday. Usually, the black satin or velvet waistcoat would accompany a patterned skirt that mimics a bed covering. Today, though, she and Emmanuel wear new threads, and their matching peasant dresses make me choke on the laughter that almost bursts out. I play it off as though I'd swallowed wrong, but really, I'm dying. I've never seen anything so ridiculous.

Emmanuel Superior flips a long brown curl from his shoulder—one of his worst wigs yet—and beckons to me with his usual purple fingernail.

"Another glorious day at the Tree Factory!" Mona Superior sings, lifting her skirt and stepping over Diaz's blood. Then, she sneers. "Now get to work, before I turn the jumpers loose."

With that, children hop from their seats to get in line. Most of them have never seen the jumpers the Superiors keep in their bunker as "pets-of-use." Not many of them would like to. Except for Johnny, maybe; he has a fascination for stalking things in the dark. One night, he tracked something for three hours, only to find it was the smallest rat in the history of Bygonne. He ate it anyway, though, grumbling the whole time.

I brush my arm against Jax's; our usual greeting or departing gesture when we're being watched. At the door, he takes his place at the front of the line. With a protesting Baby Lou, I start up the catwalk steps beneath flaring nostrils, a hairy nose-mole, and fake locks that may have nested families of vermin in their past life. Baby Lou whimpers, and her lip quivers. I brush a teeny curl from her eye as I reach the halfway point. That one act alone, I'm sure, makes the Superiors' toxic blood bubble and churn beneath their skin.

"Aww," says Mona Superior once I've reached the catwalk. "Isn't that precious?" Then, she smacks my face so hard my ears ring.

"Ow!" I yell, flinching. "What was that for?"

"For being such a filthy little trollop. I'm sure you've done something to deserve it."

Emmanuel Superior laughs, his pointy Adam's apple bobbing above a choker of pink pearls. "Take your nasty excuse for a human being into the office. I don't know why, but Your Madam Superior has decided to spare its life—this time."

When we finally get to the office, I'll admit, I'm scared. Below me, Mona and Emmanuel Superior disappear behind the doors that lead to the Superiors' bunker. They rattle shut as the smell of burning flesh greets me—unfortunately, a familiar smell when you've built trees your whole life. I know this stench well. A quick set-n-sear job on Diaz Superior's ankle, maybe.

I knock swiftly, and Arianna Superior answers. Her son lies still in the corner on the floor, eyes closed, his freshly set, bandaged foot propped up on two pillows. I watch his chest for breathing.

"Oh, he isn't dead," says Arianna Superior, "but he may be soon." She glides over to the corner, and I swear her legs aren't moving. Her skirt's thick, sure. Still, it appears as though she's... floating off the floor. I blink and refocus. She reaches a tall shelf, lifts an arm, stretches up and keeps going, like her body's made of rubber.

I need sleep.

I blink again, rub my tired eyes. She's returned to normal height, a bottle in each hand, shaking one with a small amount of liquid in it. The other's full. "Two drops, every four hours for the fever." She hands me the nearly-empty bottle, then crosses to another corner of the room and picks up a pile of clothes. "When these are adequately washed and mended, you will get more medicine." She drapes the clothes over my free arm.

"Thank you, madam," I say. "I'll get them mended tonight before bed."

By the time I get back to the girls' dorm, my arms are aching from the weight of Baby Lou and Arianna Superior's atrocious clothes. The smell radiating from them is so grotesque, I don't think I'll ever eat again. Hard enough to eat in the first place.

I drop the pile beside my bed, and lay Baby Lou down. She begins to cry, rubbing at her eyes with a shaky fist. "Shh, Baby, it's okay. You'll feel better soon." I squeeze two drops of medicine into her mouth and hold it closed, puffing a quick breath into her nostrils to make her swallow. Then, I dip a small cloth into water, and soak down her curly hair and face, her trembling body. She cries from the chill.

"I wish I could do more, sweetheart." I affix her into the blanket sling on my back, where she'll stay for half of the day until I can't take the weight any longer, then I'll lay her down in the playpen and hope she doesn't cry the whole time. My options are extremely limited.

Guilt and anger make me burn with fury, because I find myself thinking, *Maybe she'd be better off dead.*

§

By the end of the day, I've reached a new level of exhaustion, barely able to hold Baby Lou in my arms. Or even move my arms. My feet ache, and my back and neck throb with hot, sharp pains. My eyes struggle to stay open.

And I have ratty corpse's clothes to mend. *Ugh.* But I'm doing it for Baby Lou, not for Arianna Superior, I have to remind myself of that.

You take the dark with the light and build on.

Some days, it's easier than others. Today is not that day.

"What story are you gonna tell tonight, Momma Joy?" Chloe asks.

"No story tonight. I'm sorry"—I yawn—"too sleepy. And I have a lot to do before bed."

Both rooms fill with groans and complaining, but I'm too drained to care much. Two more drops of medicine go into Baby Lou's mouth, and she wrinkles her nose at the taste, but swallows on her own this time, without the blowing.

"Good girl, Baby." I pat her forehead. Still hot, though

not like earlier.

"What's with the mountain of rags?" Aby asks.

"Corpse woman gave me the 'privilege' of mending them for Baby Lou's medicine. I have to finish them before she'll give me any more."

"That's ridiculous! How could she be so heartless?" Aby lifts a shirt from the top of the pile and sniffs it. "And—ew, gross—where did she get these? Off of dead people?"

"She is the corpse woman...."

Aby sighs, and plops down onto my bed, next to the pile. "Well, I guess we have a lot to do, then."

"Oh no, Aby, you don't have to—"

"Don't be silly. Of course I do. She's my baby, too. And you're exhausted. There's no way you'll get these all washed and mended tonight." She points at the noisily ticking clock, hung slanted on the wall. "It's already late. Let's get everyone in bed, then you mend, I'll wash. We'll get it done in no time."

I grin. "You're a great sister." I kick off my daddy's boots and peel my dirty socks from my stinky feet. "Thank you."

"Hey, no problem." She smiles back.

Serna takes over spray duty for me tonight, because she sees how tired I am. I rock Baby Lou to sleep while she gets the little ones hosed down, and almost fall asleep myself, sitting there. I should hose down, too. I'm filthy. I lay Baby Lou in her crib, grab a change of clothes, and stumble to the washroom, as clean little girls scramble out in fresh pajamas to hop into their beds. Chloe and the other littlest ones steal hugs and kisses from me on their way past.

"Sorry I'm not telling a story tonight," I say to them.

"It's okay, Momma Joy," Chloe says. "You look tired. You can tell us one tomorrow." She pops a thumb in her mouth and smiles.

"Thank you for understanding." I crouch down and kiss her cheek. "Now get some sleep, little sweethearts. Pleasant dreams."

They trot off in a line of whispers and giggles and jump into their beds, and I continue on to the washroom.

"Want me to hold the hose for ya?" Aby asks.

"Sure, thanks."

The hose-down wakes me right up, so for once I'm happy about the cold water. I may be able to make it through the late-night clothes mending now. Plus, it feels good to be clean. Once I'm washed, Aby and I take turns slurping from the nozzle, then she turns the squeaky faucet off and tosses me a towel. I dry my skin and wrap the towel around my head as the remnants of dirty water from my body swirl down the drain in the concrete floor.

"Feel better?" Aby asks.

"Much." I put on my clean clothes—articles we found in the Bunker A warehouse storage—and we tiptoe out.

We stand staring at the nauseating mound of dead people's clothes that Arianna Superior probably stripped from the carcasses herself. I shiver.

"All right," I say, steeling my resolve. "You ready?"

"As ready as I'll ever be," Aby says with a sigh.

After removing the needle and thread from the drawer between Aby's bed and mine, I get to work on the first shirt and have it mended in a couple of minutes. Aby skips off quietly to the washroom to wash it, while I start on the next garment: a skirt with stains on it. My stomach churns as I fumble with the tear caked with dried blood. I set it aside and, trying not to think about how the woman died, move on to the next item. Aby returns with the damp shirt and drapes it over the line that runs through the middle of our room. I hold up the bloody skirt. "This one will need washing first," I tell her.

"Yuck." She makes a face. "What do you suppose—?"

"I don't even want to think about it."

Pinching a tiny section of the fabric, she holds it at arm's length, head turned to the side, scowling. She'd be much louder with her disapproval, I'm sure, if there weren't rows of little sleeping girls nearby.

"Do you want to trade jobs?" I ask.

"No, it's okay. I'll just wash it with my eyes closed."

I giggle. "I don't know how well that will work, but, okay...."

"It'll have to work, or it won't get washed," she whispers loudly, carrying it as far away from her body as possible, all the way to the washroom.

When I agreed to this chore, I had no idea what I was in for. Never has there been such awful, repulsive shreds of clothes. And to think, Arianna Superior will be wearing them with no care for the dead she violated by stealing them. This makes me hate her even more. She's a filthy, rotten soul, and I'll never understand why *she* gets to live thirty years past the average life span, when good people like my parents—like all of our parents—barely even reach thirty.

At eleven, I give Baby Lou her medicine, relieved her fever has come down. Aby and I are only halfway finished; it's going to be a long night. We work tirelessly—me, fixing tear after tear; her, running from me to the sink to the clothesline—until I've knotted the last strand of thread and handed off the last piece of clothing. She trots over to the washroom, and I check the clock. One-thirty. I lie down next to Baby Lou, and a couple of minutes later, after hanging the last wet item on the full clothesline, Aby collapses onto her bed beside us.

"So, what's the secret?" she asks.

"Huh?"

"You said you'd tell me later, remember?"

"Oh. Right."

"Well, tell me, then."

But I consider not telling her. How do you describe something like that without sounding insane?

"I'm not sure how to explain it—"

"Was it something you found in the bunker?"

I nod.

"Well... what? What did you find?"

"We found... paradise."

"Paradise?"

"Yes," I say. "I think it's... somehow... a portal to the Other Side."

SEVEN

THE SECOND I CLOSE MY EYES, it seems, the rise-alarm rings from the wall. I force myself awake to find Baby Lou's fever is back. I give her the last two drops of medicine with some water, and she gulps it down, trembling from the open air on her hot skin. She whimpers and cries feebly. Not only will I be running the chopper on a few hours of sleep again, but I'll also have Baby Lou to deal with all day. Again.

"Aby," I call over.

Still wrapped up in her blanket, she peeks over at us and sits up. "Morning." She yawns and stretches. "How's Baby?"

"Still hot. Will you hold her while I get ready? Then, I'll hold her while you do?"

"Sure." Aby swings her feet over the bedside and ties her long red curls up in a knot. "Poor thing." She runs her fingers along Baby Lou's soft, warm cheek.

"Yeah, thank goodness I'm getting more medicine for her." I scan the clothes on the line. "Thank you so much. There's no way I would've finished without your help."

"What are sisters for?" She winks, then nuzzles her nose against Baby Lou's neck. "You sure you'll be fine with her today? You didn't get a lot of sleep...."

"You didn't either."

"I know, but—"

"I'll be fine."

"Well, let me know if you need anything. You know where to find me."

"Okay."

"Paradise," she whispers, smiles, and scrunches her shoulders like she does when she's excited. "Can we go tonight? Pleeeeeease....?"

"Maybe."

She taps her feet on the floor, and bounces on her bed. "We can get one of the other girls to watch Baby while we go. Serna's good with her."

"We'll talk about it later," I say with a yawn. "I'm too tired to think right now. Let me talk to Jax."

Soon, I'm changed into work clothes with my boots laced up tight, ready to face Arianna Superior with her washed and patched-up garments. Still a disgusting, ratty mess, but much less so than last night.

With Baby Lou slung on my back and Arianna Superior's clothes draped over my arm, I lead the girls from the dorm when the door opens. To our surprise, Diaz Superior—on crutches—waits to guide us to breakfast in an unusual moment of semi-sobriety. The fire in his eyes gives it away. When he's able to walk straight, he likes to be close instead of up on the catwalk like the others, in case any of us acts up. That way, he's within arm's reach. The familiar coil of thornwhip, strung through his belt loop, peeks out from behind him. Today, he wants someone to take out his anger on. God knows he won't take it out on his mother. She'd kill him with no remorse. With the flick of a finger. Not sure why she hasn't yet, it's obvious she despises him. That could explain why he doesn't have his own oxygen tank.

Jax nods slightly as we reach the common area door. I breathe deep and prepare myself. You never know with Diaz. He's flinching with each step. *Why on Earth is he mobile?* He shouldn't be up for at least another week. Either his mother put him up to this, or his bloodlust was too great for him to stay still. He sways at the door, and I move aside to let everyone pass. With a whimper, Baby Lou tucks her face down behind my back.

"What the hell do you want?" Diaz spits a fat lump of mucus onto my boot toe—on my daddy's boyhood boots. I could breathe fire. But I tame it. For Baby Lou.

As if it never happened.

"Madam Superior had me mend her clothes for medicine," I say. "And I'm finished. I need to take her the clothes and get the medicine now."

He snarls a laugh, leans back against the wall, resting a crutch against it, too. "Well, now… ain't that sweet?" He snatches up a shirt and inspects the stitch. "It seems you missed a spot." Then, squeezing the cloth in both hands, he yanks outward until the fresh seam tears open again, the thread endings reaching out like little arms, begging for justice.

I'm frozen, speechless. Baby Lou cries, and white hot rage burns inside me. He snatches up another article and rips it in two. Then another, and another, and another, until the weight has lifted from my arm and transplanted itself into my heart. Every item is torn in two.

I start to walk toward my table, numb.

"Hey!" he calls behind me. "I didn't say you could go anywhere."

I turn back toward him while Jax and everyone else watches. Once I'm near him again, he slaps me and I fly backward, knocking Baby Lou from her blanket. She screams, and I scramble to scoop her up. My face is throbbing and wet, as Diaz Superior moves closer, thornwhip raised to strike.

Jax erupts from his chair and slams it against the wall. Diaz pauses at the sound, and in seconds, Jax is between me and

Diaz Superior, fists ready, chest heaving, body bent forward. I imagine his eyes, dark and brutal, valiant and fiery, like a hero from the stories I've told and read to the children in the past.

Only now do I see that hero in Jax.

"Go ahead," he says coolly. "Do it. I dare you."

Diaz snickers and teeters on his crutch. Then, he cocks back as if to bring the whip down hard, until an unbearable screech makes us all cover our ears.

"What are you doing!" comes the howl of Arianna Superior as she bursts through the doors leading to the Superiors' bunker. I've never seen anyone move that fast. Like she has wheels for feet. Her sparkling tank struggles to keep up, as Aby steals away Baby Lou into the common area, to safety.

"Are you aware he's the best oxygenizer we've ever had?" Arianna looms over her son. "Explain to me what's going on here!"

"I had your clothes all sewn," I say, "but he ripped them all—"

"She's lying," Diaz counters. "She brought them to me, just like this—"

"No"—Jax shakes his head—"she didn't. He ripped the clothes, then he slapped her and cut her face, and he was going to whip her and the baby to death. And if that happened, who'd run the chopper? Sure as hell won't be me. I have solenoids to make."

What a sly boy he is.

Arianna glances from the pile of clothes up to her son, and I swear her eyes glow red. Diaz grumbles as he disappears, hobbling toward the corridor to the Superiors' bunker.

"Please, madam," I say. "I stayed up until nearly two o'clock washing and mending everything. I need more medicine—"

"No." She lifts her golden mask and inhales deep into it. "Once you have adequately mended these garments, like we agreed—"

"But . . . but I already did!"

She swoops down into my face in one swift motion, tip of her nose a splinter from mine—the closest I've ever been to her. A dark energy swirls around her, mixed with the smell of rust and salt—tears, maybe?—like she alone is responsible for the world's pain, suffering, and decay.

"Do you like to breathe?" she asks.

"Doesn't everyone?"

"Are you aware that it's extremely disrespectful to answer a question with a question?"

"Is it?"

Her face flushes blood-red. "Do you know what happens to those who do not respect and obey their Superiors?"

"They get the easy way out?"

I stare into her dead eyes, and she stares back into mine as I invite her to kill me. In this moment, I've silently defeated her. Not caring—or bluffing that you don't—makes the threat of losing your life a flimsy weapon.

"I'll mend the clothes again tonight," I add. "Thank you, Madam Superior."

"Yes. You will. And you'll do it hungry. Humphrey!" she calls. "Do not serve Miss Montgomery any slop today."

I almost thank her.

Humphrey grumbles in response, and Arianna Superior turns swiftly, gliding up the catwalk steps. When she reaches the top, she's joined by Mona Superior, who whispers something to her, then Arianna goes on toward the office.

"Beasts!" Mona laughs. "It is now time to discuss a change in quota."

We collectively hold our breath. Even the smallest of us knows what that means.

"You have been producing many fine trees as of late," she continues. "We are very satisfied with each of your positions and feel you all know your jobs well. Which is why we have decided to increase production. You will be expected to produce one hundred trees per day now, as opposed to the prior seventy-five. The line will move quicker, so be prepared. And do not lose quality. We have signed a contract with Taborton. Their salvagers will supply us with extra materials, and in return, we will give them a third of our production." She takes a deep breath in her oxygen mask, then continues. "If you perform adequately, you will be rewarded with one hour of evening free time in the cellar. And I pray I don't need to remind any of you what happens if you do not perform adequately...."

At the words "free time," the energy in the room changes. It's been months since we went down there. The Superiors are definitely up to no good.

"And if the rest of you expect another meal today," Mona Superior adds, "get yourselves to your stations and begin work immediately. In five minutes, work will be double-time."

Jax helps me pick up the clothes, while everyone heads to their stations, excitement plain on their faces. No one cares that they'll be working harder. They've been offered a small taste of freedom, and now they're dancing in the clouds. How cleverly evil of the Superiors. This will increase production much more than threats, starvation, or beatings.

Aby joins us with Baby Lou. "What do we do?" she asks.

"We take these clothes back to our dorm," I say, "drop them off, and get to work."

Jax and I head down the hallway with Aby at our heels. "But... but what about Baby? She needs medicine."

At the dorms, Jax slips something into the clothing pile.

"Eat it fast," he whispers.

"Thanks," I whisper back. He stays at the threshold while I take the clothes inside, dig out the lump of bread, and cram it into my mouth in two bites.

"Joy?" Aby follows me in, frantic with worry.

"She'll have to go through the day without it," I explain through my chewing. "Just the day, though. I have a plan."

She tries to read in my eyes what it is. "You'll tell me later?"

"Yes. Now, help me get her changed. I'll keep her for the first half of the day, give her plenty of water and keep a bucket and a cloth nearby to cool her down when she needs it."

Aby nods and changes Baby Lou into a clean diaper, then wraps her shivering body in a blanket.

"I need to go," Jax says from the doorway. "Is your face okay? You might need antiseptic."

"It's fine. I'll brush some on before I go out."

"Okay. I'll catch up with you later."

"Thank you, Jax. For... saving us."

"Of course." And with a quick half-smile, he's gone.

Aby hurries the first-aid kit out from under her bed as the warning alarm sounds. A quick brush of rubbing alcohol later, I grab a stack of rags, a bottle and a bucket, and we both hurry to our stations.

I barely have enough time to get Baby Lou into her play-pen with a fresh bottle of water before the chopper begins to beep at me. Hopefully, she'll let me leave her there for a while, because my body can't take her weight much more with this lack of sleep. Maybe I'll be lucky. I breathe in deep, and press the "ready" button.

When all of the lights are lit, the line starts. One good thing, I suppose—the adrenaline will keep me awake today. The first slab of titanzium slides down, and I rush it to the gridlines and count, using the second hand of the window's wall clock.

One.

Two.

Three.

The blade falls, slicing two perfect halves.

Three seconds isn't bad. I can handle it.

An hour into production, and I was right about the adrenaline; I'm more alert, even if my stomach begs for nourishment. I'm used to that, though. The exhaustion will catch up eventually, but it'll be replaced by adrenaline again tonight when I risk my life for my Baby.

Twenty minutes later, shrieks erupt down the line. Samurai is engulfed in flames. I slam my hand on the emergency stop button, grab my bucket, and rush to him, dousing the fire with what little water is left. It's hardly fazed. Frantic, I rip off Baby Lou's blanket sling and attempt to wrap it around Samurai's writhing body, but he's swinging his arms, the flames ever-growing. Without thinking, I punch him in the face. He drops to the ground, and I cover him with the blanket. The fire dies immediately, leaving him burned and bloody, but alive.

"Someone get Mona Superior!" I cry. "He needs medical attention!"

Johnny sprints toward the catwalk stairs and punches the emergency alarm. Samurai moans, then it's drowned out by the shrill siren. I feel faint. Too much blood.... In some spots, the skin is gone completely. Charred muscle and bone peek through, tinged with hints of red.

"It's okay, Sam," I tell him. "We'll get you all fixed up." I cradle his head in my lap as Aby and Miguel approach.

"What happened?" they ask.

"I don't know. I heard him screaming, and saw he was

on fire."

"It was too fast," says Miguel. "Too fast for him."

"I'm sorry I hit you, Sam," I cry. Burnt hair and flesh stench hangs in the air, bringing with it memories of the day Molina died in this very spot. "I had to make you still to put the fire out." Lips, nose, and ears are gone completely. He rocks his head from side to side, slowly, then, his chest falls for the last time. I sob harder as feet trample the catwalk and down the stairs. Soon, Jax is crouching beside me.

"What happened?" he asks. "Is he dead?"

I nod, clutching Samurai's head to my chest.

Another brother... dead.

§

With Sam's death taking up the Superiors' "precious time," and an older boy learning how to use the sun torch, in order to reach our quota, they made us work two extra hours. Half of the little ones were crying on the way to dinner, weak with hunger and fatigue. But for me, the hunger was a fine distraction.

The Superiors kept their promise, though. We have our free time in the filthy cellar playroom. But none of us feels much like celebrating. Chloe and some of the younger children chase each other around, half-heartedly, while others play with the few raggedy toys in the corner. We olders sit in pairs and groups, gathered here and there, chatting softly, talking about Samurai, and Toby.

Aby and Miguel sit in a dark corner, their fingers exploring each other's skin, while a few of the older girls pass Baby Lou around, slathering her with kisses and get well wishes. Though she manages the faintest smile, she's fading fast, having refused even water for the past few hours. If the bad air and fever don't get her, the dehydration will.

Jax takes a seat next to me on the broken machine part that is now our playroom bench. He rests his elbows on his knees. "Man... I can't believe it."

I nod and kick at the concrete through a layer of dust. A leaky pipe drips water down a nearby wall, next to a flickering oxygen light, leaving a trail of green slime. The squeaking echo of rats through the vents makes me shiver.

"You okay?" he asks.

"This is no place for children to be," I say loudly. Emmanuel Superior probably waits within earshot on the other side of the door, but I don't care. Let him hear my blasphemy.

I'm old enough now to know what keeps us going each day: the unsaid hope that someday we'll be free. That we'll be rescued, adopted by people from another town, or even bought by less demanding, less abusive owners, ones who'd let us be children in the hours outside of work. It's a hope we keep private, too afraid to be told we're being silly, that we'll never get out of here. We'd be stripped of our fantasies, working for a breath we resent taking. Strip us of our hope, and strip us of our desire to live; steal away the delusion of future freedom, and drain what little willpower remains to spend another rotten day building trees.

But Toby and Sam don't even get the possibility of freedom now. They died with their dreams still silenced. Or—

I laugh out loud, and Jax shoots me a curious glance.

—maybe they were the lucky ones. Maybe that's the true freedom.

Death.

Jax takes my hand, pulls it to his chest, probably thinking I've lost my mind. Maybe I have. He caresses my skin with his thumb and says nothing. But he doesn't have to, the gesture is enough. A warmth grows in me, and I realize I have much to live for. Even now. Even here, in this hideous, foul, lifeless world. I have Jax, Aby, Baby Lou, and the rest of my brothers and sisters. I have love. And love itself, if nothing else, is enough to wake me up tomorrow. That, and the possibility that we may all soon be rid of this place for good.

"Tonight," I whisper into Jax's ear, my lips brushing his earlobe. "We have a mission."

He shivers and moves into me, squeezing my hand. "Ooh," he whispers back, lips hovering over mine. "Tell me more." I remember their silken warmth when he kissed me . . . how he stood his ground between me and the thornwhip today . . . and I tremble with desire for the first time.

"Thanks again," I say, "for—"

He interrupts me with a kiss.

I wrap my arms around him, draw him closer, our heat igniting a fire between us.

"Ew, gross!" a little voice yells from nearby, and I back away, embarrassed.

I try to take my hand from Jax, but he grips it tighter and shakes his head. "I'm not letting go," he says. "Let them stare."

After a tense moment, I relax and lay my head on his shoulder. "Tell Humphrey we'll have him something real good if he'll let us out tonight."

"I don't know if he'll go for it."

"Promise him. Tell him we'll have it within an hour after we leave."

"Seriously? How are we gonna do that?"

"Diaz probably has some liquor stashed in the office, right? And it just so happens . . . that's where Baby Lou's medicine is."

EIGHT

EMMANUEL SUPERIOR BARGES into the playroom in his lacy negligée and satin house robe, and escorts us back upstairs to our dorms to be locked up tight.

"What, no goodnight kiss?" I mumble as our door slams. Pieces of the wall crumble to the floor.

"What's the plan?" Aby offers to take Baby Lou, and I gladly hand her over. My arm muscles are about to give out from holding her so much over the past two days.

"Jax and I are going to break into the office."

She gasps, clapping a hand over her mouth. "Joy, no—"

"We can't risk mending these clothes again, to have something else happen and get no medicine. Plus, I don't want her to go through the night without it."

"We're not going to mend the clothes, then? Won't she know?"

"No, you and Serna, and whoever else knows how to sew, will get started on that, while Jax and I go."

In the washroom, I fill the empty brown medicine bottle with water and screw the lid on tight, then hurry back to Aby. "I'll take the full bottle, and replace it with this. Then, tomorrow, when she gives it to me—*if* she gives it to me— she'll never know."

Aby blows out a fast breath, tugs at her tattered black shirt. "It's crazy. You know that, right?"

"I know, but it's time for crazy. We're not playing their games anymore. From now on, they'll be playing ours. They just may not realize it. Yet."

"Did you see what Arianna did to her son's ankle, Joy?"

"Yes. But we're different; we make her trees. Without us, they wouldn't have their precious canned air to breathe. And she wouldn't have all of Bygonne at her mercy. That makes us more valuable than her son."

Aby kisses Baby Lou's nose. "What a monster," she says.

"Yes she is."

There's a knock on the door.

"I have to go," I say. "Start the girls on the sewing. It shouldn't take very long with a group. At least we don't have to wash them again."

She sighs. "Okay, Joy. Please be careful."

Jax waits for me on the other side of the door, vibrating with anticipation. Humphrey's perched on the side of his cot, hands clasped together, worry on his face.

"Ready?" Jax says.

I nod, and close the door behind me.

Humphrey shakes his head. "You kids must have a death wish."

"Quite the opposite," I say.

"Well, you better not get caught—" He hacks for about a minute straight, the veins around his face and neck bulging under bright red skin. "Not that it would matter much on my end," he goes on when he's finally caught his breath. "My days are numbered anyway." He holds out the heavy key ring, balanced on one finger, and I take it from him.

"Which one's for the office?" I ask.

He stares in disbelief. "Brave tonight, aren't we?"

"Which is it?"

He shrugs, points. "The smallest of the lot, with the blue dot on it."

I search through until I find that one. "Thanks, Humphrey, for helping us save a little girl's life."

"Whatever. Just don't get caught."

We take off toward the stairs and ascend them swiftly. With no light on in the office, a bit of relief mixes with my fear and adrenaline. I grip the office key in one hand, the rest in the other to silence their jingling. My eyes dance from the office door to the corridor doors, where I expect them to fly open any second and spit out all four Superiors to our demise.

But we reach the office door with no incident, and at one easy turn of the key, we're in, closing it soundlessly behind us and rolling the flap over the window. Our hearts and breath are a symphony in the stillness, beating and breathing a dangerous song of freedom in a servant's world. I've never felt more alive. The promise of possible death clashes against the realization of power over the Superiors. I refuse to follow their rules any longer.

Jax removes two light sticks from his pocket, cracks them, and hands me one. I shake it, making the light glow brighter. "You find the liquor," I whisper. "I'll get the medicine."

He gives me a thumbs-up, and we split. He crosses the room to the cabinets in the far back corner which store who-knows-what, and I size up the towering shelf that harbors the medicine at its peak. Like a princess in a high castle on a mountaintop, I must now figure out how to scale it and retrieve. I thought I was delirious when Arianna Superior seemingly elongated her body to reach up there. Now, as I stare up at the shelf I know the medicine's at... maybe I wasn't so delirious. It's an impossible height.

I move a wobbly chair in front of the shelf and climb up onto it. Standing on tiptoe, my fingertips barely reach the other bottle. As soon as I have it in my hand, I replace it with the water-filled one and step back down, nearly falling off of the chair as it jerks off-balance.

"Got it," I say, inspecting the full bottle.

"Me, too," says Jax, and he holds up a large bottle half-filled with auburn liquor behind a burgundy-and-gold label. "And it's good stuff, too. Humphrey's gonna be pleased with this, for sure." He unscrews the lid, takes a whiff, and makes a face. Then, he wipes the rim with his shirt and gulps some down. He cringes, then hops, then takes another gulp and holds the bottle out to me.

At first, I shake my head—

"Come on, try it. It's good," he says.

—then give in, take the bottle, down two huge gulps, and hand it back to him with a wince as I swallow. "Happy?" I say. "Can we go now?"

"It's good, right?"

"I guess. I just really want to go."

"Hand me the light stick."

I give it to him, and make sure the bottle of medicine is safe in my pocket. He tucks both light sticks away, along with the bottle of liquor and, after I fold the flap back off of the window, we finally exit the office. I lock the door behind us.

Mission accomplished.

We hurry down the catwalk stairs, but as soon as we pass the chopper, Jax steals me away behind it. He removes the bottle from his pocket, unscrews the lid, and smiles. I smile back.

"We did it," he whispers, then gulps the liquor for a couple seconds before passing the bottle to me.

I hesitate, but victory wins me over. Like my daddy after his own winning streak, with enough to trade for food and medicine for Mother, and some left over. . . . I take the bottle and gulp, and gulp, until I'm floating in a warm, giggly place. Swaying, I hand the bottle back to Jax.

"We better save the rest for Humphrey," I tell him.

He screws the lid back on, then takes my hand and guides me through the main factory room, and down the steps we came up earlier in the evening.

"Where are you taking me?"

He doesn't answer. Instead, we sneak the rest of the way swiftly down the stairs until we reach the unlocked playroom and slip inside. As soon as we're behind the closed door, we collide into each other, an aching wave of longing.

"I want you, Joy Montgomery. I always have." And he kisses me feverishly.

I push back, though only enough to speak. "Then have me."

§

Stumbling up the stairs, pausing every other one to steal another kiss, Jax and I finally make it back to the dorms. Humphrey's in the same position we left him—sitting up, hands still clasped in front of him, except now he's snoring.

"You aren't fooling anyone," says Jax, and he drops the third-full bottle of liquor onto the cot, startling Humphrey awake.

"Took you long enough," he grumbles and snatches up the bottle. He unscrews the cap and has it emptied in seconds, with hardly a cringe, then hands the drained evidence back to Jax. "Get rid of this."

A flash of purple light flickers from the chopper window. Jax heads toward it, returning the empty bottle to his back pocket. I follow, still swaying from the liquor and the evening's events. When we get to the window, lightning rips through the sky—an electric web of destruction, promising to split the clouds open any second to spew toxic filth onto Greenleigh and the rest of Central Bygonne. It rains here more than anywhere else, and depending on the severity of the storm, the stability of the Tree Factory's power is questionable.

"Nice," Jax says. "That's what we need, more excitement."

"Trees have to fill with water somehow," I mumble. "Come on, I need to get Baby Lou her medicine."

Jax takes my hand, and we travel back down the hallway. "Okay, but then we're going out again."

"We are?"

"Yup."

"Where?"

"You know where. Miguel wants to bring Aby."

"You told him?"

We approach a reclined, temporarily silenced Humphrey.

"We're going in for a couple minutes," Jax says to him, "but we're coming right back out."

Humphrey shrugs. "Don't get caught."

"I wish you'd quit saying that."

Another shrug. "It'd be game over if you did."

"Thanks for that constant reminder." I shove Jax into the shadows on the other side of his door. "You told Miguel?" I repeat.

"Well, you told Aby. Of course I told Miguel. He's my best friend."

"I thought I was your best friend." And I make a dramatic pouty lip, one he'll only witness when there's liquor in me.

He tugs me closer, takes the opportunity to nibble on the lip softly. "You're more than that." He slaps my backside. "Now come on. The night's young. Get Aby. Wear that sexy black dress." Then he winks and disappears inside the boys' dorm as I float to ours and pour through the door like water.

"Joy!" Aby guides a needle into a piece of fabric, tugs the string through the other side. "What took you so long? I've been worried sick. Did you get the medicine?"

Besides Aby, only Serna and another girl are still sewing. The pile of ripped garments has shrunk to only a few remaining, and the stack of neatly lain, freshly re-mended clothing is tall by its side.

"Yeah, I got the medicine. And we were... sidetracked." I can't hide my grin. "Awesome job on the clothes! I can't believe you're almost finished."

Aby's eyes widen with knowing, and her mouth gapes. She covers it, then quickly removes her hand. "You didn't!" She stands and sniffs at my breath. "Is that... liquor I smell? Joy! Tell me all about it. I want details. But not too many, that would be—"

"There's not much left, right?" I interrupt.

"Huh?" She blinks. "Oh, no. Just three things. These girls are sewing maniacs over here." And she winks at them. Their eyes are heavy and glazed from the extra hours of monotonous work after twelve hours of hard labor. "The others kept dozing off mid-stitch and poking themselves, so I sent them to bed."

"Nice work, girls. How's Baby?"

"Still hot and dry. She drank water, but not much."

I go to her crib with the medicine bottle and pick her up. She stirs, but doesn't wake. "Hey sweetheart, I have your medicine." Her cheek's hot against my lips. I unscrew the bottle, drip two drops into her mouth, then blow into her nostrils to make sure she swallows.

"She needs a doctor," Aby says.

"I know."

But we both know that's silly-speak. The cost of taking her to a doctor in Taborton—the nearest living, breathing city, ten miles west of here—is twice as much as buying three new orphans. And leaving the Tree Factory with Baby Lou... someone would have to go along to care for her. The Superiors sure won't. That would mean showing someone the way to the trolley tunnels... the way *out*. Totally out of the question.

"Can you two finish up these last three things?" I ask the girls.

They nod.

"Why?" Aby asks.

"We're going out again," I whisper.

"What? Where?"

"You're coming, too."

Her eyes light up, and she claps her hands.

I give the bottle to Serna, who tosses me a concerned glance.

"If we're not back... when you wake up, make sure Baby Lou gets two drops every four hours. And don't let the Superiors find this bottle, whatever you do. Hide it at all costs, got it?"

"I won't let anything happen to it," says Serna. "But you'll be back, right?"

"Yes." I kiss Baby Lou's cheek and lay her down in her crib, covering half of her body with a blanket so she doesn't catch a chill. "But... just in case."

I retrieve my box of belongings from under my bed and dig through it; a deck of cards, scant clothing, a few tattered books of fairy tales, and Millie, the animal my mother made me, until I find the slinky black dress I hid underneath it all. I take it and Millie out to inspect them both. Many things my mother made with her hands, but this I remember most. She removed half of her own bed pillow's stuffing and cut a pattern out of an old skirt, coughing the entire time. It wouldn't be much longer until she was gone from my life forever.

"What kind of animal are you making?" I asked her.

"Does it matter?" she responded.

I trace Millie with my fingers—droopy, uneven ears; four short appendages; a long tail where the stuffing has gathered in a fat lump at the end—and remember that day, her words.

"What matters," she continued, "is that you're going to find one. You're going to make it out, Joy. You'll be free one day." Then, she tossed a long brunette wave of hair over her shoulder, and showed me how to sew. My first—and last—lesson. Like with reading. Daddy taught me what little he knew, and I taught myself a little more. One last deep inhale into Millie's smooth, stale fabric, and I lay it down next to Baby Lou.

In a way, I suppose my mother was right. Though no one could've guessed what we'd find twenty-three levels beneath the earth. I wish I could tell her I witnessed a real animal roaming free beneath the sun....

I hold up the slinky black dress to inspect it. "Do you have any dresses?" I ask Aby.

She nods. "An old one of my mother's. Why?"

"Wear it," I say, "Tonight, we're celebrating."

"Oh? Celebrating what?"

"Freedom."

NINE

ONCE ABY AND I ARE SPOT-CLEANED and have nervously slipped into our too-snug-and-too-revealing dresses (with our everyday work boots), we quickly comb each other's hair and fidget. Neither of us has ever dressed up for a boy before.

"This is, like, a real date!" she says, clapping quietly.

The *tap-tap-tap* at the door says it's time to go.

"Ugh—I'm changing," I say, and go to peel the thing off of me. But Aby slaps my hand.

"No, leave it. You look incredible. Besides, they're here. Come on."

We wave to Serna and the other girl finishing up the last two garments, and they wave back. I mouth a 'thank you,' and the younger one rolls her eyes. Obviously jealous. Definitely understandable. This is the most excitement we've had in, like, well... ever, as Jax said. And leaving them behind to sew clothes for Arianna Superior... I probably wouldn't be too happy about it, either.

Aby and I pause to do a last minute tug-and-straighten, then Aby opens the door, despite my frantic head shaking.

"Hey!" she whisper-yells and jumps straight into Miguel's waiting arms, wrapping her legs around him.

Jax, on the other hand, struggles to pick his jaw up from the floor while I stand there like a big dumb lump of awkwardness. I kick a boot toe at the ground, and catch Humphrey peeking at me from under the sagging fat of his arm. He quickly hides his eyes when I glance his way.

"Wow," Jax whispers, "you look…"

"Fantastic, right?" says Aby.

"Uh-huh." He nods and takes a slow step forward, as if afraid to break me with too swift of a touch. "Gorgeous," he says, while he slips both arms around my waist and lifts me up off the ground. He squeezes me tight, plants a soft kiss on my lips.

"Thanks." My cheeks burn with the embarrassment of my embarrassment. "Can we get going now?"

"Certainly, mademoiselle." Jax winks and takes my hand. "I feel like I need to be all formal and whatnot with you dressed like that."

We all laugh.

"You look fantastic, too, Aby," Miguel says.

"Thanks."

"Man"—Jax rubs his hands together—"do we have a night to remember ahead of us, or what? Here…." He passes out breathers, which we strap to our heads.

"A fine addition to this ridiculous dress," I mumble.

"It's not ridiculous," Jax counters. "You could take over the world in that thing."

I giggle. "Well, thank you. Maybe it'll come in handy one day if we ever find a way out of here."

At the wash station shelf, Jax and Miguel move it away from the door, and in seconds, we all have our breathers on and air-locked, and have ducked into the darkness. I quietly close the door, feel for my spear and, finding it in the same spot as always, finally let out my held breath. Jax hands Aby and Miguel the two dimming light sticks from earlier, then cracks a new one. A bright bluish-white globe of luminescence glows brighter, becomes zig-zags as Jax shakes it vigorously.

The ground grumbles with the thunder outside; a dark, low

vibration that raises the tiny hairs on my arms.

"Let's hope the power doesn't act up," Jax says.

"Seriously? Why'd you have to say that?" I ask. "Remember last time, the jumper?"

"That was a coincidence."

"You guys saw jumpers last time?" Miguel asks.

"One. Right after Jax mentioned how it'd been a while since we saw one."

"Maybe we should stay—"

"Nah, man, it was just one." Jax runs his fingers through his hair. "And I speared it. So now, it's none."

"Always more where that came from," I say.

Jax holds his light stick above my face. "You aren't scared, are you?" He winks, but I merely stare back until I have to turn away. Now that the little bit of liquor has worked its way through my body, a fuzzy faded feeling surfaces. Embarrassment finds me unable to fend it off. Embarrassment and fear… interesting combination. Kind of like fruit and death.

"No," I finally say. "I'm not scared."

A total bluff, though my want to not be scared wins out. Mind over matter, my daddy used to say all the time.

"Hell no, you're not," Jax says. "You're one tough girl. Wanna lead?"

"Let's not get too carried away." I hand the spear over to Jax and take my place behind him in the cramped passageway. Aby trails me, then Miguel, taking up the rear; our usual order when we come down together. The one time I led was the one time a jumper landed on me. Luckily, Jax has good reflexes.

Before long, the passageway ends and opens up to the larger area that branches off into different corridors and stairwells, elevators and doors—all of which have been explored—and I fan my fading light stick in a semi-circle around me, keeping alert for jumpers.

A small white rat scurries by, startling us.

"Johnny would have the time of his life down here," says Miguel. "He won't quit bugging me to ask you to let him come."

"Yeah, I'd bring him," Jax says, "but..."

"He's a live wire?" Miguel finishes for him.

"Yup. Love the guy, but he's loco. And I don't want to have to search him down in this place."

Miguel laughs. "You got that right."

We pass up the warehouse, moving quickly through the connecting tunnel between Bunker A and Bunker B. When we get to the stairwell door to start down the stairs, Aby breathes in deep behind me. "Ugh," she says, "I hate going down here."

"Aw... I'll keep you safe, baby," Miguel says.

"Evenin'," says Jax as he steps over Old Jonesy's legs.

For the hundredth time I, too, step over him, and wonder how he died, right here in the stairwell, up against the wall.

"It's not the jumpers I'm worried about." Aby shivers dramatically, easing over his legs behind me.

"You ain't afraid of him, are ya?" says Jax. "He's such a sweet fellow. Shy, quiet..."

"Funny."

Something slides against the concrete steps behind me, and I stop, shine my light stick to illuminate Miguel with Old Jonesy's boots in his hand. I smirk.

"What?" he says. "I need some new boots, man, look." And he points his light down onto his own with holes cut in the toes to allow room for his feet, which probably outgrew the shabby things years ago.

"You go right ahead," I say. "I'm sure he won't mind."

Jax inches up behind me. "Yeah, better a few sizes too big, than too small."

"And Old Jonesy's got some big-ass feet," Miguel says. "You know what that means."

Jax snickers.

"Oh my God," I mumble. "You're joking, right?"

Old Jonesy is now slumped over entirely, his body blocking our way back up. Once Miguel has on the dead man's boots, laced-up and tied, Jax helps him reposition Old Jonesy like he was, setting Miguel's raggedy boots beside him.

"Thanks for the trade, man," Miguel says.

"Better?" Aby asks, shivering again.

"Definitely."

"I do not even want to know how those smell."

"Probably a lot like those clothes you washed for Arianna Superior," I say.

"Ick. You should wash those," she says to Miguel. "Really."

Once we descend the remaining flights of stairs, the citrus smell greets us, stronger than before, and triggers my heart-pounding. Almost there. None of us makes a sound as we traipse down the last dark and hollow corridor where the elevator lies. The closer we get, the stronger the citrus scent, vastly overpowering the normal mildew-and-musty smell of every underground bunker we've explored.

"What's with the smell?" Miguel asks.

"The smoke smelled like that, real strong," says Jax. "In that room, before we went to... wherever it is we went to."

"The Other Side. It has to be."

"All right, Momma Joy. If you say so."

"There's nothing else it could be," I argue. "At least I... I don't think there is."

The rhythm of our eight feet stepping softly toward the known-but-still-unknown is teetering on too much to handle. Nervousness brings a slight nausea, but it could be from the liquor. Last time Jax and I found liquor in the kitchen, I was nauseous for two days. Soon, our globes of light shine in the reflection of the elevator doors a few feet down the otherwise dark corridor. Adrenaline makes me shudder.

"Well?" I say. "Go on then, Jax...."

He steps forward, fist clenched, knuckles raised to knock, when the light above it lights up and the elevator dings. The door whooshes open.

Aby jumps into Miguel's arms, and I take a step back.

"Jax," I say, "you didn't even—"

"I know, I know. More importantly, though, I didn't even press the button. Did you?"

I shake my head.

"You two?"

They shake their heads.

"Someone's definitely down here," I say.

The light goes dark again and the elevator doors begin to close. "Come on." Jax pushes them open again with the spear, holding them in place. "If whoever it is wanted to hurt us, we'd be hurt already." He gets on the elevator, spear still against the door.

Aby, Miguel, and I stand frozen.

"Okay." He shrugs, moves the spear, and the door begins to close.

"Jax!" I grab the door, which pops back open again. "What are you doing?"

"Going to the Other Side ... or whatever. You three comin'?"

"What have we got to lose?" Miguel says.

He's got a point.

We enter the elevator with Jax, and he lets the door close.

"Enter destination," the computer voice says, making us all jump.

"I forgot about that," I say, trying to catch my breath.

"Does it matter what we enter?" Jax raises his head toward the ceiling. "Won't you take us where you want to anyway?"

With a small lurch, the elevator begins to descend, rattling and screeching like before, if not more, because of the extra weight.

"This is totally creepy," Aby whispers.

"This is nothing," I say. "Wait until we get to twenty-three."

Again, like before, after a long descent and much ear-popping, the light to sub-level twenty-three glows and stays lit, while the elevator comes to a stop. The door opens to the frail, grasping cobweb on the overhead fixture. The right-hand corridor is still entirely dark, but straight ahead is lit up with flickering yellow bulbs and green oxygen lights. Jax and I remove our breathers, echoed by a cautious Aby and Miguel, and we're greeted by the citrus-and-rot stench.

Jax leads the way, moving purposefully down the long hall, and when we reach the paintings, Aby and Miguel get caught up in their brilliance and mystery, as Jax forges ahead to our green-lit door. I press my hand in my print from before and find it dry. I half-expected it to be some kind of miracle, never-dry paint, which someone from years and years ago used to paint these here. But no. There's no denying it. Someone is definitely down here.

Someone who's a superb artist.

"Will you please come out?" I'm surprised by my own voice making its way through my unusual trepidation to find the Joy I know. The Joy my daddy raised to be a survivor, a fighter; the Joy who gives fear a swift kick to the jaw and pushes onward.

"Your art is marvelous," I continue.

Aby gives me a fearful glance.

I squeeze her hand. "Jax is right. I don't think whoever's

down here would hurt us. Whoever painted this... is someone good. Someone we want to meet." I nudge Jax.

"Um, yeah," he says. "My favorite is the dancing ladies. Sexxxxxy." He winks.

Miguel snickers. "Yeah, how 'bout some nudes next time?"

Aby kicks him.

"Ow!"

"Could you please tell us if this is the way to the Other Side of The Wall?" I call out. "There are almost forty of us. The youngest is a year-and-a-half old. She's sick, and we're starved, and... and if this is it, please... we need to know...."

We stand silent for a short eternity before it's apparent we won't get an answer.

"Well, then," I add, "will you at least make sure we get back? If we get stuck there, nobody would take care of the children." And as these words come out of my mouth, I consider this fact for the first time.

Jax reaches for the green button.

"Jax, wait," I say. "Let's get them."

"Who, the children? That's crazy! What if we get brought back again? We can't bring thirty-something children down here in the middle of the night on a whim. No." He shakes his head. "Bad idea."

"But what if we go, and get stuck there?"

"Then we get stuck there. We'll have to risk it. I've thought about it, and I have some speculations I want to check out."

"And they are...?"

"I've been thinking about what you said, about the whole portal thing. If that were true, then this would be point A, and the hut would be point B. We need to check out the hut for controls. We didn't inspect it too well when we were there last. This time, we need to find if there's a way to control it."

"Portal?" Miguel says. "Seriously?"

"There's no other logical explanation," I say. "That we know of, anyway."

The book my daddy taught me to read from was a science-fiction one about wormholes and transports and traveling at light speed to far-off galaxies.... I thought it was the stuff of an overactive imagination, but now... I'm considering the possibility that this "stuff" might actually exist. Maybe our world holds things we don't know about because we haven't experienced them yet. We've lived in the bunkers of Greenleigh, most of us, and in the Tree Factory. What wonders and magic and truths lie beyond the grasp of our fingertips and the understanding of our minds?

My guess is now many, many things.

"Are we in agreement?" Jax says. "We go check out the hut and hopefully find out how to control this thing, then we come back and plan our escape."

I look to Aby and Miguel, who both appear as frightened as they do exhilarated. They shrug, and Miguel nods.

I sigh. "Okay. But please bring us back!" I yell. "I have my Baby Lou to take care of."

Jax pushes the green button, and as the door slides open, the same fog pours from the room, beckoning us to another world. I take Aby's hand, she grabs Miguel's arm, and we follow Jax into the room.

"Let's leave our breathers here by the door," I say. "We won't need them where we're going." And we drop them in a pile. "So you'll know what to expect," I add, "it'll feel like you're flying through space, alone, before it spits you out into a wooden room."

"That sounds terrifying," Aby says.

"A little," I say. "But worth it."

Blue-and-green specks of light flicker from the walls and the ceiling, growing brighter as the fog clears. The door behind us closes, and we huddle together in the middle of the room. The long, whitish-blue line of light moves down vertically, again blinding me for a second as it passes my eyes, then back up.

"Scan complete," it says.

Hissing smoke fills the room, and with a flash of bright light, I'm sucked into the vacuum of space, spiraling through a whirling kaleidoscope of silvery-white, dress flapping and hair twirling in the airstream. When it finally stops, I'm sitting in the same spot as last time, with Jax a few feet away, and Aby and Miguel on my other side.

"Shit!" Miguel jumps up, and helps Aby to her feet. They sway in astonishment.

"That was amazing!" Aby says. "Where are we?"

"This is the hut," I say.

"Is that... a window?" She points.

"Yes," I reply, as Jax helps me up. "With the best view you'll ever lay eyes on."

They rush over to it, and I follow them, while Jax searches the room, sliding his hand along the walls, carefully surveying each and every crack and crevice. Once I reach the window, I find both Aby and Miguel crying. Even my eyes fill with tears when I gaze out again. How could you not get emotional, every time, from this vast, incredible world?

"Maybe we're on another planet," Aby whispers. "Because, how could this be in Bygonne?"

"Yeah," Miguel adds, "this isn't the world we know."

"But the world we know is tiny," I tell them. "Think about it: we've lived most of our lives trapped behind a wall, underground, or locked in bunkers with foggy purple windows. How do we know? How do we know what's really out there? This world is huge! So much we haven't even witnessed! So much potential for life we didn't even know existed."

"Nothing," Jax says. "Not a damn thing here. I know electrical, and there's absolutely nothing—no wires, no buttons, no screens, not even lights, which is very unusual—"

"Yeah," I say. "The room was lit up at night last time, like there was light inside."

"But there is no light. Not even capabilities for it."

"Can we... go... outside?" Aby asks, trembling from the magnitude of her question. Before now, it was a question you'd ask only if you wanted to die. Here, it's something entirely different.

"Wow." Miguel takes her hand. "Yeah, can we?"

And I nod through my tears. Jax sighs and shrugs, giving up his search and giving in to paradise. Together, we go to the door, and I open it slowly. We shield our eyes from the brightness that seeps through, simultaneously inhaling the salty-sweet air as it swirls in past us. Then, we step outside.

TEN

THE FOUR OF US FACE THE HORIZON over a patchwork sand-and-grass hill rolling downward to the sapphire sea.

Aby grips my arm tight and motions to the faraway shimmering blue mass. "That's the ocean?" she asks.

"Think so."

"How? How is that the ocean?"

"Like I said... I think this is the Other Side, it has to be. All those stories when we were younger... they had to have come from here."

Miguel shields his eyes from the sun. "But it doesn't make any sense," he says after a moment of silence.

"No, it doesn't," says Jax.

"When we get back, this time we'll find whoever brought us here," I offer, "and make them tell us what's going on. Then, we'll bring the children with us, and... whoever it is, will have to let us stay."

We stand motionless for another silent moment, and I'm bursting inside. There's so much beauty. Too much to process all at once.

"Whatever you say, Momma Joy." Jax kisses me. "You ready to take over the world?"

"What do you—?"

He grips my waist with both hands, and I squeal as he lifts me high into the air, up over his head. At first I tense, afraid he'll drop me. But after a few seconds, I relax, taking in the view, eye-level with a blue-gold and orange-cream horizon.

The wind caresses my skin, tousles my hair as it passes by on its way to somewhere else magnificent. I stretch my arms out as wide as they'll go and smile, breathing in deep the sensations of weightlessness and wonder. My stomach flutters as Jax finally drops me down into his arms, feet back on the ground.

"That was wonderful," I say.

He winks. "Told you you'd take over the world in that thing."

"I don't know about taking over the world . . . but definitely on top of the world."

We start down the hill, the grass tickling my bare legs beneath my dress, startling the same deer from the same spot as last time.

Aby covers her mouth as it scampers away. "Animals? There're animals here?"

I nod. "That's a deer, I think."

"Paradise!" She swoops down, plucking a handful of tiny yellow flowers from the grass. She stuffs her face into them, inhales and smiles wide, then throws them into the air, twirling as they shower down around her. A little farther down, and the mighty, swaying group of trees come into view to our right. Aby screams with delight and astonishment. "Are those trees—like, real trees?"

Miguel kneels in the grass, one hand on his chest and one over his mouth. His eyes water as he struggles to breathe.

"Yes," I say. "Real trees."

"Well, let's go see them!" Aby grabs my hand and tugs.

Jax takes my other hand. "I want to see the ocean first."

My heart leaps at the thought. "Me, too," I say through quivering lips.

For three generations, grand stories have circulated through Bygonne about this seemingly infinite, enchanted world called the ocean. Strangers would come from miles away with these tales—stowaways in Haulers, prostitutes, and peons—and as a tiny girl, I'd sit and listen to them in awe and disbelief, attempting to imagine things barely conceivable: water so deep, everyone in Bygonne could stand foot-to-shoulder and still not reach the surface; vast underwater forests, teeming with brightly-colored life and a million species of animals—and all able to breathe!

"Ocean first," I say, "then trees. Is that okay, Aby?"

"Whatever you say, Joy." She claps and hops in place. "Ocean, then trees, and then, oh my God there's so much to see!"

"Okay," I giggle. "Let's go then!"

"Anyone want to take bets on if it's salty, like the stories say it is?" Jax asks.

"Bet I can beat you all there to find out!" Aby races off, her red curls and mother's dress flapping in her tailwind.

We follow her, carefree and howling into the sweet blue place angels are born and nothing's lain to rest. For once in my stupid life, I'm somewhere where I suspect nothing horrible awaits me each time I blink. Only glorious explorations and discoveries of life. Maybe I'm being naïve, but as we wander through the unknown, a swirling pure wind urging us onward, I'm reminded of my parents' belief that I would be free one day....

And it's hard to imagine anything terrible occurring in this dream-come-true.

When our feet touch white sand, the rushing crash of the wet opus before us, we shed our clothes and boots. With the ocean at our fingertips, none of us is too worried about being in our skivvies. I pant, catching my breath—*It feels so good to run!*—and my right hand grips Jax's tightly. My left hand finds Aby's, and on her other side, Miguel shivers in his pinned-to-fit boxer shorts.

Standing here at the mouth of the roaring sea, I feel microscopic before its vast, dazzling beauty. Its intensity washes over me and I cry; I'm witnessing the most spectacular thing that has ever existed.

Aby clutches my arm, her wet, salty-blue eyes matching the water and sky perfectly. "That's the ocean!" she says, lips quivering.

"I know!"

Jax breathes in deep and squeezes my hand. "On three...."

"Wait," Miguel says. "I can't swim."

"None of us can swim, man. It's fine. We'll stay where the water meets the sand."

"Hold Aby's hand," I say with a grin. "She'll keep you from drowning."

"One!" Jax calls into the sky. "Two!" He kisses my fingertips and hops in place, tossing his straight black hair from side to side, psyching himself up.

"Three!" I yell and take off toward the water, gripping Jax's and Aby's hands tightly. The sand is hot, squishing between my toes with each flying step. Then, it's cold as we reach the watery sand, jumping from it into the waves. The second my face touches the water, I open my mouth for a taste.

"Salty!" I let go of Aby's hand to grip Jax's shoulders.

"I knew it!" He wraps his arms around me, kissing me eagerly as the waves slosh and swirl and slap against our bodies. My feet sink in the mush beneath us, and something brushes past my leg.

"I just felt something...." I glance down at the clear blue water and a group of tiny blue and purple creatures pass by us. "Fish!" I tap Jax's arm. "Those are fish!"

"I see them, they're awesome!"

"Aby, Miguel—!"

"We saw some, too!" Aby says.

Jax slides up behind me and wraps his arms around my bare waist. He holds me tight, and I relax against his body, swaying back and forth with the rhythm of the waves. And ask myself for the thousandth time: How is this even possible?

Soon, I start to shiver. "Gets a little cold after a few minutes, doesn't it?"

"I'm not cold," says Jax, "but we can get out if you want."

"Not yet." I dip my hands into the water, scoop some up with my palm, and the sunlight reflects like little diamonds in the tiny pool of saltwater. In my peripheral, Aby and Miguel have their lips fused together. I give them a good splash.

"Hey!" Aby screams, and she and Miguel attack in full splash mode.

"Jax, help me!" I yell.

He comes to my aid, slapping huge sheets of water at them. We tumble onto the shore and lie there laughing, while waves crawl up to lick our toes then drag tiny sand particles back down.

"I heard people used to make things with sand," Aby says.

"Yeah, me too," I say. "Castles and things."

She scoops a moist pile into her hands and wrinkles her nose at it. "I don't get how that's even possible."

"Me, neither." I, too, scoop up a pile of the brown mush, but instead, plop it right down onto Jax's head. "Now hats, maybe."

Everyone—except for Jax—erupts in laughter as the sandy goop drips down around his ears and eyes. Then, he cracks a smile, which soon becomes laughter as he surprises me with his own mush to my head, smearing it around like some earthy hair lather.

"This is the best day of my whole life," says Aby. Her laughter shifts to happy tears, and Miguel wraps his arm around her.

I spy a tiny treasure buried beside my feet, and I dig it up, brush off the sand, then trace its blue-and-white speckled spiral shell. "I think we could all say the same thing." Again I shiver, flinging wet sand from my head. "Let's find a spot to dry off before we head to the trees. I'm cold."

Once we're somewhat air-dried, we slip back into our clothes and boots and begin the trek back up the hillside and over—to the left now—where the trees are. This time, we don't run. We savor every last step that takes us to the extraordinary phenomena. Sure, the ocean is vast, powerful, inconceivable... but these... I am near speechless. Too much emotion behind how I feel about these, now that the initial shock from seeing them for the first time has worn off. I haven't quite sorted it all out yet. I'm not even sure there are words to describe how I'm feeling.

Aby embraces the smallest one, her cheek mushed up against its base, tears trailing over a smile tinged with sadness.

Miguel loses his ability to stand and collapses in the sandy grass. I haven't heard him cry like this since Pedro was sent away. What at first seem like happy tears turn to sudden rage and he explodes onto his feet. "Why!" he screams into the blue. "If this is here and this is real, why are we in goddamned Bygonne? Why did my brother lose his hand building trees for the Superiors, when they're growing right here? Why? And where are we? Where the hell are we!" He drops to his knees again in a sobbing heap, and Aby goes to comfort him.

"Jax, should we—?"

"No, just let Aby. There's nothing we can do. Besides, he's right, isn't he?"

"Yeah. He has every right to be upset. We spend our sorry lives building trees when there are some growing right here, and none of this makes any sense. Anyone would have a hard time with this."

"But especially him."

"We've all lost loved ones."

"True."

"His is still fresh, though," I add.

"Yeah, that it is."

Now I know what those jumbled feelings are. Miguel is right. There's anger behind this awe, and it runs deep—so deep. Someone has some serious explaining to do.

Finally Miguel calms down, and Aby urges him to come over to us. We make ourselves comfortable, backs against the rough brown tree trunks. Aby runs her fingers along the bark's patterns, while Jax and Miguel discuss some technical possibilities and scientific speculations of how this is all possible.

I tune them out, spinning the shell I found around and around in my fingers, as if it held the secret to what this all means. I tuck it into Jax's pocket. He furrows his brow, and I shrug.

"Maybe it'll be there when we get back," I say. "It's a good experiment."

"Gotcha."

He and Miguel continue talking, and I lie back to stare into the sun. It hurts my eyes, but I stare anyway. The mere fact that I'm not burning to death right now is an unexplainable magic in itself.

Magic.

I sigh.

How awesome—and tragic—that all magic is man-made.

Being married to a magician and knowing the science behind it all, when my daddy wasn't around, my mother burned that into my mind as a teeny girl. No such thing as magic. Everything has an explanation. We didn't magically appear in some alternate dimension; there's solid science behind it. Only, I have no clue what it is, and from the sound of Jax and Miguel's ridiculous conversation, they don't either.

"Let's stay here forever," Aby says.

"Not yet." I sit up next to Jax, rest my chin on his shoulder. "We have to get the children first."

"How do we go back there?" Miguel asks.

"When we're ready," I say, "we just go back to the hut, and...."

"And what?"

"I don't know. Last time we just went back in, and a minute later we were back in the bunker room."

"Well, when do we go back?" he asks. "We've been gone for a while already."

"An interesting thing about this place," Jax says. "Last time we got back, hardly any time had passed, even though we were here for hours."

"How—?" Aby stops herself. She knows as well as we do there's no logical explanation for any of it. Yet.

"I'm starving," Miguel says, "so it must be real. If it were some sort of, I dunno, 'dreamland,' then we wouldn't get hungry, right?"

"That part sounds logical," I say.

Jax chuckles. "Anyone know how to fish? Or hunt, maybe?"

"Yeah, right." I stand and brush the sand from my dress. "We'll have to find something else."

Everyone else stands, too, and we head deeper into the trees, separating just slightly, to get a good look around.

"Hey!" Miguel calls out after a few seconds. "I think I found something edible!"

We push through the maze of trees to find him kneeling beside a tiny fat one whose branches hold bright, bluish-purple balls. He cups a few in his hand.

"Berries," I say. "Yeah, I heard you could eat certain kinds of them, but—"

And before I finish, he's crammed them into his mouth. "But what?" he mumbles.

"Certain kinds could kill you."

For a split second, Miguel pauses in his chewing, and then shrugs. "Oh, well. They're good. Probably the best thing ever. So kill me. At least I'll die with my mouth full of something delicious for once."

"Let me try," Aby says.

Miguel drops a few into her mouth, and she closes her eyes, mentally drifting away as she chews. Jax strips a branch of a dozen berries, presses one between his finger and thumb, and it bursts, staining his skin purple. He tosses half into his mouth, and gives me the other half. "Yum," he says.

I examine one carefully before biting it in two, but the second the juices touch my tongue, I'm downing the rest and joining my friends in stripping the little tree of every last berry. After gorging ourselves, we return to our spot to rest.

Soon, a white fluttering thing—a butterfly, I think—dances along on the breeze to land on my arm. I freeze. Aby taps Miguel, and the three of them watch as the delicate wings rise and fall. It crawls along my arm, tiny legs tickling my hairs, making me giggle. When it finally flies away, I notice the sky colors have changed—the sun rests on the horizon like a great reddish-orange ball, floating on the water's surface, sending richly colored rays of delicious light across its utopia.

"Sunset," Jax says. "We fell asleep last time and missed it."

We watch the sun sink behind the glittering wet horizon, leaving a cream-colored moon in its place to light the implausible Earth. The waves' mesmerizing dance lulls us as the air cools, and I feel myself getting sleepy. But I don't want to sleep. I don't want to miss any of this. The water's rushing hush breathing against the shore is, by far, the most glorious sound. Slowly, night noises replace the daytime sights, and darkness calls to be explored, its mystery yet untold. Chilling, yet wildly invigorating.

"Hopefully no creatures with fangs lurk in the dark," Jax says.

I give him playful punch. "Quit that."

"Well you never know, right?"

"But…." Aby pauses, contemplating, then continues. "What would happen if we didn't get back?"

"I wouldn't be able to live with the guilt," I reply. "Poor Baby Lou wouldn't have a chance." Suddenly, I'm in a hurry to get back to her. Which is very interesting. Here I am, with the free, marvelous, living world at my fingertips, and I want to get back to the Tree Factory of death and rot and toxic air. To my poor, sick Baby.

I guess that's why they call me Momma Joy.

After a while of lying there listening to the waves crash against the shore, lightning strikes the horizon.

"Whoa," says Jax.

"Yeah," I say, "that's strange."

"Was that lightning?" Aby asks.

I nod. "There was a storm the last time we came, too."

Lightning strikes again, closer, followed by thunder that vibrates the earth around us. Then, droplets of water splatter on my skin.

"That's our signal to get back to the hut," Jax says.

We make it back, out of breath, with raindrops beating down around us. But the moment Jax closes the door in the strangely-lit hut, it goes dark, and I'm spinning through space, alone. I open my eyes in citrus-and-rot darkness, concrete against my back. The pounding in my head and my intense thirst and nausea make me cringe. "Jax? Aby?" I try to raise myself up. I'm weak, woozy.

"Right here," Jax says from my left.

On my other side, fingers find my arm. "Joy?" Aby says. "What happened?"

"We're back."

"That was intense," Miguel says from Aby's far side.

Next to me on the floor, a faint glow rises up from the light stick that was in my hand before we left.

"Our light sticks are almost dead," I say.

"Yeah, that's not good," says Jax. "Means we've been down here for a while. We have to hurry back up."

Then, I remember. "Jax, the shell! Check your—"

"Nope, empty. It's not there."

Aby curls into a tight ball. "I feel horrible."

"Me, too."

"Was it the berries?"

"No. We felt sick the last time we came back, and we didn't eat any berries."

Jax wobbles to the door and presses the dark button beside it, but it doesn't open. He bangs it with his fists. "Come on! We have to go, man, let us out!"

"If I let you out," a girl's voice rises up in the darkness from the back of the room, "you have to promise never to come back."

"Who's there?" I say. "Show yourself."

Jax gathers the spear up from the ground and grips it tightly, walking toward the voice in the dark.

"Stop," she says. "Don't come any closer."

Jax does, beside me, Aby and Miguel close behind us.

"Why not?" I ask. "What is this place? Is it the Other Side?

And who are you?"

"I'm no one. You... you have to leave. Now."

"We're not leaving until you show yourself to us." I take Jax's light stick with my own and forge ahead.

"Please," she says.

Another two steps, and a figure comes into view—a girl about my age, with short brown hair tucked under a boy's hat and a string of black letters and numbers imprinted on the side of her neck.

"I'm Joy. Are you the one who painted the stuff in the corridor?"

She peers at me with sad dark eyes, and tosses a pebble onto the ground. Then, she nods. "Now you must go. And you must never return."

"Okay, will you tell us why?" I ask. "Please. We have over thirty children, forced to be slaves. We're half-starved, and in need of medical attention. Please, you have to help us. We need to bring them back here."

"No." She stands up, brushes dust from her pants. "You cannot bring them here."

"You led us down here, twice," says Jax, "and now you want us to leave and never come back? That doesn't make any damn sense."

"I'm sorry, but you have to go." She straightens, probably to seem more intimidating, but doing a lousy job of it.

"Okay," Jax says. "Then how do we get out? The door's closed, and there's no power. And how is there electricity down here anyway? Could you tell us that?"

The girl stares at the door across the room. "No more questions," she says. The button next to the door lights up green, as well as the red lights along the outer edge of the ceiling that indicate harmful oxygen levels. She holds her hand up slightly, the air in the room moves in a gust, and the lights turn green. "Now go. When you get to the elevator, it'll be ready to take you back."

"How'd you do that?" Miguel asks.

"Go!"

"Okay, we're going," I say. "Come on, guys." I usher them to the door, trying to be subtle with my amazement. After we collect our discarded breathers by the doorway, I turn to the girl, who scratches her nose with paint-stained fingers. For a couple of seconds, I hold her gaze, reading her eyes. Confused. Lonely. Conflicted. Strong, yet fragile. Things I'm not sure how I know. Things my daddy knew about people, too. There's also a strange sense of connection to her that's difficult to pinpoint.

"Could you at least tell us your name?" I ask.

At first, she doesn't answer, kicks her boot toe at the ground and leans against the wall. Then, she glances at me and fidgets with the hem of her shirt. "Smudge," she says.

"Smudge? That's your name?"

She nods.

"Well, it's nice to meet you, Smudge. Maybe we'll see you again sometime?"

"No," she says. "You won't."

ELEVEN

None of us say a word until we get back into the elevator and strap on our breathers... then we all speak at once.

"How'd she do that thing with the door?" Miguel says. "She just looked at it, and the light lit up."

"Magic?" I shrug. "I bet she's the reason there's electricity and oxygen down here—"

"That's not even possible," says Jax.

"And the portal to paradise is?"

We fall silent while the elevator rattles and screeches toward sub-level six.

"You know," I continue, "I think there are things going on here that are beyond our comprehension. There's a reasonable explanation for it all."

"I thought it was magic?" Jax says.

"I was joking. There's no such thing as real magic, only man-made illusions. Smoke and mirrors."

"Well, she had me fooled," Miguel says, leaning against the wall.

Aby rests her head on his shoulder. "Me, too."

"All of the best tricks do," I say.

The elevator comes to a stop, and the door opens.

"Do what?" Jax asks.

"Fool you."

Once we've hurried down the long corridor and back up the six flights of stairs, my stomach twists into knots. We have no idea what time it is, and as we pass the warehouse, a rumbling boom makes us all jump.

"Thunder?" I whisper.

Jax nods, holding the dim light stick out in front of us. The Tree Factory door is ahead, through one more corridor.

"Maybe that means it's the same storm as where we just were...?" Aby offers.

I lay my hand on Jax's arm. "I don't know, but... what if it's daytime?"

He pats my fingers. "Then we're in big trouble."

"Well, that's comforting," Aby says.

Silently, we tiptoe toward the Tree Factory door. Sweat drips around my face where the plastic of the breather meets my skin, and as Jax reaches out for the handle, Aby takes my hand and squeezes it, tight. I squeeze back.

Jax opens the door. Darkness from inside the factory gives me instant relief. If it had been daytime, they'd have the lights on. I lean the spear back against the wall in the corner, and the four of us exit the bunker door. Jax re-locks it. Then, we move out from behind the shelf, which he and Miguel lift to place back against the door.

"Looks like we're safe," I whisper.

A cackling in the dark raises chill bumps all over my body. We huddle together as bright lights flicker on over our heads.

All four Superiors stand before us.

"Well, well...." says Arianna Superior.

Her son steps forward, gripping his thornwhip.

"Diaz...." Arianna motions for him to fall back. "Save it. You'll have your fun soon enough." She flicks a finger at Mona and Emmanuel, who step toward us, holding chains with shackles attached. "Speaking of fun," she continues, "I hope you enjoyed your adventure. It's a wonder you're back here at all. You are braver—or stupider—than I gave you credit for."

While Emmanuel shackles Jax, Mona Superior locks shackles around my wrists, ankles, and neck, and then moves on to Aby, who's openly sobbing. Diaz lunges, punching her mightily in the side of the head, and she drops to the floor in a still heap.

"Aby!" I scream.

Miguel fights to help her, but Emmanuel restrains him inches from her. He locks the metal cuffs around Miguel's neck, ankles, and wrists, runs a purple fingernail along his jawline, then grabs him between the legs.

"What the hell, man!" Miguel tries to jerk away, and Emmanuel's face, painted with gratified power-lust, makes my insides burn. I lock eyes with Miguel, sending him a silent message: *Wait. It's almost time.*

He struggles to calm himself; his heaving chest slows, and Emmanuel Superior removes his hand. I watch Aby's chest to make sure she's breathing.

"Oh, she isn't dead," says Arianna Superior, "but she may be soon. As well as the rest of you." She flicks her finger again, and Diaz digs down into Jax's pocket, takes out the key ring, and tosses it to his mother.

Mona and Emmanuel tear the breathers from our faces, then drag us behind them by our chains. Diaz rips off Aby's breather, grabs a handful of her hair, and begins to haul her, chains jingling against the floor, following us. A visible shiver ravages my body, because I know where they're taking us. By the door to the stairwell, they leave their oxygen tanks and fasten on their own fancy breathers. Then, it's down a flight of stairs, past the cellar playroom, down three more, and through a doorway to the dungeon. Last time Jax and I were here was a year ago, when we rewired the Tree Factory's electrical, which took a specialist from Taborton three days to fix—three days in which no trees could be built. The first and only real break the treemakers ever got. Well worth the few days down here.

I have a feeling this time won't be as easy.

Aby's never been down here; she won't handle it well. Jax will be fine, but Miguel's three days after Pedro was sent away, changed him. He now has night terrors nearly every night, Jax says. I make quick eye-contact with them beneath a dull, flickering yellow bulb, and watch where Diaz puts Aby, before Mona Superior pushes the green button beside my own cell door. It screeches open, disappearing inside the wall. The light on the wall's oxygauge changes from green to red, back to green, then to red again as I enter the foul, rot-smelling darkness. Same cell as last time. How nice.

My head immediately begins to spin from the bad air. Mona Superior attaches my chains to the wall and locks them with a giant key, then laughs as she heads toward the exit. "I'll be back," she sings. "We wouldn't want you to be too lonely down here." With a bang, the heavy iron door rattles closed behind her, leaving the long orange shadow of the barred window stretched out on the floor in front of it. Enough light to barely make out the thin lines of dirt beneath my fingernails.

After the other three doors echo shut, and the stairwell door slams, I perk up my ears in the pitch-black stillness. My head pounds, and my stomach begs for food. I'm parched already.... Not good.

"Jax?"

"I'm here." His muffled voice calls faintly through the thin stone wall between us. Like the wall between the two dorm rooms—unstable, with ancient, crumbling grout. Last time, one cell stood between us, so we couldn't communicate. There's one plus, at least.

"What do we do?" I ask.

"I don't know."

"Can you talk to Miguel?"

"Maybe if I yell. He's on the other side of me—"

"No, don't yell. We have to think of a plan to get out of here without drawing their attention."

"And then what?"

"We kill them, and we go find Smudge."

"That's your plan?"

"I know, I know... let me think. It's all I've got for now. Do you have—?"

The stairwell door slams, and I freeze. Footsteps approach, then a cell door screeches open—either Aby's or Miguel's.

Aby screams, and tears fill my eyes. I fight to free myself. "Leave her alone!" I cry. "Please, don't hurt her!" Foolish to beg, because I know that's what they want.

"No, please!" she wails from four cells down. "No! Please, no, don't! Please, noooooo!"

A moment later, her cell door closes again, followed by the stairwell door slamming.

"My hair!" she cries. "My hair!" Then, she screams, and screams, until her spirit's shattered. I feel the break, a catastrophic loss, the death of something pure and irreplaceable.

"We have to get out of here," I say to Jax. "Can you get out of your shackles?"

"Not unless I bite through my own hand," he replies. "Which I am not doing, by the way."

I spit on my wrist to lubricate the metal, but with its rough finish, it's not slick enough. It's too tight anyway, almost cutting off my circulation. Curious, I stick my pinkie into the keyhole. "These things are ancient," I tell Jax. "I bet it wouldn't take much to pick the lock."

"You got anything to pick the lock with?"

"Um... no."

An hour or so passes before Jax speaks again, and I'm grateful for it. The faraway sobs of Aby are becoming too much.

"When they come into your cell," he says, "be ready. You know what they're going to do."

"I know. I'll be ready."

"They jump, you jump. Until they're flat under your feet. Think of it as a dance, baby. You can do it."

"Okay," I whisper.

"Joy? You hear me?"

"Yeah, okay," I say, louder. "Got it."

The Superiors know from last time how terrified I am of jumpers. I made the mistake of verbalizing it with panicked screams and pleas for help. I learned a lesson then: no matter how scared you are, don't let your enemy know.

Though maybe that was a good thing. Because now I know what they'll do to get that reaction from me that seemed to please them so much. They'll wait until I'm exhausted, delirious, and too weak to fight, then they'll set a couple of jumpers loose. Or maybe they won't wait that long. Maybe they'll make sure the jumpers have been good and starved for a few days first, that way, they'll go straight from the cage to my throat. They might do that just to insure what happened last time doesn't happen again. I must've surprised them when they came back and found two jumper carcasses and a crazed girl with a blood-smeared face. Won't be any different this time. Except now, I know what to expect, so I'll be more prepared.

I don't know how much time has passed when the slamming echo of the stairwell door jerks me awake from a wretchedly uncomfortable sleeping position. A cell door rattles open, closer than last time.

Miguel's cell.

I hold my breath and say a prayer in my mind—or maybe it's more of a curse—that whoever's about to do evil unto him, dies the most horrible death.

Miguel yells, then his voice is silenced, leaving only the sound of jingling chains and an exaggerated moan, followed by Emmanuel Superior's laughing.

I close my eyes and cringe. If what my imagination tells me is actually happening, then he's more of a psychotic sicko than I thought. Of course, I should've guessed all along he'd go as far as violating boys for his own gruesome satisfaction.

God, I hope I'm wrong, though.

Miguel's door closes, and seconds later, the stairwell door slams shut again.

"Jax, did what I think just happened... happen?"

"Didn't sound good—at all. I think I hear him crying—"

Then, Miguel begins to scream, thrashing around in his chains as he howls and curses... it's enough to rip my heart out. Aby's crying, too, saying something to him, probably trying to console him. But after that, I wouldn't be surprised if he could never be consoled again.

"Oh my God, Jax, what if you're next—?"

"If he tries to stick that thing anywhere near me, I'll rip it off."

"But—"

"Don't worry, I'll be fine. I promise."

§

Ravenous hunger and thirst tell me another day has passed. Reeking of urine and bloody from the strain of trying to slide my wrist from the shackles, I'm a fine feast for a family of jumpers now.

"Jax?"

"I'm here."

Every couple of hours, I call over to make sure he's still alive.

"You heard Aby or Miguel at all?" I ask.

"No. You okay?"

"Um … is that a trick question?"

"Joy?"

"Yeah?"

"Will you marry me?"

"What?"

"I mean, I know I don't have a ring or anything, but—"

Laughter crackles out from a stale place inside me, and transforms into tears. "Let's get out of here first, and talk about marriage later, okay?"

"So, you don't want to marry me?"

"I didn't say that, I—"

The stairwell door slams and keys jingle down the corridor, closer, closer … and stop at Jax's door. A lump rises in my throat and more tears make my vision swim as his door clicks and screeches open.

"What do you want, you psycho?" says Jax. "What the—?"

"Do you like it?" Emmanuel Superior's voice reverberates through the air like a noxious gas. "I made it myself."

"You're sick, man. You should get help, you've got serious issues. That whole women's clothes fetish … ? Not attractive. People are saying things.…"

Emmanuel Superior laughs. "You know, I've always liked your spirit. So feisty.…"

Jax's chains rattle. "Touch me again," he growls, "and I promise you'll regret it."

"Leave him alone!" I scream.

"Ooh, we have an audience," says Emmanuel. "How nice.

Let's put on a good show, shall we?"

I think I hear Jax spit. Then, the sound of flesh hitting flesh and a thud against the wall makes me go rigid.

"Jax!" I scream.

Emmanuel laughs again. "Don't worry, tramp, your excitement is coming soon." But in a split second, his laughter turns to a howl. "You bit me! You filthy wretch!" Another punch or slap.

"There's more where that came—*mmph*—!"

"Oh, I don't think so," Emmanuel says. "Now, it's my turn."

"Stop hurting him, you monster!" I shriek. Sounds of pain through waded cloth will forever be burned into my dark reservoir of hatred for the Superiors. Finally, I surrender my futile fight and let my body fall against the wall. I'm powerless to save him.

For now.

A plan for revenge sets ablaze inside me. I squeeze my fists, pressing my fingernails into my palms, crying silent tears for my best friend. They're going to get what they deserve. I'll make sure of it.

Part of me believes Jax knowing I hear his abuse makes it all the more humiliating for him, so I hum loudly to myself; it helps muffle the noises. Soon, my humming becomes a song my mother used to sing to me. She'd hum the parts she didn't know. Unfortunately, I only remember one line now… something about sunshine and love.

Jax's screeching door snaps me back into reality.

"Did you enjoy the show, little tramp?" Emmanuel Superior calls from the corridor. "It was nearly as enjoyable as your mother. Sweet dreams now…."

I try to let his words pass through me like vapor, but my mother's ghost and her haunted past still linger in the room, along with some stench of truth. My mother never would've—*would she?*

I press my ear to the wall and hear sniffling. I've never witnessed Jax cry before.

"Jax?" My voice shakes. "Are you... okay?"

More sniffling and chain rattling answer at first, then a long, heavy silence follows before he speaks again.

"So... you'll marry me, then?" He's broken and weak, not even faking strength.

"Of course, Jax," I cry. "Of course I will."

TWELVE

THE MOST INTENSE AND MIRACULOUS ACT I ever witnessed was done by my daddy in Bunker C's saloon and performance hall. He told me I couldn't go; it was past my bedtime, and my mother needed me there. Each breath for her rattled death and she'd be gone any day now. He didn't want to go either, but with my outgrown shoes and nothing to trade for Blue Notes to buy more, his eyes shimmered with the regret of no choice. He kissed my forehead as I lay beside my mother and tucked the blanket under my chin.

"I don't really need any shoes, Daddy—"

"Nonsense. You haven't had a new pair in years." He gave my head a soft pat. "Hush now, and get some sleep. I'll be back in a little while."

"What if Momma doesn't make it through the night?" I whispered.

"She will. And I'll be back soon, anyway." He smoothed my hair back, and gave her a kiss.

"Okay. Night, Daddy."

"Night, sweetheart."

I closed my eyes, pretending to surrender to sleep, but after the door to our room shut, I rose and tiptoed down the corridor behind him. He moved sleekly, silently in his long black cape and tall black hat. But being barefoot, I had no trouble moving silently as well. I followed him all the way to the performance hall, snagging a big brown coat from the full coat rack on the wall. I waited until the doorman, who was nearing end-of-days, moved down the hall to hack his lungs where he wouldn't disrupt the show, and then I slipped through the door, past the fancy, hand-painted sign that read: Zephyr the Magnificent – Performance tonight! Ten Blue Notes.

With the heavy hood covering my head, I sat near the back, shivering with nervous excitement as scantily dressed young women bound him with seven heavy chains and seven thick locks. His expression was of calm strength and confidence as a clear cube rose up from the stage and enclosed him. In seconds, channeled water from underground began to fill it quickly as he struggled against the chains. It rose past his knees, past his stomach and chest—and when the water had reached his chin, he still hadn't broken free of one chain or lock. Once it had risen over his head, I counted the seconds and played with the fear of his death for but a moment. I knew my daddy better than that. It was just another illusion.

He'd put on a good show, holding it until the very last second, and then, when the audience thought all was lost, he'd shockingly free himself to an explosion of amazement. I'd never watched him perform for an audience before, but I could accurately guess how it would happen.

Sure enough, at a minute twenty-seven, he shed the chains and shot up from the water, to the roar of an awe-intoxicated crowd. He'd miraculously freed himself, again.

But that, like all of his tricks—like freedom in life itself—was an illusion.

"Joy?" Jax calls out, startling me from my reminiscence.

"I'm here."

"You alive?"

"Yes. Are you all right, Jax?"

"Dandy."

I shift into another uncomfortable position. How would

my daddy have gotten out of this one? There's no illusion in these very real shackles and chains, no audience watching in the dark, cheering me on, other than the memories of those who loved me, and the fear that those I love now may be dead as well—or soon.

Now is my time to shine, alone.

But not entirely alone.

"Help me, Daddy," I whisper.

And he's next to me, whispering back: *Fear is the greatest illusion of all. Face it, fight it, and be free.*

When the stairwell door opens again, I know my time has come, and I'm ready for it, welcoming it, even. I get into position, sitting with my back against the wall, lifting my shackled feet high off the floor and, steadying my breathing, try to remain perfectly still. Though my legs begin to shake, I hold them in place, gritting my teeth against the exhaustion that wants me to give up. My door slides open, quieter than the rest. The dim light from the hallway illuminates a figure from behind, though I can't tell who it is, and I remain silent as two large rectangles—cages—are placed right inside the doorway. With the flick of a wrist, they rattle, and my cell door quickly closes again.

It only takes a few seconds for scurrying sounds to reach my ears. I hold my breath, steady my trembling legs, and hope against hope that at this moment, twelve hours on my feet, building leg muscle every day, will pay off, like last time.

Two enormous white jumpers come into view, and I cringe. They could eat me in three bites. The Superiors must've been overfeeding them... until now. With a shrill hiss, they lunge. The first one gets right under my feet, and I bring my boots down with every ounce of my strength and all of the hatred I have in my body—and crush its skull.

The second backs up, hissing and bearing its fangs.

"Joy?" Jax calls out. "You okay?"

I prepare for strike number two. The jumper circles me, and I lift my skull-stompers back into the air. "Come here, sweetie," I sing to it. "I won't hurt you."

"Joy!" Jax is frantic now, thrashing in his shackles.

"I'm fine," I say calmly. "Handling it."

Jumper Two decides he's too hungry to wait and rushes toward me, right over the body of his friend, and I bring my boots down in one swift, crunching blow.

I have to stop myself from shouting my triumph for the whole Tree Factory to hear.

Now is where real victory will be born, where I'll finally become something. In the dark and silent promise of death, I'll make a way for us—a life. I'll keep my promise to Miguel and put an end to this—for good.

With my heels, I drag the fat body of one jumper into my lap. My fingers shake, and I fight nausea. I've done this before, though for different reasons. Last time, I hadn't eaten for days; this time, I need a way out to save my friends—my family.

Trying not to breathe in the filth-smell of the rodent's fur, I raise it to my mouth and, pausing for one last nerve-gathering, I bite into it. Warm wetness drips down my chin. I gag, sputter, and spit the nastiness from my mouth, then dip my fingers into the tear and spread the warm skin apart until I rip the hole wide enough. I dig through the creature's slimy entrails until I've curled my fingers around a rib bone. With a jerk and twist, it snaps, and I extract it from the animal's body, then toss the carcass aside. I trace the bone with my fingers, its pointy tip, and say a prayer.

Then, I jostle it in the keyhole of my shackles... and they click open.

My blood is fire in my veins as they drop and dangle from the chain attached to my neck shackle. I feel for the keyhole there and carefully insert the bone. This time it takes some wiggling, and after a half-minute of panic, it too, clicks open. I carefully remove it from my neck and set both shackles onto the ground to start on my ankles. With a quick jiggle of the bone in the keyhole, they clank open to the ground.

My daddy would be proud.

But I'm not free yet.

The shackles were easy, but the door... I'm not feeling good about.

Sure enough, there isn't even a keyhole. I steady my breathing to calm my panic. This room is ancient, probably about to collapse. There has to be a way out. I tiptoe back to the wall where Jax is on the other side.

"Jax?"

"Joy, are you okay?"

"Jax, I'm out of my chains and—"

"Shit, really? How?"

"I'll tell you later. Right now, I need to get out of this room. Any ideas?"

"I have no clue."

"I'll have to wait until they come back and open my door."

"Then what?"

"Uh... kill them? Is there any other choice?" I squint into the window's scant light and run my hands along the stone wall's crumbling grout.

"Did they put jumpers in there?"

"Yes. But I took care of it."

"I love you so much."

Somewhere in a dark corner of the Earth, a flower blooms, opening itself to the toxic world around it. I stamp it with my feet. It has no business here now, clogging my mind when I need to focus on escape. Besides, those return words don't flow freely in a mouth still quivering from rancid jumper blood.

"I'm going to search for a way out," I say instead. "Maybe the bars are loose on the door." I take off before hearing his response and inspect all four bars, pushing, pulling, and yanking on them. Not so much as a jiggle in any direction. I shove my shoulder against the door—*Maybe I can force it open?*—but it's secured deep in the wall.

I give up and decide waiting is the only choice left. I step back over the bloody mess of the two jumpers, lift the heavy bodies off the floor by their tails, and discard them in the far back corner. Then, I position myself inside my shackles without re-locking them, gripping the bone tight in my hand. I'll need to make it appear like I'm still chained when the Superiors come in, which should be any time now. Or perhaps, a long time from now.

I try to imagine piercing the bone through the body of a Superior, and where the best place would be. Slipping my left hand from its shackle, I press different areas of my chest and neck, finally deciding the soft indention at the base of the throat would be the best—and easiest spot to aim for.

I spend the next hour or so filing the bone on the rough concrete, rotating it to get it from all angles. The tip was pointy to begin with, but not sharp. It'll need to be as sharp as possible, I've only got one shot to make things right. Zero room for error.

"Jax?"

A few seconds of silence passes before he answers. "Yes?"

"I'm going to get us out of here, okay?"

"Okay, Joy," he says, voice drained of all hope and faith in me. I envision his eyes, lacking the light they'd have if he actually believed in me. But I'll show him. I'll show them all.

For a while, I drift in and out of sleep, fighting the urge to pull out of the shackles and curl up into a more comfortable ball. Giving the impression of helplessness at a second's notice will be my saving grace. I can't give in to exhaustion now. Soon....

On cue, the stairwell door slams shut again. My eyes snap open wide, I grip the bone tight. A cell door squeals—either Aby's or Miguel's.

I take a deep breath.

"Thanks for dinner!" I yell. "It was delicious! Best meal I've had since the last time I was here—Oh!—and if that's you, Emmanuel, I've been meaning to tell you how absolutely ghastly that scar looks. I mean, you'd think after seven years it'd fade some—but, no!" I laugh. "The more bad makeup jobs you try to cover it with, the more noticeable it gets!" Then, I explode with my best possible fake laughter, until I hear the just-opened door close again and my own door rattle open. Sure enough, the flowing silhouette of Emmanuel Superior's satin house robe twirls behind him as he moves through my doorway.

I stand, faux shackled arms up over my head, as if protecting myself from a coming blow, but when he gets close enough, my breath catches. Framing the scarred and hideous face of Emmanuel Superior... are the long red curls of my sister.

"We'll see how much you have to say in a few minutes," he snarls, and grabs my left arm. I whip my right wrist from its opened shackle and pierce his throat with the sharpened rib bone. Zero error. He grapples at it, falling to the ground, blood oozing from his neck.

I slip out of my other shackles and scramble for the key ring in his bulging robe pocket. Instead, I find a handkerchief and a wad of cloth. He swats at me, but his widened eyes and his gasps for gurgling breath tell me he's near-gone. I push him onto his other side and fish the key ring from his other pocket, then yank Aby's hair from his head. First time I've ever seen his real hair—white around the edges of a giant bald center. No wonder he always wears wigs.

When I finally leave him, his body has stilled. I rush next door to Jax's cell, Aby's hair folded up under my arm, and my heart races as I push the button.

"Joy?"

I run to him and throw my arms around his neck, squeezing tight.

"Did you kill him?"

I nod, my shaky fingers fumbling with the keys.

"That was brilliant, how you lured him to you."

"Thanks. I wasn't sure if it was going to work."

After trying two different keys, the third one unlocks his shackles and he's free in seconds, too. He enfolds me in his embrace, as if he'd never loved anything or anyone so much.

"I told you I'd get us out," I whisper.

"I believed you."

"Come on, we have to hurry."

We slip quietly from his cell. My head swims with too much adrenaline, and not enough sleep or food and water; everything's surreal. In Miguel's cell, he doesn't believe his eyes, either. "How did you—?"

"He's dead," says Jax. "She killed him."

"Was that why you were screaming those things, to make him come to you?"

"Joy?" Aby calls over from the next cell. "Is that you?"

Miguel points to the wig of red hair still tucked beneath my arm. "Is that... what I think it is?"

"Yes," I reply.

His eyes fill with rage and hatred.

"But he's gone now"—I click the key in the shackles around his feet—"and he'll never hurt anyone again."

Together, we rush out of Miguel's cell and on to Aby's. The sight of her filthy, sunken face topped with hacked-off hair snaps my heart in two again.

"Joy?"

"Yes, we have to hurry. Emmanuel Superior's dead."

"Dead?"

I nod, and in less than ten seconds, I've freed my sister, clutching her trembling frail frame tightly. "And I got you this back." I hold up her hair.

At first she smiles, then cries as she cradles it. "How'd you get out of your chains? Is that blood on your face?"

"I'll explain later."

Aby and Miguel fall into each other's arms.

Jax tugs at me. "I think I hear someone coming."

We race out of Aby's cell and, closing the door, duck behind a protruding wall on the other side. We hardly breathe for what has to be at least three minutes, listening for another Superior coming down the stairwell. But there's only silence.

Jax finally breaks it. "We need a plan."

"We need weapons," Miguel adds.

Out of habit, Aby goes to tug a strand of her hair, but finding it missing, clasps her hands together instead. Anguish and rage distort her face into one I hardly recognize. "It'd help if we knew what time it was," she says. "Then we'd know if they were in their bunker or not."

"It's night," I say.

"How do you know?" Miguel asks.

"He was wearing his satin house robe. He only wears that

at night."

"Good call," Jax says. "They're probably in their bunker, then. Maybe asleep."

"They may have Humphrey guarding," I say, and hand him the key ring, which he inspects before stuffing into his pocket.

"If he's alive," he replies. "I don't know how the Superiors found out we were gone, but I have a feeling Humphrey didn't get off lightly for not 'performing adequately.'"

"We need to get to the spear."

Jax shakes his head. "I'll bet it's gone. They'd make sure to get rid of it, or take it to their bunker. Besides, we can't risk going back through that door yet. We'll have to use what we have around the factory and the dorms—"

"What exactly are we going to do?" Aby asks.

"We're going to put an end to this," I say. "Kill the other Superiors, get the children, and go find Smudge."

"Smudge?" Miguel repeats, tucking his stringy black hair behind his ears and crossing his arms. "Why?"

"I have a feeling she knows the way out of Bygonne, whether it's through the portal or another way."

"She told us we'd never see her again," says Aby.

"She was bluffing. Maybe she wanted to believe it, but her eyes and body language said otherwise. I think she wants to help us, though she's conflicted for some reason."

"Why do you think she wants to help us?" Jax says.

"Not sure; I sensed it. And we don't have much of a choice, so it's worth a shot."

"How did you get out of your shackles?" Aby asks again.

"Uh…" My gaze falls to the ground. "I used a jumper's rib bone…."

"How'd you get a jumper's rib bone?" Aby cries, disbelieving.

As I explain, I feel their stares on the dried jumper blood

smeared across my face.

Miguel whistles softly, impressed.

Aby gapes.

"A little Zephyr," Jax says with a weak smile.

"Any of you would've done the same thing," I say.

"Um, no." Aby shakes her head slowly. "I'd be dead right now, because those things would've eaten me alive." She reaches a shaky hand up to her ragged hair, and we share a silent moment before she speaks again. "I suppose I should be grateful, then, that's all he did... to me." Her tears swim. "After all, it grows back, right?" Then, she cries into her hands, guilty shroud visible to the world, until her head darts up, hand over her mouth and eyes wide. "Oh my God...." Her gaze flits between Jax and Miguel. "Was he wearing my hair when he... when he...?"

They both look away, unable to mask the truth and the pain.

"Oh my God!" Aby begins to sob uncontrollably. "Now I can never grow it back!" Her fists clench and her face turns red, like she's holding back a scream. "Because you'll think of him!" she cries. "And... and what he... what he did to you!"

"No...." Miguel pulls her into his arms, holds her tight, shushing, rocking her. "No, Aby. I won't let him take that from you. Ever."

"Me, neither," says Jax. "Don't ever think that."

I give Aby's arm a squeeze. "We have to be strong now, sister."

She peeks up at me from Miguel's chest and stares absently for a few seconds, before she nods and wipes her eyes as if she'd come back from somewhere far away. Holding the wig of her hair at arm's length, she inhales deep and, with a grimace of hatred and disgust, tosses it through the bars of her cell door window. "Let's give them what they deserve," she says through gritted teeth.

"Yes…." I crack my knuckles, rub my sore wrists. "It's time for revenge."

THIRTEEN

THIS TIME, I LEAD. Jax rests his hand on my hip, following close as we creep up the stairs, past the playroom and the memory of love, which, even though happened only a couple of days ago, feels like another life. We weren't entirely innocent, of course, but now I realize, even in the darkness, a certain amount of innocence was there. The events over the last two days have changed us all; we'll never be the same four people we were.

At the top of the stairs, we pause to breathe in a silent prayer.

"New plan," I whisper. "Get the children underground first, then devise some means for annihilating the Superiors."

"You sure about this?" Jax says.

"Yes. We can't risk anything before we have them safely underground."

"It's not exactly safe underground, Joy," says Miguel.

"Please, you have to trust me."

I don't wait for a response. Instead, I put a finger to my lips and push down on the handle. The door creaks open, and I cringe as the sound echoes through the factory's main room. Then, I peek out, straining to make out the shadows. After a minute, and still no sign of the Superiors, we slide out, moving swiftly along the wall toward the dorm room corridor.

When we get to the right turn before the dorms, I stop and hold up my hand. They all stop behind me, and I glance around the corner, then whip my head back with a start when I find Humphrey standing at attention against the wall, right where his cot once sat. Humphrey's never actually *stood* guard before... and the way his body is awkwardly erect, like stone, sends a chill through me.

"What?" Aby whispers. "Is Humphrey there?"

I nod, whisper back, "But something isn't right with him."

Jax nudges Miguel and points to the far wall, where a rack of hollow poles for tree branches are stored. "Weapons," he mouths, and motions for me and Aby to stay down while he and Miguel move swiftly, zig-zagging past various machines. Once there, they each take a pole and head back to us. Not the best weapons, of course, but they'll work for now.

Jax motions that he and Miguel will go first. They grip their poles and tense up, then take a breath and round the corner. Aby and I follow close behind. Humphrey doesn't even glance in our direction. After a few feet, Jax stops and plugs his nose. Then, we smell it, too—the stench of fresh rot. Jax points at Humphrey's feet, and the hairs on my arms stand up. Below him lies a strange black shadow. We inch toward him, the overpowering smell getting stronger and stronger.

At a few feet away, the source of the smell becomes apparent: Humphrey's dingy white shirt now matches the rest of him—riddled with red gashes, festering with rot. His hands are nailed to the wall, metal spikes stake his feet to the floor, and his eyelids are stapled to his eyebrows in a state of perpetual terror. After the initial shock comes the sadness. He may not have been family, but he was the closest thing to a grown-up friend we've had in years. But then I'm relieved for him, once I realize that he, too, has been freed.

Whatever. Just don't get caught, was the last thing he said to us.

I told him to quit saying that.

"Damn," says Jax. "Looks like Diaz had his fun."

"Oh my God," Aby whispers, pinching her nose. "Poor guy."

"At least he's not suffering anymore," I say. "Come on, we have to hurry. You guys get the boys up and ready, and we'll get the girls. Two minutes, up and out. They'll be wondering where Emmanuel is soon."

Jax unlocks the girls' dorm room door and I hold my breath. I'm envisioning everyone pinned to the wall like Humphrey, but when I flip on the light, I'm relieved to discover wiggling bodies, startled awake. Baby Lou stirs in her crib.

"Hurry," I tell Jax.

He nods, and they disappear inside the boys' dorm. Aby and I step into ours, and I close the door quietly. Already, wide eyes and smiles greet us from a handful of beds. I put a finger to my lips. "Everyone get up now. Quietly. We have exactly two minutes to get our belongings and get out of here."

"Momma Joy!" Chloe hops down from her bed and runs to me, knotted blonde locks bouncing on her head. "Where were you? What happened to Aby's hair?"

I lift her up, squeeze her tight. "Shh, we have to be quiet. We'll explain everything later." And I set her back down. "Get your bag and put your stuff in it. We have to really, really hurry."

She runs off to her bed while the other girls scurry to pack their things.

"Where are we going, Joy?" Serna asks.

"Underground. We've found a way out. No more questions now, we have to get out of here in one minute. If we don't, we're all as good as dead." I scoop up Baby Lou, surprised her skin's a normal temperature. She opens her brown eyes and smiles at me, then bats at my face.

"We thought you were dead," says Serna, snapping her knapsack and tossing it over her shoulder.

"We thought we were, too. Thanks for taking care of Baby."

"You know, a few hours after you left, the oxygauge in here started acting strange. In both dorms. A couple hours later, she started getting better. I only gave her the medicine twice. I hid the bottle in the washroom."

"The oxygauge was acting strange?"

"Yeah, go look. And I'll take Baby if you need me to, so you can get your stuff."

"Okay, thanks. Will you carry her out, too?"

"Sure."

I go to the oxygauge and read the dial. If it's right, it's the freshest air we've ever breathed. But there's no time to ponder why. I fetch the medicine bottle from the washroom, gulp water from the hose for a few seconds, then rush back to my bed for a quick change of Baby Lou's cloth diaper and out of my disgusting dress, which I toss into the corner. Never felt this good to change. I shed my boots to change my socks and put on my daddy's old T-shirt, my mother's jeans, then slip my boots back on and tie them up tight.

Aby tucks her mother's dress into her bag and ties a scarf around her ragged hair. Her black cotton shirt and black work slacks match her face's mixture of seriousness with a touch of sadness. "Feel better?" she asks.

"Yes, much better. You all right?"

She nods. "Ready to be rid of this place for good."

"Aren't we all...."

Once I have Baby Lou tied snugly on Serna's back, I dump the contents of my box into my daddy's old magic bag and sling it over my shoulder. "Time to go, girls. Everyone line up. Take a breather from the wall as you get to the doorway, and put it on."

Jax and Miguel have already begun to line up the boys, each with a breather secured in place. I try to put one on Baby Lou, but she wiggles and makes a face, as though to start screaming. She hates wearing them. I'll wait to put hers on when we get underground, we can't risk the tantrum right now.

The sight of Humphrey again makes me hurt for all the little eyes; the stuff lifelong night-terrors are made of.

"Don't look at him," I say. "Keep your eyes on the person in front of you." I do a quick headcount, and when I'm sure we have everyone, I signal for Jax to start the procession. He returns a thumbs-up and, quickly, quietly, the long line begins to move down the corridor, past the window and the chopper, and around the corner.

Miguel falls back to take up the rear, next to Aby and a couple of younger girls, gripping his pole and surveying the area behind and above us. Johnny ties his bandanna around his head, his shirt around his waist, then punches a fist into his palm. He puffs out his muscular chest, crosses the room to snatch two more poles off the shelf, spinning them around with the vengeance of a boy who's ready for war. I halfway expect him to yell obscenities as we escape through the forbidden door.

Miguel rushes up to help Jax move the shelf, then Jax clicks the key in the lock and swings the door open. He whispers something to the boys in front, and they move into the corridor's shadows. Twenty-something bodies later, my girls disappear into the shadows of safety, too. Aby and the younger girls go ahead of me, and I wait until all of them are down first. When it's finally my turn, Jax greets me at the door, placing something heavy, cold, and surprisingly familiar into my hand, along with a light stick.

"The spear?" I tuck it under my arm and crack the light stick, illuminating the cramped passage full of uneasy faces.

"Yep, looks like they didn't come down here after all."

Miguel and Johnny move the shelf back as close to the

door as possible without completely blocking it, then they join us in the dark.

"What now?" Johnny says. "Oooh, nice piece of artillery...." He flicks the spear tip. "That could do some serious damage."

"It has," Jax says, cracking another light stick. "And it's gonna do some more, too."

"You believe they had that new kid running the chopper?" Johnny laughs, giving the boy a playful smack on the back of the head.

"Quit that," he says.

"I'm surprised he has any hands left."

"What happened?" I ask. "How did they find out we were gone?"

"The storm," Johnny replies. "The power went out, and Arianna came looking for Jax to fix it. Woke us all up, screaming something awful. Searched the girls' dorm, too, and found out you four were gone. That's when they took Humphrey away and questioned him."

"And then they killed him?"

"After they threw you four down into the dungeon. They made us all watch—"

"Oh my God, no... they didn't...."

"Yep. Said if we didn't 'perform adequately' now that you four were gone, the same would happen to us."

"How could they be so horribly evil?" Aby whispers.

"But these guys did awesome." Johnny spins around, searching the blue-lit shadows. "Come here, little man."

Jax's apprentice slumps over to us.

Johnny throws an arm around his shoulder. "He stepped up and did some fantastic work. I was extra proud of him." And he gives the weary boy's head a quick rub.

I shake my own head, and lean the spear up against the

wall to fasten Baby Lou's breather onto her. At first she fights me, but she soon gives in, and I secure it to her face. "Everyone make sure your breathers are air-locked," I announce quietly. "Did Baby Lou witness what they did to Humphrey?" I ask Johnny.

"She was there, but—"

"I covered her eyes," Serna says. "And her ears."

"Thank you."

She nods.

"So, everything ran smoothly while we were gone? With the machines, I mean?" Jax asks Johnny.

"Ha! Hardly. It was crazy, man. They had to pull children from the scrap rooms to cover for Aby and Miguel—it was nuts. You people must've really given 'em a rash."

"We need to get moving," I say. "We can chat about things later. Right now, we have to get the children somewhere safe and hidden, then plan our next move."

Jax plants a quick kiss on my cheek, and hands me the light stick. "Wanna lead?"

"Yes." And I place the spear into his hand, securing my breather and activating the airlock. "With you," I add. "You're faster with that thing than I am." Then, I start walking, light stick held out before us. "I'll be the light."

"Yes you will," he says. "And a mighty bright one at that."

§

When we clear the corridor leading down to the main bunkers, we stop, dumbfounded by the green lights lining the ceiling. Here and there are also dim, flickering bulbs, which give the place more life than it's had in a very long time.

We find an oxygauge on the wall and check it, before

announcing to the children that the air is—somehow—safe to breathe and they can remove their breathers.

"Keep them on your heads, though," I say, "just in case."

As we pile into the warehouse, seeing what lies in the once-dark corners and crevices for the first time, curiosity makes my stomach churn with both fear and excitement. Arianna Superior said something when they caught us, that it was a wonder we'd made it back at all. . . . Surely she doesn't believe Old Jonesy's silly monster superstitions. . . .

Whatever the reason, they obviously don't come down here. What she said proves that even more, though the relief we're safe from the Superiors is sharply met by the dread of something possibly dangerous down here. But even that's snuffed out by the truth. We know what's down here. We've been through enough times. The only thing to watch for are jumpers, and the Superiors keep those caged up in their bunker, so . . . what are they afraid of?

"No jumpers tonight," says Jax, reading my mind. He winks at me. "I bet you scared off every jumper for ten miles."

"Let's not talk about that, like, ever again."

"Come on, girl, that's gotta be the single most—"

I grab Jax's arm and squeeze as I notice something by the door.

"What?" he asks.

I bend over to pinch it with my fingers and, sure enough, it is: sand. I fan the light stick around, illuminating the area.

"Is that—?"

"Yeah, and there's a trail of it. . . ."

I leave Johnny and Miguel in the storage room with the poles to guard the children, while Jax and I take the spear and follow the trail—past rows and rows of shelves that we believe used to hold food and water and other goods, past the ransacked dusty crates and all the way to the back, to a dead-end at a wall.

"Okay...." says Jax. "It took us to a wall."

I guide the light stick along the stone until something else catches my eye—something tiny, poking out from a vertical crack. I pluck it from its spot.

"What is it?" he asks.

"I think it's a... paintbrush...." I survey the area. Jutting up and down from the tiny hole are more cracks in the stone, which I trace with my finger. "This wall opens," I say. "Someone put this here so we'd know."

"What if it's a trap?"

"It's not a trap."

"How do you—?"

"I just know."

"Okay... how do we open it, then?" He presses against the wall, and nothing happens. He pushes with his shoulder, and it doesn't budge.

I tuck the paintbrush back inside the hole, and give it a push. Something clicks, then one side of the wall pops forward, enough to grip. We tug on it, and the heavy section draws open to reveal a room about the size of the storage area across from the warehouse, except this one's empty. Almost. In the middle sit three large brown crates. Two are together, the other a little farther from the first two.

"Hello?" Jax calls into the room.

"Smudge?" I say. "Are you here?" We stand in silence, waiting for a response that doesn't come.

"If she's the one helping us," Jax says, "why does she have to play the mystery game? Come out already!"

"I told you, she's conflicted."

"About what?"

"I don't know." I step into the room, shining the light stick above us.

"Hey, what does that say?" He points over to a sign pinned to one of the twin crates, and I remove the thick sheet, curious.

"These crates are made of wood," Jax says. "Not old wood, either."

"And this is paper." I trace its painted lettering, trying to place its familiarity. "These two are for us."

"How do you know?"

"It says, 'For the Treemakers.'"

"Oh. Well, let's open them."

After some prying, the first crate's nailed-on lid comes off. We lean over and stare in disbelief. My stomach grumbles in response.

"Food!" Jax says. "A ton of it! And water!" He removes a glass bottle and unscrews the cap, not even testing it before gulping half of it down. He hands it to me. "Drink it. There's like fifty of those in here, at least."

I gulp down some of the delicious water, then pick up a strange bundle of yellow things and pluck one free. I know I've seen these in a book before....

"Bananas!" says Jax.

"That's right. I couldn't remember.... How do you—?"

He snatches it from my hand, takes a bite, and makes a face. "You gotta get this outside part off first." After messing with it for a minute, he peels back the outside to reveal a delicious, slender morsel. We both smile. He offers it up, and I take a giant bite, floating away to banana Heaven. Jax peels the rest and shoves the whole thing into his mouth.

"Oh my God," he says, muffled, "we gotta get these to the children—"

"Hey," says a voice behind us, making me jump.

"Johnny, jeez… warn us next time," I say.

"What's all this?" He leans over the box, and his eyes widen, confused. He rips a banana from its bundle. "What are these?"

Jax swipes it from him and peels it like he's done it a thousand times. He winks at me, then hands the peeled banana to Johnny. "Eat it."

Johnny takes a cautious bite, chewing slowly at first, but soon he's swept away, too, and gobbles it down. "What are they?" he asks, mouth full.

"Bananas," I reply.

"Well"—he wipes his mouth—"babanas are the best things ever. Where'd they come from?"

I giggle at his mispronunciation. "Smudge, I think."

"Smudge? I don't get it."

"It's someone we met down here last time we came."

"You met a guy named Smudge? Down here?" He points at the floor.

"A girl, actually."

"A girl? Is she cute?"

"She may be your type," says Jax. "Likes to wander around in the dark and whatnot…."

"And she knows where to get more babanas? I have to meet her. Where's she at?"

"Down here, somewhere," I say. "Maybe."

"You lost me."

"It's complicated."

Johnny points to the other unopened crates. "What's in those?"

"We're about to find out," Jax says. "Help me with the lid to this one."

They go to work prying the lid from the second of the pair and toss it behind them.

Jax digs around inside. "Supplies."

I lean over to find more light sticks, a few boxes of matches, blankets, clothing, a few toys, and other random stuff.

"It's like she knew what was going to happen." I pick up a doll with a hand-painted face, and think of Chloe. She's never had a doll before. I tuck it away, and walk over to the other, separate crate. "Guys, come here. Help me with this lid."

They hurry over, and together, we pry the lid from the third crate, letting it clatter to the ground. The three of us lean over.

"No way!" Johnny yells. He and Jax grab up two of the three items, which I have no idea what to call.

"What are they?" I ask.

"Crossbows," Johnny says. "My dad had one of my grandpa's."

"They shoot arrows?"

"They're called bolts, actually. Same idea, though."

"What about that?" I point to the last item pinned with another paper message, and when I remove it, a black screen lights up with red numbers on a strange, silver box.

"How did that happen?" Johnny asks.

"Are those numbers counting down?" Jax leans in for a better view. "Yeah, they are. I think that means one hour, fifty-nine minutes and forty-eight seconds. Forty-seven, forty-six, forty-five—"

"What happens when it gets to zero?"

"We have to take it upstairs," I say, "to the Superior's bunker. I think I know what happens when it gets to zero."

"What?" Jax asks.

I show them the paper in my hand with the red, familiar, painted lettering I can't quite place.

"What does it say?" they ask.

"It says: 'For the Superiors—Boom.'"

FOURTEEN

WE PUSH THE TWO CRATES OF FOOD and supplies back to the storage room and introduce the children to bananas. Most of them have only had slop their whole lives, and them cramming their mouths full of the yellow mush, I'm positive, justifies what we're about to do.

I go to Chloe and a group of the youngest girls in the corner, my arms filled with dolls. Coincidentally, there are four dolls, and four little girls who are in need of dolls. They squeal as I pass them out, and Chloe even cries. She kisses her doll's yarn head and rocks her.

"Thank you so, so, so much, Momma Joy," she says. "I love her."

"Don't thank me, thank our guardian angel."

Johnny and Jax are in the warehouse learning to use their crossbows. The weapons are simple enough, and they're quiet. Smudge isn't too conflicted about us killing the Superiors, that's for sure.

"When are we going?" Miguel asks.

"Soon."

Aby excuses herself from the doll-circle and joins us at the storage room door, Baby Lou in her arms. "You're not going, right?" Her blue eyes beg Miguel to stay.

"Aby, you know I have to."

She turns away.

I place my hand on her shoulder. "We won't let anything happen to him, I promise."

She whips her head to me. "You're going, too?"

"Yes, of course I'm going. It's my responsibility to—"

"What—die?"

"No. To make sure they never hurt any of you ever again." I kiss her cheek, then Baby Lou's. "Now, please . . . we have to go. We'll be fine, I promise. Back in thirty minutes or so."

"And if you're not?"

Miguel hugs her tightly, kisses her cheek. "We will be."

"You boys professionals yet?" I call into the warehouse.

"Pretty much," Jax calls back, "as long as the target doesn't move."

"Good enough." I hand the spear to an older boy. "Guard this door," I tell him.

He nods and, gripping it tightly in his fist, repositions himself by the doorway.

Aby takes something from her pocket. "You'll need a weapon, then." She drops the item into Miguel's palm.

He holds up her daddy's tiny pocket knife, chuckles, and clicks it open to reveal its two-inch blade.

"Hey, it's better than nothing," I say.

"Thanks, baby." Then, he closes it, slides it down into his own pocket.

"Let's move out," Johnny says.

Jax slowly makes his way from the other side of the ware-house with the silver box, when Johnny raises his crossbow, face deadly serious, closes one eye, aims, and shoots. I let out a startled cry as the bolt misses Jax by about three inches and spears a large rat in the gut.

"Shit," Jax says, "you scared the hell out of me, man."

"Me, too," I say, heart now slamming in my chest. "Good aim, though. You're a great shot."

Jax sets the box down gently on the floor between us.

"Who's carrying this thing?"

"I am," Miguel and I both say at the same time.

"No," I say. "You have a knife, you cover me."

He nods.

I take Jax's hand and reach for Miguel's, then motion for them to close the circle with Johnny's hands. After an awkward split second, they realize this isn't the time for childishness, and the brothers clasp hands as well.

I clear my throat. "Um, God? Or... Whoever You Are.... I know we haven't spoken much over the years, but in my defense, I didn't know what to believe. I'm not entirely sure now, either, but I think I'm closer to the truth than I've ever been, truth being, nothing is entirely understood or explained, even if you look deep into it. But there's something that shines bright in the dark—something strong, hopeful, something to live for, to die for... and even kill for: Love.

"And if you are indeed the Keeper of all that is love, then you'll help us protect the little lives who are counting on us. After the pain, humiliation, and suffering those people have inflicted on my brothers and sisters, I ask that you allow us to take justice and vengeance and love, and do something extraordinary, to be free... to live together in love and peace, without evil, forevermore."

My words flutter off into the air, and after a silent moment, we say, "And so it is."

"That was nice, Momma Joy," says Jax.

"Thanks. Let's hope it worked." I smile, and he returns it. Taking a match from one of the boxes, I strike it on the rough concrete and light the "Boom" paper with it, then drop it to the floor. The flame crawls along its edges and finally devours it, leaving behind a smoldering black skeleton. I spit a couple of times and rub the saliva around in the ash, dab my thumb into the wet soot and streak my cheeks and forehead with it.

"What are you doing?" Jax asks.

"Come here." I dab my thumb again, and he backs away.

"Why?"

"A long time ago, people painted their faces before going into battle. The paint was believed to hold magical powers of protection and strength, and make the warriors appear more ferocious." I smear some black around his face, and we silently hold each other's gaze for a few seconds before he speaks.

"Joy…" His drops his head.

"What?"

"Never mind. Let's just get this over with."

Miguel and Johnny streak their own faces, and we're ready to go. With a few deep breaths, I rub my hands together and pick up the box. It's lighter than expected.

"How much time do we have?" Johnny straps his weapon to his back.

"One hour, thirty-two minutes and forty-three seconds."

"We better hurry."

"Johnny and I will go first," I tell them. "Jax, you and Miguel in the back."

Jax salutes me, Miguel withdraws his tiny knife, and I readjust the box in my hands. "Everyone ready?"

Three nods.

"Let's go."

At the factory door, sweat trickles down my hairline as I watch the numbers count down, smaller and smaller. Johnny clutches the door handle and, with a finger to his lips, pushes open the door. It creaks, and I sense we're about to get caught like last time. Except this time, we aren't defenseless. Maybe that would be better. Then, we could get this over with.

Johnny opens the door all the way and swings his crossbow

out in front of him. We file out slowly, though once we find the space empty, we move more quickly to the rusty double doors leading to the Superiors' bunker. Once we get there, my chest swells with nervous fear. We've never been past this point. Jax slides ahead of us, crossbow in one hand, jingly key ring in the other. He tries key after key, until one finally fits into the slot, and he turns it with a click. Both he and Johnny nod to one another, and each takes a door handle, crossbows ready.

They swing the doors open, aim their weapons down the long, empty, sparsely lit space. Faint outline of a doorway at the other end. Green lights dot the perimeter, signaling good air. I check the oxygauge. Of course it's good air, we're entering the Superiors' territory now. The cleansing powers of fresh oxygen fill my starving lungs.

Johnny takes off, and Jax brushes past me to his side. I make tense eye contact with Miguel, and see fire in him. He smiles, and when I remember my promise, I smile back. A part of me can't even believe this is happening; we're doing it. We're going to end this, tonight, and they're all going to get what's been coming to them for a long, long time. Like Emmanuel Superior.

After what seems like a mile, we stop at the entrance to the Superiors' bunker. Both Jax and Johnny press their ears to the door for a few seconds, then lean back and shake their heads. No noise on the other side. Jax pushes down on the handle. Locked. He searches the key ring for the key that opened the last two doors, and tries it. The quiet click of the lock mechanism echoes in my ears, and it may as well be thunder. For an instant, my heart stops, and I sweat profusely. The boys are sweating, too, gripping their weapons as Jax pushes the handle down.

The door opens to a shadowy darkness lit only by whatever

light shines through the doorway. After checking the wide room to make sure no one's in it, we creep in and duck behind a mound of stuff, while Johnny eases the door to its frame—not completely shut, to allow easy access out—and then he, too, crouches with us. My eyes finally adjust, to piles of items everywhere, from floor to ceiling.

After waiting a silent moment, Johnny forges down a little trail in the middle of the packed room, toward the soft light in the doorway ahead. A glance around, and I think I know what this is: the Superiors are hoarding the belongings of Greenleigh's dead. From the corner of my eye, I swear I catch a glimpse of my great-grandmother's teapot. . . .

At the doorway, with Johnny and Miguel on one side and me and Jax on the other, Jax and Johnny silently communicate with their eyes and through hand motions, then take turns peeking out in the hallway. Jax points left, then leans over to whisper in my ear, "Bedrooms to the left. Stay here with the box and Miguel. We'll check their rooms."

I shake my head. "No way," I whisper back. "We're going with you."

He shrugs, then waves to Johnny, and each takes one side of the hallway, aiming the crossbows down them as Miguel and I emerge. Once we're out, the four of us travel down a corridor lit by two fancy light fixtures and packed with as much random junk as the room we just came from. The smell of Emmanuel Superior's rancid perfume tickles my nose, making me sneeze. I muffle it in my arm, and hold back another one coming on.

One hour, twenty-six minutes, fifty seconds.

When we reach the first bedroom of the four—two on the left, two on the right—I tap Jax's elbow with mine, nod to the box, then toward a pile of clothes between the two left-hand doors. He gives me a thumbs-up, and we crouch down together.

Then, he slings the crossbow over one shoulder and, with both hands, lifts up a mountain of stuff that's probably been sitting there for years. I slide the box into place, underneath, relieved to have it out of my hands, and Jax, with a smile, lets the clothing fall to cover it. You'd never know it was there.

Johnny raises four fingers, points to the four doors and to each of us and himself—four doors, four of us. We nod. Jax and I take the doors on the left; Johnny and Miguel, the right. Johnny silently counts to three and we all take a collective deep breath, then turn our doorknobs.

As soon as I open mine to peek through the crack, I close it again. In his bed, Diaz Superior lies naked in a puddle of his own puke. I could've gone the rest of my life without witnessing that, and will likely spend the rest of my life trying to erase it from my mind. The boys join me, and we scurry back to the room by our exit, ducking behind a mound of stuff in the corner.

"My room was empty," Jax whispers. "Full of women's wigs and stuff. Probably Emmanuel's."

"Mine was empty, too," Miguel says. "Like, really empty."

Johnny frowns and curses silently. "I had Mona in mine. What about you, Joy?"

"Diaz."

"Not good," says Jax. "We're missing one."

"Should we check the rest of the place?" I ask.

"Maybe we should just kill them," Miguel says. "I mean, why not? We have weapons. Why wait for the box?"

"We don't need to risk it—"

"Hello?" Mona Superior's voice calls from the hallway, and startles my blood cold. "Emmanuel?"

The sound of a closing door and feet shuffling toward us makes me panic. Johnny stands with his weapon, but Jax pulls him back down. He holds a finger in the air and, taking the key ring from his pocket, gives it a jingle. "Yes?" he says in his best Emmanuel Superior impression. "I'll be right back."

Mona's footsteps stop. "You going down there again?" She yawns. "Haven't you had enough fun for one night?"

"Not yet," Jax replies, face filling with rage.

"Well, all right. But remember, Arianna wants their minds intact for the transfer when she gets back. No head injuries."

Jax hurries to the door, gives it a good slam.

"Whatever," Mona Superior mumbles.

Seconds later, her bedroom door shuts again, and we all breathe a sigh of relief. We meet Jax by the back door. He quietly reopens it, and we slip away down the corridor, through the rusty double doors and into the Tree Factory, racing across the main room and around all of the machines we'll never operate again. I take one last look at the chopper and the window.

I can't say I'm sorry to see them go.

Then I remember: my daddy's gloves. "Wait!" I whisper-yell. "I'll be right back." I leave them in the middle of the main factory room and dart to the chopper.

"Joy, what are you doing?" Jax whispers loudly behind me.

I snatch my daddy's gloves from the grid and bolt back through the room. "Can't leave these," I say when I return.

When we get back underground, our relief is only slight. Arianna Superior could be anywhere. Down here, for all we know. My imagination tries to plays tricks on me, but I feed it with reason to keep it under control.

If she were down here, we'd know it.

"Anybody have a clue where she might be?" Johnny asks.

"No clue." Jax holds up a hand, ears perking up in the dark.

Johnny glances over at Miguel and me, and we both shake our heads. How would we? There've always been periods of

Arianna Superior's absence. Sometimes weeks; once, for a few months. Rumors that she was on the Other Side circulated as much as rumors that she was in the Far West Bygonne, or visiting the eastern cannibal tribe, and so on....

No, Arianna Superior has been an unsettling and unsolvable mystery since the beginning. Seems like ten lifetimes ago when she first came in with a group of fading vagabonds a couple of years before my mother got sick. I was fascinated by her white hair and wrinkled hands, and her eyes, a cloudy blue sky. Occasionally, she'd smile, though it appeared painful; one of those broken ones that pinches your heart and makes you wonder, even as a child, what made her so sad. And always, that inevitable break... it would happen someday; something would push her too far, and she'd snap in two on the inside. I didn't have words back then, but I do now. Like nightfall after a toxic daytime storm, one day her eyes turned black and her broken smile faded forever.

Soon after, Micah Greenleigh—the mayor for which our town was renamed—on his death bed handed her the keys to the Tree Factory. Then, everything changed. People grew ill, died younger. My daddy worked his fingers to the bloody bone for years without a day of rest.

Only now am I seeing the smoke and mirrors here.... For how long has Arianna Superior been stashing aces? What secrets does she know, of Bygonne and the Other Side, the keys to our freedom—or our demise?

"Transfer," I say. "I wonder what she meant by that...."

The warehouse comes into view, and the whispering of children in the dark is music to my ears.

"I don't know," Jax says. "I'd feel a lot better if she were up there, sound asleep in her bed right now."

One at a time, we step through the broken doors of

the warehouse, ducking through the silent wreckage and stirred-up dust.

"How much time do we have left?" Miguel asks.

"Maybe an hour and ten or fifteen minutes," Jax says. "Hard to say."

"We'll know when it happens," says Johnny, "if your friend's message is right."

At the storage room door, the older boy with the spear stands at attention, in the exact same spot we left him. I smile, and he salutes me. I salute back. "Any excitement while we were gone?"

"None. But I have a feeling there might be some soon, now that you four are back." He hands over the spear and yawns.

Aby rushes past him and throws herself at Miguel. They hold each other tight, and only then do I relax a little more. Corpse woman might be missing, but at least we're together and safe. Soon, we'll have two fewer Superiors to worry about.

"I'm thinking we should move," Jax says. "No way to know for sure how powerful that blast will be—"

"But the box is so small...." I peek in at Baby Lou and most of the others asleep on the blankets, curled up together comfortably.

"Doesn't mean the blast will be," he says.

After another few seconds of thought, I make my decision. "No, we should stay and let them rest." I tuck my daddy's gloves down safely into my bag. "We have no idea what we're doing next. We should use this time to plan. Plus, we need to make sure it goes off. If it doesn't, we'll have to go back and take care of them ourselves. If the explosion was dangerous to us, way over here, I think Smudge would've warned us."

Jax tugs a handful of hair, shaking his head. "Are you sure about this? We don't even know her—"

"She gave us food, water, and supplies. And weapons. And toys, for crying out loud! Why would she do that, if we couldn't trust her?"

Still, he shakes his head slowly with a sigh. "All right, you got me there...."

"Let's make ourselves comfortable and wait for the boom, then. We'll sit here in the doorway and keep an eye on things."

"Wait for the boom," Johnny repeats. "Intense." He slides down the doorframe, resting cross-legged with his head against the wood.

The rest of us join him to create a circle in the doorway.

"Well?" Aby asks. "How'd it go? Did you get inside their bunker?"

"Yeah," says Miguel, "but Arianna wasn't there. And we almost got caught by Mona, until Jax faked the most excellent Emmanuel impersonation I've ever heard in my life."

"Wow...." She clasps Miguel's hand between her own two. "Nice going, Jax."

"Thanks."

Jax lies down with his head in my lap, gazing up at me. I brush some hair from his face, trace the outline of his lips. "Soon, we'll be in paradise," I say.

"You really think it's a portal to the Other Side?"

"Yes. I mean, I... I think I do."

Jax sighs, heavily this time, and again tugs at his hair. "I can't even comprehend how that would be possible."

"I wish you people would explain this 'portal to the Other Side' thing," Johnny says.

Miguel's eyes widen, then cloud over with confusion. "The smell...." He stares off into nothingness, like his thoughts scampered away into the dark.

"Yes?" I say. "The smell what?"

Johnny grunts an irritated chuckle, and tosses a rock. "Am I here? I think I'm asking a question, but maybe I'm too idiotic to realize I'm not actually saying anything…?"

Jax puts up a hand to silence Johnny's rant. "Hold on, let him finish."

"The smell," Miguel begins again. "In the empty room I checked… it just occurred to me. The room was weird—no furniture or anything. Not like the rest of the bunker crammed with junk. Empty… and a little smoky…."

"Okay, what's so strange about that?" Johnny asks.

"The smoke… smelled like citrus."

Jax and I make startled eye contact.

"Are you sure?" I ask.

"So what?" says Johnny. "Who cares if it smelled like citrus?"

"Okay, Johnny, listen. I'll give you the quick version…." And Jax sits up, cross-legged, hands in his lap. "Twenty-two floors below us is a smoky room that smells like citrus. When you go inside, a bright light flashes, and suddenly you're in a wooden hut overlooking the ocean. Real trees, blue sky, animals… paradise."

"Get outta here."

"It's true," I say. "And the more I think about it, the more I believe it has to be the Other Side. Nothing else makes sense."

"And *that* makes sense?" Jax says.

"None of it makes any damned sense to me." Johnny tosses another pebble through the open door.

"Why would it smell like that in Arianna Superior's room?" Miguel asks.

"Probably a coincidence," I say.

"You sure it was the same smell?" Jax asks.

"Pretty sure."

"Ugh!" Jax yanks on another handful of hair. "None of this

makes any sense!"

"I don't know…" Miguel says. "Maybe it was a coincidence."

"Maybe." I search my mind for the words to describe what I'm thinking. "Or… maybe we can't understand it. You know, because, well… imagine if an alien came to Earth from some distant galaxy—would it be able to comprehend our world?"

"That depends," Miguel says. "If they were smarter than us, then—"

"Okay, bad example. I mean, if we've never experienced something, or never been told or taught about it and don't even have a clue that it exists, and suddenly we're thrown into it, how likely is it to make any sense?"

Jax scratches his head, furrows his brow. "So… okay, you think we should go back down to twenty-three? What happens if we can't get there? Smudge said never to come back—what if we can't even get down there? Or what if we do, and can't get into the room? Or we go there, but come right back? Then what?"

"Then, we search the bunkers until we find the trolley tunnels," I say. "She wouldn't help us escape and kill the Superiors if that was her intention, though. She's obviously leading us to safety, otherwise she wouldn't have manipulated the oxygen levels and turned the lights on, and everything else."

"How'd she do that?" Johnny asks. "She some kind of electrical wizard or something?"

"I don't know. But when we find her, maybe she'll tell us."

For a while, we sit in silent contemplation, listening to the rhythmic breathing of the sleeping children—and a few snorers—until a roar-and-rumble above startles us. Shock waves roll through the walls and the floor and the ceiling, shaking the whole room and showering dirt and debris onto us. My heart beats a thousand miles an hour, sparked by the adrenaline surging its metallic fire through my veins. We jump up as the children are jolted awake by the earthquake.

"Woo!" Johnny yells.

Then, we're all cheering, jumping around, celebrating. That boom was the snap of two more chains binding us to a life-long miserable existence.

FIFTEEN

BABY LOU BEGINS TO CRY from the noise and excitement. I scoop her up into my arms. "Shh, Baby, it's okay. One step closer to freedom." I rock her and Millie while the celebration continues.

"Goodbye, Tree Factory!" Jax hollers into the air, along with the rest of the cries of celebration.

But Chloe isn't celebrating. Instead, she cradles her new doll in the corner, a sadness in her face. I sit down next to her, pulling her into my lap next to Baby Lou. "What's wrong, sweetheart? Did the noise scare you?"

She shakes her head.

"Well, then why are you sad? We don't ever have to build trees for the Superiors again. Doesn't that make you happy?"

Still, she peers up at me with the eyes of a wounded angel. "Yes," she says hesitantly. "But who's gonna build trees now?"

"Well... no one. At least not anywhere around here."

At this, she leans into my chest and cries.

"Sweetie, what's the matter?"

"Now we won't have any air to breathe, and we're all gonna die, and... and I want my mommy!" Then, she cries and cries... more than she ever has before. Like she's only now learned how to grieve for the parents she barely knew and will never remember. She was a surprise baby, born too late. Her mother was already approaching thirty.

I hold her tight and let her cry, feeling somewhat foolish. How did I not consider this problem before a five-year-old did? What will become of Bygonne now, with no one left to build trees? Rumors once circulated of another Tree Factory somewhere, but no one knows if it actually exists. What'll become of this place now? Have we unintentionally sealed the fate of certain death for Bygonne?

"I've got you, sweetheart." I rock her and Baby Lou. "We'll have air to breathe; we're going to find paradise, like Billy, remember?"

She nods, rubbing a balled fist into a tired, teary eye.

"You have to trust me now, okay?" I kiss her forehead, squeeze her and Baby Lou tight. "Momma Joy will take good care of you, and all of your brothers and sisters. I promise, I won't let anything bad happen to you."

She has every right to be scared. All of us do. We're sailing blindly through the dark, unsure if the light at the end of the tunnel is merely a mirage. And if we are stuck in Bygonne, we've destroyed our possibility of survival. If we don't get out of here, we have less than a year to live.

We find a few large backpacks in the supply crate, along with a first-aid kit and some peel-back cans of strange, edible goods. Paper labels with funny names like "Brussels Sprouts," "Artichoke Hearts," and "Garbanzo Beans" call us to a strange and delicious new world of tastes. There are even a few rolls of toilet tissue. Smudge thought of everything.

We load up the bags and get seven older boys to carry them. The food and water we have will get us through the next twenty-four hours, at least. I peel a banana for Baby Lou and Chloe to share. They devour it in under a minute. They've never eaten anything but nutrient-fortified slop; everything you need to survive, minus the appeal. They've never been happier than they are right at this moment, yellowish-white mush and bliss spread across their faces.

Jax slides an arm around my waist. "What now?"

Smoke smell drifts down through the ceiling.

"I need to make an announcement," I say. "Aby, will you take Baby Lou?"

"Sure."

She puts Baby Lou on her hip, and I stand in the doorway. "Everyone listen up. Olders, find a younger buddy. You'll be responsible for them from now until further notice. We'll be walking through a lot of corridors and down a few flights of stairs. Help them if they need it. If they get tired, let one of us know, and we'll stop the caravan to rest. I don't want to stop too much, though, until we get to our next destination. It isn't far."

Jax moves beside me. "There's a box full of light sticks right over here." He points to a crate beside the door. "Everyone take two. We don't know if there'll be light or not in the corridors."

Murmurs rise up as everyone shuffles around. Chloe tugs on my arm. "Will you be my buddy, Momma Joy?"

"Of course." I crack a light stick and hand it to her. "Shake this up real good, and help light the way with me."

Her eyes widen with excitement as she shakes the stick with two tiny hands.

"Baby Lou needs changing before we go," Aby says.

"Okay, and if anyone else needs to use the washroom… well, there isn't one. But any boys, follow Jax outside to the corridor across from us. Any girls, go with Aby to the storage room across from the warehouse, where we found the supplies. We'll meet back here when everyone's relieved, then we'll head out."

I hand a toilet tissue roll to Jax, and a small group of boys follows him out the door. A larger group of girls gathers around Aby. She hands a whining Baby Lou back to me in exchange for a roll of tissue, then she leads the girls away to the secret storage room.

"Johnny," I say, "I need water and cloth. Be my assistant."

"Um...."

"Come on, it's fine. You don't have to watch, just dig through that crate and find me a thick shirt."

"Gotcha." He takes a bottle of water from his bag, then digs through the crate of old clothes.

"Do you have anything to cut the cloth with?"

"No." He hands me the water, then holds up a gray shirt. "Will this work?"

"Yeah, that's probably thick enough." I notice Miguel standing right outside the door. "Hey, Miguel?" I call over. "Hand me Aby's knife."

He tosses me the closed knife, which I use to cut Baby Lou a diaper, then I get her cleaned up and swaddled in the fresh cloth. Her dress is filthy. She's been wearing the same one for a few days.

"Okay, now find me the smallest shirt you can," I tell Johnny. "She needs a new dress."

Again he digs around for a few seconds, and Jax returns with his group.

"How about this?" And Johnny holds up the ugliest shirt I've ever laid eyes on, a strange man's face on the front and words printed beneath it.

"Let me see."

He tosses me the shirt, which would fit me big, and I read aloud the words below the man's face: "Only you can create a better future." I flip it over to more words on the back. "Make your eternal sacrifice for Lord Daumier—before it's too late! What does that mean?" I mumble.

"No clue," says Jax. "What a strange place this world was once, huh?"

"Yeah, definitely strange." I replace Baby Lou's dress with the huge shirt. It swallows her, but it'll keep her warm and comfortable, and her skin protected.

Aby and the girls return, giggling and gossiping. This is the most time any of them have ever spent with the boys, outside of working with them in the Tree Factory. Their heads are so in the clouds, they probably don't even realize where we are, while they're busy eyeing each other with flirty glances. It makes me happy, because even though we're underground, we're freer than we've ever been.

I tie Baby Lou onto Serna's back so I can spear something—or someone—easily, if necessary. She cries at first, but once I give her Millie and her bottle, she rubs her eyes and yawns. Our walking should put her right to sleep.

"Everyone get with your buddy," I say. "Chloe, next to me. Jax and I know the way, so we'll lead. Johnny—you and Miguel take the rear with the other crossbow and protect us from the back. A few poles are left for any older boys who want to carry them for added protection, if necessary."

After everyone is situated in pairs with various weaponry, Jax and I start out of the storage room, Chloe between us. "Where are we going, Momma Joy?" She holds the light stick high, a noticeable fear in her eyes.

"To find a friend. We have to walk for a bit."

"You have a friend down here?"

"Yes."

"What's her name?"

"Smudge."

"Smudge? What kinda name is that? I never heard a name like that before."

"I'm not sure. We haven't had much time to talk to her."

She stares off into the distance, her little mind

contemplating big things. We pass through the busted ware-house doors behind Jax, who's moved a few feet ahead and whips his crossbow, left, right, left, right, searching for a target.

"Momma Joy?" Chloe finally says.

"Yes, Chloe?"

"How come she's your friend if you haven't talked to her much?"

"Chloe, honey, we're going to have to save this conversation for another time, okay? Right now, I need to pay attention to where we're going and what's around us."

She lifts her light stick back up. "Okay."

"Good girl. You're a fantastic light-shiner," I whisper, and she grins up at me.

We follow Jax down the familiar corridors, yellow and green lights shining around every turn. Every oxygauge we pass ticks noisily, as if they hadn't moved in years, but they tell the truth: miracles are occurring here, tonight. Illusion or not, Smudge somehow makes electricity happen... and air, and food, and weapons... and she's nowhere around to take the credit.

We forge on through the connecting tunnel between Bunkers A and B, and when we turn down the corridor that holds Old Jonesy's stairwell, I jog a few quick steps forward and catch Jax's arm. "We can't take them over Old Jonesy," I whisper. "They'll freak out."

He stops, and the procession stops behind us. "What do you propose we do, then?"

"Whatcha talkin' about, Momma Joy?" Chloe asks.

I stare Jax down. He already knows what needs to be done.

"Ugh." He sighs. "Okay." Then, he whistles down the cor-ridor behind us. "Miguel, Johnny, come here."

"Someone has to stay out here with a crossbow," I add.

Johnny and Miguel make it to us. "What's up?" Johnny asks.

"You stay out here and guard everyone, Johnny. I have to take care of something in that stairwell with Joy and Miguel. We'll be right back."

"What is it?" Johnny asks.

"It's nothing, man," Jax replies.

"Come on! You guys have been coming down here forever, and I never got to go one time. Let me go."

"How do you use that thing?" Miguel points to the crossbow. "Show me, and I'll guard so you can."

After Johnny gives Miguel a quick lesson and I leave Chloe with Aby, I hand my spear to an older boy, then Jax, Johnny, and I head to the stairwell. Behind the closed door, I'm still surprised by the glow of green and yellow lights along the ceiling and walls, revealing Old Jonesy's every rotted detail.

Johnny jumps back.

"This is Jonesy," Jax says, chuckling. "Also known as 'Old Jonesy.'"

"It's a… it's a…"

"Corpse," I finish. "And we need to move him so he doesn't terrify the children."

"Where do we move him to?" Jax asks.

"All the way down the six flights," I say, "and put him in a corridor opposite the direction we'll be going."

"Man, check out that hat." Johnny crouches down next to Old Jonesy and snatches the hat from his skull. Dust flies as he gives it a few good swats. He removes his bandanna, stuffs it into his back pocket, and plops the hat onto his own head. "What do you think? Does it suit me?"

"Well, Miguel has his boots," I say, "so why not?"

"Who's going down backwards?" Jax says.

"I will. Johnny, help Jax. That part will probably be heavier."

I stoop down to lift Old Jonesy by the ankles, careful not to touch the crispy, blackened flesh of his feet, and they take him under the arms. "One, two, three...." We lift him up, and I'm surprised to find him so heavy, considering there's so much of him missing.

Five flights of stairs later, sweat trails down my spine, glistens on Jax's and Johnny's foreheads as we struggle with the weight. At the bottom of the fifth staircase, we let his body drop and catch our breath.

"Dang," says Johnny. "That's one heavy dude. Imagine what he was like when he was alive? Must've been a monster."

Jax laughs, wiping his forehead with the back of his hand. "Yeah, man. Did you check out Miguel's new boots? That Old Jonesy had some big feet...."

"And you know what that means," Johnny says, chuckling.

"You boys are incredible," I say, shaking my head. "You don't miss a beat, do you?" Taking a deep breath, I bend down again, gripping Old Jonesy's pant legs. "Come on, we need to hurry."

Still amused, Jax and Johnny stoop down and lift him up. "Where to?" Jax says.

I nod behind them, toward the corridor lit up with only green oxygen lights. The one behind me—the one we'll head down with the children shortly—is lit with both those and the yellow bulbs-in-fixtures to illuminate our path. We're definitely being led to the portal. No doubt in my mind now.

We drop Old Jonesy around the corner of the next green-lit corridor, relieved to be rid of him, then jog back to the stairwell. We start up, out of breath, but keep a steady pace. Nervous excitement and adrenaline, as well as an obviously lighted path, are our motivation to push past the fatigue.

"How come there's light and clean air all the way down here, too?" Johnny asks, halfway up the six flights. "How's that possible?"

"Smudge," I say.

"Yeah, but how—?"

"We don't know yet, but we're going to find out. Apparently, she's leading us to where she wants us to go."

"Such a mystery," he says. "Can't wait to meet her." And he winks, adjusting Old Jonesy's hat backwards on his head.

When we make it back, everyone's exactly where we left them, though most are sitting now.

"Okay, everybody up," I announce. "It's time to move again. We're halfway there."

They hop to their feet, excitement pushing them through their tiredness as well, I'm sure.

"Hey, where'd you get the new hat?" a boy asks Johnny.

"Found it," he replies, "just lying there on the ground."

"Liar!" says another boy.

"All right," I say, "listen up. Olders, help your younger buddies get safely down these next six flights of stairs. Hold their hand, if you need to. Or guide them. There's light, but it's not real bright."

Chloe slides her little shaky hand up into mine. I squeeze it tight, and smile down at her. After a headcount and quick check on Baby Lou, Jax and I move the line into the stairwell, past Miguel's old boots, and down. The echo of feet, pitter-pattering their way to paradise, brings tears to my eyes. My heart swells with joy for the first time since before my daddy died. He'd be so proud of me, I know he would be.

With everyone safely down the stairs, we wind through the corridors Jax and I have explored countless times. Everyone's quiet, waiting for the moment when they find out what's next. We turn the corner to the corridor that leads to our elevator, the tiny yellow light above it already on. Oddly, this still surprises me.

Jax stops to check the nearby oxygauge, shaking his head in astonishment. "I can't even believe it."

"Wait," I say. "What about the elevator? We can't all fit at once."

"We'll have to go in groups."

"I hate that idea."

"We have no other options, do we?"

We're halfway to the elevator now, yet something nags at me, though I can't place it. Then, it hits me. "Jax," I say, grabbing his arm, "the smell... I don't smell it, do you?"

"What?"

"Citrus."

"Oh,"—he sniffs the air—"no, I don't."

"What does that mean, do you think?"

"I don't know. You're the one with all the assumptions."

"Yeah, but you're usually the one with the speculations."

"Well, I got nothing. Let's get down there and see what we find."

We reach the elevator and wait for it to ding, and for the door to open, but it doesn't. I push the button, which finally opens the door. No citrus.

"Johnny," Jax calls to the end of the line. "Come here."

Johnny trots over. "What's up?"

"We need to go down in groups. I'll take the first group of ten with a crossbow. Joy comes down with the next group, then Miguel, then you. Got it?"

Johnny nods. "Where we going? Which floor?"

"Twenty-three," I say. "But it should take you there automatically. It did for us, the last two times."

He nods and starts back to the end of the line. "We'll meet you down there."

"You bring the next group down right behind me, okay?" Jax says to me.

Adrenaline rushes through me. It's hard to feel my fingertips. "I don't like us being separated," I say.

"Me, neither. But we'll be back together soon. Just a few minutes."

"Who are you taking?"

"The first five pairs here." And he points to them, including Aby and her buddy. She's no happier about being separated from Miguel, than I am from Jax. She kisses Miguel and hugs him tightly, then steps reluctantly onto the elevator, clasping her little girl's hand. Once everyone's on, Jax blows me a kiss, then the door slides closed between us.

SIXTEEN

After what may be an eternity, the empty elevator returns. The door dings open, and I hold it for Chloe and the next four pairs, including Serna with a sleeping Baby Lou on her back.

"All of this clean air and traveling put her right to sleep, I see." I smile at Serna as I enter the elevator, and she grins. "We'll see you guys on sub-level twenty-three," I say to the boys.

Johnny gives me a thumbs-up, and Miguel waves as I let the door close. Only after do I notice one of Jax's crossbow bolts stuck into the floor, beneath the buttons.

"Enter destination," the elevator voice says.

I yank the bolt up and push the button for sub-level twenty-three. *Why would he do that?* He wouldn't shoot a bolt into the elevator floor for no reason. I inspect it. Yes, it's definitely one of his.

"Why was that there?" an older girl asks.

"I'm not sure."

"Yeah," a boy chuckles in disgust, trying to mask his fear. "She's not sure of much—or so she says." And he elbows the boy next to him who looks one hundred percent terrified already. "You know what I think?" he goes on. "That she's just gonna take us east and feed us to the cannibals—oh!—or maybe she'll just gobble us up herself; her and her boyfriend. . . ."

This new boy—a lousy blabbermouth—was shipped in last week from Taborton. Twelve years old, with brown, fuzzy eyebrows that connect in the middle and a total of four rotten teeth in his whole fat mouth. He loves to brag about his "vaccinations" that protect him from our diseases.

Slowly, I walk over to him, peer down into his eyes... and smirk. "Yes," I tease. "And we'd start with you, except I wouldn't want to choke and die."

He shows me his middle finger.

Chloe squeezes my hand, points to the numbers. "Are we almost there?"

The twenty-two button lights up, then goes dark.

"Next floor," I say.

As the twenty-three button lights up, I move closer to the door. But instead of it staying lit and the elevator slowing to a stop, it, too, goes dark and the number twenty-four lights up. We keep descending.

"Hey!" I bang a fist on the door, waking Baby Lou on Serna's back. "What's going on?"

Twenty-four goes dark while twenty-five lights up and stays lit... except we don't stop. We continue to descend. My ears pop, and Baby Lou screams, probably from the pressure in her ears, too.

"Momma Joy!" Chloe tugs at her ears in a panic.

"Pinch your nose and blow," I say.

She does, and I pinch Baby Lou's nose, though she fights me. Her screaming should clear her own pressure. Deeper and deeper we plummet into the earth, and panic swallows me. I grip the bolt tightly, my sweat making it slick in my palm. Then, it hits me.

"Jax shot this into the floor, so we'd know this would happen," I say to myself. "It was pointing... down."

After what might have been another fifteen to twenty floors later, the elevator finally slows. "Please enjoy your travel," says the voice, as the door opens to Jax and Aby, beaming from ear to ear with wide-eyed excitement.

Jax rushes in, throws his arms around me. "You are not going to believe this." He takes the crossbow bolt from my hand, then motions to two older boys, who nod and get on the elevator as we file out.

"I'm sending them up to tell the others what's going on. I wanted to make sure it was safe down here before I let them go." He holds up the bolt. "So, you figured this out?"

"Yeah, finally, when the elevator kept going after sub-level twenty-five. What's down here?"

"Something unbelievable." Aby tries to smile, but it's overcome by a tremble of fear.

We move into the new corridor with the others, except this one isn't like those above us. The combination of smells is both alluring and alarming, because I don't know what to call them. To my left stands a stone wall with steel support beams; same, across from the elevator. Only one way to go. Slowly, my gaze drifts right, toward a strange whooshing noise. The corridor stretches out before us in an arched tunnel, with small, scurrying creatures inside that cast long shadows from the orange, square overhead lights. On the far side at its end, a green glow illuminates the unknown.

"What's down there?" I ask.

The elevator door closes with a ding, taking the two boys back up to the others.

Jax grabs my hand and tugs me down the tunnel, Aby following close behind. But Chloe, gripping my other hand tightly, plants her feet. "I'm scared, Momma Joy."

"Don't worry," Jax says. "I've got this." He holds up his crossbow, loading the bolt back into place. "And I won't let anything happen to any of you." He continues to guide us down the tunnel, the whooshing noise getting louder, the scents stronger.

I take a deep breath. "What is that smell?"

A few more feet and a crisscross-barred covering over the exit becomes visible. My heart races, pumping the liquid metal of adrenaline through me; I taste it in my mouth, and my fingertips grow numb. Another few steps, and the source of the whooshing sound is explained.

"That smell," Jax says, "is life."

We stand inches from the tunnel grate, and on the other side, leafy green plants crawl along a sloped ground, down into a rushing black river a hundred or more feet across. On the opposite side, a thick forest travels upward, disappearing into utter darkness. Above the river, and seeming to float in midair, a line of tiny green lights follows the river in both directions.

"Guess we know where our water comes from now," I say. "My daddy always said there were tunnels, deep underground...."

"Look over there," says Jax, leaning into the grate and pointing to our right.

Trembling, I lean in with him to see what he's talking about. "Is that... a boat?"

"Yep," he says. "And big enough for all of us, too. At least it appears so from over here."

The boat rests on a platform above the water, and it's almost half the width of the river, with a fat bottom and an enclosed space on top with wraparound windows.

"Anyone know how to operate a boat?" I ask.

"I'm sure it's not that difficult," Jax says. "We need to get the children on safely, and make sure they stay inside. No telling what could be lurking in that water, or in those trees. Giant jumpers, at the very least."

"Oh, that's comforting. How are there trees and stuff so deep underground? Don't they need sunlight to grow?"

"Your guess is as good as mine. I'm sure we'll figure that out, though. Probably related to how there's fresh air way down here, you know?"

"Yeah"—I nod—"maybe."

On the wall is a rotating lever attached to a chain pulley, which I suspect raises the grate when turned. If it actually works, I'll be amazed.

Chloe's hand trembles in mine. "I'm cold," she says.

"Yeah," I say, "it's much cooler down here than what we're used to. Come on, I'll give you a ride." I crouch, and her clammy arms slide into place around my neck as she climbs on. I wrap my hands under her knees. "Let's go—" I start, but Chloe suddenly shrieks and thrashes around on my back.

"Get it off, *get it off!*" she screams.

Jax swings, and something thumps against the wall. I'm horrified by a huge, wriggling creature lying on its back, feet dancing in the air. Chloe wails, strangling me with a panicked grip.

Jax aims, and plants a crossbow bolt in the creature's middle, which releases a thick ooze, silencing its dance. "That's one big-ass cockroach," he says.

"I wanna go home!" Chloe cries. "I wanna go home, and I want my mommy!"

I slide her down to cradle her. "Shh, honey, it's okay—"

"No!" she sobs.

Jax removes the bolt from the bug's midsection with a crunch, returning it to its holder. Then, he takes my arm and guides us back up the tunnel, excitement replaced with fear. Both his and Aby's thoughts, plain on their faces, match mine: Sure, it's a way out… but what's out there?

§

When the other two groups make it down, and we have Johnny with the second crossbow and Miguel with the spear, I feel better, but not much. I hadn't really planned on a dark, underground forest with a black river and roaches the size of my hand. I had my heart set on a lovely, bright, blue-and-green paradise... not a ghost ship waiting to take us straight into the slimy, rotted mouth of Hell. Why Smudge would lead us down here, and not to the portal, is a thorn in my side. I wish she'd just show herself already and explain everything. This mystery's getting old—fast.

Jax, Johnny, and Miguel, along with a couple of older boys, discuss security measures, while I keep an eye on the tunnel and reassure the terrified youngers, rocking Chloe in my arms. Thirty minutes, and she still hasn't let go of me. My neck and back ache from her weight.

"Chloe, I need to set you down, honey—"

"No," she whines.

"Yes, just stay here by me." And I set her on the ground. My muscles thank me. I'm at least thirty pounds lighter now. Still, she grips my leg and sniffles.

"All right," Jax says. "Let's move out."

"Olders," I say, "stay with your buddies, and hold their hands if they're seven or under." Younger hands dart up into olders', to the great reluctance of the older boys. But I give them a stern look. "We don't know what to expect once we get that grate open, so we need to be safe."

Stay on guard. Be aware of your surroundings.

Together, we travel down the arched tunnel in silence, Jax and Johnny sweeping their crossbows back and forth in front of us. When we reach the end, Miguel gives the pulley's handle a crank, producing a screeching echo from dry metal, followed by the grate rising a few inches. Miguel waits as Jax checks the area then gives him a signal, before turning the lever again. It rotates easily, though the squeal is enough to pierce through your bones, not to mention alert everything within a mile radius that naïve newcomers, who probably taste pretty good, are down here in time for dinner.

Once the grate's raised halfway, Miguel snaps the chain into a latch that holds it in place. Jax and Johnny cautiously duck under to examine the area, before waving us out behind them. We follow onto a platform a few feet wide with a railing, thankfully, to keep people from falling into the river. Who knows how deep it goes, or what lies beneath the surface? Behind and above us, slanting upward, mirroring its opposite side, the dark forest rustles with life and disappears into the black background. No way of telling how far back it goes, or how high.

"Stay away from the railing," I say. "To be safe."

We walk the downward-sloping platform toward the boat, and when we get to it, I'm surprised by its size. From the tunnel, it was hard to tell, but close up, it's at least fifty feet long. Plenty of room for all of us, with some to spare.

"Let's hope something doesn't already live here," Jax says under his breath.

I want to kick him. He has a bad habit of bringing up the worst possibilities. Instead, I glare at him, finger to my lips.

Holding the brown-and-white boat up out of the water, a platform disconnects from where we're standing, attached to a cable stretching to another pulley lever tied to a steel guardrail. On top of the boat is another platform surrounded by a railing, a square groove sunken into the floor, complete with a silver latch.

"Everyone gets on, except for one person," I say. "That last person has to release the pulley to drop the boat into the water, then hop on the deck."

Jax examines it, nodding. "Smart girl." He carefully pulls the worn black handle, and the door clicks open. I shine my light stick inside, and we both lean in.

"What do you see?" Aby asks.

"Hey," Johnny calls from the end of the line, "can we hurry it up already? Something just moved over here. Sounded big."

A circle of benches line the wall inside the boat, and toward the front, a doorway to a smaller room, where a chair sits behind a giant wheel with handles poking out all around it.

"Hey!" Johnny yells.

"Everyone on, now!" I say. "Carefully! No pushing—"

But pairs of olders and youngers near-trample each other to get onto the rickety boat. The wood floor moans at the sudden weight.

"I'll let the lever down," says Jax.

"No," Miguel says. "I'll do it. You can stand up top and cover me with your crossbow."

Jax nods and disappears inside, heading to the front room with the wheel. Seconds later, footsteps echo overhead, and Jax leans over the rail above me. "Nice view up here," he says, clicking a bolt into ready position.

I help the last few children on, and Aby pushes Baby Lou into my arms, shoving past me in the doorway. "Aby, what—?"

She begins ranting at Miguel for "endangering" himself again.

"Get on the boat," he yells at her. "Now!" I've never seen his face so serious and scolding.

Aby stops dead in her tracks, stunned, then backs through the doorway. Miguel cranks the lever and the boat shifts down a few inches. I close the door to find Aby crying in the far corner. We lower a few more inches, and Baby Lou whimpers in my arms. A few more, and the sensation of floating, the resistance of water pushing against the boat, parting to go around it.

"Come on!" Jax yells from above us.

Through the door's window, I watch Miguel fumble with the chain in its latch. Sweat trickles down his face, and his hands shake. Finally, he gets it to lock into place. He wipes the sweat from his eyes, gives Jax a thumbs-up, and steps toward the edge to jump down. Then, he disappears. But his feet don't hit the ceiling above me. Instead, I hear Jax's frantic yelling. I thrust Baby Lou into Serna's arms and race to the front, up the stairs to the roof.

What I see cannot possibly be real. Something enormous and as black as night has pinned Miguel to the ground, slashing at him with claws the length of my arm. Five crossbow bolts already stick out from its giant body. Jax takes aim and fires again—his last bolt. The monster yowls as the bolt grazes him, and the crunch of bone fills the air as it bites into Miguel's shoulder. Miguel screams—a bloodcurdling, soul-piercing sound—as the monster picks him up, shakes him like a tiny, fragile, bleeding doll in his massive jaw.

"We need more firepower—now!" Jax cries. "Johnny!"

But Miguel grows still, and the monster drops his limp body onto the ground in a bloody lump. Johnny races up the stairs, shooting before he's even cleared the top step. The monster howls as Johnny's bolt embeds into its enormous jaw. It stops the mauling long enough to see its attackers, then sinks its teeth into Miguel's chest.

Then, its body flies into the air.

A dark figure throws Miguel over one shoulder and races to the edge, leaping and landing almost on top of me.

"Go!" The black hood's pulled down to reveal Smudge's

face. "Downstairs, now!" she yells.

We charge down the stairs, and Smudge lays Miguel gently onto the floor, then hurries to close the hatch and push the heavy deadbolt into place. She yanks a lever next to the wheel, and the boat's released, moving forward in the water.

Aby bursts in. "Oh my God!" She falls to her knees beside Miguel, hysterical.

I kneel down on his other side. His eyes are closed, body ripped to shreds, covered in blood. I place two fingers on his neck, praying for a pulse... but knowing the truth. Even if he's alive, his wounds are too great to heal with our meager first-aid kit. Feeling nothing at his neck, I try his wrist, while Aby's eyes beg me to find life.

None.

I shake my head and cry.

Our brother, Miguel, is dead.

SEVENTEEN

My head flushes with heat, sweeping black spots through my vision. I brace myself against the wall, trying to steady my breathing so I don't faint. It'd be easy for me to give up here, to give in to the weakness. My heart's been broken too many times. Everyone I've loved has died horribly, far too soon.

Then, I remember what my daddy told me as my mother was dying, moments before the Superiors came and took her away: "No one is ever... really dead." He put a finger to his lips and touched it to her heart.

After they took her, he held me tight in his arms and said with quivering strength, "You must be strong, my daughter. No matter what happens, don't just survive... *live.*"

I love my brother, but now he's dead. And life must go on. There are people who need me.

Aby takes Miguel's hand and pets it. "He can't be dead. Miguel!" She collapses to the floor, while Johnny punches the wall and Jax erupts from the room.

"Aby—"

"You let him go! I tried to stop him, but... but... Why did you let him go!" She wails hysterically, banging her head against the wall.

I stand, whip round to face Smudge, who steers the boat solemnly. "You have a lot of explaining to do."

Still, she focuses straight ahead. Does she not hear me?

I go back to Aby and try to lift her from the floor. But she shrieks and jerks her arm away. I don't know what else to do, so I follow Jax out. The rest of the children stare, terrified, but I can't form words to tell them anything. I keep walking, barely feeling my feet on the floor.

Jax stands at the back window, hands stuffed into his pockets, empty crossbow discarded to the floor. I stumble to his side, and he drops his gaze, shakes his head. "It should've been me—"

"Well, I'm glad it wasn't." I squeeze his hand. "Don't do this, it's not your fault."

"It is my fault." He takes his hand from mine.

"No, it isn't. Did you see the size of that thing? You shot five bolts into it, and it wasn't even fazed. You did everything you could do."

Again, he shakes his head.

"Oh my God...."

He looks up at me.

"Jax, the monster...."

"I know."

"The rumors were true...."

He exhales a disgusted, desperate laugh. "What I want to know is"—he faces me squarely—"how come your friend in there brought us down here, when there are flesh-eating monsters the size of ten men who aren't even scathed by the weapons *she* gave us?" His face flushes red. "Now she's taking us where, exactly? You're really going to trust her?" He starts toward the front, but I grab his arm.

"Wait," I say, "let me talk to her. Please."

He yanks his arm away. "Talk to her? Miguel's dead because of her, and you want to talk?" He snatches up the spear leaning against the wall and pushes past me.

I chase him to the front, watch in horror as he cocks the spear back, and aims it at Smudge.

"Jax, no!"

"Tell us what's going on!" His knuckles whiten from his death grip on the spear. Veins bulge in his neck and forehead, as if he's about to explode. But Smudge acts as if he's not there. She adjusts her hat, pulling her hood up over it.

I take the spear from Jax, and he storms back through the cabin, screaming obscenities. Aby's still curled up by Miguel, sobbing, and on the other side of the doorway, Johnny stares blankly at the black water before us. I stand quietly next to Smudge.

"Sunrise," she says.

"What?"

"The sun will be up soon. It's safer then."

"The sun? But aren't we deep underground?"

"Yes."

"Then how is there sunlight?"

"The aboveground tunnels filter sunlight through millions of mirrored, oxygen-filtering pipes installed seventy-five years ago when the river was discovered. That was when the aboveground tunnels were built."

"How do you know all of this?"

"I just... know."

"Where are you from? And where are you taking us? Is it the same place? Was it you who left all of those supplies for us?"

"It would not be possible for me to answer all of those questions at once."

"Fine. Where are you from?"

"Alzanei, originally."

"Never heard of it. Is it on the Other Side of The Wall?"

"Yes."

"Well, you have to take us there, then!"

"I am taking you... to someone who will offer you safety."

Aby erupts in shrieks and begins throwing herself against the wall.

"Johnny," I yell over her screaming, "help me get her out of here!"

He snaps to, and we attempt to secure her floundering body. She claws at me, scraping my cheek with her fingernails, and I swing back, planting my fist into her temple. I see Samurai, and guilt floods me as her eyes close, body going limp. Panic-stricken, I feel for a pulse while Johnny holds her steady. Her heart pumps wildly, but slows down as I'm holding my finger there.

"Nice shot," says Johnny.

"Let's take her out of here."

We carry her to the back, set her down in the corner by Jax.

"Momma Joy, what happened to Aby?" Chloe asks, thumb in mouth, knees pulled to her chest.

"What happened to her?" Jax asks.

"Joy knocked her out," Johnny says.

"She was hysterical, I had to." I show him the scratches on my face. "Now I need to finish my conversation with Smudge, and figure out what to do... with Miguel." I head back toward the front, Johnny following, still gripping his crossbow, which holds three remaining bolts. We were never a match for that monster.

"Why'd you bring us here?" I ask Smudge once I'm back through the doorway. I avert my eyes from Miguel's lifeless body. "Why? When you knew there was no way we could fight that thing?"

"Things—there are more than one. I tried to guide them away from you, but—"

"Guide them away?"

She glances at me, then back to the water before us, which

has become a lighter gray color. The surrounding black forests are turning a dark green, mottled with shadowy pink and yellow flowers, and hanging vines. Bright twinkling light dots the area far above our heads, making it impossible to see a ceiling.

"There are a lot of things you don't know," Smudge says, "and there's no way I can tell you all of them now. You'll find out everything when it's time."

We share a moment of silence while a thousand different questions fight their way to my mouth. I pick one. "You said it's safer during the day?"

"Yes. The... monsters, as you call them, are... nocturnal. They... hibernate during the day. We must watch out for other creatures, though. Most things here have become either poisonous or carnivorous. But the... largest threat we only need to worry about after sunset."

She has a strange way of speaking, hesitant and pausing, like she decides against using a certain word at the last minute, for whatever reason.

"Is that room—the one you took us to—was it a portal to the Other Side?" I ask.

"It would be too... difficult for me to explain that to you now. But I will... soon. I... promise."

"I sure could go for a nice swim in the ocean," says Johnny. "Please say it's real, and not just something these people dreamed up."

"It is real," she says. "To an extent."

"What does that mean, exactly?" he says.

"I'm not sure how to explain it... in a way you would understand."

"Is that an insult to my intelligence? Wow, we haven't even been formally introduced, and already you're insulting me."

"I'm sorry. It wasn't meant as an insult."

He steps forward, holds out his hand. "I'm Johnny."

Smudge glances at it, and I read fear in her face. You'd think she never shook anyone's hand before. She dips a small hand into his and, giving it a quick shake, retracts it just as swiftly to its position on the wheel. "Smudge," she says.

"We need to find a place to bury Miguel," I say, "and we need to make it fast. I can't keep looking at him, and Aby sure doesn't need to again."

"The water is the safest place," Smudge says. "You should not spend any more time on land than you have to."

"But won't he... float?"

"We'll dock up at Gomorrah Grande and drop him in while we're docked. Avert the children's eyes. The body will be... devoured in seconds."

"De—*devoured*?"

"Yes. The water is filled with Teuridons."

"With what?"

"Smaller cousins of the Liopleurodon. They've been here since the prehistoric era."

"Awesome," says Johnny, pumping his crossbow in the air. "Do they taste good?"

"You would not be able to catch one to eat it. They are half the size of this boat, with jagged teeth a meter long."

"Well, damn. I guess we definitely don't want to fall in, then, do we?"

"No," she says. "Definitely not."

"So, this river has been here since the prehistoric era?" I ask.

"Yes. It was untouched by humans for millions of years. Until recently."

"How's that even possible?" I say. "I mean, that before there was light down here, there was life. And what about oxygen?"

"Some things cannot be easily explained or understood. Certain creatures and other life forms do not need light or perfect air to survive. They... adapt over time."

"That's amazing," Johnny says. "Who would've ever thought all this was down here?"

"Yes," says Smudge, "it is... very amazing."

§

With the sun fully risen, the dark forest has become a lush green jungle, where I expect a man in a loincloth to swing from a tree at any minute, like in the book my daddy read over and over to me when I was younger. "Oh to be free," he'd mumble, closing the tattered thing and placing it back onto the bedside table.

I don't think this would've been his idea of freedom, though, had he experienced it firsthand. What kind of freedom is hiding from bloodthirsty prehistoric monsters who want to gnash you to bits?

I peek through the doorway to check on Aby, who's now awake, and Jax, sitting in the boat's back corner. Occasionally, their whispering floats to the front, laced with hostility and mourning. When I meet their eyes, they look away.

"They ain't too happy with you, are they?" Johnny says in a low voice.

I shake my head. It's true. They've obviously drawn a line between us, with me on the opposing side. But I can't find it in me to care as much as maybe I should. Their out-of-control emotions make them react blindly, and they resent me for not being more distraught over Miguel's death. I see it in their eyes, unable to hold my gaze for long before breaking away.

They're wrong, though. It's not that his death hasn't ripped me apart inside. I just have no choice but to accept it, and move on. It's what strong leaders do. It's what strong mothers do.

You take the dark with the light and build on.

"Your friends," Smudge says. "They... don't trust me. Why do you?"

"Your eyes. I can read a bluff a mile away. I get that from my daddy."

"I trust you," Johnny blurts out. "You know... in case you were, uh... wondering."

She steers the boat closer to the high bank, then tugs back on a lever. It clanks against something and falls still in the water. Smudge looks me in the eye. "Your father.... Yes...." Her eyes sadden, and she turns away. "We're here."

"Where? And did you know my father?"

"Gomorrah Grande. And... no, I didn't." She rises from the chair and climbs the stairs to the roof, and I follow her, trying to ignore the blood everywhere. When I clear the hatch doorway, I'm astonished by the view. In every direction, the underground jungle goes on forever it seems; a complete impossibility, yet here it is—man-made magic, together with Mother Nature, in all of their brilliance. In the distance, huge pink and red flowers cover an archway almost entirely. It lies at the end of a long stone pathway, similar to the one we traveled down to get to the boat. I make out the shape of a stone-and-steel elevator shaft, though I can't see how high it goes, vines and greenery blending it into the background.

"What is this place?" Johnny asks.

Smudge tightens her hood's string, tying it in a bow beneath her chin. "It used to be a hotel."

"What's a... hotel?" he asks.

"A place where people would come and stay for a while during their travels. Many years ago, it was known by everyone in Bygonne for its elegant balls for the elite. Anyone with one hundred Blue Notes and evening attire could attend." Without hesitation, she jumps from the railing to the stone platform, then winds a squeaky pulley attached to a huge rusty chain. The boat rises out of the water, the children squeal, and in seconds, we're level with the platform. Johnny goes next, and I follow, leaping from the top of the boat to the platform. My feet hit the ground, and I'm met by Jax, who now holds the spear in one hand and cradles Baby Lou in his other arm.

"Where does that elevator go?" he demands, pointing the spear at Smudge.

"To an old hotel called Gomorrah Grande."

"We're going there. Now. We're not staying out here."

"Jax, what about Miguel?" I ask. "We have to do something—"

"What? Throw him in the river? You go right ahead."

Aby collapses into him, sobbing deeply. He wraps his spear-holding arm around her and Baby Lou whimpers.

"Grab your bags and strap your breathers to your heads!" Jax yells. "Everyone off the boat!"

"Jax, wait, we don't know what's in there—"

"But we know what's out here!" Tears well in his eyes, and he swipes them away. "Open the gate—now!"

"Open it yourself," Smudge says. "I'm going to help bury your brother."

I've never seen Jax look so murderous. This isn't the Jax I know. Something's snapped in him; something irreparable. His maniacal eyes are the mouth of a volcano—hot and deep, teetering on the brink of annihilation.

"Please be careful with Baby Lou," I say.

He shrugs me off and heads down the path, guiding Aby and a trail of terrified children.

"Wait for us inside the gate," I say. "We'll be there in a

couple minutes."

"I'll help, too," Johnny says to me, tipping Old Jonesy's hat.

While the three of us go back inside to collect Miguel's body, the tears that I've kept down now push their way to the surface. I kiss his cheek, and they sprinkle his matted black hair.

"Out the window, portside," Smudge says.

"Portside?" I repeat.

"Left. Further from shore. And I suggest you don't look once we drop him in."

We carry him to the window and set him down, and my tears continue to fall as Johnny and I kneel beside him. Smudge slides the window open. A small lump in Miguel's pocket catches my attention and I reach my hand in. Aby's father's knife. I slip it into my pocket, while a vice grips my heart. Even if he'd had it in hand, he wouldn't have stood a chance.

"I'm gonna miss you, bro," Johnny says, voice shaking. "Damn...." He chokes up, wiping his eyes with a sleeve.

I lean to Miguel's ear, struggling to breathe. "We did it," I say. "You're finally free. And no one ever really dies." Then, I touch my finger to his lips and place it to my heart, as it splinters into a million pieces. I nod to Smudge and Johnny, and together, we lift him up.

With one push, he's out of our lives forever.

EIGHTEEN

JOHNNY AND SMUDGE FOLLOW ME off the boat and down the path, toward Baby Lou's cries and the children waiting on the other side of the gate. Jax has it lowered almost all the way down, so we have to toss our bags under first, then crawl through. I take Baby Lou from Serna and rock her as Jax lets the gate hit the ground behind us.

"It's okay, Baby," I say. "Momma Joy's got you." Instantly, she settles down in my arms. Jax leans against the wall near Aby, and when I meet his eyes, he turns away.

"I can't even look at you," he mutters.

"We can change clothes when we get inside," Johnny says, and he brushes my arm with red-stained fingers. "Share a bottle of water to get cleaned up."

Jax leads Aby gently by the arm, forging ahead in the dark tunnel, spear at the ready. In their older-younger pairs, the children follow. Chloe's hand finds my arm, and I'm startled. I didn't realize she was next to me. "Are you all right, Momma Joy?"

I nod. "I will be."

Johnny follows the group, waving us on behind him.

Smudge leans against the wall, facing the other direction.

"Aren't you coming?" I ask.

"If I don't, you won't be getting inside, and your friend may... bring harm to us because of his anger. But if I do, I may lead you into danger again. And if I leave you..." She shakes her head, retreating inside her thoughts. "So strange, these human emotions," she mumbles.

"What? What do you mean?"

"Never mind." She pushes from the wall and heads toward the group.

I walk beside her, sensing it's now become my job to protect and defend her, too. And hopefully solve the mystery that surrounds her, an impenetrable veil.

For a split second, she wears a faint smile as if she'd remembered a happy thought from long ago. But it vanishes just as quickly when Jax bangs on the elevator door.

"So how'd you do it?" he demands, glaring at Smudge. "Are you going to wave your magic wand for us and open this one, too? Or are we stuck out here?"

Smudge focuses on the elevator door, and a moment later, the light above it flickers on—then pops inside its fixture. We all jump as we're met with semi-darkness again. Then, the elevator button glows orange. Jax studies Smudge, awe nearly tipping his rage, though he manages to right it before slamming his finger on the glowing, dusty button.

"You're going to have to tell me how you do that," I whisper.

Smudge says nothing, but at the corner of her mouth, I see the wanting of a grin.

The elevator door slides open, much to the astonishment of the children. I have my own dumbfounded moment as they file in, two by two, until every single pair has loaded on. I reach the doorway and find an elevator the size of a small room; twice as big as our group.

"These were made for large numbers of people to travel up together," Smudge says, "so no one would have to wait down here for too long. Gomorrah Grande was known for its hospitality and comfort."

Inside, the elevator is by far the fanciest I've ever seen. A thick layer of dust coats the mirrored walls lined with a smooth gold railing. In one spot, the dust was wiped away, the clear spot eerily resembling fingerprints.

Notice the nuances.

The tiny hairs on my arms and legs stand up straight. I shiver.

"Comfort, huh?" says Johnny. "Let's hope they have a few nice comfortable beds for us to sleep in, then."

"The air-quality in there is questionable," Smudge says. "Until I activate the air-flusher and oxygenation system, it would be best for you all to wear your oxygen masks."

"Breathers on, everyone," I say. "Olders, help your buddies, make sure they're airlocked."

The elevator doors close and we begin to ascend while everyone fumbles with their breathers. I get Baby Lou's into place, then Chloe's, and then pull mine on.

A boy in the corner curses, fighting with his strap. "It won't tighten!"

An older boy helps him, and finally, everyone's secured. At least that's one thing I can protect them from—bad air. The walls creak and the cables squeal, but not nearly as badly as the bunker elevator. The last numbered button says forty-five; Gomorrah Grande goes twenty floors deeper than Bunker B does.

"This is a lot of weight," I say. "Are you sure—"

"Yes," says Smudge. "It is built with indestructible material. The cables are somewhat dry, but fine. Sturdy."

"Don't you need a breather?"

"No."

I catch Johnny gazing at her in quiet wonder. So many things I want to ask her, too, starting with how she can breathe bad air. And how she knows so much about things over here, if she's from the Other Side. And how she does that thing with the electricity. But I'm afraid if I start questioning, Jax will join in and get fired up all over again. He still holds Aby close, though now I sense it's less about comforting her, and more about getting back at me, for... whatever. My tiniest bit of jealousy is doused by the ridiculousness of such a thing in these circumstances.

The forty-five button illuminates, the elevator slows, and the door rattles open, letting bright light pour in. Smudge jumps in front of us, holds out her arms, as if to protect us. When my eyes adjust to the light, I'm both intrigued and slightly terrified. It appears the jungle decided to take over the hotel. A giant pillar in the middle of the room stands entirely covered in greenery and bright flowers. Something flutters through the air, past giant golden birds hanging from thick chains. Along the edge of the elevator doorframe, a strip of green light shines down, signaling good air.

"What's wrong?" I ask Smudge over the curious murmurs of the children.

"The power is on."

"But I thought you—?"

"No. Not this time. I have to see the exact location of the circuit to send the signal."

"Okay...? So, then—?"

"Someone is here. Whoever it is has activated the generator."

"Let's go," Jax says, pushing past us.

"Wait," says Smudge. "It might not be safe."

Jax glares and grips his spear tight. "Safe doesn't seem to be an option anymore, does it?"

At that, she's silent. He's right. We aren't safe anywhere.

He taps something on the wall outside of the elevator. An oxygauge, probably. "It's good air," he says, and takes off his breather, inhales deep. "Yeah, it's good. Everyone strap your breathers to your heads. Have them handy, just in case."

"I wish you would come with me," says Smudge, as everyone follows Jax's orders. "Please, trust me. I'm positive Raffai would be happy to take you in. All of you. Give you a safe place, a home...."

"Who's Raffai?" I ask.

"He is... one of the good guys. He..." She messes with her hat, kicks her boot toe at the ground. "He saved my life."

"Oh, yeah?" Jax laughs. "So now you're down here in the dark, leading children to their deaths for fun? Some life he saved."

"That's not fair," I say, "it wasn't her fault. She was only trying to help—"

"Well, I don't want her help, okay? Everyone, off the elevator."

Reluctantly, the children join him, leaving Smudge and me with Baby Lou and Chloe. I step off, and Smudge follows. Jax holds his spear in front of her. "No. You're going back where you came from. Square?"

"Jax, what the hell are you doing?" I say. "Stop—"

"We don't know her, and we sure as hell don't need her help. As soon as we make our way up, we'll take the aboveground tunnels east—"

"You know that's suicide," I tell him. "And she's staying. She's part of our group now, so deal. Move the spear." I lock eyes with him, dare him to argue. If he's separating us, fine. But he's going to know who's leading this split family. "Move the spear," I say again.

After a heated standoff, Jax finally huffs and turns his back on us.

"Everyone stay close," I say. "We need to be careful. We don't know what's in here. Or who. Come on," I tell Smudge.

A moment's hesitation, and she crosses the threshold. She and I, with Baby Lou and Chloe, pass up Jax and Aby and join Johnny at the front of the group, where he stands guard with his three crossbow bolts. I hope he doesn't have to use them.

"We good?" Johnny asks.

"As good as we can be, for now. Let's check this place out. We need to find a safe room for everyone to rest together. No splitting up."

We move farther into the room, past a wall that marks the entrance to a giant common area that towers above us, all the way to an enormous, light-filtering purple dome. The hotel is circular, with forty-five levels enclosing this open section in the middle. Each floor has a gold railing, like in the elevator, and a staircase that travels to the next one above it, where the rooms are. Hundreds of red doors face outward, and everything's covered in greenery. Lots of places for things to hide.

A trickling waterfall pours over the side of a partially-collapsed floor a few levels up, feeding a small stream formed in the deteriorated tile floor. The stream disappears into a thick group of trees in a corner, though it isn't the only water flowing. Everywhere, water drips, giving life to all that flourishes in this forgotten place.

Jax launches the spear across the stream, and a rat scurries away. Johnny takes aim with his crossbow, but the rat disappears around the corner.

"Do you know your way around in here?" I ask Smudge.

"No. I've never been here before. I've only heard stories."

Jax forges ahead to retrieve his spear, hopping carelessly over the tiny river, silently daring something—or someone—to step in the way.

"Where's all of the water coming from, then," I ask, "when we're so far above the river?"

"I would assume the water is from pipes that burst long ago when the earth shifted. Could have been an earthquake, perhaps. And with no one here to repair the breakage, the water, along with the light from the dome... made life possible."

To our left, red double doors stand next to an area filled by a long counter with chipped blue paint and a striped red-and-gold awning. Behind this sits a dark space and the faint outline of a door with a circular window.

"Quit it!" a boy yells.

Apparently, he and the new kid have decided now's a good time for a shoving match.

"He keeps stepping on my heels!" the boy tattles.

"You keep stopping in front of me," the new kid mutters with a smirk.

"This really isn't the time," I tell them both.

We reach the counter, and something springs from the darkness and flutters off through the air. I jump, and a girl screams. Chloe cries, buries her face in my side.

"What the hell is that?" Johnny aims his crossbow at the thing flying away in a semi-hovering manner, thick reddish-brown wings held high above a fat, ribbed body. It disappears inside the pillar's thick leafy covering that rises up to the sky dome.

"That's one of those giant cockroaches," Jax says. "They're probably all around here."

Chloe claws to climb up into my arms, screaming like she's covered in them. Baby Lou cries along with her, though it might be partially because her diaper's completely soaked through, and I'm sure she's uncomfortable. She's long overdue for a changing.

"I can't carry you, Chloe," I say.

"I'll take her." I'm surprised by Aby's weak voice behind me.

Sobbing, Chloe jumps into her arms, and Aby fights the urge to cry with her. Tears caught in her eyes reflect her misery from inside.

You have to stay strong.... I hear my daddy's voice so clearly, like he's standing next to me. It's what he'd say if he were here. *There's a time and a place for weakness, and now's not the time.* Everything he told me as we watched my mother die, everything I tried for so long not to think about, all floods back. It's been there always, waiting for the perfect time. As if he knew....

He did know. He always told me I'd be free, and fed me full of blue skies, green leaves, and clean air, while preparing me to journey through Hell to get there. So this can't be the end. I have to talk to Jax, convince him to give Smudge a chance. Maybe after some rest... time to reset his thoughts... he'll be more receptive. Hopefully he'll agree to meet Raffai, once he sees this place is nothing but a dead end.

"What does that say?" Johnny asks, pointing to the space behind the counter.

Squinting, I take a step closer to a wall sign with worn printed letters. "Nightly Rate, fifty Blue Notes. Then, there's a list of items you can buy from the kitchen."

"So, the kitchen must be back there, then." He motions an elbow toward the door with the circular window.

"Must be," I say. "That might be a good place to rest and find things we could use. I doubt there's anything edible, though there might be knives or something else useful. Let's make sure there aren't any creatures in it, then we can rest and plan our next move."

Jax obviously doesn't want to give in to my being leader, but he knows I'm right. With a heavy sigh, he motions to Johnny and an older boy. "Let's go check it out."

The light above the counter blinks, then glows brighter to illuminate the area. I glance at Smudge and see a glimmer of magic. "Did you—?"

"Yes. It's safer with the light on."

Jax moves hastily through the kitchen door with Johnny and the other boy at his heels, and they return a quick moment later. "Come on," he says.

"Yeah, seems like a good place to rest," Johnny agrees. "Just some greenery on one side of the room. We poked, but nothing scurried out."

"Be careful what you touch," says Smudge. "Some of it is highly poisonous. We'll have to make sure it's safe enough before we bring in the children." She looks at Jax. "May I?"

"Be my guest."

She slips around the counter, disappears into the back room, and she's back a second later. "Common jungle ivy. It isn't poisonous."

"Come on, everyone." I motion them forward, and we file into a kitchen three times larger than the one at the Tree Factory.

"Stay away from the vines." I won't say it aloud, but I'm still not sure what might be living in them. Halfway across the room near the wall, I choose a spot to set down my bag, as well as Chloe's and Baby Lou's. The new kid decides to be rebellious and lie down by himself, next to the ivy. I doubt telling him to move would do any good. I'd be wasting my breath.

Chloe yawns beside me. "Momma Joy?"

"Yes?"

"What happened to Miguel?"

"He... got hurt."

She glances up at me, her youth knowing more than it should. "He died?"

I take her hand, tears in my eyes. "Yes, sweetheart. He died."

She scratches her nose with a tiny hand and stares at the floor. After a few seconds, she looks up at me again. "Momma Joy?"

"Yes?"

"Are we gonna die, too?"

I crouch, knees aching from exhaustion and Baby Lou's weight in my arms. "No," I say. "I will not let that happen. Okay?"

She nods. "Momma Joy?"

"Yes?"

"I'm hungry. Can we eat now?"

At this, Baby Lou cries louder. She definitely knows that word—eat—and obviously agrees. Time for a changing, a meal, and a nice long rest.

"Is anyone else hungry?" I ask. Mostly "yeses" come in reply. Johnny and I, as well as Aby and Jax, may very well go the rest of our short lives without eating.

"Those with cans of food and water in your bags, take out five of each," I instruct. "Two bites, then pass."

"Hey!" Johnny yells from the front corner of the room. He props a small door open with his foot. "Washrooms, and they look decent. Nothing alive in here, at least."

Soon, a group of children line up to use the washrooms. I lay Baby Lou down on a blanket and take a bottle of water from my bag, along with a few pieces of the T-shirt from the warehouse. I fill her own bottle and hand it to her, but she kicks her legs and screams, swatting and fighting me, because she's so tired and cranky. After some wrangling, I get her cleaned up and re-wrapped snugly in a fresh cloth diaper, when Aby brings me a can of something called "mashed potatoes."

"Looks like stuff she can eat," she mutters, handing me the

can and walking away before I can thank her.

I lift the spoon out and inspect the sticky white fluff. Smudge grins at me. When I catch her, she turns away. What a strange girl. Strange, yet intriguing. Kind of like this cloud-in-a-can. I spoon some out and taste it.

"Oh my God," I say. "This stuff is delicious." Of course, anything would be. I offer a small portion to Baby Lou, and she takes a careful bite. As soon as she tastes it, though, she grabs the spoon. She's never wanted to feed herself before. With Tree Factory slop, that's not so hard to understand.

I manage to get in a few bites before Baby Lou, Chloe, and another girl finish off the can. With food this delicious, I might be happy to eat again. And it may have the power to heal a broken heart—may. I'm not ruling out the possibility.

After mealtime's over, I roll Baby Lou up in a blanket. In my arms, she gulps on her water, eyes growing heavy, and I hum in her ear as Johnny digs through a couple of cabinets. The rest of the children get comfortable on the rotted tile floor.

"Jackpot!" Johnny calls out, startling Baby Lou and a few others. "Ooh, sorry. Jackpot," he says again, quietly. A cabinet he's opened in the back corner by the ovens and the refrigerator is full of folded blankets. Dust flies as he beats one with his fist. "They'll work." He passes them around while I tuck Millie into Baby Lou's blanket with her. I lay her down next to Chloe, who hugs her new doll tightly, and cover them both with another blanket. In seconds, they surrender to sleep. Two minutes, and they're snoring.

Three more little girls lie on Chloe's other side, snuggling with their dolls, while another line of girls are on the far side of Aby, who's chosen, strangely, to lie down right beside me, facing the opposite direction. At our feet, the boys make themselves comfortable, creating a wall between us and the rest of the room. Except for the new kid, of course, who's sprawled out in the open.

Jax stands before us all. "Listen up, older boys. We're going to take shifts. Everyone needs rest, but someone also needs to keep watch. Groups of two." He peers around the room. "No clock in here, so… when you can't hold your eyes open any longer, wake up the next pair. We'll start at that end"—he points to our left—"and work our way down."

I consider talking to Aby, but it's probably best to leave her alone, let her rest. Doesn't seem like she wants to talk to me anyway, seeing as how I knocked her unconscious minutes after her boyfriend died. An "I'm sorry" might be good. But maybe it's too soon for that.

Smudge sits near the door, back against the wall, not looking the slightest bit tired. The lights dim—thanks to her, I'm sure—just enough to see by, though dark enough to sleep. If I wasn't so tired, I'd sit next to her for hours, asking a million questions, probably faster than she could ever answer them.

Johnny timidly walks over to Smudge and crouches to offer her a piece of cloth and a bottle of water to wash with. She stares at him curiously for a few seconds, then takes them and says "Thank you." Johnny tips Old Jonesy's hat and grins, then heads toward me. "Here you go." He gives me a half-bottle of water with hastily cleaned hands.

"Thanks, Johnny." I pour the water into my own hands, and use a square of cloth to wash off Miguel's blood. The remnants in the grooves of my fingernails will have to stay for now. I can't waste any more of our drinking water. I'll just try not to look at my hands. Shouldn't be too hard; I have so many other ones to focus on.

"Is Jax taking the first shift?" I ask quietly.

"Yeah, him and two other guys. Would you feel better if I

took the first shift?"

"No, it's fine. Thanks, though."

And here, for the longest time, I thought Johnny was the unstable one. We all did. Now, I'm seeing a whole different side of him. Different sides to everyone I thought I knew. Johnny's become a confidant, a leader; someone I can trust and depend on. The others, Jax and Aby... their masks have crumbled, dropping pieces here and there for us to trip over as we try to navigate the storm. You really don't know someone until they've been pushed to the edge. *Will they fall... or fly?* Or maybe, sometimes, it takes falling to learn how to fly.

Johnny clears his throat. "Okay, well... I'll be right over there if you need me." He points a few people down.

"Okay," I say. "Get some rest."

"You, too, Joy." And he walks back to his blanket to lie down, with a split-second glance at Smudge before he does.

I dig through my daddy's magic bag to find the pants and shirt my mother slept in every night. I've never worn them, but I guess now's the time. Taking them from the bag, I cross to the washroom when one becomes available, and before I close myself up inside the stale-smelling space, Johnny gives me a reassuring nod.

Inside, it's apparent the washroom was once a luxury. Gold peeks out from underneath grime on all of the knobs and handles. The once pristine white-with-gold-swirl countertops are now dingy, fractures crawling along the surface. In the blurry mirror, I briefly take in my reflection, then look away. Bruised, scratched, and scabbed. Filthy. A wretched mess.

I shed my daddy's work shirt, plastered hard with Miguel's dried blood, then my mother's jeans, which aren't as bad. Maybe once we're on the Other Side, I can wash most of it out with good soap. Can't bear the thought of discarding them.

Quickly, I wash my face with the rest of the water in the bottle, then change into my mother's night clothes, surprised to find they fit me perfectly. Perhaps too perfectly. A tiny pink bow dots the V-neck that swoops down to show more of me than I'm used to. The soft, pink-and-white fabric brings back so many memories... lying in bed next to her; listening to her labored breathing; feeling the cloth, hot with fever from her skin; praying for her pain to go away, though at the same time, praying for another day with her. I know how it is to be conflicted. I suppose that's my connection with Smudge.

When I come out of the washroom, Johnny's eyebrows arch, and he grins at me. He gives me a thumbs-up, and my face flushes hot. It's a nice gesture, though I'm not concerned with how I look, other than being free of blood and dirt. Quietly, I lie down on my blanket next to Baby Lou and Chloe, and Aby again turns her back to me. Jax's eyes dart between the two of us, and I shift my back to them both. I can't think anymore right now. So I drape my arm across Baby Lou and a snoring Chloe, and I, too, give myself to sleep.

NINETEEN

It seems like seconds after I close my eyes, screaming jolts them open again. I sit up to find Chloe flailing by the wall. Inches from her and Baby Lou crawls another mammoth cockroach. Immediately, I yank up Baby Lou, and Johnny plants the thing to the floor with a crossbow bolt.

"It was on me, Momma Joy!" Chloe cries, swatting at her head. "It was on me, *again!*"

"Look!" Someone to my left points across the room at another cockroach perched on top of the new kid's head.

"Hey, new kid!" Johnny calls over. "Wake up!" He aims his crossbow and cautiously moves toward the boy, whose stillness beneath the heavy insect makes my blood run cold.

With one swift kick, Johnny sends the disgusting bug flying across the room, though a part of its ripped-off head remains attached to the kid's scalp. The headless body stills its squiggling, and Johnny crouches to take the boy's wrist in hand. He drops it, shakes his head. "Jax, where are you?"

I leave Baby Lou and Chloe with Serna and rush over to Johnny, glancing around on my way. Jax, Aby, and Smudge are all missing.

"What happened?" I ask.

"That thing sucked out his brains or something, look...." And he points to the piece of insect still attached through what appears to be a tube inserted into a bloody hole in the top of his head. His sunken eyes and cheeks show something's obviously missing behind them.

"Oh my God...." A wave of nausea hits me. I turn away. "Where are Jax and Aby, and—?"

The door opens, and I'm relieved to see Smudge. I repeat my question to her.

"They left a couple of hours ago," she replies. "He left two boys to watch, and told me not to follow, so I... respected his wish. But then, two hours passed, and I was... worried and went to search for them. I came back when I heard the screaming. What happened?"

I address the group. "Who did Jax leave in charge? Come here, please."

Johnny joins us at the door and tells Smudge what happened. "So I'm thinking the quicker we can find Jax and Aby and get to your Rabbi friend, the better," he says.

"Raffai," she corrects. "And I agree."

Two boys approach, staring guiltily at the ground.

"What happened?" I ask.

One boy shrugs. "He left us in charge. Said they'd be back soon."

"Okay... so weren't you supposed to be watching?"

"We fell asleep," the other says.

Irritated, I wave them away, though I might've done the same thing, too. In fact, guilt bubbles up to the surface, and now I'm thinking it's my fault. I should've stayed awake; I should've been watching.

"So, they just... left?" I ask Smudge. "No explanation?"

"Not directly. I heard them discussing finding a way out through the aboveground tunnel, and..." She bows her head.

"And, what?"

"I think they... wanted privacy."

An ember of jealousy sparks inside, hotter than before. The thought of them alone together angers me for so many reasons.

Is now really the time for that? They must be losing their minds.

"We have to go find them," Johnny says.

"What about the children?" I ask. "Did Jax take the spear?"

"Yes," says Smudge.

Johnny motions to the far end of the room. "Look at all those drawers." The dusty ovens and refrigerators sit nestled among a ton of cabinets, like the one he found the blankets in, and rows of drawers beneath them. "This is a kitchen. There have to be knives somewhere." He retrieves his bolt from the insect, slinging guts from it, and clicks it back into place while the three of us cross the room to the drawers. But after digging through every one of them twice, plus all of the cabinets, we don't find a single knife.

"Someone's already cleared them out," says Johnny. "They had to. Nothing useful anywhere." He removes a thick sheet of paper from a drawer and arches an eyebrow, whistles softly. "Here, check this out. This is what this place used to look like." He holds it up, worn around the edges, with a picture and words on the front. "What does it say?"

I take it and trace the fancy lettering below the most stunningly elegant structure I've ever seen. Words that are nearly impossible to conceive.

"Read it out loud," Johnny says.

I take a breath. "Gomorrah Grande: Give Your Ultimate Sacrifice today, in luxury, and live forever the life of your dreams."

"What does that mean?" he asks.

"I'll explain everything once we are out of this place," Smudge says. "We need to find your friends, and quickly. Leave the weapon with someone here. The three of us can go."

"Without a weapon?" Johnny scratches his head. "I don't think that's such a great idea, do you?"

"Please," says Smudge. "I never use weapons. You have to trust me."

Johnny looks at me, but I'm remembering the monster flying back into the air, moments before Smudge slung Miguel over her shoulder and jumped onto the boat. "We have to trust her," I say. "She knows more about this place than we do. And she's survived down here alone, without weapons."

For a moment, he stands in frozen contemplation, before shrugging and trotting off to a group of older boys, one of which he chooses and gives a quick crossbow lesson to.

"Are you sure they'll be safe down here?" I ask.

"No. As your friend said, we are not entirely safe anywhere. But if you give them metal cooking pans and utensils, they could either fight off more insects or get our attention if they need help."

"Good idea."

Johnny returns after he and the other boy move the new kid's body to the farthest corner of the room. He's uneasy without his crossbow, stuffing his hands into his pockets, shrugging. "What now?"

"Help me get some pans and utensils to pass out," I say, and I explain to him what Smudge told me.

Johnny shrugs again. "Okay, sounds like a plan."

So we clear the cabinets, the most deadly utensil being a sharp, three-pronged fork, which I hand to an older boy.

"Seriously?" he says.

"Seriously." I squeeze his shoulder and whisper, "Let's just hope you don't have to use it."

Johnny, Smudge, and I take a step back to view our pathetic little army. I want to laugh, but I'm afraid it would become tears. All of the children I've grown to love and have become protector of… defending themselves with ordinary kitchen items. Chloe grips her wire whisk as if her life depends on it. She isn't so far from the truth.

"Everyone listen up," I announce, "we have to go find Jax and Aby so we can get out of here. Lock the door behind us, and do not open it unless you hear three knocks." I motion to the boy with the crossbow and he comes forward. "Guard the door," I tell him. "And if we're not back—"

"We'll be back," Smudge says.

Chloe cries, then Baby Lou starts to cry, too. My anger at Jax and Aby flares into silent rage. If anything happens to these children while I'm gone... I don't know what I'll do. I give Baby Lou a hug and Chloe a kiss. "Be a strong girl," I say. "I'll be back soon."

Chloe nods her blonde head and sniffles.

"Take good care of my Baby," I tell Serna.

She nods, too, cradling a frying pan beneath her other arm.

"Come on," says Johnny, "we need to hurry. They could be in trouble."

"Oh, they're in trouble all right," I mumble. "Big trouble."

§

As soon as we cross the threshold, the door closes swiftly behind us, and we hear two deadbolt clicks.

"I'm thinking we should've grabbed one of those pans," Johnny says.

And I'm thinking I agree with him. Surveying our surroundings—leafy vines that have swallowed the walls, twisty jungle trees that have pushed right up through the tile floor—I feel so small and vulnerable.

"It's fine," Smudge says, removing her hood from her head. "It's your friends out here we should worry about." She moves ahead, waves a hand behind her. "Stay close. When I came out looking for them earlier, I thought they may have gone upstairs to search for a ground-level exit. I took the elevator up, but didn't see or hear them anywhere. So we should start our search down here."

"There's another elevator?" I ask.

She nods. "For inside the hotel. It begins on the next level up."

"Should we call for them?" Johnny asks.

"No." Smudge shakes her head, voice low, almost a whisper. "It's best to be quiet, especially when others are around. We don't want to alert them to our whereabouts more than we already have."

"You really think others are here?" I ask.

"Yes. I know there are."

"Well, that's comforting," says Johnny. "Let's hope they're nice."

"That is not extremely likely." Smudge scratches her neck near the black string of letters and numbers printed there.

"What does that mean?" I ask, pointing at the tattoo.

She starts at the question. "Oh... that...."

We head in the opposite direction of our entrance, passing rustling leaves and shuffling sounds that may be critters scurrying around, trying to find the best angle to attack from. A dark doorway set in the far corner comes into view, and Smudge heads toward it. To our left and out from under a massive mushroom sticks the bent legs of a fallen golden bird. High above, and caught in thick, dangling vines, the chain which once held it.

"So, are you going to tell us, or not?" Johnny asks. "Because I'm a little curious myself."

"Curiosity...." Smudge's eyes shift around the room. "That's one of the more dangerous ones...."

"You know, you're something else," says Johnny. "Don't get me wrong, you're cute—real cute—but sometimes, I have no idea what you're saying."

"My name," she says.

We stare, confused, as we reach the shadowy doorway.

She stops and faces us slowly, points at the tattoo. "This is my real name."

"I thought Smudge was your name," I say.

"No, that's kind of a... nickname."

"So"—I lean in to get a better look—"7ZS3-22Y is your real name?"

She nods.

"Man," says Johnny, "things must be real diff—"

Smudge holds up a hand, puts a finger to her lips, and motions for us to get between her and the wall. We scurry behind while she stands as still as stone, eyeing the thick leaves a few feet ahead. Something swishes them, and they wave slightly.

Smudge raises her left hand, arm outstretched, palm facing the hidden intruder.

I hold my breath.

The leaves wave again, then something leaps through—furry and brown, with yellow eyes and a long striped tail, sharp fangs in a frothing mouth. An invisible force knocks it back into the leaves, and it howls as it smacks the wall behind the thick vines.

After a few intense seconds, Smudge tugs her sleeve down over her hand.

"How did you do that?" I ask.

"Yes," rises an unfamiliar voice from within the vines. "How *did* you do that?"

The leaves move again, and this time, the shape of a person—a leafy person—moves forward. I make out brown eyes set in dark-brown skin, almost entirely hidden by leaves. A long, silver kitchen knife in his hand reflects the light. Then, a second figure steps forward, holding the creature that tried to attack us, a second silver knife in its own hand.

"Well, we found the kitchen knives," Johnny says.

"What the hell did you do to Tallulah?" a girl's voice demands. I make out pale skin, slits of angry black eyes, jet-black hair.

"It will not die," Smudge says calmly. "It's only temporarily stunned. It will be fine in about an hour."

"She. Tallulah's a she. And in an hour, I think I'll let her gnaw on your face." The girl, covered from head to toe in leaves, comes closer. She stops in front of Smudge, towering over her by at least three or four inches.

"Then I may have to do more than stun her next time," says Smudge, without a hint of intimidation.

"Look," I say, "we don't want any trouble. We're trying to find our friends so we can leave, then we'll be out of your way."

"Where did you all come from?" the boy asks, his deep voice sweet and soothing, like a well of sleeping angels.

"I'm Joy, and that's Johnny. We're treemakers from Greenleigh. And that's Smudge. She's…"

"From the far east," Smudge says.

"Far east?" The girl laughs. "Yeah, right. More like, what planet are you from?"

"Treemakers, huh?" the boy says, ignoring the girl's accusations. "What are you doing down here in the jungle?"

"We escaped," I say. "There was an… accident. An explosion. We barely made it out alive with the children."

"Children?" the boy says. "Was that the screaming we heard

coming from the kitchen?"

Johnny gives me a look of warning, but the boy's kindness makes me want to trust him. Not so much the girl. Him, I trust, though.

"Yes. Over thirty of us altogether. Two from our group disappeared. That's who we're searching for now. Our youngest is only a year-and-a-half old."

They glance at each other, then back to us, and the boy emerges from the leaves, holding out his hand. "Emerson." I shake it, and he offers me a warm smile. "That's Vila. There are two more of us. We'll introduce them to you shortly."

"Where are you from?" Johnny asks.

"Northeast Subterrane. We escaped from there just last week."

"Why?" I ask.

"Long story."

"Where are the other two?" Johnny's eyes dart around. "Hiding in leaf-suits like you two were?"

"None of your damn business," Vila spits.

"Vila, calm down," says Emerson. "These people aren't the enemy."

"We'll see about that," she mumbles, petting her animal.

I study Tallulah. "For the longest time we thought the only animals left were rats," I tell them. "Obviously, that's not the case. How did you get that one to be your pet?"

"I found her when she was a baby, near the Subterrane."

"Hey," Johnny interrupts, "can we all get to know each other *after* we find Jax and Aby?"

"Your friends went in there." Emerson points to the dark doorway. "Well, we think, anyway. We heard crying earlier and came down to check it out. After a while, we heard screaming from the kitchen and figured there were a few more of you."

"What's in there?" I ask.

"The pool, and a few more rooms. Some sort of entertaining rooms, probably. They're kind of strange."

"Come on," Smudge says, "We have to find them—now." She moves on through the darkness, while Johnny and I follow her.

"We'll wait for you out here," Emerson says, "and keep watch."

The moment we step into the dark, everything lights up, and Smudge nods when I glance her way. Inside, the walls are mirrored, dotted with splotches of grime over a layer of dust, yet our reflections still ripple in them. The red-and-gold light fixtures with soft-yellow old-fashioned bulbs in them—the two that actually work—are so detailed and perfect, someone obviously put a lot of time into making them.

When we leave the hallway, the light changes from red and yellow, to blue and deep purple in a room with shimmering walls. At first I'm confused, until I realize the light's reflected from an enormous pool that fills most of the room, with tiny mirrors dotting the entire edge in a swirling wave. Greenery adorns certain sections, while two lights in the water illuminate flowing things beneath the surface.

"Wow," says Johnny.

"Wow is right," I say.

Together, we spin slowly, taking it all in, until Johnny points to the wall beside the door where words had been beautifully painted in purple and blue, now chipping, and edged in thin lines of gold.

"What does that say?" he asks.

I clear my throat. "Whosoever immerses themselves in these waters shall have eternal life."

Johnny laughs. "All this stuff about living forever, and

they're all dead. Idiots."

"This way." Smudge leads us around the corner to another doorway already lit up, and into a sparkling dusty-gold hallway with ten, fancy red-numbered doors.

"Shall we?" I say.

Johnny nods and opens the first door to darkness. The light blinks on to shine over a neatly made bed with an ornamental covering. We move on to the next room, and the next, and the next. The first nine are all identical, and all empty. We stand before door number ten, and my chest heaves while a sickness sits in my gut like rotten slop. Johnny goes for the door.

"No," I say. "Let me." I twist the knob, and Smudge turns on the light.

And there they are, startling awake in each other's arms.

TWENTY

I PIVOT AROUND, FIGHT BACK RAGE, and Smudge turns off the light.

"Um... you guys might want to get up," Johnny says to Jax and Aby.

Cursing and heavy breathing cuts through the darkness as they scramble to put themselves back together again. "What are you doing here?" Jax mutters.

Something snaps inside me. I spin back around. "What are we doing here?" I yell. "While you two were 'comforting' each other, a boy died! And we've left the children alone with kitchen utensils to protect themselves so we could hunt you down! So what are you doing here?" Light from the hallway shines onto their guilty faces.

"Could we... turn the light on?" Aby says softly. "I can't find my other boot."

I flip on the light switch, shining truth down onto the messy bed. Tears fill my eyes, and I push my way past Johnny and Smudge, back through the pool room, to the fancy corridor. When I emerge through the entrance doorway, Emerson and Vila are still waiting in the same spot—Emerson, concerned; Vila, amused.

"Trouble in Lovetown?" Vila snickers, crossing her arms, and I want to rip her to shreds. Instead, my tears betray my strength, and stream down my face.

"Ah, honey...." Emerson plucks handfuls of leaves from his camouflaged suit, then pulls me to his chest and squeezes tight, like he's known me all of his life. "Love is heartache, sister. Ain't nothin' easy about it."

"Thank you." I wipe my eyes, push away from him to gather my shattered heart from the floor. "I'll be fine."

Footsteps approach from down the hallway, and I take a deep breath, see Vila's pet twitch in my peripheral.

"Is that thing safe around children?" I ask.

"Yeah, once she gets to know you," Emerson says. "I'm sorry she jumped out at you. She was just protecting—" His eyes focus behind me as Johnny, Smudge, Jax, and Aby come through the doorway.

Jax grips his spear. "Who are they?"

"That's Emerson." Johnny points. "That's Vila, and Ta... Ta—"

"Tallulah," Vila finishes. "And she's hungry. Come on Em, we need to get back."

"Did I hear you say someone died?" Emerson asks me.

"A twelve-year-old boy." I glance at Jax. "Some giant cockroach sucked his brains out through his skull."

"Bloodbugs," Emerson mumbles. "Yep. Hate those damned things. You have to clear the vines out of the room before you go to sleep, because they get up in there and hide—"

"Why are you talking to them like they're welcome here?" Vila demands. "This is our place."

"No, it isn't." Emerson holds a stiff finger in the air. "They found it, just like we did. They're welcome to stay as long as they damn well please."

"Whatever." She retreats with a sigh. "I'll be upstairs."

"You stay upstairs?" I ask.

"Yeah, second floor. Well, technically it's forty-four, but... second floor's easier to say." He winks. "Anyway, there's less greenery and things for critters to hide in up there. You're welcome to bring the children up. It's safer. We've cleared the greenery out of a few rooms for ourselves, but we can clear a few more. Doesn't take long at all. Plenty of room for your group."

"Thanks," I say, "but we won't be here for long."

"Where're you headed?"

I look over at Smudge for permission to tell.

"I'm taking them down the river," she explains, "to meet a friend of mine from the Other Side. From there, we may head under The Wall with him."

"The Other Side?" he says. And when I think he'll ask if his group can come along, he adds, "Why on Earth would you want to go there?"

"Why wouldn't we?" I ask.

"From what I've heard, things aren't much different there."

"Things are very different there," says Smudge.

"Why do you say that?" I ask Emerson.

"Well, we've heard some stories… hard to say what's rumors though." He shrugs. "I don't know, I suppose it might be worth it to check it out."

"What kind of stories?"

"Em, you comin'?" Vila calls down from the second floor.

He waves a hand in the air. "Yeah, V, gimme a minute." He plucks a remaining leaf from a buttonhole in his shirt, then looks back at me. "Never mind. You never know at the Subterrane. Sometimes things get passed around to scare people so they don't revolt. At least, that's what we think, anyway. I probably shouldn't put so much weight on them. If your friend says it's the place to go, then I'd trust her."

I scrutinize him for a moment, struggling to quell my curiosity. "Okay, well… we're going to get back to the children," I say. "Mind if we come up soon?"

"Not at all."

"But what about... her?"

"Vila?" He scoffs. "Oh, she's a little rough around the edges, sure, but... kinda like Tallulah, once you get to know her, she's a sweetheart."

"A sweetheart," Johnny says with a smirk. "Right."

"We'll be up there soon," I say. "Once we get everyone together."

Emerson nods and, gripping his knife, jogs up the stairs. I start back toward the kitchen, deciding it best to pretend Aby and Jax don't exist. At least until I can wrap my mind around things.

"Joy?" A soft hand grips my arm, a voice now razor-sharp, when once it was a healing balm.

I yank my arm away, fighting against tears.

"Please, Joy," she begs. "I'm so sorry. It's just... Miguel—"

I spin around—a world of pain on a tiny, fractured axis—and glare at her. "So you thought you'd have your way with Jax to make things all better? Well, nice going. Because now, not only have we all lost Miguel, but you and I—we've also lost a sister." I turn my back on her, adding over my shoulder, "Oh, but that's okay. Because now you have yourself a nice replacement for me *and* Miguel."

"Joy, stop it," says Jax. "It wasn't her fault. We were just talking and... one thing led to another."

"It takes two, you know," I tell them. "It was both of you. Hers, as well as your fault, Jax. And you've done a great job of splitting us down the middle. What a fine example for the children to follow. Hey, with any luck, all of them will grow up to be just like you two, tearing apart the hearts of everyone they meet, like paper. Because—who cares, right? We're all gonna die young, so why not go out with a bang?" My last words sting as I stare into Jax's eyes, a goodbye. Because I'll never let him in again.

"Oh, and Aby"—I dig into my pocket—"you might want this back." I extract her father's knife and place it in her hand, knowing it's the best, and worst, possible revenge. At that moment, there's not a spec of guilt anywhere in sight. Aby holds the knife in a shaky, outstretched hand, afraid at first to bring it in close. Then, she cracks and begins to weep, hugging it to her chest. And I hope it hurts. Right now, at least, I do.

"Johnny, Smudge." I whirl around, my invisible magic cloak sweeps the pain into nothingness. "Let's get the children ready to meet our new friends."

§

I knock three times on the kitchen door, and the boy with the crossbow answers. "Thank goodness," he says. "Where were they?"

"They were... exploring. They're fine."

Best not to bring the troubles of love-gone-wrong into their lives. They're already faced with defending themselves from monsters and mammoth, brain-eating cockroaches with kitchen utensils. They don't need anything else to worry about. But the split's obvious—Johnny, Smudge, and I walk in first, with Aby and Jax trailing guiltily behind us. The older children can see it like a spark in the dark, I'm sure.

I find Serna, and kiss Baby Lou's cheek. Then, I kneel down to Chloe and take her hands. "Thank you for being brave."

She nods, still clutching her wire whisk.

I move in front of the group, while Jax stands off to the side, leaning against the wall to stare at the boy whose death he's partially responsible for. Jax, the one I might have loved just hours ago, seems so much smaller and weaker. Fallen. Aby, too.

Maybe they're meant for each other, because I won't be that. I refuse to fall. I'm flying from this place, like my daddy always said I would, and I'm taking my brothers and sisters with me.

"We met some people," I announce.

"Out there?" someone asks.

"Yes. Two people. Our age. And there're two more. They've cleared a few rooms on the second floor, and they've invited us up."

Even before I get the last word out, everyone's picking up their bags and blankets and moving toward the door.

"Wait." I hold up my hands. "So we're all clear: as soon as the sun comes up tomorrow, we're leaving here with Smudge. We'll be meeting her friend, Raffai, and hopefully get to the Other Side."

The room erupts in a mix of cheers and murmurs of disdain.

"I know," I say, "but we don't have a choice. The only way to get anywhere completely safe is to go back out there." The words sink in for a moment before I continue. "We'll be sleeping upstairs tonight as guests, so everyone, please, be polite and gracious in their letting us stay with them."

Once we've gotten everything packed up, the pots and pans and most of the utensils put away, we line up at the door. Chloe won't let go of her weapon, though, and possibly never will again.

"Can I keep it, Momma Joy?" she asks.

"Of course you can."

I take Baby Lou from Serna, change her, then wrap her up in a blanket and hold Chloe's hand. Jax stands off to the side, while Aby drifts down the end of the line, alone.

"Johnny," I instruct, "you guard the front half."

He takes his spot by the door.

"And you"—I glance at Jax—"guard the back half with

the spear."

He gives me a slight nod, eyes still swimming in guilt.

"Okay," I say to Johnny. "Open the door."

He reaches for the handle... right as someone knocks on the other side. "Hey, it's me, Emerson. Thought you guys might need an escort."

Johnny opens the door to a freshly-dressed Emerson—tall and handsome, with chiseled features, like he was carved from wet wood. He smiles when he sees me, and it's contagious, actually drawing up a sliver of my own.

"That's very kind of you," I say.

"Wow." He surveys everyone, bright eyes bouncing from face to face and offering more of that smiling warmth. "Big group." He tickles Baby Lou's chin, and she giggles. First time I've heard her giggle in days. "What a cutie," he says.

"Bah." Baby Lou reaches for him, wiggling her fingers.

"I think she wants you, which is strange," I say, "because she... well, she doesn't know you."

"Ah well, come here, sweetie." He holds out his hands and she goes straight to him, without hesitation, babbling and tugging at his black-collared shirt. "Yeah, Pia calls me Papa," he says, chuckling.

"Pia?"

"You'll meet her in a minute." He glances down at Chloe. "She's about your age, little missy. She'll be excited to have a friend. She's never had one her age before."

Chloe's eyes light up. "Can we meet her now?"

"Yep, she's upstairs on two."

Chloe jumps up and down, and waves her whisk around, then stops. "Are the bugs up there?"

"Not like down here."

"Everyone ready?" I ask, and everyone answers "yes"

in unison.

"All right, Emerson. Lead the way."

"You want the baby, or the knife?"

"She seems happy with you, so...." I shrug.

Emerson slides the long silver knife out of his back pocket and hands it to me with a nod. "It's all yours."

With Emerson holding Baby Lou, me with the knife and Chloe—whisk and doll in one hand, gripping my fingers tightly in her other—and Johnny with the crossbow at the front of the line, we all move swiftly to the stairs. The carpet, once a delicious, deep red-rose, is now a decrepit brownish-red where mold has feasted and microorganisms have festered for who knows how long. Stony bones of the steps peek out in spots, like flesh burned away.

But time has been the only flame here; time, and light streaming in from the dome overhead, which now shines brightly with a glowing ball high above, and water that found a way through the path of destruction. What has been destroyed here, has also been brought to life. Same as the Treemakers of Greenleigh.

Everything dies, yet, nothing's ever really dead.

I play with the possibility that Miguel's spirit went to some Paradise in the Cosmos, as my daddy used to say. And he'll meet Toby and Samurai there. They'll swim amongst the galaxies, wade in the glow from an eternal sun, tossing star dust down upon the Earth for us to always remember them. I don't know. But one thing I do know is: when we get to the Other Side—the real paradise here on Earth—I'm taking him, too—*all of them*—alive in my mind.

Halfway up the stairs, Vila comes into view, also free of leaves, with short black hair that shines like a dark, raging abyss. "They're here," she calls over her shoulder. Tallulah peeks her furry head up from the knapsack on Vila's back, then tucks herself inside again.

A tiny bouncing blonde girl with lopsided pigtails and a smile that could breathe vibrant life into a dead world, points and claps her hands. "Bubba, look! Lots of 'em!"

Behind them approaches a boy with a walking stick, limping slightly, and beneath a brown hat a tad too big for his head, is hair as white as clouds in pictures from the old world. His eyes are the sky, or the unbridled ocean, warm and wild, inhabited with too much to ever discover in their depths. The moment I see him, I fall into them, helplessly. When he grins—the hint of a dimple on his left cheek, lopsided like the little girl's pigtails—I stumble on the last step up.

He laughs, then covers his mouth. "Sorry, I don't mean to be rude." He holds out his hand in greeting. "I'm Mateo." His grip is firm, and my whole body warms.

"And this is my sister, Pia."

"Nice to meet you, Pia." I try to hide the tremble in my voice. "This is Chloe. She's excited to have a new friend to play with."

"Come on!" says Pia. "I'll show you my room!"

Chloe looks up at me, wanting to go, but not sure if she should. I nod, let go of her hand, and she trots off after Pia, dropping her whisk behind her. I slide it down into her bag.

"Can we go, too, Momma Joy?" asks another little girl.

"If it's okay with them."

"Oh, of course," says Mateo. He waves us up to the balcony encircling the wide open space with the massive pillar in the center. "Room two-twelve is Pia's room. It should be open."

A group of girls skips off down the balcony and disappears, one by one, into a room a few doors down.

"So... Joy?" Mateo says.

"Huh?"

"Your name. It's Joy?"

"Oh yeah, sorry. I'm Joy."

"All right," Emerson announces, "anyone who wants the grand tour of Gomorrah Grande, level two, follow me."

I'm still astonished that Baby Lou is completely at ease with him. Most of the children follow, including a straggling Jax and brooding Aby. But I can't move. Or maybe it's that I don't want to. Something about Mateo is so comforting... as if he's a long lost part of me that's finally found its way home.

"I'm Johnny." Johnny shakes Mateo's hand firmly. "And that's Smudge."

"The sorceress," Mateo says, chuckling. "Yes, my friends said you're a special one."

"She is," I say. "In fact, she was just about to tell us all about that."

"I was?" she says nervously.

"Yeah"—Johnny winks with a smile—"I think I remember her saying that, too."

I swear I see Smudge blush. She turns her head.

"Well," says Mateo, "we're in luck. I have the perfect spot for the revealing of secrets."

"You do?" I ask.

He nods. "Yep. I call it, the sky hammock."

TWENTY-ONE

AFTER MAKING SURE ALL OF THE YOUNGEST GIRLS are safe and occupied with Aby nearby, I tell her we'll be back soon.

"Where are you going?" she asks.

"To show them around a bit," says Mateo. He gives me a wink where she can't see, then leads us down the balcony to a long hallway.

Aby watches us, curiously, same as Jax when we come to what looks like a weapons room where he and a few other boys are talking to Vila. Lying neatly on the bed are rows of knives and sharpened wood spears. Vila chatters away, but Jax seems more interested in what I'm doing with Mateo.

"Hang on a second." Mateo slips through the doorway and takes two spears. "Sorry to interrupt, V. We'll be back soon. Going up to twelve."

"Why?" she asks. Tallulah peeks out from her bag and hisses at us, then tucks herself out of sight.

"I want to show them the hammock," he tells her, and walks back out, holding three spears. "Here," he says, "not that we'll need them, but it's best to be prepared. And they might be a little more effective than that thing." He points to Johnny's crossbow.

Johnny takes the spear, inspects the craftsmanship. He touches a finger to the sharp tip. "Nice. Yeah, I'm a decent shot, but I like this, too. The more, the better."

Mateo's fingers brush mine as I take the offered spear. His touch unearths my vulnerable core; a warm, sacred place where truth and magic lie. And I don't even believe in magic.

But I do believe that one touch could light up this building for years.

Or maybe… I'm delusional from the traumatic experiences over the past few days. Maybe these feelings are weakness, disguised as the lie of love at first sight. After all, I found my best friend and boyfriend with my other best friend and sister, mere hours after someone we all loved dearly had been viciously slaughtered.

I'm completely unstable.

"I didn't get you a spear," Mateo says to Smudge. "Em and V say you don't need a weapon."

"True," she agrees.

Farther down the hall, Emerson, still holding Baby Lou, exits through a doorway, followed by a line of children. "The life room," he says to us, pointing behind. "Where we keep the different specimens we find. Unbelievable how much is here, really. We're always discovering new things." We enter the room, and over the children's heads hang rows of different types of insects, including the carcass of a giant "bloodbug," which rests between a long, black spiky thing and another insect with brightly-colored wings, possibly a butterfly.

"We have ten extra rooms good for sleeping," Emerson says to me. "How do you want them separated?"

"Boys' and girls' rooms, with at least one older in each. I'll have Baby Lou, Chloe, and one more younger girl in with me. The younger boys can be in Jax's room." *As long as he doesn't go "exploring" again.*

"Adventurers!" says Emerson. "Make yourselves comfortable in our rooms, or out here on the balcony while we get a few more rooms cleared. We'll be serving lunch shortly."

"And no one leaves this area!" I announce.

"You can be in here, Joy, if that's okay." He points to the door we're standing next to—room two-sixteen. "It'll be cleared by the time you all return."

"Perfect. Thanks for your help. I really appreciate it."

"Oh, it's no problem at all. It's nice to have more around. Gets too quiet here sometimes."

The children scatter, and I peek inside my room. Leafy vines cover half of one wall, and the ancient, smelly bed covers are made of the most exquisite cloth that'll ever have touched any of our skin. Unfortunately, they're identical to the ones shed to the floor during Jax and Aby's "explorations." Something that won't be easily forgotten—or forgiven.

"They're pretty nice rooms, aren't they?" Mateo asks me.

"Yes, they are. Beautiful," I say.

"Yes… beautiful." His eyes swim in mine, past the point of assumption he's still talking about the rooms. My face grows hot, and I dip my chin. Mateo chuckles warmly, and it soothes my writhing insides, like he'd curled up in my soul to take a nap for a while. I struggle to breathe steadily.

"So…." Emerson grins at his friend. "Where you off to?"

"The sky hammock. Will you be okay while we're gone?"

"Oh, yeah. Me and my new little friend here will be just fine. We're about to go check out Pia's room, see what we can find to play with. Then, we'll get lunch started."

"Okay, we shouldn't be too long."

"Yell if you need me." And he takes off down the balcony, Baby Lou happily perched on his hip.

With his walking stick in one hand and a spear in the other, Mateo continues the opposite way down the balcony corridor with us at his heels. "Em's dad worked on generators his whole life." He laughs. "How lucky is that? Only took him a few hours of tinkering around with the thing to get it going again. Don't ask me how it all works; I wouldn't be able to tell you much. Runs with water and electricity both, but that's about all I know."

We get to a smaller interior elevator and Mateo reaches for the button.

"Wait," says Johnny, who gives Smudge a grin.

But she starts, like she got caught stealing cookies. "What?"

"Come on, do the thing," he says. "Please?"

"Do what thing?" Mateo asks.

She breathes in deep and focuses on the elevator. A second later, the button lights up and the door opens by itself.

"Wow!" Mateo says. "That's great! How in the world did you do that?"

"Would you believe me if I told you... magic?" She laughs nervously.

"No such thing as real magic," I say. "So, no. You're not getting off that easy."

Mateo steps onto the elevator, and we follow. The door closes, and he presses the button for sub-level twelve.

"What is 'real,' anyway?" Smudge asks. "Does that mean it needs to be explainable, that you have to know exactly how and why it works, what connects A to B? Can nothing unexplainable in this universe be... magic? It's all semantics, you know...."

"There she goes again." And Johnny pats her on the hat.

Smudge whips out, grabs his hand. "Don't touch my head—ever."

"Whoa... sorry. I didn't mean to, uh... offend you."

She relaxes, releases her grip with a sigh. "No, I'm sorry. I shouldn't have reacted like that. I... have a thing about my head."

"Is that part of the secret?" I ask, while the elevator creaks and shimmies as it ascends. Before long, we've reached our stop.

"I suppose, yes," she replies.

The door opens, and we exit the elevator. It's warmer up here, closer to the dome, but fewer vines and things, likely because of less water.

"Leave the spears in the elevator," Mateo says, dropping his with his walking stick before limping out ahead.

We leave ours near his and follow him out. On the balcony, Mateo climbs up onto the railing.

"What are you doing?" I ask.

He winks and, spreading his arms wide, falls backwards.

"Oh my God!" I yell.

"What the hell?" says Johnny.

We rush over, and when we get to the railing, we see him suspended in mid-air, hands behind his head and grinning up at us. I squint, making out a semi-transparent netting that stretches around the area's circumference from railing to center pillar.

"Come on!" he calls up to us. "It's super sturdy." And he rolls to the far side, giving us room to free fall from what might as well be a million feet high.

"Hell, yeah!" Johnny hops onto the railing, then jumps off like it's two feet in the air. "Woo!" he yells, landing on his side. The net expands, then retracts. "He's right! Sturdy! Come on, you two!"

I read something unsettling in Smudge's eyes.

"What is it?" I ask.

"I don't know what to call this one," she says quietly. "It's... very confusing. I mean, all of the other ones are so easy—guilt, sadness, anger, all forms of fear... happiness, joy, excitement, bliss... those, I understand. But this one... it's a mix of everything, all in one. There's fear, excitement, nervousness, curiosity… happiness.…" She stares longingly at Johnny.

"Oh!" I laugh. "I think I know exactly what you're talking about."

"You do?"

"Yes." And I gesture to Mateo.

"Interesting.…" she says. "So what do you call it?"

"Well, I'm not one hundred percent sure, but… I think you call it … love."

"Love?"

I nod. "And what do you call it when you're about to jump a million feet down into a questionable net, to love waiting below?"

"I don't know. What?"

"Absolute insanity."

Smudge smiles wide; the first real one I've seen from her—soft, innocent, and so natural it surprises me, coming from someone so full of mystery.

"Yes," she says. "That makes perfect sense."

I hold out my hand, and she places hers into mine.

"On three?" I say.

"On three."

We climb onto the fat gold railing and teeter there for a second, while Mateo and Johnny observe from a distance. They sit talking low to each other, possibly amused by the whole ordeal.

"What do you think they're talking about?" Smudge asks.

"I don't know, but—three!" I jump, tugging her with me, and we scream, laughing a second later as we land in the net. The boys roll back to us, sitting up with their legs crossed. Smudge and I do, too, with her across from Johnny, and me from Mateo. Though I tell myself not to look down, I, of course, immediately do, and my vision sways as I make out the treetops and the splotchy greenish brown-and-white tile floor far below. Dizziness overtakes me, and I realize I'm holding my breath.

"Breathe...." Mateo pats my hand with his own warm one. "It's safe, I promise. Sometimes when I'm bored, I jump up and down, and flip and roll around on this thing until I get tired. I've even brought my sister up here. Really, it's fine." A short squeeze, and he slides his hand away, leaving my skin longing after his.

I squint up at the bright sky twelve stories above us, behind the massive light-purple dome I'm amazed to find so clean. "Why is this net here?" I ask.

"Probably so people couldn't jump," says Mateo. "There's another one twelve stories below us."

"True," says Smudge, as she pulls her hood over her hat, then hugs her knees. "A suicide pandemic hit Bygonne many, many years ago. Most people took their own lives in one form or another. If not, then they were *giving* them. The Ultimate Sacrifice. Good thing your friends downstairs were more interested in each other, than in the room's wall dials."

"Why?" The only thing I'd noticed about the room were the birds printed in frozen flight on the bed covering tossed recklessly to the floor.

"Gomorrah Grande was once the largest cultivator of donors. People would go to those rooms to be transferred."

"Transferred?"

"Yes. It's... hard to explain...."

Hadn't Mona Superior said: *But remember, Arianna wants their minds intact for the transfer when she gets back. No head injuries.*

Were we to be transferred?

"So... 7ZS3-22Y?" says Johnny.

"Yes?" Smudge replies.

"Wow, you actually answer to it!"

"How'd you do that thing back there with the elevator door?" Mateo asks. "Is that how you all came up here? Em was wondering, since he deliberately shut off the breaker to the jungle elevator."

Smudge expands her fingers out, then closes them into a ball in her lap. "If I tell you, you won't believe me."

"Why not?" I ask. "We've already seen what you can do. Why not believe how you do it?"

"Because your mind cannot easily conceive that which you know nothing about."

"Try us," says Johnny. "We've seen some stuff."

Smudge sighs. "Okay. But bear with me. I've never... done this before."

"Done what?" I ask.

"This. Any of this. I've never had... friends. I've never talked openly to... your kind before."

"Our kind?" Mateo says.

"Yes. Humans."

"Whoa...." Johnny slaps his knee, eyes wide.

"So, you aren't human?" I ask.

"Not entirely."

"Well, what are you, then?" asks Johnny. "An alien or something?"

Smudge giggles. "No. I am an OAI—an Organic Artificial Intelligence. I am part human and... part machine. Some from Alzanei—the Other Side—who aren't so fond of us, refer to us as 'Synthetic Humans,' or 'Synths.'"

We stare in silence, and she flexes her hands again.

"Wow," says Johnny. "That's intense."

"Is that how you can control electricity?" I ask.

"Yes." She nods. "I send signals to manipulate electrical

current. It has its limits, though."

"Are there a lot like you on the Other Side?" Mateo asks. "I've heard some stories, but never anything about... um... machine people."

"Hundreds. In fact, last time I heard, we were nearing five hundred."

"How do they... make OAIs, and why?" I ask.

"We are the 'pure ones,' the followers of The One who'll bring the dead Earth back to life. We're developed with manipulated human DNA and grown for three years in artificial wombs, rapidly reaching our full young adult size. While our human bodies grow, fragile organs are removed, recycled, and replaced. Except for the brain. No matter how hard they try, they cannot mimic that miraculous operating system. So, instead of removing it, they add another section—the Nirvonic System. It targets the amygdala and hippocampus to block emotional drive, with programmed responses to certain life-threatening situations to replace the lack of the emotion and fear that helps protect humans from danger."

"Wait," I say. "So, they program your brain?"

"Kind of. With the rapid growth rate of OAIs, we don't learn the things human children learn. Mind maps from donors are imprinted onto the fresh brain, with the knowledge it needs to operate in this world. The Nirvonic System keeps the mind 'pure' from the so-called 'impurities' of emotion. It also creates an amnesia of sorts; we may remember bits and pieces of our donor's past, but we feel no connection. We become the perfect servants of the One True Lord, the 'Messiah,' come to bring back peace and purity to the Earth. I once had no choice *but* to believe that."

"Whoa, you totally lost me there," says Johnny.

"Me, too," I say. "Kind of. Let's back up. What's 'organic

artificial intelligence'?"

"Mechanics that mimic life. They grow and heal themselves, except faster and better than a human body can."

"What do you mean by 'donor'?" Mateo asks. "And 'transfer,' and 'mind maps'...?"

"A mind can be mapped. Everything a human mind has ever learned can be uploaded onto an OAI liqui-drive—billions of neuroconnections and electroneuro patterns are stored for a short time, usually about five years. Donors are those who give the Ultimate Sacrifice, also called a 'transfer'; they give their lives for an OAI. After a transfer has taken place, the donor's mind is wiped clean, inducing a vegetative state."

"So... they die?" Johnny asks.

"Yes. They are told this sacrifice is the only way they'll get to live forever, though they are only told a partial truth."

"Basically, this guy thinks he's God," says Mateo, "and he's tricking people into suicide so he can build an army of mindless followers...?"

"Not entirely mindless," Smudge says, "but missing many human aspects, yes. OAIs are not curious, envious, angry, selfish, boastful, fearful, or traitorous. They are loyal, intelligent, honest, graceful, strong, confident, and, best of all for Lord Daumier, programmable. The Nirvonic System receives direct override commands. OAIs can be completely controlled, and often are."

"But, Smudge," I say, "you're here, and you have feelings; like, real human emotions. You're not controlled. How can what you're saying be so?"

"That's where Raffai comes in. He's the leader of the Revols, a group who oppose Lord Daumier and are doing everything they can to make things... right. As right as possible, anyway. Servants of the One True Lord are sometimes captured and awakened."

"Awakened?"

"Yes. With a simple surgical procedure, Raffai rewires and reprograms the Nirvonic System, removing the brain blocks, which relinquishes the control of Lord Daumier and his Clergy. We are then open to the full spectrum of human emotions, as well as the memories of the ones who sacrificed themselves for the lie of making a better future on Earth." Smudge breathes in deep and meets each of our stares, until her eyes drift back down to her hands in her lap. "After Raffai's Revols capsized our fishing boat, they paralyzed the five of us and took us back to their city where they awakened us, then gave us three options: to continue to serve Lord Daumier, to stay with them, or to go rogue and live life on our own as we chose."

"Free will," I say.

"Yes. He made us human. And then, he set us free."

TWENTY-TWO

"LUNCHTIME!" Emerson calls up, a tiny brown speck-of-a-person below, still holding an even tinier speck on his hip. "And I think Little Missy needs a changing!"

"Guess that means we have to go," Johnny says. "That's too bad, 'cause this is great. Best time of my life."

"Just a minute!" I yell back to Emerson. "Mine, too, Johnny," I sigh, "but Baby needs me. Now how do we get down?"

"Just roll on over to the side, and climb up onto thirteen," Mateo says. "Once you get there, you'll find a handle to help you up over the railing."

Sure enough, there's a brass handle bolted to the support beam that runs from sub-level thirteen to sub-level twelve. Mateo climbs over first, then helps the rest of us.

"So, you never told us," Johnny says to Smudge. "About your head, I mean."

"Oh. Right. Well... OAIs are almost immortal, if it wasn't for this fragile brain...." She shakes her head slightly. "Once I was awakened, I realized just how fragile it made me, especially once I decided to remove my helmet."

"You wore a helmet?"

"All OAIs wear helmets. We're hated by many people, and the only way to kill an OAI is to... remove the head or the brain." Smudge rubs the back of her neck. "I guess I'm... still getting used to being... so exposed."

Johnny slowly reaches a out hand, and she studies it as the fingers come closer to make contact with the skin of her neck. He gently massages the spot. "We won't hurt you," he says. "You can trust us."

Smudge closes her eyes, melts beneath his touch. "I know you won't hurt me. And it's not that I don't... trust you... but I'm still learning all of these human emotions. They can be tricky."

"That's the truth," I say.

"You remember what it was like?" Johnny asks. "Before you were awakened?"

She nods and makes the elevator door open for us. Johnny stops his massaging as we climb on, retrieve our spears, and Mateo, his walking stick.

"I remember everything," she says.

The door closes.

"You don't know until after you've been awakened that it was like...." She trails off, lost in reminiscence.

"Like...?" I coax.

"Being a prisoner in your own body and mind; being alive, but not really alive; human, but more machine, more... programmable. Lord Daumier calls it 'pure,' but that's not purity. It's purely evil."

"What's the truth about the portal to paradise?" I ask after a long silence. At the second floor, the elevator door opens to Emerson and a crying Baby Lou.

"I'll tell you more later," she says. "Take care of your Baby." But for a moment, she stares hard at Baby Lou.

"Is that him?" I ask after following her gaze to Baby's shirt. "Is that Lord Daumier?"

She nods, shuddering in disgust.

"He looks like a big time ass." Johnny holds out his hand. "Join me for lunch?"

Smudge grins and slides her own small hand into his bigger

one. Together, they walk down the balcony, and I take Baby Lou from Emerson, once again inspecting the ugly man's crackled face on the front. Only now do I notice how strikingly similar his features are to Diaz Superior's. The thought doesn't sit well.

"She's been a good girl," Emerson says, "and a couple of your boys helped clear out a few more rooms. I think they're all getting situated in them."

"Thanks again for all of your help. I really appreciate it."

"Hey, it's no problem. You enjoy the sky hammock?"

"Yes, wow. It was incredible."

"Lots of incredible things going on around here," says Mateo, who glances at me with a grin, then looks off down the balcony. "So what's for lunch, Em?"

"Artichoke hearts, beans, and mashed potatoes. Along with whatever that stuff is you found in that tree."

"I guess we're running pretty low on supplies now," I tell them. "Thanks to Smudge, we've been eating decent since we left."

"Well, this is from our supply," Emerson says. "We raided the food storage before we left the Subterrane. Terrible how awful the guards are. All brawn and no brains. Deaf, too, prob'ly."

"You had food like that where you lived?"

"Yep. Came from the Other Side, three times a week, usually. The Subterrane's a salt-mining community, with mines a mile down almost. We traded salt for food, then shipped it across Bygonne to whoever had a decent trade in their specialization... diamonds, cotton, other kinds of food, precious metals, etcetera."

"Why did you leave?" I ask.

Emerson and Mateo make uneasy eye contact for a moment.

"Because my sister was chosen," Mateo says.

"Chosen? What does that mean?"

"Uh... let's eat first," he says. "Then, I'll explain everything."

§

After I change Baby Lou, I join the others, who are scattered here and there on the balcony in groups of three and four, eating lunch in the first real relax-time since we left the Tree Factory. Their contentment in such a short time after Miguel's death makes me both hopeful and downhearted, though I shouldn't expect them to shed tears about it forever. Or at all. Children are like titanzium—so strong, resilient, and they can take so much before their spirits finally break. A good thing, really. Most of them have a chance at future happiness, once we get to the Other Side.

But I'm dying to know more about Smudge and the world she came from. As I feed Baby Lou mashed potatoes, sneaking a delicious bite here and there, a thousand questions flood my mind: Does she eat? Sleep? How is it over there? Is there clean air? I'm kicking myself for not having asked all of this while in the sky hammock. Can't ask her now. No way Jax and the rest of them will take her story lightly. She'd be an outcast, whether stated openly or not. Already Jax is probing for a reason to throw her into the river. He definitely doesn't need to know Smudge's truth. Sooner or later, though, I'll need an explanation. A good bluff may be in order.

Jax sulks over, sits down onto the floor next to me and Baby Lou. A few feet away, Mateo eyes me from beside Emerson, where Vila blabbers on to a few younger children while her strange animal sniffs the air around her head, maybe to learn the smells of these strangers in her home.

"Can I talk to you for a minute?" Jax says.

"Talk away." I spoon more mashed potatoes into Baby Lou's mouth.

"Listen, what happened between me and Aby... that was a mistake—"

"Yes, it sure was."

"We were just talking about Miguel and... and then we were crying together. I was comforting her, and...."

Aby peeks up from her spot alone by the distant wall, where she's decided she doesn't need to eat. For a split second, my sympathy rises for her... then it's gone. "I don't want to hear anymore, Jax. It happened, it's over, let's move on."

"Yeah, you already have, haven't you?" And he glares at Mateo, who locks onto his stare without expression, without turning away. Jax shifts back at me. "So, why shouldn't I?"

"Why shouldn't you?" I sneer.

He scrambles to his feet and storms away to pace along the balcony, where he tosses me one last glance, then goes to sit down next to Aby.

After a moment's struggle with his walking stick, Mateo rises and joins me, favoring his outstretched right leg as he sits down. "You okay?" he asks.

"Fine. What happened to your leg?"

"Mining accident. Fell in a hole, busted up my knee. Never did heal correctly."

"Wow. When did it happen?"

"Three years ago, when I was fifteen."

"So you're eighteen?"

"Yep. At least I think I am. Lost track of time since we've been here. May be my birthday today, and I don't know it. It was coming up soon...."

"Well, happy birthday, then."

"Thanks." He smiles. "How about you?"

"Sixteen last May."

"No way! You seem much older than that."

"Really?"

"You're very mature for sixteen."

"Well, I've been like a mother to these guys for a few years already." I run my fingers through Baby Lou's hair, meeting tangles that will need to be cut out. I shake my head. "I do the best I can."

"That bad over there, eh?" He lifts his head, eyes shielded under the brim of his hat from everyone but me, giving himself to me alone.

"It's bad," I say. "We've been running the factory ourselves for about three years now, with only the Superiors to answer to. It's been horrible." Then, I lean in to whisper, "It wasn't an accident. The explosion, I mean."

"I didn't think it was," he whispers back.

"How did you know? Usually I'm a pretty good bluff."

"Anyone sane would do whatever it took to get away from that place. The Superiors—" He shudders. "The few times they traded with the Subterrane, I could practically taste the evil dripping from them."

"How did they get there?"

"The trolley. Or a rover, maybe."

"A rover?"

"Free-range vehicles built to travel in the harsh, open-air climate. They're usually only used at night, when it's not as hot outside; it can get pretty toasty inside, even with the air-cool system."

"How do you know all of this?"

"My father. Best thief the world has ever known, I'm sure of it. He had ways of discovering things."

"Your father was a thief?"

"Well, yes and no. He was primarily a salt miner, but also a thief. He'd tie pouches of salt to his legs to trade in small quantities in exchange for information from people who wanted more than their meager rations."

I giggle.

"What's so funny?" Mateo asks.

"Oh, it's just... my daddy was a gambling magician; the best *liar* the world has ever known—"

"Wait—was he Zephyr the Magnificent?"

"Yes!" I blink. "How in the world did you know that?"

"Come on... not many gambling magicians around Bygonne lately."

"True... but how? Did you hear about him?"

"I saw him perform once."

"Really?"

He nods. "I was about ten or so, and my father had saved up Notes for two whole years so I could see him...." We lock gazes, and the desire for his hands in mine grows. But young eyes, and angry ones, watch in my peripheral and make the physical connection impossible, though this non-physical one is almost as intense. "Your father was an awesome man," he continues. "Freeing himself from those chains, when he should've long been drowned—"

"Oh my God," I laugh again. "You know what? I think I was at the same show. Only time I ever saw him perform in front of a crowd. I'd stolen a man's coat and snuck in—"

"That was my father's coat!" he blurts.

"What?"

"Yeah, when we left, it was gone. Did you put it back?"

"No, I ditched it later in a storage closet when I got near our quarters."

"Was it brown, with a hood?"

"Yes! Oh my God, are you serious?"

"Yes!"

Everyone's staring now as our voices rise in excitement.

"That's unbelievable," I say, as tears well in contrast to my smile. "I'm so sorry I stole your father's coat."

"Don't be. Why are you crying?"

"Well, I . . . I miss him so much, and I've only been able to share his memory with one other person." I glance over at Jax. "But now I've just realized something. . . ."

"What's that?"

"Real magic exists after all."

Mateo takes my hand, and I let him. No longer can I withstand the inevitable: fate or God, or the ghosts of our fathers, have brought Mateo and me together—at the perfect time. No denying it, the awe of how it's all happened, and now this undeniable connection between us, like stars that have orbited together for years, finally colliding to make a bigger star.

"Magic is real," Mateo says. "Ever since I saw Zephyr the Magnificent perform that night, I knew it was. Never a doubt in my mind about it, either."

Tears roll down my cheeks as I openly sob, hiccuping against swirling emotions, everyone watching as my revelation comes. Baby Lou's face grows serious, concerned, as she watches me. I kiss her cheek. "Momma Joy's okay, sweetheart," I say. *More than okay.*

Smudge was right about the magic. It was there all along. But I failed to see it, because . . . I was a part of it.

I was the smoke, the mirror, the muse. . . .

I see that now.

At once, I throw my arms around Mateo's neck and, squeezing tightly, kiss his cheek, then whisper into his ear,

"Thank you, so, so much."

He kisses my own cheek. "I knew it when I saw you," he says, voice low so no one else can hear. "Something in your eyes...."

"What?" I say. "What did you know?"

"That I'd fall in love with you."

The urge to kiss him is so strong, too strong to withstand, almost.

He gazes at my lips, then winks playfully. "There's plenty of time for that later."

My skin grows hot with embarrassment; he suspects my thoughts, and I've never wanted to kiss anyone so badly. And not just kiss—mesh into him, disappear inside his skin to become one. I've never felt that way about Jax; his was more of a comfort thing. This is a force of nature, a connection only death could break.

Thankfully, Emerson squats down near us, because I can't put these feelings into words.

"You tell her yet?" he asks Mateo.

"Uh, no. Not yet."

"You gonna?"

"Yeah."

"Dah." Baby Lou reaches for Emerson.

"Well, hello there, little lady." He picks her up, sets her in his lap, and she babbles to him.

Mateo adjusts his outstretched leg. "Okay, so, my sister was chosen as a sacrifice by Queen Nataniah. At three 'choosing ceremonies' a year, she supposedly speaks to 'the gods,' who tell her which children will be sacrificed. But unlike the Ultimate Sacrifice Smudge told us about, this particular sacrifice isn't as pretty, or as complicated. The 'chosen ones' are kept in a separate room and fed extremely well until their twenty-fifth birthday. Once they come of age, the 'bloodletting' ceremony is held, when they're slowly drained of their blood, then they're cut open."

"That's horrible," I say. "Why would they do that?"

"That's not even the half of it," he says. "After they're cut open, the townspeople feast on the organs, and the fat and flesh is ground up, fortified with nutrients, put into cans... and shipped to Greenleigh. To the Tree Factory."

His words take a moment to register. "Hold on, are you saying—?"

"Yes. Slop is one hundred percent human fat and flesh."

I fight to hold down my mashed potatoes. All those years, shoveling that filth into my mouth. My stomach churns. The curly black hair I found was not Humphrey's. Then, other pieces click together, a nightmare jigsaw puzzle.

"Those are the cannibals!" I say. "The Superiors weren't lying!"

"No, definitely not."

"They sent our brother there! Did you meet him? Pedro, missing his left hand...?"

"Uh, no... doesn't mean he wasn't there, though. Pia!" he calls toward the group of giggling girls down near Aby, then adds to me, "If they bring them on a rover at night, everyone's asleep, and sometimes the Queen sends them straight to the fattening chamber."

Pia jogs over, pigtails bouncing. For an instant, the nightmare multiplies tenfold. Could we have eaten our own brother, unknowingly? Then, I remember the age limit, and I'm relieved. He wasn't quite twenty-five yet.

"Yes, Bubba?" Pia asks.

"Before we left, do you remember a boy named Pedro? He was missing one of his hands."

She bites her lip, trying to remember. "Oh yeah," she cries.

"Pedro! He was nice to me, and he was so sad 'cause he missed his baby brother."

"That's him!" I say. "We have to go back, Mateo. We have to save our brother."

TWENTY-THREE

"No, WE CAN'T GO BACK THERE," says Emerson. "We wouldn't stand a chance."

"We have to go back," I insist. "His brother, Miguel, died down there in that jungle. We have to. For Miguel."

"You don't understand," Mateo says. "Not only is going back there risky, but the river only goes one way; the opposite direction. And the trolley doesn't work very well with four people on it, much less thirty-something—"

"Trolley?" I say.

"Yeah, a trolley tunnel exits from the twentieth floor. It used to operate with electricity, we think. An antenna sticks up from the top, and wires run along the tunnel. But there's also a pump jack, as a power failure back up."

"What's all the excitement?" Johnny asks, as he and Smudge join us.

"Remember what the Superiors used to tell us about the eastern cannibals?" I say. "Well, it's true." And I proceed to explain what Mateo told me, though I stop short of revealing the Tree Factory slop's ingredients. Probably not the best time to tell him. Or anyone. Ever.

"Eat Pedro? Hell no," says Johnny. "Where is this place? We have to get him—"

"Listen," Emerson says, "it took us two days to get here by trolley, but we kept stopping to rest, with only three of us pumping. Probably wouldn't take as long with more muscle, but... what about the children? We can't take them there.

They'll get us all caught. Killed, eaten, held captive, tortured. Like I said, we wouldn't stand a chance."

"We'll take them to Raffai," Smudge says. "To safety first, before we attempt a rescue."

"I agree," I say. "But... how are we going to do this?"

"Who's Raffai?" Emerson asks.

"A friend of hers, on the Other Side," I say.

"The Other Side? You know how to get over The Wall?"

"Under it, actually," she replies. "And yes, I have that knowledge. The passageway is right next to where you all came from, near the Northeast Subterrane."

"And you've been through there?" Mateo asks.

"Yes."

"Smudge, I'm curious," I say, "why did you lead us to the jungle if we could've taken the trolley?"

"I didn't know for sure if you'd all fit in the trolley. The boat can hold more. And Arianna Superior sometimes goes to the Subterrane using the trolley tunnels. I felt it would be safer using the boat, as long as I led the... monsters... away." A sadness sweeps her face of its youth. "I'm so sorry," she whispers.

"Smudge, don't." I pat her knee. "Guilt and regret won't do you any good. You did what you thought would save us, and I appreciate that. We all do." Jax glares over at us, Aby by his side. "Well, most of us, anyway. But tell me something..."

She nods her assent.

"How were you planning to lead them away?"

Smudge sighs. "I suppose I should tell you the truth about them, now that you know my truth."

"Wait." Emerson holds up a hand. "What truth? Fill me in?"

"Smudge is part machine, part human," Mateo whispers. "I'll tell you the rest later."

After a serious inspection of Mateo's face, then Smudge,

who nods, Emerson whistles softly. "Well, I'll be damned...."

"The monsters, as you call them, are also part machine," Smudge explains. "Many years ago scientists from this side managed to get the genetic coding for OAIs, and instead of humans, they created weapons, bred them and programmed them to destroy. Only, the organic intelligence they generated had done something they did not anticipate—it grew beyond the confines they'd created and took control of the Nirvonic System, which they renamed the 'Wild Adaptation and Reprogramming,' or 'WAR' System, and the creatures learned how to take advantage of it. They learned how to fool the host into thinking it had control, until the host was within reach and vulnerable, then they would attack. And because these creatures were part machine, they could also think with near-human capabilities. They could plan, calculate, and some believed they could even mimic reason. They have three downfalls, though: large size, so they cannot hide or move as stealthily as they'd like to; they have to recharge every day, for at least twelve hours—"

"How do they do that?" I ask.

"Migrate to the highest point in the jungle where the heat from the sun is most intense, and they hibernate. The heat-energy helps them regenerate quickly, though they still could without it. It would just take longer."

Johnny eyes his three crossbow bolts. "How many of those things are out there?"

"No one knows for certain," she says, "but it's believed their numbers, though not particularly large, are enough to do serious damage. Especially if they ever make it to the surface."

"Give us a rough estimate," he says.

"Approximately one hundred. And similar to OAIs, they are nearly indestructible. Terminal brain damage has to occur for them to become inoperative."

"You said they had three downfalls," Mateo says. "What's the third thing?"

"Oh, yes." Smudge wiggles her two thumbs in the air, smiling. "They do not have opposable thumbs."

"So, how again were you planning to lead them away?" I ask.

"They do not have breeding capabilities, but since they were created using animal DNA—Black Bear, Panther, and primate, to be exact—they do have instincts. I waited for three days, and when I heard the explosion, I simply manipulated their brain stimuli to activate their hormones. I figured if I guided them as far away and as high up as possible from the river, it would give you plenty of time to get into the boat. Once you all were on the river, they would not be a threat; they are... scared of the creatures that live there. The WAR System keeps them from getting hurt."

Silently, we let everything sink in, though I'm sure I'm not the only one who didn't understand half of it.

"But it didn't work...." I sigh.

"Not entirely, no. The Reaper that killed your brother... his hunger was more convincing than his hormonal pull. Four were easily led away, but he turned, unexpectedly. After stunning the other four, I got there as soon as I could."

"Is that what they're called on the Other Side? Reapers?" I ask.

"Yes."

"How fitting," I say bitterly.

"So, two ways to get to the Other Side?" says Emerson. "Through the trolley tunnels, or up from the jungle?"

"Yes. At first, there was only the one secret entrance in the trolley tunnel, but a few years ago, a second one was added in the jungle."

"Thank goodness for the one in the tunnel," Johnny says.

"Yes, it is very fortunate."

"How do you know about Arianna Superior?" I ask.

"There is... more to her than what's apparent."

"I knew it." I snap my fingers. "Is she part machine, too?"

"Yes, but not OAI. She wishes to become one, and has been altered gradually over the years. Lord Daumier uses her desperateness to be Head Saint of Alzanei to his advantage, filling her with lies of how she can become 'pure,' if only she keeps at it long enough. She doesn't realize he does this... to get more transfers. He is a very good liar. And she wants it badly enough to believe him." Smudge drops her gaze to her hands, then continues, in a more somber tone.

"Arianna Superior alone is responsible for thousands of suicides; she manipulated, lied to, threatened, and beat the naysayers into submission until... no one was left. Except for the children. Because there is a great chance of faulty transfer, or even fatality, with donors under thirty years of age, she waits until they come of age, and have gained the neuro-strength and knowledge needed for a faultless transfer, then they, too, are sacrificed."

"What a monster," I mutter.

"Yes," Smudge says. "She is an evil, evil human."

"Alzanei. That's where you said you were from, right?"

"Yes. The last eastern city... an island of sorts."

"Question," Mateo says. "Can those things, those Reapers, get into the tunnels?"

"Not that I'm aware of. I've never seen them in the tunnels, and I've been throughout all of them. If we do come across one, or even a group, though, I can stun them, just not kill them."

"Why not?" Johnny asks.

"A stipulation of my awakening. Raffai programmed me

to be a creature of peace who supports all life; I cannot intentionally kill. The Earth is dead enough already."

"Yeah, and we'll all be dead if we come too close to those monsters," Johnny says. "Or Reapers, or whatever they're called. I think there's a flaw in your friend's reasoning, there."

"I did not say I entirely agree with his... reasoning. My human mind can see many rules are made to be... broken... or at the very least, bent. But in this one area, my programming overrides my free will. Everything else, though... I am free."

"Well, then"—Johnny readjusts Old Jonesy's hat and taps his crossbow—"you do the stunning and we'll do the killing. Fair? That won't go against your programming, will it?"

"No. If you decide you must kill, I cannot stop you."

"One question, though." Johnny leans forward. "How do we kill them?"

"You must pierce the frontal cortex, through the eye," says Smudge. "That is the... quickest way."

"Okay.... But will you be upset?"

"No. Not if you are defending those you... love." She glances at him, then back to her lap. "Love. What a powerful force. Perhaps, the most powerful force that exists. I'm still calculating this..." She takes us all in, gaze lingering longest on Johnny. "... new information."

"I think you're right," I say.

"Okay." Emerson rubs his hands together. "While you gals are gettin' all philosophical, my wheels are spinning on a plan."

"We need to get Vila over here," Mateo says.

Johnny stands, dusts off his pants. "Jax needs to know, too." He stretches out his legs, twists his spine, wincing as it cracks in a few spots.

"Are you in pain?" Smudge asks.

"Yeah, I injured my back lifting titanzium last year. It gives me a lot of trouble."

Standing, Smudge rolls her right sleeve up over her wrist. "Close your eyes. This will be somewhat... shocking."

"Okay...?" Hesitantly, he does.

Smudge goes behind him, where only Emerson, Mateo, and I see her bring the reddish glow of her fingertips to the base of his spine. She touches him, and he flinches.

"Whoa, what the—?"

"Shh...." She moves up his spine a few inches, touches him again, fingers glowing brighter still as they make contact with his cotton shirt.

Johnny tenses, then relaxes.

Smudge steps back. "How do you feel?" she asks.

For a moment, he twists—left, then right—and his face lights up with amazement. "It doesn't hurt... at all!" He whips around to face her. "I could kiss you."

Her cheeks flush crimson as she tries to hide a grin.

"That was incredible," I say. "What about Mateo's knee? Can you fix that?"

"How was it injured?" she asks him.

"Tore some ligaments and dislocated my kneecap—I think. It healed all wrong; it's a big mess in there. But I'm used to the pain."

"Well, I could alleviate some of the pain, but not much. Electro-therapy only heals certain things. Others would take more intensive treatment."

"I'm fine," he says. "Let's just figure out what we're going to do next, because honestly, I'm curious as hell now about what's on the Other Side. If we have a safe place to go over there, we need to go to it, as soon as possible, like you said, Joy. This is no place to spend the rest of your life. Unless you have no other choice, of course. But it appears we do now."

"How is it over there, Smudge?" I ask. "Clean air? Real trees? Animals? Food?"

"Yes to all. It's much better than here."

"Well, hell," Emerson says. "You've got me convinced."

"Johnny—" I move closer to talk quietly. "We can't tell Jax about Smudge yet."

"We gotta tell him something."

"I know, but something other than the truth. For now."

"Okay, well... what do you suggest?"

"Direct any of his questions about her to me. I won't offer any information until he requests it, though you can fill him in on the Subterrane and Pedro, if you want, and the plan to leave in the morning. And bring them over here afterwards."

"Got it." He skips off along the balcony, past restless children finished with their meals. Jax eyes us suspiciously. I observe as Johnny begins to explain everything to them, and I see the exact moment he tells them about Pedro—both of their faces animate with emotion, and Aby begins to cry tears of joy and desperation. Seconds later, they're making their way over to us.

"V," Emerson calls over to Vila.

"What?"

"Come over here."

She rolls her eyes, makes a clicking sound with her mouth. Tallulah jumps from her knapsack into Vila's arms, and the two of them join us. The animal's yellow eyes bounce from face to face, and she hisses.

"What is it, Em?"

He plops Baby Lou up onto his shoulders and she laughs. "You should be a part of this talk," he says, squinting as Baby bops his face with Millie's floppy ears.

Vila mumbles something, and Emerson glares sternly.

I breathe in deep to calm my wild emotions. So many things are going on inside at one time, it's maddening. So I focus on Pedro, and the children—Baby Lou happier than she's ever been—as Johnny, Jax, and Aby join our circle. For a moment, no one speaks, and I don't know how or where to begin. But then, an inner nudge—my daddy's spirit—tells me to be strong, to be bigger than any silly games or troubles and imaginings of the last few hours. Time to move on.

I clear my throat. "In order to move forward," I say, "we need to think about a few things. First, we have common goals: we all want to be free, fed, and safe. We need to get the children to safety and rescue Pedro, then get back to safety ourselves, and to do this successfully, we can't let the recent events break us. We have to move past it."

I let my words sink in, and Baby Lou babbles some more, trying to be in on the conversation. "We need to come together now," I continue. "Which also means fully accepting Smudge—"

"If we're going to fully accept her," Jax says, "then she's got some explaining to do."

"Exactly," Vila agrees.

"She doesn't have to explain anything to either of you," I tell them. "You've both been vicious and threatening. Whatever you want to know, I'll tell you, so you can get over your animosity toward her."

"Okay, where's she from?" Jax asks.

"The Other Side."

"Why did she lead us underground to the flesh-eating monsters?"

"She was trying to help us. She thought it was safe. An honest mistake."

Jax snuffs a disgusted laugh, but sucks it back when all eyes train on him, waiting for him to release his judgment. "Fine," he says. "An honest mistake. But what about everything else? That stuff she does with electricity?"

"That," I say, "is electro-telekinesis."

"Electro what?"

"She can manipulate electricity with her mind."

"That's not possible," he says.

"It is. You've seen it with your own eyes, all of us have."

"What a joke!" Vila yells. Tallulah scrambles over her shoulder, back into the knapsack.

"How is it possible then?" Jax asks. "Tell me."

I grin at Smudge, and then at Jax as I flitter my fingers in the air. "Magic."

"What? Joy, you don't even believe in magic!"

"Actually—" I sneak a glance at Mateo, see a twinkle in his eye. "I just became a believer."

TWENTY-FOUR

Jax and Vila aren't fooled. Even Aby seems suspicious. My bluff wasn't quite convincing enough this time, but it'll have to work for now. Once everyone's safely on the other side, I'll tell them the truth. Or, maybe Smudge will. When they see she's a good person, they might better accept that she's "not entirely human."

After a few games of charades, a couple of hours playing musical rooms to see whose bed is bounciest, and a back-and-forth relay race across the second floor balcony, we've killed enough time to get us to dinner. With the children fed, I'm ready to put them to bed so we can plan and prepare for our rescue mission.

But a few of the younger ones have other plans for me.

"Momma Joy?" Chloe says. As usual, they've nominated her to be their spokesperson.

"Yes, Chloe?"

"Can you tell a story tonight? Please? Pia's never heard a story before."

Pia's sad blue eyes and pouty lip beg me to end this story-deprived injustice as she tightly grips her new friend's hand. How could I say no?

"Okay, I'll tell one."

Cheers erupt behind them, surprising me. Even the olders seem excited. I suppose it's been a while since I've told one. They were used to one every night. Now they're missing them. Through all of this chaos, that's their stabilization: Momma

Joy will tell a story, and everything will be all right.

"You're a storyteller, too?" Mateo asks. "Wow. Is there anything you can't do?"

"A few things," I tease.

Vila rolls her eyes. "I'll be in my room," she says, and walks away. Without her knapsack on, for the first time, I notice her long slender neck and how sharply it contrasts her broad muscular shoulders. As if she'd been doing manual labor her whole life, like we have. Not surprising. A salt mine doesn't sound any less of a hell than the Tree Factory.

"Everyone get comfortable," I say. "I'll tell a short one tonight. But before I do, I have an announcement."

"We already know," says a boy. "Pedro is with the cannibals, and we're going to the Other Side so you can rescue him before he gets eaten."

"Yeah, we heard you guys talking," a girl says.

"Oh. Well. Word travels fast around here, doesn't it? And that's why I have to keep it short tonight; the olders will be planning and preparing, then we'll need plenty of sleep before we leave tomorrow. We don't know when we'll be able to sleep again, in beds at least."

Baby Lou gulps something called "coconut water" from her bottle, as content as I've ever seen her. But her weight's breaking my arms.

"Aby, can you take her?" I ask.

"Sure." The second Aby's arms are opened, Baby Lou goes to her.

With the release of her weight, I feel like I'm floating. Who knows how long I've been holding her, afraid to put her down in this place. Can't wait until we get to somewhere safe; to see that light at the end of the tunnel. The open sky that awaits us. Seems like the perfect place to pull tonight's story from.

Once everyone's comfortable, I close my eyes and try to forget about the new people. But Mateo's gaze burns into me, much more than the others', and my insides flutter. I wash the sensation away into the ocean that fills up my mind, deep and blue and magical, blanketed by cloud-dotted skies with no beginning or end. My story begins with a mermaid who soon discovers she can fly. Her wings are soft and feathery, painted with rainbows. The sky and the sea are both hers to fly in and swim free, in and out, up and around, as far as she can go, forever. In my mind's eye, there's a mountain peak hidden in the clouds where she likes to sit when she needs to rest. There, she can perch herself at the top of the world, pet the clouds and tell them stories of her life beneath the sea.

She is the Butterfly Mermaid.... After years of being free, she's lonely and bored with her infinite playland. She flies straight up for days, until she finally reaches where the blue sky meets the black of space. Once she gets there, she realizes she's actually at the bottom of the ocean. Infinity has circled back around, brought her to the beginning again. Was there something she missed? A reason she was cursed to be trapped in this illusion forever? Had she been born in the wrong world, the wrong time? Perhaps she was meant to live in another dimension, with others like her....

She weeps for days, and floats aimlessly, letting the current take her, seeing the clouds who were once her friends, passing by without a care. She wonders how she could've given up so easily. Surely, there's something more....

She's startled when her head bumps something. There, before her, lies an island, and in front of her hovers the most handsome butterfly merman.... She could never even imagine such a smile.... "Welcome home," he says, offering her his hand.

And at that moment she realizes, once she surrendered, letting the current take her, she was led home....

I embellish the story so much, I almost believe it's real and forget where I am, that horrible things happened today. That my life's been a mess of sorrow. I become the Butterfly Mermaid who's found an impossible light in the darkness, a hope she never realized she was without, until it found her.

I open my eyes, half-expecting faces glazed over by boredom. Instead, bright, excited ones stare back, starting beneath my nose. Chloe and Pia, and a few other youngers, moved closer during my imaginings.

"Did you enjoy the story?" I ask.

"Yes!" they cheer.

To my left, Mateo claps softly. "Well done! That was incredible. Where'd you come up with that?"

"When I was younger, my mother used to read me fairy tales, and when she died, my daddy taught me to read using his science-fiction books."

"They did well," Emerson says. "I've never heard a story like that before. You've got a gift, sister."

"Yes," says Smudge, "you do. That was fascinating."

"Yep, she's got an imagination on her, doesn't she?" says Johnny.

"Thanks." My cheeks warm. "Now it's time for bed, everyone."

The children groan and whine, but the collective yawning says their little bodies agree.

"Hey, no complaining," says Jax. "This'll probably be the best night's sleep you've ever had. These beds are—" He stops, realizing too late what he's about to imply. Instead, he shrugs, and mumbles, "Really comfortable."

Any anger that might want to resurface is diffused by

Mateo's staring at me in awe. I find it more invigorating than disturbing. No one's ever looked at me like that before. Like how you'd look at Heaven if you could inspect it with your naked eye, touch it delicately.

Serna and another older girl shuffle the younger ones into their correct rooms, while Aby disappears with Baby Lou into ours and Jax helps the boys remember which are theirs.

"I need to help tuck everyone in," I say to Mateo. "Where should we meet when we're done?"

"In my room—two-nineteen." He moves closer, lowers his voice. "I'll be waiting."

"I'll be there soon."

He brushes his fingers against my arm and chill bumps crawl across my skin. "See you soon."

"Where are we going to discuss things?" Johnny asks, sliding a hand into Smudge's. She hides a grin by bowing her head.

"Two-nineteen," I tell him. "You two can go ahead. I'll be along with Jax and Aby, once we get everyone situated, though I'll need to get Baby Lou to sleep first, so they may be in before me."

"Gotcha." He tips his hat, and he and Smudge head over to Mateo's room.

In my room, Aby has already tucked away Chloe, and another girl, and is changing Baby Lou into a fresh cloth diaper.

"I'm going to lie with Baby for a few minutes," I tell Aby. "It's a new place, and I don't want her rolling out of bed. Would you check the rest of the rooms and do a head count while I get her to sleep? We're meeting in two-nineteen to plan."

"Sure." She turns to walk out, a lingering guilt on her face.

"Aby?" She glances back, and I almost tell her I forgive her . . . but something won't let me do it. Not yet. "Never mind. I'll see you in two-nineteen."

"Okay. Joy?"

"Yes?"

"Do you think he's still alive?"

"Pedro? Yes."

"Do you really think we'll be able to rescue him?"

"Yes. I mean, I think so. Smudge will be with us…"

"Does she really control electricity with her mind, Joy? Is that the truth?"

"Yes."

A partial truth. The slightest bit of guilt creeps in, but Aby can't know yet, either; she's too unstable, and I wouldn't put it past her to tell Jax.

"Okay," she says with a sigh. "Whatever you say."

After she closes the door quietly behind her, the little girls in my room giggle and whisper softly between yawns and stretches. I kiss their foreheads, then slip into the musty, yet luxuriously comfortable sheets next to Baby Lou. She stinks. Wherever we end up tomorrow, I hope there's a washtub, decent soap, and an open fire, so she can have a warm bath.

Baby Lou bats at my face and lips as her eyelids grow heavy. I hum the song my mother used to hum to me every night, trying not to think about the last time I hummed it—to drown out Jax's sounds in the dungeon. But it's no use. My thoughts go there, and to the question he asked me, following the abuse by Emmanuel Superior.

So, you'll marry me then?

And in that moment, it was me and Jax, from then, until forever. If only we could be free, we'd get married and live out our fairytale, finding love and freedom beneath the pure blue sky.… Yet it was an artificial light, illuminating the darkness just long enough, giving us hope strong enough to motivate us to fight for survival and freedom. Hours later, with freedom came death, lies, lust, betrayal, and a long list of possible catastrophes. Most horrible of all is the sickening in my gut and the quickening of my heart that points to what my mind already suspects: that we're not even past the half of it.

I cuddle Baby Lou as she drifts off to sleep. Snoring from the second bed tells me the other two are asleep, as well. Dislodging my arm from beneath Baby Lou's neck, I rise slowly, tucking pillows to either side to keep her from rolling off. Then, I sneak out without a sound, closing the door behind me.

Out on the balcony, I'm startled to find Mateo waiting there. He smiles, raises an elbow—a handle for me to grab hold of. "I thought you might want an escort. You know, someone to protect you from the bad things?"

"Thank you." I smile nervously and, hooking my arm through his, we head toward his room.

"I wanted to tell you how much it means to Pia—and me—to have someone around to tell stories, and be kind of, you know, motherly. Ours died in labor with her. She's never had a mother figure."

"I'm so sorry to hear that."

He turns and kisses me, igniting an inferno inside, then pulls back, leaving me breathless, aching for more.

"You're a damn amazing girl," he says. "I . . . in case tomorrow doesn't go well . . . I needed to do that."

"Can you do it again?" I whisper.

He glances at me, then tugs me gently, swiftly, past two-nineteen, all the way to two-twenty-two. There, he opens the door, flips on the light and inspects it briefly, before whisking me inside. Instantly, our bodies fuse together against the closed door, like crashing waves against a hungry shore. Never in my life have I wanted to be so close to—so a part of—someone. After a few breathless minutes, I push away, as he clutches my body tightly against his. Together, we tremble with desire, and though I want nothing more than to spend a few hours alone with him, logically, that's not possible.

"We have to go," I pant, his lips a breath from mine.

"I know." And he kisses me again, with fierce passion, a downpour in paradise; an eternal freedom in his fingertips, which explore my skin like an excavated diamond. His lips are a safe harbor for all the love in the world. And he gives every bit of it to me.

I push away again, with so much thirst for him, it's painful. "Really," I say, "we have to. I don't want to, but we have to."

"Promise me we'll be alone together. After this is all over. Promise me."

"I promise. There's nothing I want more than that."

"Okay," he says. "Then, we have no choice now. We have to stay alive."

TWENTY-FIVE

MY HEART'S STILL RACING when Mateo and I exit the room. I don't know if what just happened will be a bigger motivator or a distractor. At the moment, it's accomplished both, simultaneously. On the one hand, I now have more reason not to get myself killed. On the other hand, I'm finding it hard to think about anything other than when we're finally free, what we'll do with our "alone time."

It's crazy I'm even thinking this, feeling this, about someone I just met. But no matter how much I want it to stop... I don't want it to. Makes no sense, but feels right. More right than anything has in a long time.

Mateo's fingers brush my hand as we approach two-nineteen. Soft talking echoes through the door, and he pauses to listen. Then, he sneaks a quick peck to my lips before clicking the handle. I shiver as he pushes the door open. Smudge, Johnny, Jax, Aby, Emerson, and Vila all wait for us inside. Little Pia has curled up, asleep in one of the beds. Tallulah peeks at us from a blanket-bed in the corner.

"What took you so long?" Jax asks, obviously suspicious.

"It took a while to get Baby Lou to sleep," I reply. "What have you discussed so far?"

"Well," says Vila, "you mean, other than how I'd take an afternoon stroll in the sunshine before I'd ever step foot back in that flipping salt mine? Or, how going back there's basically like putting yourself on the menu?"

"V," Emerson says.

"What?"

"Chill."

"I'm not going back there."

Mateo and I sit down at the foot of the bed his sister sleeps in. He clears his throat. "Vila, you know we can't do it without you—"

"I don't care! You people are insane! There's no way you'll get me to go back there, so don't even—"

"If you don't go," he says, "we might not make it out."

"Oh, don't you even try to pull that shit, Mateo. Don't go, then!" Her voice raises to a near-shout, stirring Pia.

"There's no need to yell," Mateo says. "Put yourself in their shoes. What if it was me, or Em there? Wouldn't you want someone to help get us out? There's no way they can do it alone; that place is a giant maze. And the Chamber is hidden. Not even the townspeople know how to access it."

"Then how did you find out where it was?" I ask.

"Vila's father and grandfather were both militia," he replies. "She knows everything about warlike situations, and how to escape from them. We wouldn't have made it out without her rat-like ability to creep around unnoticed."

"And now you want to go back." Vila shakes her head in disgust. "Unbelievable."

"We can talk more about the rescue later," I say. "We need to discuss taking the children to safety now. Smudge, how long do you think it'll take to get there on the trolley?"

"Depends on how well it travels with everyone's weight," she says. "Originally, I believe it was built for twenty-five people. We should be able to fit fine, though a few may have to sit on the floor."

"Is that how you got to the Tree Factory with all of the supplies?" I ask.

"Yes."

"How long did it take you?"

"Four hours, at top speed."

"You got the electricity to work with your electro... electro..." Emerson snaps his fingers.

"Electro-telekinesis?" she says.

"Yeah, that's it. Electro-tele... whatever. That."

"Yes, that is how. And since we are already halfway between Greenleigh and the Subterrane, I expect it'll take no more than three hours. We should be able to go seventy to eighty miles per hour."

"You know, I've been meaning to ask," Jax says. "Why the hell would a person want to go to Greenleigh anyway? It's a ghost town."

Smudge looks away. "My... grandmother... was an artist. She lived in Bunker B, where you first found me. Those were her paintings on the wall—the dry ones. The beautiful ones."

"They were all beautiful," I say. "Some were just darker than others."

"The darker ones were mine. I found her old paints in her quarters, still hidden beneath the tile flooring in a dug-out hole with... a few other things. First time I'd ever painted."

"Well, it was fantastic," I tell her. "You're a true artist."

"How did you know where her quarters were?" Jax asks.

"My... mother... told me." She fidgets with a shirt string, avoiding his gaze. I see the bluff a mile away, but everyone else buys it, except for Johnny and Mateo. They already know the truth. Smudge has no mother, or grandmother, for that matter.

"Did you take the trolley that time, too?" I ask.

"No. I went through the jungle—"

Vila laughs out loud, slaps her knee. "Yeah, right. I've heard about the creatures that live down there. There's no damn way you—"

"Why?" Jax says. "Why would you do that, when you could take the trolley?"

"When I left, I was... angry, and did not know how to deal with it. I went into the jungle... to die."

Silently, we stare at her, blatant truth in her gaze, which meets each of ours without waver.

"Then," she continues, "I remembered my grandmother, and what my mother had told me of her. My curiosity made me follow the river by day, and hide at night. I spent nearly two weeks following that river, until I finally found Greenleigh."

We all share another moment of silent awe, though Jax and Vila still remain skeptical.

"Well," says Mateo, "I'm sure I don't just speak for myself when I say this: I'm glad you decided to live. You're a great girl."

"Agreed," Emerson says.

Vila crosses her arms. "Electro Girl, I'll go, if you can prove that we're not gonna die."

"I'm not sure how I could... prove that to you," Smudge replies, "but I'm sure we stand a very good chance, if we work together. Besides, you aren't the only one who knows her way around the Subterrane."

"Oh, yeah?" Vila perks up, curious.

Smudge turns to me. "Those supplies I gave you—?"

"You got them from there?"

"I knew you'd need things when you were ready to leave, and transporting enough food and other items, as well as explosives, from Zentao would not have been possible."

"What's Zentao?" I ask.

"The Revols' city on the eastern coast."

"How did you know we'd be ready to leave when we did?"

"I didn't, exactly. But I hoped you would be soon. Bananas

only stay good for a short time."

"Mmm," Johnny says. "Bananas...."

"Hold on," says Vila. "You got into the supply room and stole food and explosives?"

"Yes. And water, and clothes. And a few dolls."

"Uh-huh. And how exactly did you do that?"

Smudge shrugs. "Magic?"

"Show us some magic, then," Vila insists.

Smudge's face flushes red with embarrassment. "I'd rather not."

"She doesn't need to prove anything," I say. "To you, or to anyone."

"Oh, yeah?" Vila steps forward, puffing out her chest.

"You don't scare us," I say.

"Vila, you seriously need to relax," says Emerson. "These people aren't our enemies."

"Whatever. I'm not going, unless Electro Girl here shows me something spectacular."

At this, Smudge stands tall, looking Vila fiercely in the eye. "If I were to show you something spectacular, then you would regret it. I assure you."

"Is that a threat, Sparky? Because I'm feeling very threatened right now." Vila cracks her knuckles, balls her fists. As if sensing her owner's vicious vibe, Tallulah hops up onto Vila's shoulder and hisses.

"You know, for someone who's supposed to be a nice girl," I say, "you're turning out to be quite the b—"

"She's scared," Smudge says. "And this is how she hides it. She's afraid of what's out there, of what she doesn't understand. The only way she knows to handle her fear is to attack those who compromise her safety. Those who she is not able to fully grasp . . . or control."

Vila's face turns bright red, and she squeezes her fists so tight, her knuckles turn white. She marches to the door, swings it open hard, the handle punching a hole in the wall behind it. Tallulah scrambles back into her knapsack.

Smudge looks down at her hands.

"Wow," Mateo says. "You showed her who's boss."

"That wasn't my intention. I only wanted to remove the veil that obstructs reason—the illusion brought on by denial. Once light is shed on it, there's no going back to hiding. Now that I've shined the light on her fears, they have less power over her. Over us. She'll come around, eventually."

"You're brilliant," I say.

"What's interesting," Smudge says, "is that figuring others out seems simple. But as far as my own emotions go... not so... brilliant."

Emerson stretches his legs. "That's the truth for all of us, sister. You know, you hit it on the nose, though. About Vila. She will come around. Give her time, she's a fighter. She may say she won't go, but she will. She'll be right there, out in front, leading the way. She hates not being the leader. Probably one reason she's having a hard time. Competition. She calls a lot of the shots around here, but now she's gotta share that, and she has to adjust."

"So," Aby speaks out of her silence. "We leave in the morning?"

"Yes," I reply. "We'll wake up, eat, get packed, and then get out of here."

§

Of course, when I finally get to bed next to Baby Lou, I can't sleep. My mind keeps switching from visions of the Reaper killing Miguel, to my kissing Mateo, to our finding Jax and Aby together. So much has happened in the last twenty-four hours, it doesn't even seem possible for one day.

"How are you?" Smudge asks from the floor between our two beds.

"Weird," I say. "Too many thoughts and emotions. Makes it near-impossible to sleep."

"I wouldn't know."

"You don't sleep?"

"I rest. But no, I do not sleep. My mind and body are constantly regenerated. OAIs have no need for sleep, but it does us good to rest here and there."

"You are so intriguing. I could ask you questions for hours, and not get bored of your answers."

"I'd like that. But I do believe your human body might feel otherwise."

I yawn, then giggle, which makes her giggle, too. "Yeah, true. Can I ask you one question, though?"

"Sure."

"Have you figured guilt out yet?"

"That's a difficult one. I'm still… struggling with it. No matter how much I logically know and reasonably explain things to it, it insists on resisting."

"I kissed Mateo," I say.

"Really? What was it like?"

"Amazing. But now, I feel guilty. Miguel just died, and then that thing with Jax and Aby…. So, maybe I shouldn't have done that. Like, bad timing or something."

"You know, Joy, I'm learning something fascinating about humans: they're creatures of comfort. When they experience negativity, they seek out comfort. I see nothing wrong with you finding comfort in Mateo. He seems like a nice boy."

"But, I just met him."

"Humans don't trust their intuition enough. Don't get me wrong, I'm not saying what Jax and Aby did was... acceptable. I understand why they did it, though. But, as far as you and Mateo...? The energy between you two is remarkable. You are extremely compatible."

"You can tell? I mean, you can feel it?"

"Yes. I am very receptive to vibes and energy. That's how I knew what was going on with Vila. So much of the human body is energy—positive, negative. It's very easy for me to read people."

I smile into the dark. "Thank you, Smudge. I feel better, hearing you say all of that."

"You're welcome," she says. "What are friends for?"

§

I wake to Baby Lou crying in a puddle of wetness, diaper soaked through completely. At first, I forget where we are. Then, I see Smudge, smiling at me from where she sits against the wall, and everything floods back. The two other girls sleep soundly in the second bed.

"What time is it?" I ask, and pick Baby Lou up from her wet spot.

"Six a.m., and I made more diapers while you were asleep." She hands me a tall stack of white cloth squares.

"How did you—?"

"I used a bed sheet from a few rooms down. Should be enough to make it to Zentao. They'll have plenty more once we get there. Ms. Ruby is a wonderful caretaker. Baby will be well cared for, along with the rest of the children."

"Ms. Ruby?" I repeat. "Can't wait to meet her." I pour water from a bottle on the bedside table onto a cloth square, clean Baby Lou up, then tie another cloth around her.

"Ee, ee," she says.

"What, Baby?"

She cries, frustrated I don't know what she's saying.

"She's never talked before," I tell Smudge.

"Is she saying 'eat'?"

"Ee!" she cries again.

Smiling, Smudge holds up a can and a spoon. "I thought she might be hungry when she woke up."

I take them both, and read the label. "Squash? That's a funny name."

"I think she'll like it."

"She'll like anything, after eating slop her whole life." I peel back the lid, dip in the spoon, and shiver. For the past few years of my life, I've been eating nutrient-fortified recycled human. My stomach lurches from the remembrance of its taste, texture, and smell. Thank God we didn't know the truth about it, though. Otherwise, we might've all died of starvation long ago.

"What about you? Do you eat?" I ask, scooping a spoonful of orange, lumpy mush into Baby Lou's already open mouth.

"Yes, but it's not necessary on a daily basis. If I eat once a week, my body will sufficiently store enough nutrients."

Baby Lou grabs the spoon, stuffs it down into the can. Yes, she definitely likes the squash.

"She's precious," Smudge says.

Her words resurface a fear I've tried desperately to hide. Of all people, though, I think Smudge could call my bluffs.

"What's wrong?" she asks, as if on cue. "You're afraid

for her?"

I nod. "But I shouldn't be, right? Because you said the tunnels were safe?"

"Well... safe from the Reapers, yes."

"And not safe from...?"

Smudge shakes her head. "It's possible, but not probable."

"What?"

"That we may run into Arianna Superior."

"You think we will?"

"I don't *think* so. With the Tree Factory gone, I believe she'd have no choice but to beg Lord Daumier to let her stay in his Alzanei Monastery. It wouldn't make much sense for her to be down here, unless..."

"Unless what?"

"Unless he turned her away. In which case, she may be very angry. She may be looking for you."

Heart in my throat, I help Baby Lou finish off half of the squash, until she reaches for her bottle lying next to Millie in the bed. I set the can onto the table and hand her both. She hugs Millie and gulps her water, snuggling against my side.

"Could you stun her?" I ask.

"Arianna Superior? Probably. But I'm not sure what she's capable of. Her mechanical modifications are extensive."

Now the thing in the office makes sense—her stretching for the medicine bottle—and her overall strangeness that's increased over the years.

"Well," I say. "Let's hope he accepts her, then."

"Yes. Let's hope."

I wake the other little girls and help them change into fresh clothes, pack all of our belongings, then give them the half-can of squash to finish up.

"I'll be back." I walk to the door. "I need to make sure

everyone else is up and okay."

Smudge waves at me, sitting next to Baby Lou. "We'll be here."

Out on the balcony, Mateo's looking over the lobby jungle and turns when he hears my door close. His hair's slicked back, showing his handsome features that much more. My stomach flutters.

"Morning," he says.

"Morning. Your hair's wet. Did you wash it somewhere?"

"Yeah, you remember the pool?" He points downstairs.

"You went in there? *Alone*?"

"Yeah. So, I guess I'm immortal now."

"Funny." I step up beside him at the railing. My arm slides against his.

He glances at it, then stares back out across the lobby. "Do you want to wash? I have soap and a towel. I'll stand at the door and keep watch—"

"No, thanks. I'd rather wait. As intriguing as that pool is, it totally creeps me out."

"Aw, come on." He grins, side-glancing. "Don't you wanna live forever with me?"

I giggle. "Yeah, but…"

He slips a hand into his pocket and takes out a glass flask containing a thick pale-yellow liquid. "You sure?" he says. "This stuff is straight from the Monastery. Vila snuck right into the Queen's chambers and stole it out from under her nose." He twists off the silver lid, waves the bottle under my own nose. The most divine scent ever calls me to the pool.

"Mmm. That smells great," I say.

"It smells even better on skin."

"Oh, yeah?" I move closer to breathe in the fragrance radiating from his bare chest, which I inspect for the first time. Not only do I melt from the aroma, but my knees also shake from the desire to run my fingers along Mateo's sculpted muscles. The ripples that call my name. The arms and shoulders that have seen thousands of hours of hard labor. The rough hands that turn velveteen because of his gentle touch. These things clog my mind as I try to form words. I pivot to grip the railing, too overwhelmed with longing.

"You okay?" he asks, chuckling.

I nod. "You'll have to save some of that for me. I don't want to leave this floor until it's time to head out."

"I'll save it for that alone time you promised me," he whispers with a wink, and tucks the flask back into his pocket.

My face and body burn with embarrassment and yearning, until a door closes behind me. Jax and his younger boys are packed and ready to go. He nods at Mateo, though his eyes linger on me.

"Can I talk to you?" he says.

"For a minute. I want to get everyone out of here as quickly as possible." Leaving Mateo, I follow Jax to the top of the stairs, where I inspect the rotted red carpet and gold railing laced with vines, waiting for him to speak. Yet he only stands there silently. "You... wanted to talk to me?" I ask.

He whips toward me, fury in his face. "I was stupid, Joy. I screwed up. I couldn't sleep last night because I kept thinking about how you... you never said it back."

"Said what back?"

"I told you I loved you, in the dungeon. Did you never love me, Joy? Because I thought you did...."

I turn away. In my silence, the children's stirring in their rooms is deafening. Golden birds sway above us on their chains, while high above the purple dome, a cloud snuffs out the sun, casting a gloomy shadow at the perfect time.

"Say something," he says.

"I made a mistake, too." And I look him dead in the eye. "Because you were my best friend, and it should've stayed that way."

"But, Joy, I—"

"Jax, no. I wish things hadn't turned out the way they did, but they did, and there's no going back. I'm sure I'll eventually forgive you and Aby—probably soon because you both mean a lot to me. But you and I weren't meant to be more than friends. I see that now."

"Joy—"

"I'd rather not talk about this anymore. It's time to focus on what we have to accomplish today."

"It's him, isn't it? Your new 'friend'?"

"No, he has nothing to do with this."

"Oh come on, you're not fooling anyone. I've seen the way you look at each other. Tell me the truth. If you're my friend, then be honest with me. Do you have feelings for him?"

"I barely know him—"

"*Do you?*"

"Okay, yes. I do. Is that what you want to hear? I know it's crazy, but I can't help it. Kind of how you and Aby couldn't help it, I guess."

Those last words cut him deep. With a wounded heart displayed on his face, he walks away.

"Jax, wait."

He stops, but doesn't turn. Mateo watches on from where I left him. The words forming now in my mouth taste sour. Still, I force them out as I reach his side.

"I think you and Aby are better for each other anyway," I say.

He grinds his teeth behind his cheek, looks me in the eye. "I don't want her." Then, he storms away, slams the door to his room.

A sniffle off to my right catches my attention. Teary blue eyes peek out from a nearby door opened a couple of inches. Then, that door slams, too.

TWENTY-SIX

I TRY TO IGNORE THE AWKWARDNESS as we line all of the children up on the balcony. But Aby stands at the far end of the line, with Jax a few people up from her, and Mateo on the near end. Not exactly the best way to begin the day, but we'll have to work around it. Even my feelings for Mateo have been subdued in the light of our mission. I have to focus. Too many lives balance in my hands to let a small thing like this clog my mind and cloud my judgment.

"What do you need me to do?" Smudge asks.

"Can you wait here with Baby Lou and the youngers, while I help Emerson, Johnny, and Vila with the weapons?"

"Sure."

I head to the weapons room, where the three of them disappeared to load up the spears and things. Mateo follows me in.

"Everything okay?" he asks.

"Yeah."

Emerson finishes securing a bundle of spears with twine, while Vila practices throwing the silver kitchen knives. At least a hundred holes dot the wall across the room. Tallulah peeks at me through the semi-tied opening of the knapsack.

"You've decided to join us?" I ask Vila. "You and Tallulah?"

"Do I have a choice?" She makes a face like I'm ignorant and removes the knives from the wall. "And Tallulah goes where I go."

"We have eight spears," says Emerson.

"Three bolts." Johnny taps his crossbow. "And three knives."

"And Smudge," I say.

"Oh, she's classified as a weapon now?" Vila snarls. "What, is she a god or something?"

"Of sorts," I say smartly. "Come on, let's get out of here. We have everything else packed, and the children are lined up."

"Listen," Emerson says. "We ain't cleared the twentieth floor—at all. Might be bloodbugs there, but they move slow. As long as you're not sleeping, they aren't much of a threat. As far as we know, there shouldn't be anything else dangerous. But we'll keep the knives and two spears handy, just in case."

"I'll take a spear," Mateo says.

Emerson grabs one of two leaning against the wall, and tosses it to him.

"I'll have to carry Baby Lou," I say, "but I'm sure Jax will be fine with the other spear, or a knife—"

"Are you kidding?" Johnny says. "He's got murder in his eyes. I think we're better off keeping the weapons distributed right here."

"Yeah, true."

"We'll go up the elevator in groups," says Vila. "Mat and I will stay on twenty with the knives and a spear, while everyone else comes up."

"Sounds good," I say.

Emerson picks up the spear bundle and a giant brown duffel bag. Vila peeks into her knapsack's tightened opening and makes a clicking noise. Tallulah's nose pokes through, and Vila touches it with her own. Then, she tucks her three knives in a makeshift knife-belt, while Johnny slings his crossbow over one shoulder and his backpack over the other. We file out, and I find my bag by the railing, locate Baby Lou's sling and tie it around me. Smudge tucks Baby Lou down inside it.

"Hold her in place while I tighten the knot," I say.

Smudge does, and I loosen the knot enough to retie it tighter. Once Baby Lou's secured, I affix my daddy's magic bag and Baby Lou's own bag to my shoulder, then do a quick headcount. Chloe and Pia have become joined at the hip. Chloe's even shared her doll. Aby gazes melancholically into emptiness, as if she has nothing left to live for. Again, the urge swells inside to tell her I forgive her, though I don't know why I don't. Perhaps because it's sharply contrasted by the urge to scream at her.

"Everyone make sure you've made your beds and gathered all of your belongings," I say.

Cover your tracks.

Always be prepared.

"And have your breathers in ready-position on your heads," I add.

"That's stupid!" a girl says. "Why do we have to make our beds?"

"Yeah," a boy adds. "We're not even coming back here."

"Just do it, please. We don't want it obvious that we were here. In case anyone comes… looking for us."

A few children scramble back into their rooms to hastily make their beds, and I do a quick check for belongings. "Okay," I say. "We're all clear and ready to move out."

Mateo and Vila, followed by me and Baby Lou, Smudge and Emerson, head the group toward the hotel elevator. Johnny must've noticed Aby's sadness, too. He passes up Jax on his way to her, and whispers softly, giving Aby a nudge with his elbow. The hint of a smile fades in the blink of an eye. She stares past him, over the balcony railing, with dreamy, lackluster eyes, as if trying to imagine what a free fall down into the lobby jungle would be like.

The elevator door opens before we get to it.

"How in the hell?" Vila says. "Did you do that, Electro Girl?"

She nods. "It was the… polite thing to do."

Vila shakes her head. "You're a weirdo. I'm not sure if I like you yet."

"That's okay," says Smudge. "Em says you'll come around." And she shares a grin with Emerson.

"That's right," he agrees. "Now, you and Mat go up with a few others. We'll send another group as soon as the elevator returns."

Vila and Mateo and a few children, board the elevator, and the door closes between us. A couple of minutes later, it returns, and we load the next group. After that, Jax goes up with his group, and then it's down to me, Smudge, Emerson, Aby, Chloe and Pia, and two younger boys—the same two the new kid told I was going to eat them all.

"You boys okay?" I ask.

They nod, though obviously frightened.

"Hey, you boys are gonna be fine," says Emerson. "I have a good feeling about it."

"How's the air in the tunnels?" I ask Smudge.

"The trolleys have filtration systems," she says. "We should be fine. But good to have the oxygen masks… just in case."

The elevator returns, and we climb on. A minute later, we step off onto the twentieth floor and join the rest of our group. Ahead are raggedy gold doors with circular windows, and to their left hangs a chiseled sign: Trolley Platform, this way. Traveling to Greenleigh – four Blue Notes. Traveling to Northeast Subterrane – six Blue Notes. Please make sure you have acquired from the lobby adequate Blue Notes for your travels.

Vila and Mateo push open the doors to a long, dark corridor that doesn't stay dark for long. After a few seconds of staring down it, Smudge has it lit up like daylight, complete with green oxygen lights.

"You sure come in handy," says Emerson.

"She does, doesn't she?" Johnny gives Smudge a pat on the arm.

We move down the long bright tunnel, the sound of our shoes shuffling on the concrete, until an arched exit appears ahead of us. Beyond it lies a wide-open darkness spotted with lights in a high ceiling. When we reach it, I'm shocked by the platform's massive size. Three trolleys sit idle; two blue ones before the tunnel to the right, and a red one before the left tunnel. They're smaller than the boat, but larger than I imagined.

"We came in on one of the blue ones," Mateo says. "That's the tunnel that heads northeast. The other goes southwest."

"Since we know the one you four brought here works, we'll take that one back," I say.

"Number seven." Emerson points. "Right there."

"Lucky number seven," I mutter.

Emerson grips a fat black handle and yanks up. Dry metal screeches as he slides the door open. Smudge inspects the cables above, immersed in concentration. A moment later, they spark to life, and the trolley lights turn on. She grins, rubs her hands together.

"I was worried there for a second," she says. "Took longer than I expected."

"Woo!" Emerson jumps up. "You're my new best friend, Smudge!"

"Electro Girl saves the day again," Vila mumbles.

Everyone crowds into the snug trolley car and we fill the overhead compartments with as many bags as we can, piling the rest behind the trolley operator's wall. We all fit perfectly, with only a couple of the youngest sitting in laps, and four boys on the floor in the middle.

Emerson closes the door. "Okay, who's sailing this ship?"

"I think you should," Mateo says. "You seemed pretty comfortable driving it here."

"You sure you don't want to?" he asks.

"No, you go ahead."

Emerson wipes sweat from his forehead with a bare arm. "I'll be your captain, if no one objects." He glances around at the silent faces, then hops into the driver's seat, next to a T-shaped handle protruding up from a floor groove.

"I'll need to ride up front next to Emerson," says Smudge, "to maintain a strong electrical flow. These cable connections are questionable."

"Could you take out Baby Lou and hand her to me first, though?" I ask.

"Sure." She lifts Baby from the sling, hands her to me, and I survey to see where I'll fit. Interestingly, the only spare seat left is next to Mateo. He tries to hide his satisfaction as he inches closer to the boy on his other side to allow me more room.

"Is that enough?" he asks. "I can sit on the floor—"

"No, it's fine." And I squeeze between him and Chloe and Pia, who giggle. Suddenly, I realize the open seat next to Mateo wasn't a coincidence. The girls whisper, and it makes me smile. "What are you two telling secrets about over there?" I ask.

"Nothin'," Chloe says, giggling again.

"Uh-huh."

Emerson flips a few switches, and the panel in front of him brightens with multi-colored flashing lights. Smudge instructs him on how to operate it now that electricity will guide it, and he takes a breath. "Hold on, children!" With the thrust forward of a small, square handle, the trolley jerks into motion. Vila sits cross-legged on the floor behind the operator's wall, beside the pile of belongings, Tallulah's knapsack in her lap. The drawstring's been loosened enough for Tallulah to stick her head out. Vila stares off into space.

Baby Lou cries. She's never been in anything like this before.

"Shh, Baby, it's okay." I caress her, hold her snug against my chest, and when I catch Jax looking at me, he turns his head. Johnny sits awkwardly next to Aby, like he doesn't know what to say to fix her. She's broken beyond repair. She tightens the head scarf, tucks a strand of mutilated red hair back up into its hiding spot.

Baby Lou's crying slows to a whimper as we pick up speed. She's mesmerized by the wall on the other side—dots of yellow and green lights have become thin, wavy lines. Ahead, tunnel lights turn on seconds before we reach them, with the distant portions still black. Smudge holds onto the railing above her to steady herself while she focuses forward.

"How did you get to Gomorrah Grande in the dark?" I ask Mateo.

"When the manual pump is used, it generates electricity for the headlamp on the front of the car. Horrible lighting, though it worked well enough. But this is great! We'll get there in no time."

Most of the trip is silent, though dotted with quiet conversations here and there. Smudge hasn't taken her eyes from the tunnel ahead in almost three hours. Occasionally, lights surge and flicker, and I hold my breath. It's nerve-wracking to only see a hundred feet in front of us. A white sign on the wall rushes by us in a blur. I try to read it, but we're moving too fast.

"We're almost to the platform for the Subterrane," Mateo says.

Smudge whispers something into Emerson's ear, and the trolley begins to slow. We pass a large archway to our right that reads: Subterrane Station. Then, a couple hundred yards later, Smudge breaks her focus to turn around. "Everyone hold on." Then, a section of the track drops down, and we're swallowed by the ground, coming to an immediate stop. Out the windows, blackness surrounds us.

"What's happening?" I ask.

"Sensory deprivation lift," Smudge says. "It protects the location of Zentao. You can't tell, but we are actually moving relatively quickly."

"Well, it sure feels like we're not going anywhere," Vila says.

"This part can take a few minutes," Smudge explains, "or longer, depending on the guards operating the lift. An alarm sounds when the lift is loaded, and if no one's standing by, it takes a few minutes for them to get to their posts. Zentao is heavily guarded, but they do not stand by the lift. There are... not many visitors."

"Sounds more like prison than freedom," Jax mumbles.

"Unfortunately, the protection is necessary. Invaders from Alzanei will stop at nothing to learn the location of Zentao. It's hidden extremely well, but safety precautions are still taken."

Maybe twenty minutes later, a light from outside interrupts the complaining children and Vila's rants, appearing through huge double doors swinging open. Strangely dressed young men aim guns at the trolley and circle slowly around us. Smudge waves at someone approaching behind them—a man with white hair and a beard to match, wearing a large brown hat and a vest. With kind eyes, he smiles warmly at Smudge, and orders his men to lower their guns.

Smudge meets him at the door, which opens, and she immediately stares at the ground.

"You decided to come back, I see," he says. His voice is soothing, like the brush of a warm hand.

"I did," she says. "And I hope you don't mind, but I brought refugees. All children. Escapees from the Tree Factory of Greenleigh."

He pokes his head in and offers every face in the trolley a grin only a man with a golden soul could give. "Well, I'll be. . . . Just when we were thinking all was lost for the human race. . . ." He waves. "Hi, children."

A few say hello, but most are too terrified to move.

"We've been through a lot," I say. "Two of our brothers died, and . . . we've been forced to build trees for years. Our youngest worker is five, and Baby Lou here, she's only a year-and-a-half old. We can work; clean, build. Jax is great with electric stuff. We can earn our place. I promise we won't be a lot of trouble—"

"Nonsense," he says. "You're children. You may as well be royalty around here. Now, come on, all of you. Let's get you out of this filthy trolley and into the village. Ms. Ruby's going to need someone to hold her up when she gets a look at you all. For months, she's been praying for a miracle. And here you are."

Something far behind him makes me teary-eyed. Past the young men with the guns stands another door, ajar, and through it, blue. . . .

"Sky?" I ask, pointing.

He smiles. "Sure is."

"The . . . air is safe here?"

"Yes, ma'am."

I rise with Baby Lou, echoed by Mateo. "Let's go, everyone."

They don't need a second invitation. They scramble to grab their stuff, and soon, we file off of the trolley into the small, dim bunker. The little ones scream with delight as they fly toward the open door. Emerson and Vila, with Tallulah's knapsack tied shut, along with Jax and Johnny, remain cautious, scoping out the area as we walk. Aby rushes ahead with the children, and Smudge, Mateo, and I hang back with the white-bearded man as his guards form a line behind us.

"Don't go too far!" I yell to the children.

"It's okay," the man says. "I promise you, they're safe."

They disappear through the doorway, and someone gives the door a push. It swings open wide. Outside lies a sandy beach beneath a crystal-blue sky, on the edge of a vast blue ocean, much like the one we went to through the portal.

"How...?" I whisper.

The man chuckles. "Welcome to Zentao."

"Raffai, this is Joy," Smudge says. "And that's Mateo."

Raffai shakes both of our hands. "The pleasure's all mine."

"We can't stay," I say. "Not all of us. Not yet."

He glances at me, concerned, as we reach the doorway, where he relieves his guards. They disappear around the side of the building. A warm, sweet gust of wind swirls around us. Already the children have tossed their bags in the sand and are rolling around in it or splashing in the waves. To our left, strange-looking living quarters made of sticks and greenery—like the hut on the other side of the portal—are stacked along a hill, which slopes up into a dense forest. At the top of the slope, maybe a half-mile away, looms a massive wall with green lights shining up from it into the heavens.

The Wall.

I can't believe it. We're finally on the other side of it.

"You... can't stay?" Raffai asks.

"Their brother is being held captive in the Subterrane," Smudge says. "They have plans to leave the children here, where it's safe, and go rescue him. I plan to go with them. If you'll allow it."

We stop walking, and Raffai studies us. The end of a blonde braid peeks up from his pocket.

"Sadie, you know you're a free soul now," he says. "You—"

"Smudge."

"Beg your pardon?"

"Please, call me Smudge."

"Uh... okay... Smudge. You can do what you want, but I'll say it anyway: I don't like the idea. Those people are heathens. I mean, they're cannibals, for dung's sake."

"Yes, and they plan to eat our brother when he turns twenty-five," I say. "We *are* going; there's no way we're not. Please, try to understand."

After another long moment of studying me, Raffai nods. "I can't go with you; I have the people, and my granddaughter, to care for, though I can let you borrow a few decent weapons." He tickles Baby Lou's chin. "And we can definitely offer the children a safe place to stay. But a nice meal, medical attention, a bath, and a good night's rest might do you all good before you go."

Mateo gently nudges my side with his elbow.

"Okay," I say. "But in the morning, we go."

TWENTY-SEVEN

ONCE WE'VE GATHERED UP ALL OF THE CHILDREN from the beach, and Aby from her spot alone down the shore, we follow Raffai up a rocky path and past a handful of cozy little huts with people gawking through windows. Like they've never seen children before. A man cooking something on a metal grate above a fire burning in a shallow sand pit smiles, waves, and turns the blackened thing over in the curling flames. It looks nauseatingly similar to a jumper, minus the head, tail, and fur.

Up the hill, past a few more huts and clusters of trees with fruit possibly growing on them, stands a large building. It's different from the others; not made from sticks and greenery, but stone and iron, rising three stories into the sky. As I follow it up, my gaze drifts off into the impossible blue. It's all so surreal.

Of course this would all be hard to conceive, after living the lives we have. It seems too good to be true.

Raffai rings a gold bell by the front door, next to a sign that reads: Zentao Children's and Medical Center. The children bubble over with excitement. I've never seen them this happy. Even Johnny has managed a smirk from Aby when he picks a tiny pink flower from a small bush and tucks it into her scarf. Vila and Emerson stand off to the side—Vila, skeptical as usual; Emerson, trying to calm her down. Jax sits on an enormous rock, gripping his spear like we're in enemy territory. Maybe I was wrong about him and Aby; he and Vila would be a better match.

Raffai rings the bell again. "Ms. Ruby must be upstairs," he says.

I scan the surroundings until I notice a blue-and-brown hut with a brightly painted sign: Cheyenne's – Zentao's Finest Hand-Painted Shells. "What's that place?" I ask.

"Oh, I love Cheyenne's," Smudge says. "She's an amazing artist. That's where I got the idea for—" She stops abruptly. "Never mind."

"Idea for what?"

The door to the stone and iron building swings open to a thin woman with warm brown skin and eyes to match. Her long braids nearly reach the floor. When she sees us, she drops to her knees, gripping the door handle, and begins to cry. She covers her mouth with a wrinkled hand. "Oh my goodness...."

"Your prayers have been answered, Ms. Ruby," Raffai says.

She breathes in deep, and wipes her eyes with a floral-print apron. Then, she rises, trembling, from the floor. "They sure have," she says. "I never seen ana-ting more beautiful in my whole life."

"I'm Joy," I say, and hold out my hand for her to shake.

But she doesn't shake my hand. Instead, she folds me up in her arms and squeezes, like I'm her long-lost daughter. "Joy," she repeats. Then, she laughs from deep in her belly as she holds me at arm's length. "Of course you are! And who is dis precious little one?" She tickles one of Baby Lou's bare feet, making her giggle.

"This is Louanne. But we call her Baby Lou."

"Well, she's a perfect angel. Please... come in, *come in!*" She motions for us to enter.

"Thank you." I cross the threshold onto soft flooring. Carpet. And not rotted, either. We've seriously ended up in paradise.

"Everyone introduce yourselves to Ms. Ruby as you come in," I announce. "And wipe your feet on the mat, so you don't track dirt onto the carpet."

"Oh, don't ya worry 'bout that," Ms. Ruby says. "Down the hall and to the right is the common area. We can go there 'til we get rooms assigned. I'll have Suellen bring food and tea. I'm sure you could all use a good meal."

"We definitely can," I reply, as we step into the cozy lobby area. Its smells remind me of sweets and love. From a small, round glass table in front of a couch, a tiny candle flickers. On the wall above hangs a black-and-white picture of smiling, laughing children.

"Hello, Sadie." Ms. Ruby gives Smudge a hug.

"It's Smudge now," she offers with a smile.

"Smudge? Well, okay then. Welcome home, Smudge." She gently pats her on the back and sends her my way.

Mateo offers his hand. "I'm Mateo."

"No," Ms. Ruby says, giggling. "I don't shake hands; Ms. Ruby's a hugger." And she embraces him, sends him in my direction with a loving pat on the back.

Some of the older boys stiffen at her words, though it's obvious that's not going to stop her. Ms. Ruby may be the most compassionate soul that has ever existed on the planet.

I start slowly down the hallway with Baby Lou, Smudge, and Mateo, followed by the trickling group of children once they've introduced themselves to Ms. Ruby and gotten their welcome hug. Jax and Vila nod and move swiftly past her open arms, but Emerson makes up for it by wrapping Ms. Ruby into his own arms and lifting her from the ground. She squeals with delight, and he kisses her cheek, setting her down softly.

"Thank you so much for taking us in," he says. "These children deserve a good life. And it seems like you have that here."

"That we do," she says. "But don't ya be mistaken, 'tis you children who're the blessings here."

Emerson heads down the hallway toward us, as Raffai talks to Ms. Ruby quietly by the door, no doubt explaining how we all ended up here.

We arrive at a huge room with creamy walls lined with couches of all shapes, sizes, and patterned hues. An enormous rectangular window overlooks the ocean and the midday sun sitting in a sky dappled with clouds. In the middle of the area stand a couple dozen odd-shaped tables with mismatched chairs, flowers adorning vibrant vases set at their centers. Beneath a strange, flat black-and-silver square resting on a metal arm extended from the wall in one corner, sits a mountain of colorful pillows. One by one, the children run, screaming and laughing, into the room, around and around in circles, half of them finally landing in the pillows.

The olders separate into groups, sitting on couches and at tables, eyeing the common room like they've stepped into a fantasy land. We may as well have. This is the most color and comfort we've seen all in one place—ever.

Jax and Vila take seats in the far corner by themselves. Tallulah's knapsack lies on the table in front of Vila, opened enough for the animal to peek out and inspect her surroundings.

Baby Lou squirms in my arms, kicking her feet. Out of habit, I hold her tight, but then realize... I can put her down. My eyes swim with tears as I set her on the floor. She claps and chatters with delight. And I cry. She toddles away, toward the corner where most of the children have ended up, and I struggle to keep my emotions at bay. But seeing her free to roam... even as she stumbles, and rises up again to continue onward with a carefree grin on her face... in this moment, I know we've done the right thing. Even if we fail in our rescue mission for Pedro, we've accomplished what's most important.

The children are safe.

Smudge, Mateo, and I sit at one of the larger tables, after which Emerson joins us and Johnny leads Aby over, despite her want to mope around and act pathetic. Though I feel slightly guilty for thinking it, perhaps that's why it's hard for me to forgive her. Her weakness makes me want to vomit. It goes against everything inside me. She's not who I thought she was. She's different.

Or maybe… I'm different now. The last few days' events have awakened me to so many things. I don't see her—or Jax—the way I once did.

"Oh, how excitin'!" Ms. Ruby says from the doorway. "Suellen! Come an' meet our new arrivals!"

Seconds later, a tall young woman with short brown hair and glasses enters the room. She smiles, though it's reserved. Something dark hides behind it. I see it immediately.

"Children," Ms. Ruby says, "this here is Ms. Suellen. She helps out in the kitchen, and wit' the linens and tings. She'll also be around if ya need ana-ting else and ya can't find me. The whole right wing, including the two upper levels are the children's area. Level two is the girls' floor, and level three is the boys'. The left wing is the medical facility. After everyone eats themselves a good meal, we'll get ya all checked out by a nurse. Then, we'll get ya assigned to your rooms and started on breathing treatments—"

"Breathing treatments?" I repeat.

"Yes, dear. With that poison you all been breathin' your whole lives, it's twice-da-miracle you're all standin' here. We been tryin' to get the remaining children of Bygonne over here for years, but they wouldn't have it. Went so far as to tell us there weren't ana-more children. But we knew it was a lie."

She retreats into her thoughts, face hardening in anger. Then, it relaxes, and she returns to us, gaze dancing across everyone in the room. "But here ya are now. A miracle. And with nice, fresh oxygen, you'll all be feeling good as new by mornin'."

"Sounds great," I say. "Thank you so much, Ms. Ruby."

"You are so welcome, dear. Oh, and Raffai will be back in a bit. He had some tings to take care of." She winks. He must've told her we were leaving.

Ms. Ruby talks low to Suellen, who nods and leaves the room.

"She'll be back soon with the lunch cart," Ms. Ruby says. "Fill up much as ya can. If ya eat it all and want more, please, don't hesitate to ask. But don't make yourselves sick eating too fast. A little at a time. Your poor bellies prob'ly aren't used to a lot. Remember, there's always more later." She straightens her apron down over a long purple-and-brown woven gown. "Now" —she claps her hands together—"I need to notify the medical staff. I'll be back soon. Make yourselves comfortable."

She picks up something long and black from a small table by the door. "Here's the remote, in case ya want to watch TV." She tosses it to me, and I stare down, confused, at the rows of multi-colored buttons with strange words on them.

"What's TV?" someone asks.

"Ya mean... ya don't know television?" she says.

I shake my head. "I've seen the word in books, but no, we have no clue."

"Oh, well! You children are in for a treat! Come wit' me."

At the pile of pillows she takes the "remote" back, and we all watch curiously as she points it at the flat black-and-silver square on the metal arm. A second later, the square lights up with moving pictures and sound. Everyone is instantly captivated. I have no words to describe what I see. Little...

monsters... cute and furry, dancing around, singing about sharing. Baby Lou shrieks and glances around frantically. When she sees me, she stumbles over, hands held high.

"Shh, Baby, it's okay." I pick her up and rock her. "That's television. It won't hurt you."

"You?" she says, gasping for breath.

"No, it won't hurt you."

She peeks back, and with the fading of the initial shock, her eyes are glued to the television, along with everyone else's.

"How does it work?" I ask Ms. Ruby.

"Oh, I wouldn't be able to tell ya that, dear, but I do know we've got ev'ry kiddie show for a hundred years on that ting."

"It's like... a computer?"

"Somewhat, yes. Ya had computers where you were?"

"One for calibrating machines and other settings. It's the only thing I've ever seen like this."

"Well, television was very common, turn o' the century. I tink—now I'm remembering—that television and other tings of that nature weren't possible in Bygonne after the sky damage. Because of the atmospheric conditions, it was not possible to transmit a signal."

Baby Lou kicks her feet again, curiosity winning over her temporary shock at the little creatures singing and dancing in the box on the wall. I set her down, and she climbs into a lap beneath the screen.

"Now, I need to go for a bit," Ms. Ruby says, and she gives me quick instructions on how to operate the remote. "Lunch should be here within the next thirty minutes. Make yourselves at home... because ya are now."

"Are what?" I ask.

"Home."

TWENTY-EIGHT

As Ms. Ruby said, about thirty minutes later, not one, but three rolling carts full of food arrive. Suellen, along with another man and woman serve us the most delicious, extravagant meal we've ever had. Long skinny green things, slathered in a glistening sauce, drip like golden sunshine when I bring a forkful to my mouth, and we each have our very own fluffy yeast roll as big as Baby Lou's head. Our drinks have actual ice in them—*real ice*—and flavored with tastes one can only describe as otherworldly.

But perhaps the thing that excites me most are the slabs of delectable goodness clinging to a single bone.

"Is this meat?" I ask Suellen, mouth full of the stuff.

"Yes, that's chicken," she says. "We have a farm about a half-mile from here. We raise all of our own meat."

"A farm with animals?" Chloe says. "Can we see them?"

"I'm… sure Ms. Ruby will be fine with that," she replies. "But you'll have to speak with her. She should be back soon."

Suellen and the others leave us to our wonderful meal. For a few minutes, the room is silent but for forks clanking against metal plates, chewing, and ice clinking along the insides of glasses. Baby Lou is wearing most of her mushy meal on her face, but she doesn't seem to mind. "Applesauce," Suellen called it. Whatever it is, Baby Lou thinks it tastes just as good licking it from her hands. She insists on mashing them into the mess and mixing the contents around.

I eat until my stomach tells me to stop, though I still want more of the flavor. I definitely don't want to taste the awesome meal a second time. Something tells me it wouldn't be nearly as good. Probably better than the Tree Factory slop, though.

I push my half-empty plate aside and gaze out the window at the ocean... until I'm startled by something on my leg. Mateo's hand, sneaking a thigh-rub. I side-glance him and grin. He returns it. Across the room, I catch Jax sneaking a peek at us from his table alone with Vila and Tallulah. They haven't talked to anyone but themselves since we stepped into this place.

"Looks like they've become pretty friendly," Mateo whispers.

"Well, they suit each other. They're both angry."

"V's usually not. I don't know what her problem is lately. I guess she's never had competition before. Weren't many other girls our age at the Subterrane." He leans in closer. "Plus, I think she's had a secret thing for me since we were young."

"Oh? Well, that explains a lot."

"Yeah, it does."

Ms. Ruby appears in the doorway, beaming from ear to ear. "Did ya all enjoy lunch?"

Their cheering could probably be heard back at the Tree Factory.

"That's fantastic," she says. "Now, if you'll just leave every-ting here and come wit' me. We're goin' to the medical wing to get ya all checked out. Then, we'll come back here, get your tings, and I'll take ya to your rooms."

I wipe Baby Lou down with a dampened cloth, while the rest of the stuffed children make their way from their chairs, slowly, to the door. Not many of them have ever experienced a full stomach. Scanning the room, I find everyone's by the door, except for Aby, who's staring out the window.

"Smudge, can you take Baby Lou for a second?" I ask.

"Sure."

I hand her over, then head toward my sister. "Aby," I say when I get close.

She doesn't respond.

"Hello...?" I move to her side, and her blank stare infuriates me. "Are you coming, or what?"

She still doesn't answer.

"Will you snap out of it already!" I yell.

"No!" She whips around to face me. "No, okay? I won't! So just... leave me alone!" She rushes over to the waiting group, and I follow.

Ms. Ruby gives me a concerned look. "Every-ting okay?"

"It will be," I reply. "After we all get some rest, things will be much better."

Aby glares, as if my notion were preposterous, that sleep would heal her broken heart. I glare back.

"All right, then," Ms. Ruby says. "It shouldn't take too long at the medical center; an hour tops. We have a few nurses and a couple doctors on duty. Then, we'll get ya all to your rooms to rest." She turns and walks out. "Follow me!"

We trail her down a short hallway, passing a sign that reads: Medical Wing. A couple minutes' walk later, we arrive at the large, open doorway leading into the medical room. Rows and rows of thin cots and tables line the walls, neatly cluttered with various strange-looking medical supplies. Three women and a man dressed in crisp white clothing, and another man and a woman dressed in light blue, smile at us when we enter. They spread us out on the various cots and make their rounds, checking eyes, noses, ears, mouths, and listening to heartbeats. Baby Lou screams the entire time.

The woman in light blue approaches me and Baby Lou, smiling warmly. "I'm Doctor Sullivan," she says loudly, over

Baby's crying. We shake hands.

"I'm Joy. Nice to meet you."

"You, as well. One of the little girls told me you were responsible for everyone...?"

"Uh, yes. I suppose I am. Baby Lou, shh, it's okay," I soothe, rocking her.

"Well, then I need your permission to run blood tests on everyone. Most of you have never had vaccinations or medical care of any kind, I'm sure. And in order for us to know if we need to treat anything, a blood test is necessary."

I look to Smudge in the next cot over.

"It's okay," she says. "It's a common medical procedure."

"Well... go ahead, then, I guess."

The doctor takes something from her pocket. "May I see your finger? It'll be a tiny prick." I give it to her, and she places the end of a small, square gadget against its tip. The gadget clicks and I flinch at the sharp stab. Then, she pinches to collect the secreted blood. After a few seconds, she snaps it closed with a smile, and wraps my finger with a sticky bandage. "Joy, you said?"

"Yes."

She holds the square gadget by her mouth, pressing a small button. "Joy," she repeats, and the device beeps. "This will hold everyone's samples," she says. "We'll have the results by this evening, and we'll let you know what we find. No news is good news. Will you hold the baby still?"

I nod and hold Baby Lou tight as Doctor Sullivan pricks her tiny finger. Baby screams, then squirms, while she collects the fresh blood into the device.

"I'm sorry, sweetheart," she says. "I know it's uncomfortable." She snaps the thing closed, wraps a bandage around Baby Lou's finger. "What's her name?"

"Louanne."

"Louanne," she repeats into the gadget. Then, she moves on to Smudge. Smudge displays her tattooed neck, and Doctor Sullivan nods, passes her up, moving on to Mateo instead.

Another thing I'll have to ask her about later.

After everyone's been checked and blood tested, Ms. Ruby returns to take us to a surprise. She brings two rolling carts piled high with towels and folded clothes, and leads us all back toward the children's wing. She unlocks a brown door, and it opens to a ramp, leading down at a slight angle. "Follow me, children." She flips on a light, pushing one cart ahead of her, and pulling one behind.

"Let me get that," Emerson says, taking over the one behind her.

"Oh thank ya, dear, that's sweet."

The corridor is short, and I'm grateful it doesn't seem too far underground. I've had enough of underground for a lifetime—for twelve lifetimes.

The ramp stops at two archways.

"Boys to the left, girls to the right," Ms. Ruby says. "In each area, there's a community bath, and individual showers for those who prefer more privacy. These are for you boys." She pushes one of the carts toward the left archway. "The other is for you girls."

Smudge takes the cart from Emerson and we start toward the archway on the right.

"I'll be there shortly, girls," says Ms. Ruby. "Let me give the boys instructions first." She leads the boys inside.

When we step through the doorway and around the corner, I'm reminded of the pool at Gomorrah Grande. Not as extravagant, but larger, welcoming—definitely not creepy—with shallow moving water and a platform all the way around. On one end, a ramp leads down into the water, and along the back wall are narrow stalls with green curtains pulled to the side. For a couple of minutes, we stand in silent awe, until Ms. Ruby comes through the archway behind us. "All right, then. Let's get the bubbles goin' in the pool, and I'll show ya how to operate the showers.

"Bubbles?" I say.

She winks and, leaning over to a small box on the wall, punches a few buttons. The pool's water begins to swirl faster, forming bubbles on the water's surface and along the edges of the walls. They grow and move inward, toward the center, as the girls giggle, squeal, and jump up and down.

"Are we going in there, Momma Joy?" Chloe asks.

"Is it deep?" I ask Ms. Ruby.

"Four feet at this end." She points in front of us. "Prob'ly best to keep the youngest ones by the ramp. The bubbles are made from soap, so they can just get in and play, and they'll get clean."

Clothes fly through the air, and bare bodies skip to the ramp. The pool's surface is now a thick layer of bubbles, which becomes a bubbly wave as they splash into them.

"Those the showers?" Vila motions to the curtained stalls.

"Yes, dear. Do ya need—?"

"No, I'll figure it out." She rushes off, Tallulah's head sticking out from her knapsack. Aby follows close behind.

"I'm sorry they're so rude," I say.

"Oh, nonsense," Ms. Ruby says. "They're fine. They been through a lot. Now listen, when ya get to the showers, the knob on the left is hot, and the one on the right is—"

"Did you say hot?" I ask.

"Oh, *hell* yeah!" Vila yells. "We've died and gone to flippin' paradise!"

"Guess so," Smudge says, grinning.

What a glorious day.... Aside from the warm baths my mother gave me when I was small enough to fit in the wash-tub—which I don't remember, for being so young—I've never bathed in warm water.

"You want me to take Baby Lou into the pool while you shower?" Smudge asks. "I'll go in my clothes; they need washing anyway."

"You can... go in?"

"Yes." She nods. "I am... waterproof."

We share a giggle and I hand Baby over. While Smudge heads toward the ramp with her, I snatch a towel from the cart and dig through the stacks of soft, strange clothing until I find something that might fit—a long peach-and-tan dress with skinny straps at the top, and curls of longer fabric at the bottom.

"A wonderful choice," Ms. Ruby says. "I made that one myself, years ago."

"You sew?"

"Someone has to fix tings up around here." She winks.

"My mother used to sew," I tell her. "She taught me when I was young. Good thing, too, because I've been able to mend everyone's clothes for the past few years."

"Aw, well... how fortunate they've been to have ya care for them, Joy."

"Thanks."

"Now, go enjoy your shower, you've earned it. I'll be back soon, I need to move the baby crib from the nursery, to a room on the girls' floor. Ya need to be in the same room with your Baby Lou, I assume."

"Yes, thank you."

"You're very welcome. I'll see ya soon, dear." Grinning, she heads back through the archway.

A warm shower! My eagerness is barely containable. Once I'm sure Smudge and Baby Lou are all right in the pool with everyone else, I glide to the last stall on the left, three down from where Tallulah waits in her knapsack for Vila to finish. I hang the fresh dress on a hook, and step inside. With a smile, I turn the knobs, and warm water sprays my hands. I close the curtain and undress, tossing my mother's sleep clothes to the tile floor, then melt beneath my glory. Ms. Ruby was right; I *have* earned this. My entire horrid existence has led me to this one moment, a warm baptismal spray washing everything into the drain below my feet. I've done it. *We've* done it. In this moment, I could die and be at peace.

§

Ms. Ruby situates us into our cozy rooms—olders in their own, single rooms on the right; youngers in shared, double rooms on the left. I relax with Baby Lou on my tiny, soft bed in my new dress. She has fresh, new clothes for the first time, and they almost fit her perfectly, with room to grow. She also has her own crib again, except this one has lacy ruffles lining the bottom, and it doesn't creak and wobble when you touch it. I hand her Millie from her bag. She babbles to it, and I check out the view from my window. The tops of huts and trees that rise up the hill's slope stop at the base of The Wall and a couple of miles down the beach in a thick, leafy jungle. If I lean to my left, I can see the ocean, and the sun starting to sink low. Brilliant rays of blue and orange, pinks and reds, enchant the sky.

There's a soft tapping behind me. Smudge peeks in, dressed in a black T-shirt and dark pants. She's shed her hooded jacket, but her hat still protects her head.

"Hey," I say.

"Can I come in?"

"Yeah, of course. How's your room?"

"It's great. Very... cozy."

"Cozy is exactly the word I was thinking."

She sits on the bed next to me. "Are we meeting with everyone later?"

"Yes. Once we get the youngers to sleep, we're meeting down at the beach."

"It's very interesting," she says, "the dynamics among you all. I could observe you for hours."

I chuckle. "Funny, I feel the same way about you. Do you not have blood or something?" I whisper. "The nurse skipped you earlier...."

"No, I do. But I require an alternate form of medical treatment, which also addresses the mechanical side of my make-up."

Shuffling sounds by the door. I look, but see no one. Then, I place a finger to my lips, and Smudge nods.

"Baby Lou's tired," I say. "I'm going to get her to sleep, then I'll meet you in your room. Can you let all of the youngers know it's time for bed? Have Aby help, if you need to. But I'm sure they'll be tired enough to go to sleep without much trouble."

"You're probably right." Smudge rises from the bed. "I'll take care of it."

"Thank you."

She disappears out into the hallway, then comes back into view. "Would you like me to close the door?"

"If you would."

Softly, she closes the door, leaving us in the stillness.

I draw the lavender curtains closed and turn off the light. A tiny bulb protrudes from an outlet, illuminating just enough to see what I'm doing as I pull back the covers and lay Baby Lou down. She takes a sip from a fresh bottle of water—one Ms. Ruby brought from the kitchen—then stops to have a good yawn. I tuck Millie into her arms, and crawl in bed beside her. She yawns again, and I kiss her cheek.

"I love you, my baby."

"Ma?" she says, batting at my lips. "Ma ma?"

I nod, choking back a sob. "Yes, Baby Louanne. I'm your momma. And I love you. And we're safe now."

"Ma ma ma ma," she jabbers, then yawns again and closes her eyes. I pet her head and hum as silent tears fall. Only a few hours in this place, and already she's one hundred percent better.

And this is the first time she's ever called me momma.

Another tap on the door, and Ms. Ruby tiptoes in with a strange machine on wheels. She plugs it in and a green light flashes, a motor hums, then she slips quietly to the side of my bed and leans down. "Oxygen," she whispers. "You and Baby will have the best night of sleep you've ever had." She pats my arm, and I smile.

"Thank you," I whisper back.

She leaves the room without a sound.

Oxygen.

Spilling into our room and our lungs as if it were nothing.

I take a deep breath....

And smell the slightest hint of... citrus.

TWENTY-NINE

BABY LOU DRIFTS OFF TO SLEEP, but I lay there, frozen. The citrus smell fades, so it must have been my imagination. Still, something gnaws at me. Hard to place, but with that smell, a hidden fear beneath my intoxicated awe of Zentao bubbles to the surface of my mind. Its suffocating vice grips my lungs, making it hard to breathe.

What is it?

I dig through my scattered thoughts, looking for answers. I've been through a lot. This could be residual paranoia. I take in a few slow, deep breaths. Maybe it's because I suspect it isn't all over yet. In the morning, we're leaving this perfect place, going back to Bygonne. I might never see my Baby Lou again. That could explain the feeling of something not quite right.

When I'm sure she's good and asleep, I lift Baby Lou from my bed and move her to the crib. Then, I tuck the blanket around her and Millie, and tiptoe to the oxygen machine, inspecting it for signs of being something other than what it's supposed to be. Nothing. Of course, I've never seen an oxygen machine before, so how would I know different anyway?

I settle with my paranoia, leave the room, and knock softly on Smudge's door. She opens it a second later. "You ready?" she whispers.

"Yeah, is everyone in bed?"

"Yes. They were... exhausted. It didn't take much convincing, like you said."

"I didn't think it would. I need to let Serna know to listen for Baby Lou if she wakes up."

We go next door and knock. The murmurs on the other side stop, and the door creaks open. Vila peeks out. "Hey."

"We're going down to the beach," I say. "You coming?"

"Yeah. I was just asking Serna here to watch Tallulah while we go. Tallulah likes her, and she seems reliable."

"She's very reliable," I say, then I call in, "Serna, would you listen for Baby Lou while we're gone, too? She's two doors down."

"Sure, no problem."

"Thanks. We'll be back in about an hour."

Together, we leave her doorway, and I head toward the end of the narrow hallway to Aby's room, Smudge and Vila at a standstill behind me.

"Where are you going?" Smudge asks.

"To get Aby."

"Seriously?" Vila says. "That girl's unstable."

"She isn't the only one unstable around here," I mumble.

"Hey, I heard that."

We're all unstable . . . in some way.

But Aby's door is already open, her bed neatly made, without her in it.

"I wonder where she is," I say once I return to Smudge and Vila.

"Probably already down on the beach," Smudge says. "Maybe it was her we heard in the hallway earlier."

On our way down to the first floor, we cross paths with Ms. Ruby, who's reading something from a rectangular board in her hands. She almost bumps into us.

"Oh, excuse me," she says. "Ms. Joy, I'm glad you're down here. May I speak to ya privately?"

I glance at Smudge and Vila, confused, before following

Ms. Ruby into the medical wing corridor. A few feet down the hallway, she stops and, turning to face me, takes my hand. "I received all of your medical information from Doctor Sullivan."

"Is everyone okay? How were Baby Lou's tests?"

"Everyone's fine. Other than a couple of slight asthma cases and anemia, and various other vitamin deficiencies in almost the whole group, there's nothing life threatening. With fresh oxygen, breathing treatments for the asthma, iron and other vitamin supplements, everyone should be fully healthy within a couple of weeks."

The news is good, but her eyes show something more.

"So, then... what's wrong?"

"Well... nothin's *wrong* ...."

"Then tell me what else you've got."

"Joy... you're pregnant."

A sudden ringing in my ears soon becomes a whole-body numbness. "What?" I whisper.

"It's early. About a week, maybe two...."

My heart pounds. "I need to go, my friends are waiting—"

"Joy, perhaps you should tink about stayin'. Let your friends go."

"No. There's no way. I have to go." And I brush past her, returning to Smudge and Vila, shoving the information as far away from truth and reality as possible.

"What'd she say?" Vila asks.

I shrug. "Just that almost everyone needs vitamins, and a few have asthma. Other than that, everyone's pretty healthy. It's really a miracle."

"Hm. That's good. Now let's get outside. I'm claustrophobic in this place."

Vila disappears through the front lobby door, and I fidget, feeling Smudge's gaze on me.

"What is it?" Smudge asks.

"Nothing."

For a few seconds, she reads my face, and I know she calls my bluff, but she won't pry. "Okay, Joy." She smiles. "Let's get outside, then."

A flickering flame from far below on the beach catches our attention. A few faint figures sit around the fire, and another—Vila—heads toward it.

"Is that them?" I ask.

"Yes," says Smudge.

"You can see that far?"

"I can see... farther. But, yes, I can. They're all there."

We follow a winding trail down the slope, past sleepy, darkened huts and the bunker where we came in. There, Raffai leans against a post, talking to one of his young soldiers. He waves, and we wave back, and a minute later, we're the last two to join our miniature army sitting around the fire. Aby and Jax sit, hip to hip, on a log facing the ocean, talking quietly. Maybe they're righting things between themselves. My stomach spins.

"Wow," Mateo says, walking over to me. "You look... absolutely stunning." He says it loudly, without any care for who could hear.

Jax and Aby turn to stare.

My face burns hot. "Thanks," I manage to say.

Mateo's white cotton shirt hugs his sculpted chest and shoulders in all the right spots. His top half looks so good, I'm afraid to see the rest. "You look nice, too. Clean." I grin, and he returns it.

"Thanks. Saved you a seat." He holds out a hand toward one of six giant log benches that surround the fire.

"Are we allowed to be here?"

"Yeah, Raffai said it would be fine if we met here."

"Hey, Smudge," says Johnny, dressed all in black, hair slicked back. He's left Old Jonesy's hat in his room for the occasion, I guess. Good choice. Every time I see that hat, I envision the lonely corpse of that poor drunk left in the bunker. In fact, I could go the rest of my life without seeing that hat again.

Smudge and Johnny take a seat on the log bench next to Jax and Aby, who turn around to face us, backs to the crashing waves. Mateo and I sit on the one next to Smudge and Johnny, while on our other side are Vila and Emerson.

Emerson glances from face to face, briefly locking eyes with each of us. Then, after a few silent moments, he walks to the middle of the circle and throws his arms up in the air. "Paradise!" he yells into the sky.

At this, we all smile. Even Aby. Her talk with Jax—whatever it was—seems to have helped her.

"Right here, right now," Emerson continues, "we're a family. We're a team."

"We're a miniature army," I add.

He chuckles. "Yes. And in order for us to get back here, we all have to work together. This is possible. If it was possible for us to break into the Chamber, steal Pia, and then escape ourselves, it's possible for us to get back in, rescue Pedro, and escape again. We have weapons, we have knowledge of the Subterrane's layout, and the location of the Chamber ... and we have an incentive to live—this." And he gestures around.

Then, he borrows Mateo's walking stick and begins to scribble in the sand, describing to us the details of the Subterrane's layout and how we'll get in. Once it's time to discuss tactics, Vila gives us all a militia lesson.

Yet all I hear is: *Joy, you're pregnant.*

My mind wanders away from Vila's rant about killing and not being killed, to my mother and the things she told my daddy when she thought I was asleep: *I wish I'd had her when I was younger, Richard. Just think, if I'd had her at seventeen, or even eighteen, I would've had twelve years with her! Why did we wait? Why?* Then, she'd cry so hard, it would start another coughing spell, ending in blood all over the place again. My daddy would clean it up and cry, too, telling her how sorry he was, that if only they could go back to do things over again... they'd have more time.

But I don't want that. I have my Baby. Actually, I have more babies than I can handle. And this? This is too much. It means Jax will be a father. He can hardly take care of himself, much less a baby.

And what about Mateo? What will he think?

And Aby?

My head spins, and I'm nauseated. Everything grows silent, and I realize Vila has sat down and everyone's staring at me.

"Well?" says Emerson. "What do you think? You want to add anything, Joy?"

"No, I'm fine," I reply. "You two covered everything. We can discuss more in the morning before we leave, if we need to."

"Didn't you hear?" Mateo says.

"Oh, great." Vila shakes her head. "Captain Princess over here wasn't even listening."

"Hear what?"

"We have to leave tonight," Emerson says. "While everyone in the Subterrane is asleep. It's the best time."

"Tonight?"

"We have to," Jax says. "The longer we stay here, the more comfortable we'll get, and the more we'll forget what it's like over there. And the easier it'll be to forget... about Pedro."

"Yeah, you're right." I stand, "We don't need to get too comfortable," and glance down at my dress, flapping curls dancing in the night air. Definitely not rescue mission clothing. "I need to change and talk to Serna. And Ms. Ruby."

"See if she has some dark clothing she can loan you," Emerson says. "You too, Mat. We'll need to blend into the shadows."

"Got it."

"And as soon as we're all ready," he adds, "we'll meet in the lobby. Then, we'll have Raffai let us back into the bunker... and out into Bygonne again."

§

When I ask Ms. Ruby for dark clothing to change into, her face sinks with sadness. Still, she nods, and disappears into a large closet by the common area.

"Come and take what ya need, dears," she calls out.

Mateo and I leave Smudge in the lobby to join Ms. Ruby, while everyone else returns to their rooms to do last minute things.

"I need to leave a message for Pia," Mateo says. "Well, two, actually."

In the closet, Ms. Ruby steps aside. "I'll leave you two to find what ya need. I'll be readin' and havin' a cup o' tea in the dining room."

"Thank you," we say.

"You're very welcome." She strides down the hallway, takes a left into the dining area.

"Why two messages?" I ask, skimming through a stack of pants. I unfold a pair of huge ones, riddled with holes, shake my head, then re-fold them and set them neatly back onto the pile.

Mateo laughs. "We must be cute for the rescue mission, huh?"

"Well, or maybe not look like someone dug me up with dinosaur bones."

He laughs again. "Funny."

After a bit more searching, we both find dark garments that might fit.

"So, the messages?" I say.

"Yeah. One for if we aren't back yet when she wakes up in the morning, telling her I'll be back soon. And one for… if we don't come back."

"We're coming back. *Before* she wakes up."

"But—"

"We're coming back. We don't have a choice. Okay?"

We stare into each other's eyes before he nods, kisses my cheek. "Okay."

On our way back to the front, we stop at the dining room doorway, where Ms. Ruby pauses from her reading. Her lips form a smile, but sorrow calls its bluff. "You're leaving, then?"

"Yes. But we'll be back in a few hours."

She sips at her teacup, nods, then rises slowly, coming over to us, gown waving behind her. "Please be careful. And come back soon. With your brother."

"We will," I say. "But if we're not back before they wake up… will you tell them we'll be back soon?"

Ms. Ruby hesitates, but nods again, slightly. "All right, dear."

We leave her, heading toward the stairs, where everyone else waits, pacing, or fidgeting on the couch, or chatting nervously. Only Smudge seems completely calm and confident. I'd feel the same way if I were her, I suppose.

"We're going to go change," I tell them, "and I need to let

Serna know we're leaving. Then, we'll go."

To nods of assent, Mateo and I quickly climb the stairs. "I'll meet you downstairs," he says, and we part ways at the second floor as he continues on to the third.

I tiptoe to my room, open the door quietly, and sneak inside. I gaze at my sleeping Baby Lou, bathed in the nightlight's soft glow. Such a peaceful little angel. At once, a wave of swirling emotions threatens to sink me into the floor. I rush to shed my dress and tug on my new dark pants and long-sleeved shirt—which are too big, but fit well enough—then, I hurry out before I change my mind or weaken under the weight of my fear. Two doors down, I wake Serna to tell her we're leaving.

"Now?" she mumbles.

"Yes. I need you to sleep in my room with Baby Lou."

In a few groggy seconds, she sits up, peels the covers back, and swings her legs over the bedside. She follows me to my room, and I leave her at the door, turning toward the stairs.

"Joy, wait," she says, and I pause. "What do I do if… if you don't come back?"

"I'll be back. I promise." And I swiftly descend the stairs before Serna's worry can sway my stubborn optimism.

I'm the last one downstairs. Already, everyone else is grouped by the door, waiting, but as soon as Emerson sees me, he whips it open, letting the cool night rush in. We blend into it like black paint in a dark river. Mateo limps along without his walking stick, and panic hits me. I hadn't even thought of that. How will he be able to move quickly? I take his arm and fall behind the others with him. "What about your knee?" I ask quietly.

"I'll be fine. The adrenaline will help."

"Mateo, maybe you shouldn't—"

"I'm not a cripple. Please, don't worry. I won't let you do this alone." He takes my hand, pulls me down the winding sloped path to Raffai and the others at the bottom. Raffai has four crossbows waiting, like the ones Smudge had gotten for us.

"I don't condone killing," he says. "In fact, killing any of the Subterrane people could mean serious trouble for Zentao. But I know what it's like to lose a loved one...." Grief paints his eyes a bright, sad blue, and he places a hand over his heart, on the shirt pocket that contains the blonde braid. "And it's imperative that you children make it back here alive," he adds. "But please, use these weapons only in case of emergency." He hands me, Vila, and Jax each a crossbow, then trades Johnny his near-empty one for one fully-loaded.

Inspecting the weapon, I'm suddenly overwhelmed. Johnny will have to give me a lesson in the trolley.

"I'm sorry I can't afford you more weapons," Raffai says. "We're very short ourselves."

"We'll be fine." Emerson taps the bundle strapped to his back. "We have spears for the rest of us."

"And these." Vila pats the knives tucked into her makeshift knife-holding belt. "In fact, here, Mat. You take this." She hands him her crossbow. "I'm better with knives."

Raffai punches in a code on the bunker wall, and the doors part. Lights flicker on, and we step inside. Across the room, black doors reflect our dark, rippling forms as we approach them. There, Raffai punches in another code, and those doors open, as well, to our blue trolley on the other side. He takes a handful of breathers from a row of hooks by the door.

"The air down there is dubious," he says. "Best to wear these, at least in the tunnels." And he goes to pass them out.

But Smudge holds up her hand to stop him. "I'll make sure the air's good in the tunnels," she says, "trust me. I'll have to dim the oxygen lights, though, so we don't give ourselves away."

"No breathers?" Emerson asks.

"No," says Smudge. "I promise you they aren't necessary."

"You are very brave children," Raffai says, with that same sad expression Ms. Ruby had when she told us goodbye. "Be safe, and come back soon."

"We will," I say, but for the first time, as we pile into the trolley and close the door behind us, I let loose my own secret fear with one screaming thought:

Or maybe we won't.

THIRTY

Raffai disappears behind the closing black door, and we're left in utter darkness. I break into a cold sweat, wipe my face with my sleeve, steady my breaths.

"Can you turn the lights on in here?" I ask Smudge.

"Yes, but when we get to the tracks, I'll have to turn them off again. The light could give us away." They blink on overhead.

"I brought this." Jax holds up a light stick. "I'll keep it in my pocket if we need it."

"That will help, yes," Smudge says.

For a few moments, we sit in silent stillness before Vila takes off her knapsack and places it into her lap. Tallulah's head pops out of the drawstring hole.

"You're bringing her?" I ask.

"Have to. She's our key to the key."

"What do you—?"

"I trained her to sneak into the Queen's quarters and steal the Chamber key."

"How in the world did you do *that*?"

"Long story." She pets Tallulah's head, then gives her whiskery nose a peck. "Ugh!" Vila yells. "I hate this thing! It feels like we're just sitting here. It's infuriating."

"I assure you," Smudge says, "we are moving."

"Let's go over the tactics again, real quick, V," says Emerson.

She shrugs. "Follow my lead, stay in the shadows, don't make a sound, shoot first, and don't die. I think that about covers it."

"Where are we going to stop the trolley?" Aby asks. "We can't park it at the station."

"Once we get to the railway," Smudge says, "we should get out and walk. It'll be very close. We should not risk the sound of the trolley on the tracks at all."

After an exasperating eternity, the trolley rattles, and we're spat up through the ground. The lights blink off immediately, followed by a cracking noise and a glow from Jax's hand as he shakes the light stick.

"If we were aboveground," I say, confused, "then why does the trolley car come up *through* the ground?"

"It was the best way to build it." Smudge stares out the window. "It's only eleven p.m. We'd be better off waiting—"

"No," Vila says. "We go now, and we kill every cannibal bastard in that place, if it comes down to it. Revenge or no revenge. If more of them come to Zentao, we'll kill them, too." She's the first one to the door.

I laugh, and Vila scowls.

"What's so funny?" she asks.

"Emerson said you'd be the first in line for war," I tell her. "And here you are. He really knows you well."

"I do," says Emerson, who takes the spear bundle from his back and hands one to Aby. "You know how to use one of these, sister?"

She nods.

Smudge moves up front, near Emerson. "I need to explain something," she says to us. "It would be highly probable for more guards to be standing watch now, since there's been a recent escape. I should go first, to stun them, if that's the case. Then, we'll have one hour to get Pedro out, before they regain muscle control. We should avoid killing, if possible, to minimize repercussions to Zentao. They'll know that's where we're going, and seek revenge."

"Very true," Mateo says. "Queen Nataniah would certainly get her revenge if we kill any of her people."

"Smudge goes first," I say. "Then Vila, and then the rest of us. We only kill if necessary."

"I'll hold up the rear," Johnny says, "to make sure no one comes up from behind."

"Before we go, though, I'll need to know how to operate this thing," I say.

At this, Johnny gives me a quick lesson. I aim at the back of the trolley, and plant a bolt into the wall. Easy enough. I retrieve my bolt, fumble with it for a second before clicking it back into its slot.

Vila unlatches the trolley door and slides it open gradually so it doesn't make a sound. Then, we follow her out onto the tracks, and my heart begins to pump fire through me.

"There it is," Mateo whispers.

"What?" I whisper back.

"That adrenaline I was talking about."

"Yeah, me, too."

Smudge starts down the tunnel, followed by Vila, then Jax, who holds the light stick high to illuminate our path. Emerson and Aby trail him with their spears, then me and Mateo, and Johnny at the rear. We move quietly through the darkness for what could be half an eternity in Hell before the sound of enclosed space changes. To our right is a wide-open area, which Smudge and Vila move swiftly through.

I grip the crossbow and try to stay focused, while Vila jiggles her knife in the crevice of a narrow door, which clicks open easily to a steep, rocky staircase. She holds ten fingers in the air, points up, and starts climbing. I think that means ten flights up.

Nine flights later, our momentum has slowed to a near-crawl. I worry, of course, about Mateo's climbing, but worrying isn't going to help. Soon, we stop at a dead end, another door. Vila places a finger to her lips and jabs the knife into the crevice of this door, which pops right open, too. Obviously, not many people are stupid enough to break into this place. Until now. Thank goodness for that; it makes this rescue mission that much easier.

Vila eases open the door, peeks through the crack. Then, she holds two fingers up to Smudge. Smudge nods, pushes up her sleeves, and steps up to the door. She, too, peeks through, and my heart thumps wildly in my chest as I hold my breath. This is it. Moment of truth.

Through the crack, Smudge holds up one hand, and a second later, two thuds echo beyond the door. Vila stares at Smudge in amazement, then smiles the widest I've ever seen from her, gives Smudge a thumbs-up, and waves us behind her into the Subterrane.

The second we enter the space, something eerily familiar catches my eye. Past two huge lumps of half-naked guards lying next to giant spears, near a see-through safety railing lined with tiny yellow lights, are two trees. But they aren't our trees. They're smaller, made from a shiny silver metal, as opposed to thick gray titanzium. Beyond those, is a circular space, like at Gomorrah, but more massive. Above, levels upon levels go up, and judging by the place's considerable size, I'd say quite high.

Smudge moves along the wall through the shadows, and we all follow her lead, ducking down a left-hand passageway as four guards turn down the corridor we were just in. Vila breaks into a jog, and so do we. Another right turn, then another narrow door, which she opens, and we trail her in.

More stairs. At the top, we close the door quietly behind us, holding our breath as a low murmur of another pair of guards approaches, then relax as they get softer again, heading away from us.

We climb two more flights, and before we get to the final door, Vila stops. "This floor is where the Queen's quarters are," she whispers. "And this is where we trust Tallulah." She takes off her knapsack, loosens the drawstring. Tallulah hops into Vila's arms, twitches her whiskers on her nose. "I'll get her around the corner from the door; she'll know what to do from there."

"Can't you just pick the Chamber lock?" Johnny asks.

"No, it's a complicated locking mechanism. There's a special key, and the Queen keeps it hidden in a jar."

"I'll go with you," Smudge says. "There will be more guards."

Vila inspects her for a silent moment. "I think I've decided."

"Decided... what?"

"That I like you. You are one badass chick."

Smudge grins, looks down at her hands. "Thanks. Same to you, V."

Vila gives her a gentle slap on the shoulder, then rubs her nose to Tallulah's again. "You ready, girl?"

Tallulah squeaks in response.

"We'll be back in a few minutes," says Vila. "Stay here."

"Where's the Chamber?" I ask.

"The floor beneath this one."

That's a relief. This place is huge.

They slip through the doorway, and I peek through the crack. Smudge and Vila move quickly through the shadows along the wall, then disappear from view. I open the door a little wider and hold my breath. Before an arched doorway with a thick red curtain, three enormous guards stand erect with stone-grinding fists gripping skin-piercing spears. A few feet from them, Smudge and Vila peek around the corner. Then, Vila sets Tallulah down, and I'm amazed to see the animal travel along the wall through the shadows until she reaches the Queen's quarters. She sticks her furry head beneath the red curtain, then scurries quietly inside, unseen.

Less than one heart-stopping minute later, she's out again. At first, I think she's failed her mission, but when Vila kisses her nose, I realize it was a success. I exhale. They sneak back toward us, and my insides spin. Once the Queen discovers her key missing, we'd better be as far away from here with Pedro as possible.

"Did they get it?" Jax asks.

"Think so."

When they return to the door, I move aside, and they don't even stop.

"Come on." Vila moves swiftly down the stairs.

At the doorway one floor below us, Vila pauses to catch her breath and let Tallulah crawl back into her knapsack. "Mission accomplished," she whispers. "Once we get in, we go through to the other entrance by the fountain and keep moving. Smudge, this time you'll have to stun them. Last time, Mat spiked their liquor with concentrated Magiope."

"Can we just get this over with?" Aby shivers. "I hate it here."

"Don't we all," Vila says. "Don't we all." She opens the door, and Smudge ducks in. While Vila watches with intensity, the rest of us try to see over her shoulder into the dark room. A second later, she pushes the door open fully to three guards lying on the ground, and we share a spontaneous moment of celebration, then race to the door. Vila removes something from her pocket, places it in a hollowed-out groove in the door, then twists the design to the left. The Chamber door clicks opens. She lays a finger to her lips, and we enter the room.

It's long and narrow, with rows of silken curtains covering what appear to be beds. In the middle sit barrels full of what might be food.

"I have no idea where he is," Vila says into my ear.

We move from bed to bed, passing up ones with obvious females or people way too large to be Pedro. No way he could gain that much weight in less than three weeks.

"Who the hell are you?" a girl's voice demands.

"Your fairy godparents," Vila says. "Go back to sleep. Or no wishes."

Halfway down the room, I spy a handless stump. I wave my arms in the air, then point. Everyone stops. Jax raises his hand, and taps himself on the chest. I nod, and he moves toward the bed, where he covers Pedro's mouth. He wakes immediately, eyes wide with panic, then sees Jax, and they shift to surprise. They embrace, brothers who were never supposed to see each other again.

"Quiet, man," Jax says. "We'll explain everything once we get out of here."

Pedro nods, then sees me, and I tap my crossbow. We mean war. He jumps from his bed, and we rush through the room to the other end, past a fountain and to the other door.

"Hey!" the girl says. "Where the hell are you going?"

"The Queen wants a midnight snack, girl," Emerson says. "Now hush."

A rustling says others are waking up from the noise—our cue to get the hell out of here. Vila taps Smudge, and Smudge nods. She opens the door, and Smudge stuns two guards who see us all before they fall to the floor. We hop over them, follow Smudge and Vila around the corner and down a long hallway until we're back by the Chamber entrance. The guards there haven't moved.

Back at the stairwell that leads down and out, I hug Pedro tightly. He lifts me off the ground and kisses my cheek. Then, together, we descend the stairs as quickly and as quietly as we can. In the back of my mind, a small voice tells me it's too soon to celebrate. But I do anyway. We did it. We are brave, we are strong, we are invincible. We have freed our brother from a horribly wretched, grotesque death. Now, we're taking him home. We're taking him to paradise.

THIRTY-ONE

"Where's my brother?"

Of course, it's the first thing Pedro would ask. Even before we get down the first few flights.

"He's fine," I lie.

Aby looks away.

"He's waiting for us in the trolley," I say. "He... wanted to keep watch." The worst lie ever, and I feel horrible, but if I tell Pedro that Miguel is dead, we likely won't make it out of the Subterrane.

"Well, let's get the hell out of this godforsaken place, then. I thought I'd never see you guys, or Miguel, ever again."

"Okay," says Vila once we reach the bottom floor. "I'm gonna open this door, and we have to be quiet—move silently and quickly."

Aby tries to hide her tears as she pushes past us and Vila, places her hand on the handle, and yanks down. "Let's just go." She opens the door. "There's no one down—" Her body jerks and her eyes snap open wide.

"Oh my God!" Vila cries.

Then, I see it: shiny and silver, piercing Aby's stomach through one side and out the other. Dark red blood pours from the spot.

"Aby!" I scream.

"Go!" Smudge yells. "Go up—now! It's her!"

The door slams against the outside wall with such force, it splits in half. There, standing before us, with a metal spine ejected from her wrist and through my sister's midsection, is Arianna Superior. Smudge throws both of her hands in the air, and Arianna flies backwards into the wall. Aby slumps to the floor, and I collapse to her side. "Aby! No!"

"Go!" Smudge screams again.

Arianna flies toward us with super speed, and Smudge blasts her back again.

"We have to leave her!" Jax says.

"No! I'm not leaving her!"

"Joy, she's dead!" Smudge yells. "You have to go! You have to! Now!"

Emerson and Johnny drag me by my arms up the stairs, and I glance over my shoulder to see a blast of red from Smudge's two hands as Arianna Superior flies all the way back through the platform and to the railway.

"Go!" Smudge shouts. "Next floor up!"

We sprint up the stairs and burst through the next floor's doorway, met by guards and alarmed townspeople dressed in brown robes. Smudge blasts them all, while Johnny shoots two of the guards in the feet with his crossbow. The stunned people drop to the ground as we sprint through the main room, past everyone, to what looks like an elevator door. One glance up, and I notice so many in the Subterrane are now awake.

A handful of guards rushes to block the elevator. On impulse, I lift my crossbow, shoot one in the neck, then another in the chest. I'm picturing Aby, my sister who I never forgave, lying on the floor as a fresh meal for these people, and I want to kill them all.

Everyone from our group follows my lead. Emerson chunks his spear into the chest of one, and Vila impales two of them with a pair of quick wrist jerks. Johnny shoots three bolts behind us, into the quickly approaching townspeople. Two of them fall, screaming, grabbing at the bolts implanted in their bodies.

"I'll empty it!" Johnny screams, swinging the crossbow left, right. "So back up!"

They push back, and we dash toward the elevator, skipping over still, bloody guards. Before we even get to it, the door opens, and as we scramble on, a woman's voice bellows from above.

"Demons! You will get what is coming to you!"

As the door closes, I catch a split-second glimpse of the dark skin, white robes, and high cheekbones of who might have been an enraged Queen Nataniah. The elevator begins to move, and we all collapse into each other, heaving and crying.

Smudge stands before us, rigid and straight-faced. "I know this is devastating, but we have to be strong a little longer. We can't give up now, not yet. When this elevator gets to the bottom, we will be leaving through the jungle."

"You said there was another exit, in the jungle, right?" Johnny asks.

"Yes."

"How far are we from it?"

"Not far. A few hundred yards."

"Well, that's great," Emerson says, finally catching his breath. "We should—"

"What about my brother?" Pedro asks me. "You said he was waiting for us in the trolley."

Shit! I grow numb. My ears ring, my head spins, while black spots sweep my vision.

And then, they're tugging me up off of the ground.

"Joy?" Mateo says, hovering over me.

"She's fine," says Vila. "She just fainted."

"Joy, can you sit up?" Mateo asks.

"Yeah...."

He helps me into a sitting position.

"Where's my brother?" Pedro demands. "If he's up there, we need to get—"

"Your brother is dead," Smudge says. "Joy didn't tell you before because she was trying to save your life. It wasn't the time to tell you."

At once, Pedro's face tightens, and he drops to his knees in the corner of the elevator. He begins to weep, and I cry, too.

"No," he whispers, then yells, "No!"

"Please," says Smudge. "Don't scream. They have very good hearing and are extremely fast. If you aren't careful, you could alert every one of them in a five-mile radius."

"Alert... what?" he asks through his sobs.

"The beasts that killed your brother. They live in the jungle, where we are about to go."

"Are we stopped?" I ask, wiping away tears.

"Yes," says Smudge. "I'm holding the door closed until it's time."

Pedro shakes his head. He rubs his eyes with his stump. "Is this real? I mean, I'm not... dreaming?"

"No," Vila confirms. "You aren't dreaming, it's real."

"And if what Smudge says is true," Emerson adds, "we should hightail it out of here and make a run for that entrance."

"I am getting a signal of two Reapers not too far from here," says Smudge.

"Be honest." Vila steps up to her. "You aren't human, are you?"

"Not entirely. I'm an OAI; part human, part machine. The rest I will tell you later. Right now, we must run for our lives."

Johnny and Jax help Pedro up from the floor, while Mateo and Smudge help me up.

"I'll count to three," Smudge says, "then I'm going to open the door. Everyone stay close, but more importantly, please… you have to trust me."

We all mumble in agreement.

"One…"

I snap to, realizing what we need to do. The crossbow in my hand has three bolts left.

"Two…" says Smudge.

We tighten behind her.

"Three."

The door opens to a short, dark tunnel with a raised gate at its end. Two lonely bulbs flicker on, illuminating the area. Reaper-free. Together, we dart down the tunnel to its exit and, after a glance around, Smudge races off toward the jungle. We follow, weaving in and out between trees, hopping over rocks and fallen logs. I almost slip on a slick spot, but Mateo catches me. A few more yards, and Smudge comes to a dead stop. She turns with a raised hand, and a visible ball of white-hot energy streaks through the air, into the giant body of a Reaper just ahead of us.

"Holy shit!" Vila yells.

"More are coming, we have to hurry. Come on." Smudge takes off again, us after her. My heart pounds so hard, it feels like it's going to explode. I can't believe how enormous that thing was—twice as big as the one who killed Miguel, though maybe because we're closer. We race along the river bank, a few feet from its edge, and for the first time, I see points sticking up from the water. Whatever they are, they're racing with us, probably waiting for us to fall in.

"Almost there," says Smudge.

Another minute, and we stand on the edge of a pool that branches off from the river, where black water swirls around.

Inside, those same pointed fins poke up from the surface. Something rumbles behind us—where we just came from. We pivot around. A black wave of Reapers thunders toward us, and riding one is a beastly figure with red glowing eyes.

"It's her!" Smudge yells. "She's controlling them! We have to jump!"

"In there?" I scream. "Are you crazy?"

"It's not real!" Smudge reaches into a bush, pulls out a brown bag, and straps it across her chest. "It's a holograph to keep the Reapers out. They're programmed to stay away from the water! Please, trust me—you have to jump!"

I glance back. They're close enough now to make out Arianna Superior's features. She's on the back of the largest one, surrounded by at least twenty more, all barreling toward us at lightning speed.

We don't have much choice.

"Together!" I say.

We all grasp hands and jump into the water.

Except... it isn't water. We pass through what should've been the surface to land on some sort of cushion. A hatch above slams closed, and seconds later, a thunderous pounding makes us all push together in the corner.

The sound fades, though it feels like we're sitting still.

"We're moving," Smudge says in the green glow of oxygen lights. "We're safe. There's no way for them to get in. I'm sure of it."

"We made it?" Vila says. "We're alive? Holy shit, that was intense! Woo!" She pounds a fist into the black cushion next to her, then peers around at our faces. "I'm sorry... I know you guys lost your sister, but ... but we made it. We got Pedro, and we made it. Reason to mourn... reason to celebrate."

§

Inside the padded escape pod, the green lights blur through my tears. I collapse into a retching, wailing ball. Hands grab me, pull me into someone. And he cries, too.

Jax.

"I ... I never ... told her ... I ... forgive her," I cry.

"I told her," he says. "I told her you did. On the ... on the beach. That's what we were talking about."

"You ... you told her I forgave her?"

"Yes." He nods. "You had a lot going on, and just because you didn't say it, I told her, didn't mean you didn't."

I hug him tighter, cry harder. "Did she believe you, Jax? Because I did—I did forgive her! I don't know why I didn't tell her! I should've told her!"

"Shh." He rocks me. "She knew, Joy. She knew you did, because she knew you loved her."

I push away from him—from everyone—and into the other corner of the cramped pod. Then, I scream. I scream, and I scream, until my head feels like it might explode, my throat burns, and all of my energy is spent. I try to scream again, but instead, I lie in the stillness, hearing low sobs and murmurs from the opposite side of the pod; rolling from side to side, the pain's too excruciating. I hug around my middle and curl up into a tight ball, whimpering with agonized sorrow. A catastrophic emptiness in my heart and soul brings me to a place worse than death ... because I am feeling it, experiencing it, carrying its crushing weight on my back, forever, until my time ends here on Earth.

"It's my fault," I cry. "I shouldn't have let her go. She was too fragile—always too fragile. I should've protected her. I shouldn't have let her come."

"Stop blaming yourself," Smudge says from beside me. "It's not your fault."

The pod rumbles, and then, it spits us out into the same bunker as before, up through the floor, near the trolley platform.

Raffai, with his men behind him, charge into the room. But once he sees it's us, he sends them away.

"You made it!" he cries, as the see-through dome over the pod retracts. "You made it back alive, and with your brother!" He scans our faces, and me tucked into a ball on the padded floor. The happiness fades.

I sit up, wipe tears away with my sleeve. "Our sister...."

"Oh, no.... How?"

"Arianna Superior," Smudge says. "Somehow, she found us at the Subterrane—at the trolley platform. Aby was the first to open the door, and she..."

"Oh, no.... Oh, my dear...." Raffai shakes his head, then his face flushes a bright, angry red. "This is all my fault. I shouldn't have let you go—"

"If we hadn't have gone, we wouldn't have rescued Pedro."

"Where exactly are we?" Pedro asks. "What happened at the Tree Factory?"

"I'll tell him everything," Johnny says.

One by one, we step out of the escape pod and return the crossbows to Raffai. Mateo winces as I help him out, while Johnny and Pedro walk slowly toward the exit, Johnny explaining everything, starting from the Tree Factory escape.

"I'm sorry," I say to Raffai. "We killed some of her guards. They were standing in front of the elevator, and Aby had just died, and... I wasn't thinking, I—"

"Don't apologize." He wraps an arm gently around my shoulder. "I'm so sorry you lost your sister. And if they come, we'll be ready for them. I'll brief my militia shortly."

With Mateo limping badly, and Emerson helping to steady him by gripping under his arm, we head toward Johnny and Pedro standing at the bunker's open door. When we reach them, Johnny's at the part where we'd headed to Zentao on the trolley to drop off the children. Pedro's listening, but he's also staring at the moonlit ocean, tears streaming down his face. When he sees me, he scoops me up and holds me there for close to forever, rocking me back and forth, back and forth, to the rhythm of the waves hushing against the shore.

"Thank you," he says. "For saving my life."

"But I've lost two .... Aby, your brother—"

"You're the one who told me, when our mother died...." He taps his heart. "No one ever really dies. And your sister, my brother... they risked their lives for the ones they loved. They'll live forever in our hearts... as heroes."

THIRTY-TWO

After I've spent a whole day in bed, Ms. Ruby makes me get up and take a shower. She brings me sweet tea, which I'm sure has nectar from the gods snuck into it. Instantly, my body's rejuvenated. Not so much my mind, though. As I wash, my entire life flashes through my thoughts, and when I get to Aby, things grow dark around the brilliant smile she had before they locked us in the dungeon. Before Emmanuel Superior took her hair, and before Miguel died and her sister wouldn't forgive her for making a mistake. Guilt swallows me whole, tightens its grip around my heart. Only one person I can think to talk to now.

I find her at dinnertime with Chloe and Baby Lou. Vila, Emerson, and Pia are nearby, with Mateo close enough for me to touch. But the feeling of vitality the mere thought of his touch once brought is now gone. At least for the time being.

"Are you okay?" Smudge asks me.

I pick at my food, which smells delicious, but can't talk myself into eating it.

"No," I admit. "Can we talk? After dinner?"

"Yes, of course. I think Ms. Ruby's planning an honoring ceremony for Aby and Miguel... on the beach after dinner. Do you want to talk before, or after that?"

"I don't know. We'll see how it goes. Maybe both."

She takes a bite of her food. "Of course."

I try to help Baby Lou with a few bites, but she's determined to do it herself, now that food's delicious, not hideously disgusting. She gets it everywhere, but she's having fun, and I don't care enough to stop her anyway.

"Don't worry," says Smudge. "I'll clean it up when she's finished."

"Thank you."

Ms. Ruby announces the ceremony time as everyone finishes eating. One by one, children deliver their plates to the kitchen counter to be washed, then head outside. The sun's setting beautifully over the ocean. Seeing it makes me feel slightly better, though I'm not sure if I'll ever feel entirely so.

How do you move on from this?

How do you let go of someone you love?

How do you forgive yourself, when someone you loved died before you could even forgive them?

Through most of the ceremony, I'm numb. I hear Ms. Ruby talking, then children take turns sharing fond memories of Aby and Miguel. Then… it's my turn. My knees are wobbly as I walk over to the fire and peer into the faces of everyone I love—missing two. Then and there, I make a decision.

"To be strong in the face of weakness," I begin. "This is something our sister, Abrilynne, and our brother, Miguel, taught me. To smile, though there's pain. To laugh, though there's sorrow. To love, no matter what. And to forgive." I wipe my tears and continue with quivering lips. "Sometimes in life, there's sadness. But it doesn't take away from the love, and the joy, and the beauty, and the friendship that remains. We cannot let the loss of our sweet Aby and dear Miguel take from us the very things they wanted for us all: laughter, hope, and freedom from bondage. The surrounding darkness is gone forever; as Pedro reminded me recently, the light Aby and Miguel have given to us will forever shine brightly in our hearts."

Trembling, I sit back down on the log, having spoken

words I didn't intend on saying. Words I didn't realize I had in me. Strange how our own hearts and souls and minds know things that we sometimes can't even see.

But I see now.

I hear my daddy's words: *When the secrets are revealed, you'll see the way the magic works.*

He was right about so much.

After the ceremony, we all exchange embraces and words, and many of the olders tell me my own were beautiful and moving. Not sure how moved I am, myself, but I'll come around. Healing has begun somewhere in my heart, though the pain, I'm sure, will never fade completely. Aby will be sitting there, near my daddy in his cloak and hat, as he makes something float through the air, and with my mother, as she sews Millie's last stitch and kisses my cheek. There, Aby will stay, her smile burning like the brightest guiding star. And Miguel will be there, too, beside her, in awe of her brilliance, like always.

Jax approaches me with his head down, face wet. When he gets to me, arms crossed in front of him, I fold him up in my own.

"So... does this mean you forgive me?" he whispers.

"Yes."

He unfolds his arms to wrap them around me, squeezing tightly. "Thank you."

"No, thank you. For telling Aby I forgave her. Thank you so much for doing that."

"Of course." He pushes gently back from me, takes both of my hands in his own and squeezes them. "We'll get through this, okay? We're free now. And you're... a hero."

"We're all heroes, Jax. We did this together."

"But you stayed strong. And I didn't. We wouldn't have

made it without you being the light."

We share a smile. "Thank you for saying that," I say quietly.

Smudge leaves Johnny and heads in our direction. Jax wipes his eyes and takes a deep breath, exhaling slowly as he surveys the stars above our heads.

"Am I... interrupting?" Smudge asks when she gets to us.

"No," I say. "Not at all."

"Actually, I'm going to go chat with Johnny for a bit," Jax says. "I'll see you two later."

While the children play, and groups of olders gather here and there in small groups to talk, Smudge and I walk down to the water's edge and sit with our toes at the breathing sea. Waves curl up around them, their bubbly coolness and mystery giving me more life inside.

"What was it you wanted to talk about?" Smudge asks.

"About Aby," I reply. "About guilt and forgiveness... but I think I've worked some things out in my mind. I think I'll forgive myself... eventually."

"What you said at the ceremony was... touching. You have a way with words that is truly... astonishing."

"Thank you. I appreciate you saying that."

For a few timeless moments, we watch the waves and the children playing along the beach, until I remember some things I'd wanted to ask her. So much has happened, I haven't had the chance. Now I do.

"The trees in the Subterrane... who made them? Is there, in fact, another Tree Factory?"

"Yes. One hundred-seventy miles northwest. Larger than the one in Greenleigh."

I contemplate that for a moment. "Are there children running that one, too?"

"I'm not sure. I don't know much about that one."

Another question comes to me. "What really happened when you left Zentao, Smudge? You told Vila it was because of your grandmother, but I know you don't have a mother or grandmother. So what's the real story?"

"My donor. Her name was Sadie, and she was an artist."

"That's why Raffai and Ms. Ruby called you Sadie...."

"Yes. When I first left, I was angry. I did go into the jungle to welcome death, furious with Raffai for making me more human—all of these emotions I had no idea what to do with, or how to handle. I went into the jungle and walked aimlessly along the river, trying to decide whether I wanted to jump in and let the Teuridons gobble me up, or if I wanted to let the Reapers tear me to shreds. Right when I decided I'd have a much better chance of death by Teuridons, a white butterfly landed on my arm."

"Okay...?"

"Sadie loved butterflies. She used to paint them all the time. That was when I realized I had her memories; like I had her, living inside of me. Everything she ever thought, felt, desired, or dreamed, I had in my own mind. And that's when I discovered... my soul. At that point, I had no choice; I had to go to Greenleigh."

"Why there?"

"Because that's where she lived and where her things were, hidden beneath the floor in her quarters. Her paintings in the corridor. I had to see them myself to know it was real. That would be a... human... quality."

"But what about us?" I ask. "Why did you lead us down to the portal?"

"I... haven't quite told you everything about the... portal."

"So tell me."

"First, I want to give you something." Smudge digs into

her pocket, then drops something into my hand. I'd know it anywhere. The blue-and-white speckles, the perfect spiral.

"This is the shell I found. How did you get this?"

"What you call the 'portal to paradise' is the transfer program. The citrus smell is from the chemical used to induce a dreamlike state, in which the transfer takes place. The program can be manipulated according to what the donor wants to experience in exchange for their sacrifice. I manipulated your program to be like Zentao. I placed that shell there, because it was the first gift I was ever given by a human. By Cheyenne. She painted it perfectly. I... thought it was a nice touch."

"This is hand-painted?"

"Yes. She is an extraordinary artist."

"Wait. You led us down there. You were going to... transfer us?"

"I had an... extended... moment of insanity. Another... unfortunate human quality. I thought I wanted to return to Lord Daumier. I knew I would never belong in the human world, and I thought if I had ... an offering for Him... he would accept me back into His Clergy. I first gave you and Jax a... taste... of the transfer program, because I knew you would be back with more... bodies. More minds. And you were."

"You were going to... *kill us*?"

"Well, no, not directly. Raffai's reprogramming wouldn't allow me to do that. But yes, I was planning to transfer you, and leave your brain-dead bodies to die slowly. I justified it because, in your minds, you'd live out a whole, almost-perfect life there. Time in the transfer program is different from real life; exponential. In twelve hours, you'd spend a lifetime in... paradise. I thought it was the perfect way to make everyone... happy. But...."

"But what? What made you change your mind?"

"Three things, actually. First, I realized no matter what I did, Lord Daumier would never accept me back. I was no longer 'pure,' and never would be again. Once an OAI is reprogrammed, there is no 're-purifying' them, as far as Lord Daumier is concerned. Second, you mentioned the children, your Baby Lou. That was my first experience with... guilt."

"And three?"

Smudge looks down at her hands, then up at me. "The butterfly landed on you. It wasn't an original part of the transfer program I had set up. The white butterfly must've somehow transferred from my subconscious, into the program."

"That's it? A butterfly landed on me, and that's what changed your mind? And if your mind was changed, why'd you send us away? You told us we'd never see you again."

"All right, well... first, I told you that because I was... scared. I had never interacted with humans before. I had no clue what to do... at that moment. I felt the only way to keep you safe was to keep you... away from me. I realized though, as I contemplated things, what needed to be done." She bows her head, studies her fingertips, and then continues. "When the butterfly landed on you, that's when I remembered you. Through Sadie's memories."

"I never knew anyone named Sadie. How did she know me?"

"She didn't want to... complicate things for you. You had just lost your mother, and she didn't want you to think she was trying to replace her."

"Why would I think that?"

"Because she and your father... were in love."

I freeze in disbelief, unable to truly grasp what she's saying.

"He's the one who first called her Smudge," she explains. "Every time he saw her, she'd have something—paint, charcoal, soot; whatever she had used that day—smudged somewhere on her face. It's what made him fall in love with her, that reckless abandon when immersed in her art. Like nothing else existed. He loved to watch her work, just as she loved to watch him perform. They were... entirely mesmerized, and baffled by each other. You were so young... heartbroken from losing your mother... and there was no way you'd understand." She swings the worn-out satchel around to her lap and hugs it. "Remember how I told you I found Sadie's paints under the floor tiles in her quarters with ... a few other things?"

"Yeah?"

"I've been dying to give this to you," she says. "When I went back to the Subterrane for your supplies, I left this bag by the jungle portal. I didn't want you to discover it before I could explain everything." She gives the bag a pat. "Sadie kept it hidden, so the Superiors wouldn't have the satisfaction of claiming it after your father died. I only wish I could tell her that what she did enabled you to have it. That would make her very happy." Smudge pushes the satchel into my lap, and for a second, I stare at it before unlatching it to peer inside.

Like cracking open a memory unvisited for so long it's grown a shell, what I see opens up a channel of emotional outpouring. My daddy's magic. Sadie must've taken these out of his magic bag so they'd be easier to hide; everyone knew what his magic bag looked like, and her separately hiding these items saved them from the Superiors. As I dig through the ancient memories, I smile through my tears of disbelief. Rings and feathers, scarves and balls, flowers, and a jar of fluid—all things I remember so well, and thought I'd never see again.

I come across a chain strung with two gold rings—one big and one small—and something presses the walls of my heart. "My parent's wedding rings," I say, "passed down through three generations." I slip the chain on my neck and pluck another treasure from inside. I chuckle softly, examining the bracelet I made my mother my second year in the scrap room; merely a twisted piece of metal which I curved into a U shape to fit her frail wrist. It's snug on my own, strong wrist, but its grip brings me comfort.

"Wow," I say. "I can't believe you found all of this. I always wondered who stole everything from our quarters before I got there. Now I know."

I unfold a sheet of hand-made cardboard, the sign that hung on the door the night I snuck in to watch my daddy perform. "Zephyr the Magnificent: Performance tonight! Ten Blue Notes. It was her," I say. "She painted his signs. That's why the lettering on the notes you left on the crates looked familiar. I remember now. I remember her." *How she'd observe him from the floor between brushstrokes, eyes full of love and sadness and longing....*

"Yes. She... loved your father... deeply. And when he died, it ... devastated her. That's when she decided to give herself to the Clergy, the only way she could think of to... handle the pain of losing your father."

"She left me," I say. "If she loved my daddy so much, then why'd she leave me to rot in that hellhole?"

"She thought she was doing the right thing. Not only for you, but for the world. And you know what?" Smudge interlaces her fingers in mine. "Look." She nods toward our clasped hands.

It takes me a second to realize, then I laugh softly through my tears. "She was right," I whisper. "If she hadn't have done that..."

"I wouldn't be who I am," Smudge finishes. "I wouldn't have come to Greenleigh, and I wouldn't have aided in your escape. She may not have known exactly how everything would work out in the end, but she knew it eventually would. Like your butterfly mermaid, she gave up the fight and let her intuition guide her. Not that I agree with the transfer of donors or ending lives for the purpose of producing more OAIs... but in this instance, something dark was flipped inside out and upside down... and with the flick of a wrist, your father's spirit turned this tragedy into a miracle—into *magic*. Without Sadie's love for your father, I wouldn't be here. And neither would you... would any of you."

At this, I kiss her hand, then wrap my arms around her shoulders and hold her tight. I may have lost one sister, but I've gained another in the most remarkable way. A way no one would ever believe.

Together, we stare off into the ocean, at the sun sinking deep behind the horizon. I still can't believe this was here the whole time, waiting for us on the other side of The Wall.

Paradise. We finally made it.

"This is simply amazing," I whisper.

We sit in silence, listening to the children play while I dig through my thoughts. Now that the inner fog has cleared, my daddy's voice nags: *Question everything, my daughter.* And with it, a question does arise, now that I know the truth about Arianna Superior. "If Arianna Superior wanted to kill everyone," I ask, "then why make trees? Why not just stop making trees?"

"Joy, there are some... other things I need to tell you."

"Okay.... There's more?"

"Like I said on the boat, there are many things you do not know, things you'd find out when the time was right. That time is now."

Her serious tone makes my stomach clench. "Well... what is it?"

She takes in a quick breath, then tosses a rock out in front of us. "The trees..." She pauses to toss another rock, and looks away.

"Yes? The trees what?"

She meets my eyes. "They don't create oxygen."

"Huh? What do you—of course they create—"

"They did, before Arianna Superior. Greenleigh was well on its way to manufacturing a tree that could not only produce oxygen, but also replenish the ozone layer over Bygonne. Micah Greenleigh developed the technology before he died. His grave mistake was entrusting it, and both of Bygonne's Tree Factories, to Arianna Superior."

"But, if they don't create oxygen, then what do they do?"

"They are now anti-oxyzone devices."

"Meaning—?"

"In less than five years, Bygonne will be almost entirely oxygen depleted, the ozone hole worsening, tenfold."

"Wait, so you're telling me... the trees we've built our whole lives have actually been making things worse?"

She nods. "That is why the oxygen levels were higher in the factory after the storm cut power to half of the trees surrounding it."

I lean back onto my elbows, mind blown to smithereens. My lips try to form words as I grapple with its magnitude, but only one thought is clear enough to enunciate. "We've been helping them kill people."

Then, another thought barrels down like a train toward a dead end.

"My parents..." I wipe at my tears, hot with rage and confusion. "They could've lived longer."

"That is why I gave you the explosives. With Arianna and the other Superiors gone, and Micah Greenleigh's tree technology safe, the other, larger tree factory could be implemented in regenerating the ozone over Bygonne. It is... unfortunate that Arianna Superior was in Alzanei when the explosion occurred."

"My head's spinning."

"I know this is... difficult for you—"

"That doesn't even begin to describe it."

"But you have to move on. You cannot hang onto the past. It will only keep the pain alive. This is something... Sadie taught me."

I focus on breathing in and out for a moment while I grasp for understanding. "Wait," I say. "You said Micah Greenleigh's technology is safe?"

"Yes."

"Safe where?"

She's silent, running her fingers through the sand beside her, then she looks at me and grins. "Safe. Just like you and your brothers and sisters."

I study her hazel eyes, warm, full of compassion; the freckles that dot her nose and cheeks like Zentao's stars.... "God, Smudge, you're so... human."

She laughs. "I'm not sure whether to take that as a compliment or not."

"Please, take it that way. I may have a way with words, but you have a way of making everything seem like it's going to be all right. And I don't know what I'd do without you right now. This is a lot to process."

"I know, but you're strong. You can handle whatever comes your way. You have so much of your father in you." She gazes off into the sky for a moment, before meeting my eyes again. "Unfortunately, though, I'm not quite through yet. There's... still more to tell you."

"Oh, God, really? What now?"

She inhales again, deeper this time. "Zentao is a very special place. A safe haven for all who wish to be... free and plan for the regrowth of our future. But it's... it's not what you think."

"What do you mean by that?"

"Please, Joy, promise me you aren't going to... overreact when I tell you. And you have to promise not to tell anyone, at least not yet. It's better for most to stay... oblivious to the truth. Especially the children."

My panic rises. "What? I promise, just tell me what it is."

Smudge sweeps her hand out in front of her, toward the hushing waves beneath the gorgeous orange-cream and midnight-blue-streaked sky. "This isn't real."

My heart stops. "What?"

"We are a half-mile beneath the earth, in a secret location hidden from Lord Daumier and his Clergy. The ocean only goes a few hundred yards before ending at the wave wall, which mimics the tide. The walls and ceiling are monitors programmed with the same types of images you saw in the... transfer program."

I release her hand, jump up, and spin around in a circle. "No. No no no...."

"Joy, you said you wouldn't overreact—"

"Overreact? How am I supposed to take this? Am I supposed to be happy about it? Am I supposed to be... *okay* with this?"

A few children stop playing on the beach to stare at us. Smudge stands, comes closer to me.

I shake my head, grab a handful of my hair and tug. "I knew it... I knew there was something off about this place." I glance up the hill toward the green glow above The Wall. "So, that's not The Wall?"

"No. It isn't."

I grab her arm. "Why did you tell me?" I whisper. "You shouldn't have."

"You deserve to know the truth, Joy. I know you've been

through a lot, and this is a crushing blow to add to it, but... the longer I waited to tell you, the worse it would have been. And I couldn't risk you discovering the truth on your own; you'd never trust me again. It's been very hard to keep all of this from you, because I... love you, like a sister, and even in a motherly way because of Sadie. But I had to let the dream fuel you... to push you on to get here. If you'd known the truth, you might not have made it, might not have wanted to come badly enough to push forward."

"What is the truth, Smudge? What's it like above us, where the Clergy and Lord Daumier are?"

"The Earth is dying," she says. "The air is better than in Bygonne, but not by much. The seas are near-boiling in areas, and are receding more and more each year. The water you see here is channeled from the jungle river, with salt from the surrounding mines added periodically to keep it salty."

I collapse into the sand, letting my face fall into my hands, and I cry, because my daddy was wrong. The Earth is dead. There is no paradise. And now I know, we would have been better off dead, too.

"Get up," says Smudge. "Stop this." Her voice is strange, as if fueled by someone else's. Almost like my daddy's speaking through her. "Look around you, Joy."

And I do... slowly. The artificial sun sinks behind the faux horizon. Children scream blissfully as they splash in what they believe is the ocean. Groups of olders laugh, and play, and talk... all free. Magnificent, real-looking stars sparkle from the false sky in a deceptive no end to the space above.

"Redefined dreams," Smudge says. "It may not be what you'd expected or hoped for, but it is, essentially, freedom. They have a chance for a good life here." Then, she lays her hand gently on my stomach. "You all do."

"How did you—?"

"I . . . snooped around in the doctor's mainframe. I'm getting better at this human stuff." She winks. "You'll have adequate medical care; the doctors and nurses here are some of the best. You and your baby will be taken care of."

"Please don't tell anyone."

"I won't. But you know, sooner or later, you won't have a choice."

"I know. But I'm not ready yet." I relax into the sand, and she sits down next to me. "So, what now? What do we do?"

Smudge laughs. "Well, you see those?" And she points to a few scattered buckets in a pile nearby.

"Yeah?"

"Call the children over here."

"Why?"

"Just do it. Come on, trust me."

For a few seconds, I stare at her, and she smiles.

"All right," I say. "I'll trust you, I guess. But no more lies from here on out, promise?"

"Promise."

I stand up, cup my hands around my mouth, and call for the ex-treemakers of Greenleigh and the ex-saltminers of the Subterrane to join Smudge and myself on the shore.

"Bubba! Papa!" Pia squeals. "Come on!" She and Chloe dance around barefoot, holding hands and spinning, before they stop and sway, giggling from the dizziness. They head toward us excitedly, followed by Jax and Johnny, Mateo, Vila, and Emerson.

"Yes, Momma Joy?" Chloe says.

"Smudge wanted everyone over here," I say. "You going to tell us why now?" I ask her.

She clears her throat. "I hear you all need sandcastle-building experience. Is this true?"

The loudest cheers I've ever heard rise into the air.

Only I can hear they're echoed slightly by the hidden ceiling.

"Well, then," Smudge says, and gestures over to the pails. "Go grab yourselves a bucket. We have some building to do."

END OF BOOK ONE

LINKS

If you enjoyed this story, please help others find it, and show your support for this author by leaving a review on Amazon and Goodreads.

Amazon: http://www.amazon.com/dp/B015DC4Q5E/

Goodreads: http://bit.ly/1Nqp1iO

You can find the Audible version of "The Treemakers" here: http://www.amazon.com/dp/B014X34I6G/

Look for the second book in the Treemakers Trilogy, "The Soultakers," in fall 2015 on Amazon.

Here are some more places you can find Christina L. Rozelle and her work around the web:

Amazon Author Page: http://amzn.to/1HYTjRo

"The Rozelle Army" Mailing List: http://eepurl.com/68sS9

Wattpad: http://w.tt/1GW0lW2

Goodreads: http://bit.ly/1f4Km1u

The Treemakers on ifList: http://bit.ly/1QYc7a6

Google+: http://bit.ly/1Kua9Mb

A Spark in the Dark Blog: http://bit.ly/1NmGJQl

A Spark in the Dark Facebook Page: http://on.fb.me/1JSEmWz

The Fansite of Christina L.Rozelle: http://christinalrozelle.com/

Facebook Profile: https://www.facebook.com/cl.rozelle

Facebook Author Page: https://www.facebook.com/clrozellesouth

Twitter: **Christina on Twitter (@CLRozelle)**

Instagram: christina.l.rozelle

Spotify: https://play.spotify.com/user/christinalrozelle

Pinterest: https://www.pinterest.com/thetreemakers/

ACKNOWLEDGEMENTS

It has taken an army of wonderful people to make this story happen. Each of you have played your part in my release from a toxic wasteland of my own, into this earthly paradise. I would not be telling the whole story if I didn't give my most sincere gratitude for those who helped to make it happen. The story behind the story may be more remarkable than the actual story.

First, I'd like to acknowledge the Source that has given me the lighted path through which so many other people and experiences have come into my life and shaped me into a person I can be proud of today. Whether through one sentence or a thousand, the extent of my gratitude could never be fully expressed.

Mom and Dad, Tina and Ricky R. . . . I put you through so much and you did the best you could. Thank you for your forgiveness and your strength, and for showing me what the many faces of love look like. Without your support, both emotionally and financially, this story would not be what it is. Your solid belief that I can do this, follow my dream, has enabled me to do just that. I hope to finally be a brag-worthy daughter, because I know I've been quite the opposite most of my life. You are two very special, loving, selfless, amazing people whom I took for granted for too many years. I never will again.

Savanna, my sweet girl . . . I put you through so much in your younger years and still you grew into a young woman I look up to in awe every single day. Your tendency toward tranquility and innocent spontaneity, your natural embracing of forgiveness, and your idealistic views of people and the world are something that bring me great humility. Because maybe you're a better person, I can learn so much from you—and do—every day. The wanting to make up for time lost with you was the reason I started writing my first novel. I wanted a way to bond with you. You loved to read, and I loved to write. Those loves brought us together to create . . . shadow animal people? Oh, well. :) We moved on to bigger and better things. (Thank goodness!) Thank you for being a sounding board, for helping me with plot details and characters, and for reminding me that the quest and aching for love is underlying in (almost) any story, no matter what the "genre."

Travis R. . . . Baby brother, we haven't always had the best relationship, but as the two of us have grown, we've gotten closer, and I've witnessed some pure genius from you. Thank you for your help in fleshing out some of the sci-fi stuff in this story, and for brainstorming sessions that spawned a lot of cool scenarios and ideas. I'm in such awe of your creativity and imagination, and I'm positive you have a bright future ahead of you.

'Nanna' . . . You never gave up on me. You always knew I'd find my way, and never stopped encouraging me to put my faith in a Power greater than myself, to discover that inherent light of life. I finally did that, and just like you knew it would, my life has turned around completely. Though I know you aren't here to witness it on the physical plane, you are with me always in spirit, whispering your loving encouragement whenever I need it most. I love you and miss you dearly. Thank you for being my warm west wind.

Pat O. . . . Like my Nanna, you, too, believed in me when no one else on Earth was sure if I'd be alive the next day. You took a shriveled mess of a girl and helped her on her path to becoming a woman of strength and integrity. You'd always say, "Just keep doin' what you're doin'," and "I'm so proud of you," and though you aren't here to say it anymore, I still hear it. One of my biggest regrets in life is not coming to see you that one last time, like I said I would. And then, you were gone, and I felt lost. But you had given me a gift that will never leave me: an insight into the magic the world holds, if you only look for it. Thank you, also, for being my Zephyr.

Donna S. . . . Thank you for teaching me how to be honest with myself and the world; for showing me what it's like to "walk a free woman," and to be grateful for everything I have. Thank you for showing me what "redefined dreams" look like, and for loving me past my weaknesses and through hard times. I only wish that the winds of change hadn't torn us apart the way they did. But I know that's a part of life. Nothing remains the same. We are constantly changing, shifting, moving on. . . . "Our love is meant to catapult our loved ones into the world," you taught me. Thank you for teaching me how to just let go, to go with the flow and ride the current. And to do it with a smile, cup of coffee in hand.

Tracy F. . . . You saw me at my lowest point, where I'd even lost the want to search for a way out. But you took me in your strong, loving arms anyway, and you opened my eyes. I'll always cherish the sparks you ignited inside of me when my world was at its darkest. You are such a brilliant light, and the world is by far a better place with you in it. You told me I'd write a book one day. You're one smart lady.

Donna K., Beth H., Petra W., Irie S., Harold D., Brother ChiSing, Bree O. . . . Thank you for your light and your spiritual guidance. You all helped me find a God of my understanding in your own special ways. From the bottom of my heart, thank you for helping me to sort out, identify, tame, and eradicate the inner demons that plagued me for most of my life.

Gary B. . . . Thank you for helping me cultivate my love for words, for introducing me to people like Jack Kerouac and Sylvia Plath, and for being such an important catalyst for change of all sorts in my life. Thank you for stepping up and being a man when you were still just a boy. Despite my putting you through the wringer and bringing out your worst, I always knew your heart was gold, just wounded. Thank you for allowing me the kind of regrets that make a person strive to be the best they can be every day, from this day forward. I hope you're still writing and creating things.

Allen R. . . . You've read my work from the beginning, and even though it wasn't as polished as it is now, you still encouraged me to continue writing and follow my dreams. Your "storyteller" is moving forward, and this time, she's leaving the tunnel door unlocked.

Honour W. . . . Having friends who encourage you to follow the light on a daily basis is a special thing. Thank you for always being there to offer your advice or to lend an ear, or to just bombard me with your contagious excitement for your own achievements. With you, I feel like it's okay to be proud and talk about my accomplishments . . . because I know you'll come right back with a list of your own. Thank you for also being a true friend who listens to my worries and fears and resonates with them, then tells me to be strong and "walk away because I have some place to go." If someone would've told me that in high school, it would've saved me a lot of grief.

Amy B. . . . Thank you so much for being that friend I can go to for anything. Having a friend like you is exactly what someone like me needs. I can always count on you to make me laugh when I want to cry, and motivate me to continue on when I feel like quitting. I'm happy I can do the same for you.

Kimberly Grenfell . . . . A huge thank you to you, "Her Awesomeness." Without you, I would not have spent three months rewriting and making "The Treemakers" the best it can be. There are amazing, encouraging, kind, optimistic editors everywhere, I'm sure, but I'm positive you are the crème de la crème. You so rock.

Christian Bentulan . . . . Thank you for your beautiful work on the Third Edition cover. You are an amazing talent, a great person, and I'm excited to move on to the next project.

John Gibson . . . . Thanks for rocking the interior of this book. Your work is immaculate and amazing and I am super grateful for you being there for me at a moment's notice.

And last, but certainly not least, to my advanced readers and fans and author friends, Logan K., Jonathan Y., John G., Brea B., Casey B., Leslie C., Caelan C., Sarah N., Aria M., Cheer P., Christina M., Andrew R., Tina O., Stephanie C., Kimberly V., Veronica W., Ileana S., Devika F., Angela B., Onieta R., Ashley K., Amy B., Bri H., Martin S., Katy W., and the list could go on. . . . From the bottom of my heart, thank you for being the receivers of this story and an inspiration for me every single day. You have brought my journey full circle by reading it, being an important part of my journey, and making all of this worthwhile. I assure you, there is much, much more to come.

Made in the USA
Columbia, SC
02 March 2018